EVILE
YEAR OF
Taking CHANCES

Also by Christie Barlow

Kitty's Countryside Dream
A Year in the Life of a Playground Mother
The Misadventures of a Playground Mother
Lizzie's Christmas Escape

EVIE'S YEAR OF Taking CHANCES

CHRISTIE BARLOW

Bookouture

Published by Bookouture
An imprint of StoryFire Ltd.
23 Sussex Road, Ickenham, UB10 8PN
United Kingdom
www.bookouture.com

ISBN: 978-1-78681-139-4
eBook ISBN: 978-1-78681-138-7

This book is a work of fiction. Names, characters, businesses,
organizations, places and events other than those clearly in the
public domain, are either the product of the author's imagination
or are used fictitiously. Any resemblance to actual persons, living or
dead, events or locales is entirely coincidental.

For Sarah Lees,

Thirty-nine years later,

A truly amazing friend.

CHAPTER ONE

Staring out of the grubby window from the top deck of the 425 bus as I travelled home from the city of Becton to my house in Marbury, I watched the stopped cars below. It wasn't even a Friday night and the traffic was already backed up for miles. I'd made this journey every weekday for the last six years, usually with my foster mum Irene, but at Christmas she'd retired and was enjoying every second of it.

As the traffic lights ahead changed to green, the cars below began to crawl forward again. Roadworks had reduced this busy route to a single lane last summer and every day I used it, I willed the road workers to hurry up.

Once the bus had filtered through the lights it began to pick up speed. Then the sound of the bell rang out and to my dismay the bus slowed down once more. I sighed. A gust of crisp January air blasted up the stairway as the doors opened and I pulled the lapels on my coat up around my neck to keep warm. At this time of year the bus was always chilly.

I watched the hordes of commuters spill out on to the street below and stride away from the bus, clutching their bags tightly and dipping their chins towards the ground, trying to avoid the cold sting of the air on their faces. I pulled back my coat sleeve and glanced at my watch. It was fast approaching 6 p.m. The light of the moon was already seeping through the dark blanket of sky, and I knew I'd be lucky to be home by 7 p.m. at this rate.

I rested my head against the windowpane. The bus carried on jolting slowly up the road and finally turned on to the dual carriageway to join an even longer line of traffic. I stared at the Victorian houses lined up on either side of the road. Some of them were in complete darkness, but others were lit up. I watched strangers wandering from room to room, televisions flickering, children already dressed in pyjamas and families huddled together eating their dinner. I clutched my bag on my lap and closed my eyes for two more stops; once the bus reached the petrol station after the dilapidated pub, I knew I was nearly home.

It had been two weeks now that I'd been travelling to work at the city library without Irene. She'd been my foster carer since I was fifteen. Before then I'd been passed from pillar to post, family to family. I'd moved around the country more than a travelling circus, it seemed. I'd long since lost count of the number of schools I'd attended, and I'd never stayed in one place long enough to have any stability or make any real friends. I'd never settled at any of the allocated foster homes and never felt like I belonged until I moved in with Irene.

I smiled to myself as I thought about her. Everyone loved Irene. Her manner was always gentle and patient, something I'd never experienced with previous foster carers. She'd welcomed me into her house with open arms, and it would always be a place I considered home. Just before my arrival seven years ago, Irene's husband Neville had died unexpectedly of a coronary at the age of fifty-four. Irene often told me I'd arrived in her life just at the right time; she'd needed me as much as I'd needed her.

I'd come a long way since the age of fifteen. Now, at twenty-two, I owned my own home in Marbury and stood on my own two feet financially, and that was all down to Irene, who had guided me with love and respect.

Irene had discovered my secret after a year of living with me. I was illiterate. Over the years it had become easier and easier for me to hide it. I'd never stayed in one school long enough to be assessed or for anyone to care. Over time, and in my own way, I'd adapted and learnt to cope. Irene had secured me a Saturday job working alongside her in the local library when I was sixteen, and it was there that she'd discovered the truth. She'd taken me under her wing and, after that, she'd spent most Saturdays tutoring me. Within a couple of years I'd learnt to read, and five years later – thanks to all our hard work and dedication, and my commitment to the library – the Chartered Institute of Library and Information Professionals rewarded me for my in-job experience and offered me certification, and I was promoted to city librarian.

I owed such a debt of gratitude to Irene. She guided me to become an independent woman, and I can't even begin to describe how I felt the day she told me that she thought of me as her own daughter. I certainly loved her like she was my own mother.

CHAPTER TWO

Ten minutes later I finally arrived home. My footsteps echoed as I ran up the stone steps towards the red front door of my two-bedroom terraced house. I was freezing cold and could barely feel the ends of my fingers as I rummaged in my bag for the keys.

I closed the front door behind me and switched on the hall light. I was relieved to hear the pipes clanging, and the house felt warm. The boiler had been playing up of late, and I prayed it wouldn't break altogether because that was a cost I could do without.

I kicked off my shoes and sank my feet into my slippers – comfort at last. As I hung my coat up in the cloakroom, I heard my phone beep from the inside pocket – a message from my friend Clara, saying she had some hot gossip for me. Clara was the same age as me and lived round the corner with her parents. She'd moved back home recently after breaking up with her long-term boyfriend Nick.

Since moving into my own home, I'd enjoyed the independence, but I was never really lonely as my house was within a stone's throw of Irene's. I had the best of both worlds – peace and quiet when I needed it, and yet I was always welcome to nip over for a chat and a home-cooked meal with Irene whenever I wanted.

I stirred milk into my coffee, then cupped my hands around the hot mug as I settled down on the settee. I smiled at the old Victorian fireplace in front of me. With its original floral embellishments, it was what I loved the most about this room. Even on the darkest days, it still looked so pretty. The rest of the décor was dated too, but less pleasant. The walls were covered with woodchip wallpaper and the patterned carpets didn't do you any favours if you had a hangover. The kitchen was tiny and the bathroom was at the top of a very steep set of stairs alongside two bedrooms. The bathroom was in need of a major revamp – the taps dripped constantly, the shower had a mind of its own and the tiles were clinging on for dear life. But it was all mine, and I loved everything about it.

My fingers began to tingle as I sipped my hot drink, a sign that they were coming back to life, and I began typing a message back to Clara. Before I could finish, the doorbell rang, and I sat my coffee on the table as I moved towards the door.

When I opened it, Clara erupted into the hallway. I'd met her at work six months ago. She'd just completed her degree in librarianship and had secured a job alongside Irene and me.

When she'd first started working at the library, I'd invited her along to a book club, which for the past two years I'd attended every Thursday evening with Irene. The club is run by Mim, an avid reader who owns a beautiful café approximately fifteen minutes from my house. Mim, with her long blond hair and infectious smile, oozes warmth and made us feel welcome from the moment Irene and I ambled into her café over two years ago. The café is all things vintage with its china teacups, delicious home-made cakes and hot chocolate to die for. The ambience is perfect, with scented tea lights that flicker inside glass jam jars and floral bunting hanging from the ceiling.

I can still remember Clara's first time at the book club. When we'd arrived at the café, Mim had welcomed us warmly. The front of the counter had been open, revealing an array of beautiful cakes on numerous glass-domed cake stands, and a group of women already sat huddled together at a pine table stacked with books, chatting happily amongst themselves.

I'd ordered us all coffees and we'd settled down in the plush velvet bucket chairs in front of the window, browsing through some of the books that had been set out for us. It was my idea of heaven, a book club – a place to share thoughts on books and authors with a group of people who also loved everything bookish.

Mim had brought our drinks across and introduced Clara to the group.

The whole evening had been enjoyable, and then Mim had asked the question, 'Who is your all-time favourite author?'

'Sam Stone,' Clara and I had said at exactly the same time, and then both shrieked with laughter.

It was at that very moment we'd cemented our friendship, and I knew Clara and I were going to be friends for a long time.

And here she was now, standing in my hallway and grinning like a Cheshire cat.

'Shut that door – it's freezing out there!' she said, shivering as she edged her way into the warmth.

'Where's your coat?'

'I've only come from round the corner,' she said, walking into the living room.

My eyes followed her. 'Wow, and wearing a dress that looks like it's come straight off the catwalk. Just the thing for nipping round the corner to your friend's house in January!'

Clara beamed, posing proudly with one hand on her hip. 'I love this dress – I can't stop wearing it.'

I rolled my eyes and smiled at her. She did of course look beautiful, with her size-eight figure, legs like a giraffe and toned arms. Her blond bob bounced just above her shoulders and her big blue eyes were enhanced perfectly by her bronzer and nude lipgloss.

'You should try sprucing up your wardrobe, Evie,' she said. 'Maybe then you'll start attracting some interest from the opposite sex.' She rummaged around in her bag, then touched up her lipgloss and pouted.

I ignored her suggestion. I didn't want to encourage any such interest, except maybe from Noah Jones, who'd disappeared from my life the same afternoon he'd appeared. But he was my secret.

'And anyway, you said if I wanted to get over Nick, I needed to stop moping around in my trackies and smarten myself up.'

'I didn't mean for you to wear next to nothing. You'll catch your death in this weather. And what's with the glasses? Since when have you worn glasses?' I attempted to change the subject.

Clara glanced down at her watch. 'For approximately twelve hours! I read in a magazine that men find women who wear glasses more attractive and, working in a library, I think it makes me look more intelligent and very bookish.'

I shot her my best withering look. But Clara was very much her own person and didn't give a rat's tail what anyone thought of her.

'Anyway, what was it you wanted to tell me? Come on, spit it out!'

'So you haven't heard the latest then?' Clara was about to burst.

'Heard what?'

'Rumour has it that Nick has split up with his new woman. That didn't last long, did it?'

'Hmmm, and you're bothered because?' I raised my eyebrows at Clara.

'It's all over Facebook. His relationship status has already been changed back to single.'

'Well, it must be true then,' I replied sarcastically.

Clara pushed her glasses up her nose. 'I know what you're thinking.'

'Which is?'

'I'm completely bonkers and I need to get over my obsession.'

'You read my mind.'

Clara sighed. 'I need to get over him, don't I?'

'You do! Honestly, I know he's been a massive part of your life, but look at you! You are beautiful, young and sometimes intelligent – without the glasses – when you haven't lost the plot,' I joked.

Seeing such raw desperation for a bloke made me grateful I didn't have that kind of complication in my life.

'And thanks to him, I'm homeless.'

'You're not exactly homeless – you're living back with your parents.' Clara did like to exaggerate.

'Same thing in my book,' she answered gloomily.

'But at least you aren't living with the two-timing bastard. I know it's difficult, but if you keep stalking him, and trying to find out what he's up to every minute of the day, you're never going to move on. It'll drive you crazy. I promise, he'll soon pale into insignificance if you stop torturing yourself, and then you'll start to feel better about yourself too.'

'You're right.'

'It's just common sense,' I replied diplomatically.

'I know, I know. I wouldn't have him back now anyway.'

'So stop looking at what he's doing! What about the guy from the garage? I thought he'd asked you out?'

'Dave the rave? Have you seen the car he drives?'

I laughed. 'It's not all about the car – and at least he *has* a car. And what about what Nick drives? You could hear it coughing and spluttering a mile down the road with that dodgy exhaust. I feared for your life every time you went out in it.'

Clara laughed. 'Me too.'

'Well, I suppose what the bright blue Cortina lacked in working parts, it made up for with the cream leather seats, dangly dice and what the hell was that air freshener? Very stylish to say the least.'

Clara raised her eyebrows at me. 'Vintage would be the kindest way to describe that ancient piece of junk.'

We both laughed.

'Are there any other possible contenders?'

Clara screwed up her face.

'What about Tyrone? The guy who comments on all your Facebook posts the minute you post?'

Clara shook her head frantically. 'Dork city and, anyway, he's ancient. His profile picture must have been through every filter possible. He's over fifty, looks shifty and sleazes after every young woman out there. He's not even a twenty-tequila type of guy.'

'If you drank twenty tequilas you'd probably end up in a coma.'

Just then we were both startled by the rain battering against the windowpane.

'Jeez, I don't fancy venturing back out in that tonight,' Clara said.

I stood up and walked over to the window.

'Onesie night for me,' I said, watching the rain bounce off the pavement.

'It sounds like it's lashing it down.'

'That's an understatement.'

'What about book club?' Clara asked.

I sighed. I didn't like to let Mim down – she went to so much trouble to organise everything – but on nights like this, I'd rather curl up on the settee.

'It doesn't look like it's going to stop anytime soon.'

'Dress code for the evening will be bikini and flippers if we venture out in that. Heads would turn, especially if we nipped into the pub for a pint on the way,' Clara said.

'Good grief! I'm not sure any heads will turn if I turn up in the local wearing a fluorescent pink bikini. Is there an author booked in for tonight?'

'No, I don't think there is. Mim will understand if we miss one night, especially with the weather being so vile. I'm sure we won't be the only ones who want to stay snuggled in the warmth tonight.'

'Have you eaten?' I asked, drawing the curtains and sitting back down.

Clara shook her head. 'It's one of those nights when I just want to eat stodge.'

'How about a takeaway? Oh, and wait until you see what I grabbed from the library today! I'd almost forgotten,' I said excitedly, leaning down and digging deep into my bag.

'A takeaway sounds divine,' Clara replied. 'Come on – show me! What do you have?'

I tossed a book in her direction and the grin on Clara's face as she caught sight of the cover said it all.

'Cool! The new Sam Stone book! I've been waiting for this to be released,' she marvelled, flicking through the pages.

'It came into the library today. I thought we could read it before it gets borrowed out by the masses – perks of the job and all that.'

'Absolutely!' Clara said. 'Right, I'll text Mum to let her know I'm eating with you, and you text Mim to let her know we'll see her next week.'

I disappeared into the kitchen while I tapped out a text to Mim and retrieved the battered takeaway menus from the dresser drawer.

'Curry or Chinese?' I asked, passing the menus to Clara.

'Chicken balti for me,' she piped up. I smiled. Every time we ordered a curry, Clara always had the same old same old, yet every time she swore blind she would try something different from the menu next time.

'Not going to waste your money then?' I teased.

Clara laughed. 'I thought about it for a teeny second, but what if I didn't like it? I'd be starving and I don't like wasting food or money!'

CHAPTER THREE

It was 6.55 a.m. on a very blustery January morning. I was snuggled down deep inside my parka, my hands stuffed into the pockets. Already the bitter cold was stinging my cheeks. I leant against the glass panels of the bus shelter, shrugging my shoulders and shuffling my feet as I tried to stay warm. Clara was running late as always – the bus was due any minute. I glanced up the street and spotted her running towards the bus stop, waving her hand frantically above her head.

'Morning. Cutting it fine as usual,' I said, smiling at her.

'Why is it at the weekends I wake up at the crack of dawn, and on weekdays I have to prise my eyes open and force myself to get up?'

'Because that's life.'

Five minutes later Clara and I were sitting in our usual seats, near the back of the top deck. We placed our bags at our feet and hunched our shoulders to try to keep warm.

Suddenly Clara slapped my leg.

'Hey, what was that for?'

Clara's eyes were wide and she was staring in the direction of the stairwell. She flicked her hair over her shoulder and beamed.

'Look at that vision of loveliness,' she marvelled.

I glanced up and straight away my gaze locked with a pair of handsome hazel eyes.

I immediately looked away.

'He's coming over,' Clara said under her breath.

The man sat down on the other side of the aisle directly opposite us.

'He smells gorgeous,' Clara hissed.

We both inhaled at the same time, then giggled like a couple of schoolgirls.

'There's something about him. He's mesmerising,' Clara whispered.

'Love at first sight,' I murmured dreamily to her, giving her arm a squeeze. The hairs on the back of my neck started to stand on end and goosebumps prickled my skin, but it wasn't the stranger on the bus I was thinking about. It was Noah Jones. Irene had booked him to host a one-day writing workshop at the library for the local students. That had been eight months ago, and I hadn't seen him since.

'Where do you think he's going?' Clara whispered.

'How would I know? I don't have a crystal ball.'

'I wonder if he's got a girlfriend?'

'He's bound to,' I said wistfully.

'But there's no wedding ring, which means he's still up for grabs.'

'Maybe.'

For the next five minutes we sat trying to disguise the huge grins on our faces, and every time my gaze swept in his direction, I found he was looking straight back at us with an amused look on his face.

There were two stops to go before the bus would reach the library.

'He's getting off at this stop,' I whispered, linking my arm through Clara's. We must have looked like smitten kittens as our eyes synchronised to watch him disappear down the stairwell.

'Mmm, now he's a newbie. Have you noticed him on the bus before?' I said, turning towards Clara.

'I think we'd remember if we'd seen him before.' Clara's eyes were sparkling as she leant over me and wiped the condensation off the window with her coat sleeve.

'There he goes, down that alleyway at the side of the women's boutique.'

I blinked and strained my eyes, following his every move. He must have sensed someone was watching him, as he looked back over his shoulder towards the top deck of the bus. Clara quickly slumped back in her seat, leaving me to lock eyes with the handsome stranger. With a sheepish smile, he paused for a brief moment. Then he dug his hands into the pockets of his green bomber jacket before quickening his step and disappearing out of sight.

I'd had a few opportunities to go on dates in the last eight months, but I'd always shied away from the second date. There was no one who'd caught my eye – not like Noah had. Truth be told, it had always been difficult for me to feel completely at ease with people. My inner circle, as I called it, consisted of Irene and now Clara. But Clara had no idea that Irene wasn't my birth mother. I'd only known her for six months, and I didn't feel comfortable telling her just yet. Once Irene had taken me under her wing and I knew I would be settled with her for the rest of my life, she'd suggested that I changed my surname from Thomas to match hers – Cooper. I'd been absolutely delighted.

But as much as Irene was my family now, over the past few months I'd been thinking more and more about my birth mother. Had she ever tried to find me? Did she ever think about me? I didn't even know whether she was alive or dead. I'd tried to remember her on numerous occasions, but that was just silly. I'd been a baby when I was first fostered – how could I possibly remember?

'Well that's that, the most excitement we've had in a long time! Come on, here's our stop,' I said, grasping the metal bar to steady myself as I stood up and glanced out of the window at the hive of activity below.

The city streets were already wide awake, except for the two homeless bodies curled up on cardboard next to the busy marketplace. The street vendors lined the edge of the pavement, and a long line of customers queued and tapped on their phones while waiting for their breakfast, forcing people to walk past them in single file. I could see the city square, and as usual the large, tattered wagons packed to the brim with fruit and vegetables were parked to the side of the imposing stone lions that adorned the steps up to the library.

Clara stood up beside me and stumbled into the aisle as the bus came to a halt, losing her balance and falling on to the seat opposite.

'Steady on,' I said and laughed, trying to grab the back of her coat.

'It gets me every time!' Clara tutted.

I hauled her up, still laughing, and she smoothed her skirt down.

'Crikey, look,' I said, noticing a black rucksack lying on the seat next to her.

Clara twirled around. 'The handsome stranger has left his bag! What shall we do with it?' she said, picking it up and passing it to me before we headed towards the steps.

'We could drop it off at the police station?' I suggested as she followed me down.

'I don't think we've got time to do it now,' she replied, bending her head and flitting her eyes towards the cathedral clock through the bus's windscreen. 'We open up in less than fifteen minutes.'

'Fair point,' I said, as we waited for the doors to open. The queue of people in front of us soon shuffled along and we spilt out on to the street.

We began to weave through the early-morning shoppers in the market square, and I slung the rucksack over my shoulder.

'Are we going to have a sneaky peep inside the bag?' Clara asked with a wicked twinkle in her eye.

'We can't do that! It's someone else's property.'

'Who's going to know?' Clara looked at me, tilting her head. 'There could be something in there that leads us to the identification of our mystery man.'

I had to admit the thought had already crossed my mind.

CHAPTER FOUR

I rattled the huge bunch of keys in my hand as we strolled up the stone steps towards the library. Wilson, the UPS delivery man, was already hovering on the top step by the glass doors. Behind him stood a line of four people queuing patiently and a group of students chatting excitedly about an upcoming excursion.

'Morning,' Wilson said cheerfully.

'You're ahead of time today,' I replied, smiling as I placed the key in the lock and pushed the door open. Clara and Wilson followed me in and I locked the door behind them. There was still ten minutes until we officially opened. I paused in front of the control panel and punched in the alarm code.

Clara switched on the lights in the main foyer and we walked into the staffroom. I placed the mystery rucksack down on a flea-bitten black chair in the corner of the room that hadn't been sat on in years.

'Yes, the traffic on the back roads was unusually quiet for once,' Wilson said, leaning against the wall and smiling at Clara and me.

Wilson had been our designated driver since Christmas and had a very handsome smile. I'd never met anyone as cheery as him before. Rain or shine, he was always beaming.

'There's something different about you this morning, Wilson,' Clara said, eyeing him suspiciously before standing on her tiptoes and reaching for a couple of mugs from the cupboard.

I gave Wilson a quick glance before scrutinising today's updates, which were pinned to a corkboard that had definitely seen better days. Wilson raked his fingers through his mousy brown hair. He had broad shoulders and, according to Clara, a six-pack to die for. She didn't actually have first-hand evidence, but she'd stalked him on Facebook and had spent a whole evening flicking through every photo he'd ever posted.

'It's the stubble,' I said.

'What do you think?' he asked, stroking his chin.

'Mmm, I like it,' Clara declared. 'It suits you.'

I glanced up to see Wilson and Clara's eyes lock for a second before she looked away.

'Where do you want this?' he asked, balancing what looked like a heavy box on his knee.

'Can you place it behind the front desk for me?'

'Yep, I certainly can,' he replied, hoisting the box up into his arms. His sleeves were rolled up over his forearms and he gripped the box tightly.

I watched Clara with amusement as she hung her coat on the back of the door. Her eyes followed his every move as he disappeared out of the room.

Clara caught me looking at her. 'What?' she said and grinned, shrugging her shoulders.

'I don't know why you don't just get on with it and ask him out!'

'I don't know what you mean!'

'Of course you don't.' I rolled my eyes at her as we both left the staffroom and walked towards the main desk. I bent down and switched on the computer while Clara flicked open the ink pad and set the date stamp to today's date.

Wilson placed the box down behind the desk. 'Do you want me to let the general public in on my way out?' he asked.

'Thank you, that'd be great,' I said, watching as he strolled towards the door.

'See you tomorrow,' Clara shouted after him.

For a moment, I just stood by the desk and scanned the familiar space. Everywhere looked spick and span. There were huge front windows to the atrium that brought in natural light. Underneath those were the comfy chairs, where groups of students gathered with their friends to study during their lunch hour. Artificial trees and plants stood in almost every corner of the room, and all the books were neat on the shelves. I honestly thought I had the best job in the world. I loved everything about books, from touching the smooth bindings on new arrivals to the weight of the ancient encyclopaedias.

I glanced towards the door to see a steady stream of customers beginning to filter in from the bitter chill outside. They dispersed in every direction. A student walked quickly towards the photocopier while a group of mothers, grasping the hands of their toddlers, headed towards the brightly coloured beanbags at the far side of the room. One woman stumbled straight towards the desk, a biro clenched between her teeth.

'Good morning,' she mumbled.

Her arms were laden and she could barely see over the pile of books she was juggling.

'Steady! Let me help you,' I said and smiled, standing on my tiptoes and leaning over to stop the books from toppling on to the counter.

'Thank you,' she said. 'It's Evie, isn't it?' She took the biro from her mouth and popped it into her handbag, then glanced at my name badge. 'Evie Cooper.'

'Yes.'

'I'm Mim's friend. I've seen you a couple of times in the café when you've been having lunch with your mum.'

'Yes – Irene,' I replied. 'I remember now.'

'And I believe you see my son every morning.'

'Your son?'

'Wilson. He started working for UPS at Christmas time.'

'Wilson, yes! You've just missed him. Pleased to meet you again…'

'Jenny,' she replied. 'All these books are from Mim. I told her I was passing this morning and would drop them in for her.'

'Thanks. Wilson was earlier than usual this morning,' I said, taking the first book from the pile and stamping it before I entered the details into the computer.

'Yes, that son of mine woke the whole house up, banging and clattering his breakfast pots at some ridiculous time this morning.' She rolled her eyes. 'He's on an early start today. Wilson and Josh have their suit fittings later on this afternoon.'

'For the wedding?'

Jenny beamed. 'Yes, it's soon come round, hasn't it?'

'Yes, it certainly has,' I said, piling the returned books up on the side of the counter.

My invite to Elle and Josh's wedding was sitting proudly on the mantelpiece at home – it was less than three months away. They were childhood sweethearts who'd met at school. Elle was Mim's daughter and worked alongside her in the café. Josh was from the other side of town. Wilson was Josh's best mate – and best man to boot. I smiled, remembering Clara's reaction; she hadn't hidden her excitement when she'd discovered my invite had those vital words written inside – plus one. I hadn't asked her yet, but I knew she was secretly hoping I would soon.

'It should be a good knees-up,' Clara said.

'Are you coming?' Jenny asked.

Clara peered up through her fringe while she fiddled with the hem of her jumper. 'Nah, but I'll be OK sat at home by myself while you lot cha-cha slide over the dance floor and drink copious amounts of alcohol. I can always watch the reruns of *Take Me Out*.'

I grinned at Clara. 'Shall I just get my violin out?'

'No, it's fine!' she replied. 'Weddings are all the same – full of couples that talk about babies and stamp duty. Dull, dull, dull. And anyway, how many marriages actually last these days? I'll be better off staying in by myself while you all go and have a good time.'

I cleared my throat to smother a giggle. 'Do you think that's my cue to invite Clara to the wedding as my plus one?' I asked Jenny.

'I kind of get the impression Clara wants to stay home alone,' Jenny replied ruefully.

Clara gasped and dropped to her knees in front of my chair.

'Please, please, please let me be your plus one,' she begged.

'Who can resist those puppy-dog eyes?' Jenny said.

'Shall I put you out of your misery, Clara Lawson? Would you do me the honour of accompanying me to Elle and Josh's wedding?' I asked in my most formal, poshest voice.

Clara gave me a wide grin and squealed, jumping up and down and clapping her hands like a demented sea lion.

'Shhh, it's a library!' I hissed.

'Sorry, sorry,' Clara whispered. 'Thank you! I thought you were never going to ask.'

'Well, who else was I going to take?'

'Good morning, ladies,' a voice interrupted.

We looked up and I recognised Aiden. He was a fellow librarian, and I'd met him numerous times on courses run through the library.

'Aiden, isn't it?' I asked. 'From Claxton Library?'

Jenny touched my arm gently over the counter. 'I'll be off, see you both soon.' She smiled at us before turning round and heading towards the exit.

Aiden was grinning at us from the other side of the desk.

'I'm not late, am I?'

'Eh? Late for what?' I asked.

Aiden shook his head slightly, still grinning. 'You really don't know, do you?'

Clara and I shrugged helplessly.

'They told me they'd sent you an email. I start work here today.'

'Bugger. I'll check later – I must have missed it. Anyway, welcome aboard!' I smiled. 'So you've had a transfer?'

'Did you fall out with Claxton Library?' Clara asked.

'Not quite, but I'm sure we'll get a chance to chat later and I can fill you in then. Can you show me where the staffroom is, so I can dump my rucksack and get to work?' he asked.

'Yes, of course, let me show you around. Are you OK for a couple of minutes, Clara?'

She nodded.

'Come on,' I said, smiling at Aiden as he followed me across the library towards the staffroom.

CHAPTER FIVE

For most of the morning, Clara had sat amongst the little people in the children's book corner. Every Monday at 11 a.m. she was the voice of Rachel the Reading Rabbit. The toddlers always squealed with delight when Clara prised the puppet from the story sack as they sank into the array of colourful beanbags. They'd hug their knees and sit mesmerised by her funny voices and facial expressions while she read from the latest children's books. They barely moved a muscle for nearly an hour and the relief on their mothers' faces was clearly visible.

'Do you want my opinion?' Aiden asked as we began to wind up for lunch.

'What about?' I replied, carefully stacking the returned books from this morning into a basket, ready to be filed back on to the shelves this afternoon.

'I think that one was born for motherhood.' He smiled over in Clara's direction. 'Just look at her. She comes alive when she's around children.'

I had to admit Aiden was right as I followed his gaze. Clara looked so at ease. She had one of those faces that everyone warmed to and a personality to match.

'So what happens at lunchtime?' Aiden asked, patting his stomach and hovering at the side of me. 'I'm already feeling a little peckish.'

'Clara and I usually go on separate lunches. We sometimes nip out to the sandwich shop on the other side of the square or we bring something from home. There are loads of places round here to grab a bite to eat. It's up to you which hour you prefer – early or late?'

I'd lost Aiden's attention. He was staring into space.

I tapped his arm. 'Earth to Aiden! Are you listening to me?'

'Yes, sorry. Hearing Clara read like that reminded me of my own mother when I was a child. She used to sit for hours reading all the old classics. My favourite was always *Huckleberry Finn*.'

'The classics are always the best,' I said, nodding, and let him carry on listening to Clara. Bless him. It was lovely to have such wonderful childhood memories – something I'd been missing in my own life, though Irene had tried to rectify that.

I studied his face. He seemed gentle and caring, and already I was beginning to warm to him. I'd been worrying slightly how his working here might affect us but maybe it would be OK after all.

I looked back over at Clara. The children were clinging to her leg now, hugging her like their lives depended on it while Rachel the Reading Rabbit waved them goodbye. She caught my glance and smiled. Tapping my watch, I motioned I was off for lunch, and she nodded in acknowledgment.

Touching Aiden's arm lightly, I said, 'I'm going to go for lunch now.'

'Do you mind if I join you?'

'No, not at all.'

Clara appeared back at the main desk with a smile spread across her face and placed the story sack under the desk. 'I know it's not the norm to like Mondays, but it's my favourite time of the week.'

'Aiden was just saying what a natural you look with the children.'

'Aww, so kind. Thank you, sir. It's because I'm young at heart,' she joked, grabbing the hem of her skirt and curtsying.

Aiden smiled at her.

'We're off for lunch now – is that OK with you?'

'Yes, of course.'

'If you get a rush on just let me know and I'll come back out to help,' I said.

'I should be fine. It's fairly quiet.'

Walking side by side, Aiden and I made our way towards the staffroom.

'Have you brought your lunch with you today?'

He nodded. 'Yes, I wasn't sure what to do for the best.'

'Would you like a hot drink?' I asked, filling the kettle.

'Yes, a coffee would be great, thank you,' he answered, grabbing his rucksack from the chair and sitting down at the table.

'Here's where the tea, coffee and sugar is kept. We put a pound in here each week but please shout if you notice it running low. Clara's like a bear with a sore head if she doesn't get her morning coffee fix,' I said, shaking the rusty floral tin.

He smiled. 'I know that feeling. Here.' He flipped a coin across the table. 'My debts are paid for this week.'

I popped the money into the tin, made the drinks and grabbed my lunch from the fridge before sitting down at the table opposite Aiden.

'So what brings you here to Becton then? Why the transfer?'

His face drooped and his eyes filled with sadness.

'I didn't mean to pry,' I added hastily.

'No, it's OK. Honestly, you aren't prying. It's so I can be nearer to Theo.'

'Theo?'

'Yes, my son.'

'How old is he?' I asked.

He paused. 'He's nearly three. A handful but awesome. Look, I have a photograph,' he said, reaching inside his jacket pocket and flipping open his wallet.

I smiled down at the picture. 'He's gorgeous. Are you with his mum?'

Aiden exhaled deeply and shook his head.

'No, it's been a difficult few months. It's the usual story – a whirlwind romance followed by a pregnancy. Of course, at the time I believed we were going to be together forever, but we soon realised we weren't right for each other.'

'It must be so difficult to come to that decision.'

'It was, but on the plus side there's no animosity between Louisa and myself, and our main priority will always be Theo. Even though we aren't together, we both love him with all our hearts.'

'That's all that matters,' I said, taking a sip of coffee.

He scratched his neck and then folded his arms on the table. 'Believe me, I didn't want it to be this way, but I'll do my best for that boy.'

'Do Louisa and Theo live here in Becton then?'

'Yes, we were renting a small flat near Claxton but now she's moved in with her parents. Their house is on the outskirts of Becton, and I've rented a small terraced house five minutes from them, so I can see Theo anytime.'

'What about your parents? Are they nearby?'

'I only have my dad. My mum died when I was seven – a sudden heart attack.'

'Oh, Aiden, that's so sad to hear. I don't know what to say.'

'Honestly, don't worry about it, but she's the reason I ended up going to university to study for a degree in librarianship.'

'Was she a librarian?'

'No, but she always encouraged me to read everything and anything. It was something we always did together. After she died, my dad brought me up alone, so as you can imagine, we're extremely close.'

'I bet he adores Theo too?'

'Without a doubt, but a couple of years ago he moved down to the coast with work. It's a beautiful place, and he lives in a little cottage by the sea. I'm taking Theo for a week in the summer to visit him.'

'Sounds perfect.'

'What about you, Evie? I know I've seen you on a few courses, but I don't know anything about you. Husband? Boyfriend? Children?'

'Simple answer to that one is no, no and no!' I said, taking a bite of my sandwich.

'Parents? Brothers and sisters?' Now it was Aiden's turn to gently probe before he tucked into his lunch.

'I have Irene.'

'Irene?'

Taking the last sip of my coffee, I thought carefully about what to say.

'Yes, my mum. You know her. She used to work here – tall, lean, with mousy hair to here.' I patted my shoulders. I knew my answer wasn't strictly true, but to me she was my mum, and no one needed to know any different.

'Oh, that Irene! On the few occasions I've met her, she seemed lovely.'

'She's retired now.'

'How did you end up working here? Was it always something you wanted to do – follow in your mum's footsteps?' he asked while taking both our mugs over to the sink to rinse them out.

'No, I started with a Saturday job here and I loved it that much I stayed.'

'How long has Clara been here?'

'Just over six months,' I replied.

'Did you know her before she started working here?'

'No,' I said, smiling up at him and then glancing towards the clock. The lunch hour had flown by and suddenly Clara was popping her head round the staffroom door.

'We're just coming.' I stood up and pushed my chair under the table.

'It's fairly quiet out there. Anyway, what's the verdict?'

Both Aiden and I exchanged a puzzled look.

'Verdict about what? You've lost me.'

'The bag!' she exclaimed wide-eyed, nodding towards the rucksack on the chair.

'I'd forgotten all about it.'

'You mean you seriously haven't had a peek?'

'I seriously have not!'

'What's going on?' Aiden asked in amusement.

'That rucksack over there, we found it on the bus this morning,' I said, tossing my rubbish into the pedal bin.

'What Evie means to say is this morning a very handsome man left his bag on the bus, and I think if we take a peek inside we might uncover some sort of identification that'll lead us to our mystery man.'

'But on the flipside, what if it doesn't? I think after work we should take it to the police station and let them deal with it. What do you think, Aiden?'

Aiden shrugged. 'Surely it wouldn't hurt to look?'

'I'm with Aiden,' Clara said immediately.

He raised his eyebrows at me and grinned. 'I'll go back on to the library floor. Don't be long, you pair.'

I threw the rucksack towards Clara. 'I'm not touching it. You open it if you want to.'

'Yes boss,' she said and grinned, catching the bag with both hands and pulling rapidly on the zip before I changed my mind.

Peering cautiously inside, she reached in, pulled out a banana and laid it on the table.

'Most probably his lunch?' I suggested.

'A can of squirty cream.' Clara gazed up with a puzzled look on her face and placed it next to the banana.

'Bananas and cream?'

She extended her arm and delved in further. 'I've got something else,' she said, gripping a bottle of St Tropez. 'What's this?' she asked, sniffing the lid.

'Fake tan.' I raised my eyebrows in her direction.

'Tweezers and a dodgy magazine.'

Suddenly we both gasped, staring at the item of clothing that was currently hooked around Clara's forefinger. I couldn't take my eyes off them.

'Did you find anything interesting?' Aiden asked, suddenly appearing in the doorway.

We both looked up, startled.

He was staring at the red thong that was dangling from Clara's finger.

'I think, girls, that your mystery man must be a stripper.'

CHAPTER SIX

After work all three of us trudged along the high street towards the police station.

'Does anyone fancy a pub tea tonight?' Clara asked, adjusting the rucksack on her shoulder and looking hopefully towards Aiden and me.

'Mmm, I was thinking the same thing,' Aiden replied. 'We could celebrate my first day.'

Clara laughed. 'Ha, good plan! Any excuse and all that.'

I smiled at Clara, then paused on the steps of the police station.

'Why is it I always feel like I've done something wrong when I see a police officer?' Clara said.

'I know exactly what you mean. My heart suddenly feels like it's racing,' I replied, as a couple of uniformed officers plodded down the steps towards us.

Aiden grinned. 'Sign of a guilty conscience that, girls,' he said, bounding up the steps towards the door and looking back over his shoulder at us.

Following swiftly behind him, we reached the top and pushed open the door. This was the first time I'd ever stepped foot in such a place and hopefully it would be the last.

I scanned the room. It was very plain. There was a pinboard with numerous local leaflets attached that rustled in the draught of the door when it was opened. Straight in front of us was a counter and to the left of that were five plastic chairs lined up against the back wall.

I ushered Clara to go first. She took the bag off her shoulder and placed it on the counter. A police officer who was tapping away on his computer looked up. 'Can I help you?' he asked, sliding his chair back and standing up to face us.

'Yes, we found this bag on the bus this morning and thought we'd better hand it in,' Clara replied.

The policeman rummaged around amongst some papers on the desk before acknowledging what Clara had said.

'Did you see who it belonged to?' he asked, poising his pen over the form he'd pulled out.

Clara nodded and smiled across at me before answering, 'Tall, dark and handsome just about covers it.'

The policeman smiled. 'Well that just about narrows it down. How about age?'

'I'd say similar to us?'

'Which is,' the policeman asked.

'Early twenties.'

'All we know is he was travelling on the 425 bus this morning and jumped off two stops before the library,' I added.

'Thank you. That information is a little more helpful,' he replied politely, shaking his head at Clara in jest.

After taking Clara's name and address down, he declared he was going to take a look in the bag. Clara and I desperately tried to keep our faces under control as she pushed the bag towards him.

'Have you opened the bag at all?' he enquired.

We eyed each other warily. Aiden's eyes met mine and he sniggered. He folded both his arms and leant on the counter, watching us both with amusement.

Clara's uncharacteristic silence must have said it all. She flushed.

'We may have had a small peep,' I offered, feeling my own face turning crimson with embarrassment. The image of the handsome stranger wearing nothing but the red thong flooded my mind, and I bit down hard on my lip as I tried to suppress my smile.

The policeman unzipped the bag and the three of us watched his face while he peered inside.

Clara stifled a giggle.

The officer looked up, clearly amused, and zipped the bag up before thanking us for bringing it in.

'Is there any chance if you find out who it does belong to that you could maybe let us know?' Clara joked before Aiden grabbed hold of her shoulders and pushed her good-humoured-ly towards the door.

'Out!' he said, laughing.

The three of us giggled all the way down the steps.

'Are we heading to the pub then?' Clara asked. 'It's Monday night. Pie and chips for a fiver in the Royal Oak.'

'Absolutely!' I said, linking my arms through theirs as we strolled up the road towards the pub.

'Are we grabbing our usual table?' I asked as we arrived at the pub, nodding towards the table through the archway next to the open log fire.

'You have your own table?' Aiden asked.

'We do,' I replied with a smile. 'You pair go and sit down and I'll order.'

When I came back with the drinks, Aiden was sitting on the old church pew, his long legs stretched out before him, and Clara was perched next to him. They were both laughing. I gave them both their drinks and settled myself down on the bar stool opposite them.

'So, what have I missed?'

'Clara was just telling me the story of her first visit to book club.'

'Yes, you'd only been at the library a week,' I said, taking a sip of my drink.

'The club takes place at Mim's café on a Thursday evening. It's a lovely place, isn't it?'

I nodded.

'What types of things do you do at book club then?' Aiden asked.

' We discuss books!' I grinned while Aiden rolled his eyes, laughing.

'And not forgetting we drink tea and eat cake. Mim bakes the most delicious Victoria sponge.'

'It all sounds very civilised,' Aiden mused, sitting up straight and moving his drink out of the way while the waitress placed three plates of pie and chips on the table.

Clara picked up a chip and blew on it before popping it into her mouth.

'Aww that's hot.' She wafted her hand in front of her mouth and quickly took a swig of beer.

'Do you all tend to read the same genre at book club?' Aiden asked as he shook salt over his chips.

'No, we read all sorts. Anything from crime to romantic chick lit,' Clara answered, taking the pastry off the top of her pie and placing it on the side of her plate.

'Are you eating that?' I asked her as I took the brown sauce and vinegar from the waitress, who'd just returned.

'Of course! I'm just saving the best bit until last.'

'So do you have any favourite authors then?' Aiden asked.

'There might be one in particular we could mention.' I grinned, looking over at Clara. 'The pair of us absolutely love Sam Stone. Have you heard of him?'

Aiden stifled a laugh.

'Why are you laughing?' Clara asked, puzzled.

'You're asking a person who works in a library if they've ever heard of Sam Stone!'

'Ha, yes! Daft question.'

We all grinned.

For a moment, I just watched the pair of them as they chatted about everything bookish. Aiden's eyes were warm and from the smitten look on Clara's face, it was safe to say she was hanging on to his every word. There was definitely an instant connection between the two of them, and I smiled to myself, thinking they'd make a lovely couple.

Their chatter seemed to fade away as I stared into the flames of the log fire, and my thoughts switched to Irene. She was the only one who knew how difficult this coming week would be for me. It was the same every year. This Friday was my birthday, which always led me to wonder whether my biological mother would give me a second thought. The older I got, the more this question niggled at me.

Usually on 20 January, I wanted to bury my head under the duvet and hide myself away from the rest of the world, but Irene wouldn't let me. She encouraged me to face the day like it was any other and embrace the woman I'd become against all the obstacles that had been thrown my way.

She was right of course. What would be the point of moping about? What would it achieve? In the past, I'd spent the day staring at my reflection in the mirror, wondering whether there was another woman somewhere in the world doing the same thing – staring back at someone who looked like me. Would my mother have the same colour eyes? Would she have the same colour hair? Would she have the same mannerisms?

These questions had begun to torture me in recent years. I'd started scrutinising every female who walked past me in the street – anyone who was five foot five with brown hair. But in reality, I probably wouldn't have a clue if I was standing next to her at the bus stop every morning.

This Friday I was determined to keep hold of my emotions and go to work as normal, then spend my evening with Irene as planned. She'd agreed to cook me my favourite dish of all time – fish-finger sandwiches. OK, so you didn't need to be much of a culinary expert to shove a tray of fish fingers into the oven, but Irene's home-baked bread and the way she cut it into thick chunky doorstops and dressed the sandwich with iceberg lettuce and the finest tartare sauce was pure perfection.

I'd never really shared my thoughts about my mother with anyone else except Irene, and everyone I'd met in recent years thought Irene was my mother. I'd been close to telling Clara on a couple of occasions, but something always held me back.

The only thing I knew about my mother was that her name was Sarah Thomas; the rest was a mystery. The only possession I had from my childhood was the shawl I was wrapped up in when my first foster parents took me home. It had managed to survive every foster home alongside me.

'Earth to Evie,' Clara said, interrupting my thoughts.

'Sorry, I was miles away,' I said, suddenly realising I hadn't a clue what Aiden and Clara had been talking about for the last five minutes or so.

'What were you thinking about?'

'It's my birthday on Friday.'

'Oh no! I didn't know,' Clara apologised. 'What do you want to do? Pub? Nightclub? What do you think?'

'It's a tame one for me. Mum's invited me round for tea,' I said, smiling. 'But maybe we could grab a few drinks on Saturday or something?'

Just then we were interrupted by the sound of jovial chatter. I whirled round to see Josh and Wilson ambling over towards our table carrying a pint of beer each.

'Hey up.' Wilson smiled at us all. I noticed his eyes quickly darting between Clara and Aiden.

I smiled up at them both. 'Hi.'

'How are you, Evie?' Josh asked, grinning. 'Everything good in the land of books at the minute?' He pulled up a stool and sat next to me. Wilson perched opposite Clara.

'Great!' I replied, beaming at him.

With his piercing blue eyes, chiselled cheekbones and blond hair, Josh wouldn't look out of place on the cover of *Surfer Weekly* but he was actually an accountant and worked in the city. He was a friendly, genuine guy who everyone instantly warmed to. I'd met him at book club one summer evening when he'd popped in to pick up Elle.

All evening, Elle had been gushing with the news that she'd just got engaged and had spent the whole evening showing off the beautiful diamond now gracing her left hand. Josh's proposal was so romantic. He'd hired a pilot from the local airfield to fly over her house, trailing a banner behind the light aircraft that read, 'Will you marry me, Elle?' And of course her answer had been yes!

'How's life with numbers?' I asked him.

He laughed. 'Very numerical and boring to most folk.'

'Yes. In fact, stop there.' I flipped a beer mat at him.

'I'm not sure if you know Aiden,' Clara chipped in. 'He's started work with us today after transferring from Claxton. Aiden, Wilson is our UPS guy. I think you might have just missed each other this morning.'

With a quick nod, both Wilson and Josh introduced themselves to Aiden.

'I believe you've both been for a suit fitting this afternoon,' I said, finishing the last mouthful of my pie and placing my knife and fork on my empty plate.

'Yes, we have, and as long as I don't put on any more pounds, I think we're all done now.' Josh grinned and patted his stomach.

'Josh is getting married in a couple of months' time to Elle,' Clara told Aiden.

'Who is the daughter of Mim,' I added.

'Who owns the café where the book club's held?' Aiden finished.

'That's the one! A man who listens to what you say!' Clara grinned, obviously impressed.

Aiden leant over the table and stretched out his arm towards Josh. 'Congratulations, mate.'

They shook hands. 'Are you married, Aiden?' Josh asked.

'No, but I have a son called Theo who's nearly three,' Aiden replied proudly. 'Louisa – his mum –and me aren't together any more. It's not ideal, but we do our best for the little man.'

'Did I mention I'm now coming to the wedding as Evie's plus one?' Clara beamed at Josh and Wilson.

'Excellent,' Wilson replied, smiling at Clara with a sparkle in his eye.

'I'd love to get married one day and settle down with a couple of children and a few pets. I can't wait to bake bread, fairy cakes and sew my own patchwork quilts.' Clara's eyes were shining.

'Really?' I looked at her suspiciously.

'Yes really,' Clara mused. 'Isn't it every girl's dream to find a prince and have her dream wedding?'

'Then you best start the search for your ideal man,' I said, swerving the question while glancing between Aiden and Wilson, who seemed to be hanging off Clara's every word.

We were interrupted by Josh's phone beeping with a text message.

'Damn, I shouldn't be here. I've clearly forgotten I should be at a meeting with Elle, discussing wedding cakes. Drink up quickly, Wilson. I'll have to drop you back home.'

'No problem at all,' he replied.

'Then I've got a bit more work to do after that. The honeymoon won't pay for itself unfortunately.'

'No rest for the wicked,' Clara said, grinning at them as they downed their drinks and placed the empty glasses on the table.

'I'll see you in the morning,' Wilson said with a smile as he stood up.

'You sure will,' I replied as they disappeared through the pub door.

'Well, they seem like a couple of decent lads,' Aiden said. 'I need to make a move too. I want to nip back and bath Theo and read him a bedtime story. That'll give Louisa a break for an hour or so.'

'Aww, how lovely are you,' Clara gushed.

Aiden checked his phone before stuffing it back into his pocket and bidding us farewell. As soon as he was out of earshot, Clara caught me watching her with amusement.

'He's quite nice,' Clara said dreamily.

'Quite nice?' I grinned. 'I can tell by the look on your face that you've got your whole future mapped out!'

She opened her mouth to speak but I silenced her with my hand and laughed. 'Don't try to deny it.'

'Anyway,' she changed the subject quickly, 'I know you said you're spending Friday with Irene but what shall we do on Saturday? We could make a night of it.'

'I'd love to, I really would, but money is a little tight at the minute. I have to watch my pennies. I was just thinking when Josh mentioned he was doing a little work tonight that I might have to think about looking for a part-time job in the evening.'

'Are things actually that bad?'

'They aren't bad as such. I can pay my bills, it's just I don't have any extra for nights out.'

Clara was quiet for a moment, but then beamed across in my direction.

'What are you thinking?' I asked, intrigued.

'How about you get yourself a lodger?' she suggested.

'I've already thought about that, but it could be a lot more hassle than it's worth. What if they're messy or they drive me insane?'

'In that case, you would need to rent a room to somebody who didn't get on your nerves and was extremely tidy,' she said, throwing her arms open and tapping her hands on her chest.

Suddenly the penny dropped. 'You mean you?'

'Yes! Of course I mean me! Well,' she said, grabbing my arm, 'what do you think? It would be so much fun! Late-night girly conversations, film nights... not to mention the extra money.'

'It would certainly help me out,' I said, feeling the smile spread across my face.

'Is that a yes then?' Clara asked with a grin, standing up with outstretched arms.

'I think it just might be, Clara Lawson.'

She pulled me to my feet and hugged me tightly. 'We are going to have *so* much fun! When can I move in?'

'How about the weekend after my birthday?'

'Absolutely perfect!' she squealed before squeezing me again.

CHAPTER SEVEN

Listening to the wind and rain batter the windowpane, a shiver ran down my spine. I knew I would have trouble sleeping tonight. It had been the same for as long as I could remember. As soon as it turned midnight on 20 January, I knew there would only be one person on my mind for the next twenty-four hours – my biological mother.

I buried myself under the duvet and willed myself to go back to sleep, but it was no use – I couldn't drop off. Through my tired eyes, I watched the clock for what seemed like every second of the night. I tossed and turned until about 4 a.m., when I finally placed one weary leg in front of the other and padded downstairs to make myself a hot drink. Clutching a mug of steaming tea in my hand, I lingered for a moment in front of the hall mirror and mimed the words to myself, 'Happy twenty-third birthday.' It was when I stared at my own reflection that I knew the time had come. I was tired of the feeling of abandonment I felt every birthday, and as much as Irene loved me with all her heart, there was still a part of me that I felt was missing. I needed to know why my mother had given me up and what had happened to her. Moving between various foster homes, I'd experienced a sense of loss on many occasions, and I'd no experience of positive relationships other than Irene – and more recently Clara. Try as I might, I found it hard to trust people, so I tended to avoid relationships too; but that said, for the past twelve months of my life with Irene's help, I'd grown emotionally stronger. I knew I was ready to find out exactly who I was, and there and then I made the decision: I was going to start the search for my mother.

I climbed back up the stairs towards my bedroom. Perching on the edge of my bed, I felt a mixture of trepidation and excitement. I'd a jittery feeling in the pit of my stomach, but nothing could stop me now – the decision was made.

I drew back the curtains. The rain was torrential. It sounded like bullets firing as it grew heavier and started bouncing off the parked cars in the street below. With my hands cupped tightly around my mug, I sipped my tea. A surge of emotion ran through my body as I thought about my decision. I knew that in the coming days, weeks, even months my emotions were going to be all over the place. The wait would be painful. I needed to prepare myself mentally for what I was about to discover, if anything at all. I had no idea why I was given up as a baby. For all I knew my mother could be living in another country or even dead.

The question of how I would feel if I discovered she was dead ticked over in my mind. I didn't know, but I needed some kind of closure because the not knowing had begun to gnaw away at me.

Then of course there was the possibility of rejection. How would I feel if I managed to track her down and she didn't want to acknowledge my existence?

Whatever the outcome, I was about to embark on the biggest emotional journey of my life, and thankfully I knew Irene would be by my side every step of the way.

I finished my drink and snuggled back down under the covers. I must have dozed off for an hour or so because I was woken up by the alarm clock. I prised open my eyes, feeling like I'd just gone to bed. I was exhausted. I took a moment and then threw back the duvet, only to be hit by the chilly air brushing against my legs, and I shuddered.

Here we go again – another birthday.

Suddenly my phone beeped, startling me, and I read my first happy-birthday text of the day, from Clara.

After a quick shower and a brush of my teeth, I ventured downstairs. My stomach was already churning thinking about the day ahead and I couldn't face breakfast just yet.

I opened the living room curtains and let the morning light flood the room. I was relieved to see the rain had finally stopped – the pavement was covered in huge puddles, but at least I wasn't going to get drenched on my walk to the bus stop this morning. There was nothing worse than sitting on a cold bus soaked through.

I flicked on the television and watched the news for a moment. Why was it the news channel only ever reported the depressing stuff that was going on in the world?

I poured a glass of orange juice and settled myself on the sofa. I'd another ten minutes before I needed to leave for the bus.

The words of the newsreader washed over me. I wasn't really listening. There was only one thing on my mind: I wasn't going to wait – I was going to start searching for my mother today.

For the time being I'd decided to keep my decision to myself, except for sharing it with Irene, of course. I wasn't ready to talk about it with Clara just yet, even though I knew she would be totally supportive. She had no inkling that Irene wasn't my biological mother, and anyway there was nothing to tell yet. Once I'd filed my interest in trying to track her down, it could be a very long waiting game.

Glancing up at the clock, I saw it was time to leave for work. I was looking forward to Clara moving in, even though I'd have to spend some time this week removing the junk from the spare room. I wasn't sure what she would think of the murky pink woodchip wallpaper though. Maybe I'd suggest we decorate it before she moved in.

Fastening up my coat and slinging my bag over my shoulder, I pulled the front door shut behind me and began to walk towards the bus stop. I managed to dodge a couple of cyclists and early-morning dog walkers before spotting Clara, who for the first time in history had managed to arrive at the bus stop not only early but before me.

She was waving at me frantically and shouting, 'Good morning, birthday girl!' I could feel my face slowly turning crimson as a sea of faces looked over in my direction from the bus queue. Clara wasn't embarrassed at all by her overzealous greeting, and as I began to get closer, she burst into song. Thank God for her sake that she could actually sing. The woman standing directly behind her shuffled backwards awkwardly, no doubt deafened by Clara's sudden outburst.

'OK, you nutter. I think it's safe to say everyone standing at the bus stop now knows it's my birthday.' I couldn't be cross with her as she beamed at me and threw her arms around me.

'Happy birthday!'

'Thank you, but keep your voice down! Everyone's looking at us.'

She grinned. 'Who cares? My singing has brightened up their day!' she said, finally letting go of me as the bus arrived.

Thirty minutes later, we arrived at the library. Once inside the staffroom, Clara threw her bag down on the table and rummaged around inside. 'Here!' She pulled out a small gift that was wrapped in pink-spotted tissue paper with a bow on top.

'For me?' I asked, smiling.

'Of course it's for you! I can't see anyone else around here with a birthday today.'

'Well thank you very much,' I said, taking the gift from her and unwrapping the paper.

'Oh, they're perfect,' I squealed, staring down at the silver earrings in the shape of books. 'Thank you!' I kissed her cheek softly.

'What's all the squealing about?' Aiden asked, walking through the staffroom door and placing a large white cardboard box on the table.

'It's Evie's birthday today!' Clara said, smiling as she scooped up the ripped wrapping paper and tossed it into the pedal bin.

'Good job I bought you this then.' Aiden gestured towards the box. I lifted off the lid to reveal a mighty fine-looking birthday cake.

'Wow! It looks delicious! Thank you.'

'I know how much girls like cake,' said Aiden, displaying a dimple as he grinned at both of us.

'Oh and I nearly forgot,' he went on, pulling a slightly creased card from the inside of his jacket pocket. He handed it to me and pressed a swift kiss to my cheek.

'Happy birthday, Evie.'

'Thank you, Aiden,' I said. 'Now who fancies a slice of birthday cake for breakfast?'

'Do we have time?' Clara glanced up at the clock.

'There is always time for cake! We have fifteen minutes until opening time, so grab those plates and let the sugar rush begin,' I said, flicking the kettle on to make us all a cuppa while Clara sliced up the cake.

'Mmm, this is delicious,' I said as I sat down at the table and took an enormous bite. Clara laughed as I wiped jam and cream from my chin.

All three of us sat in silence aside from the odd murmur of appreciation at how delightful the cake was, and once every morsel was hoovered from our plates I spoke.

'That was the best breakfast I've had in ages. Thank you, Aiden.'

'Is there time for another slice?' Clara looked longingly at the cake.

'No! And you'll feel queasy if you eat any more! Save some for lunchtime.'

Clara blew a sad kiss at the leftover cake as Aiden shut the lid on the box and grinned at her.

'Wilson hasn't arrived with any deliveries,' I said, thinking that was a little unusual.

'Maybe all your birthday presents are too heavy for him to carry from the van,' Clara said, grinning as she held the door open so Aiden and I could walk past her on to the library floor.

'Or maybe it's simply because we don't have any deliveries today. I'll fire up the computers. Here, take these,' I said, throwing a bunch of keys towards Clara. 'Can you open up the front door?'

'Yes, of course,' she answered, catching the keys in her hand.

Clara disappeared towards the front door while Aiden and I walked towards the main desk.

'How was your evening?' I asked him.

'I bathed Theo, then I read him a story – which reminds me, am I OK to set Louisa up with a library card? We may as well borrow children's books from here, then I can bring them back for her.'

'Yes, of course, that's what we're here for.' I smiled, thinking how lovely Aiden was. 'Do you want me to do it for you now?' I pulled up a chair next to the computer and clicked on the new client registration page.

'Thanks,' Aiden replied. 'I'll write her details on here.' He grabbed a pad.

A small stream of customers began to file through the door. I looked up to see Wilson hurrying towards us, juggling a box.

'Here he is. Morning, mate.' Aiden reached out and took the box from him.

'Sorry I'm late!' His face was flushed. 'It's been one of those mornings.'

'What he means is that it's my fault.' Jenny rolled her eyes from where she was standing behind Wilson.

'For once, Mum, I'm not going to argue.' Wilson smiled, quickly kissing her cheek. 'I'll catch you at teatime,' he said, waving as he dashed back out on to the street.

'He'll forgive me,' Jenny said. 'The internet isn't working at home, and I was wondering whether I could use that computer over there?' She nodded towards the desk on the other side of the room.

'Of course, that's what it's there for,' I replied, noticing how exhausted she looked. 'Do you need any help with anything?'

'No, thanks, I'm fine.' Jenny walked over towards the computer, scrabbling inside her bag as she went. I watched as she sat down and placed a pen and notepad on the table beside her.

Grunting noises from the other side of the room interrupted my thoughts, and I laughed when I spotted Aiden grappling with a very large poster. It was too large to manage by himself. 'Urghh,' I heard him mutter under his breath before he thumped the poster in the middle to try to straighten it out.

I hurried towards him. 'Here, let me help,' I offered, standing on my tiptoes and reaching up towards the corner of the poster. I smoothed down the bottom half, which I had to agree had a mind of its own.

'Thank you,' he said, finally securing it to the wall with some drawing pins. We both took a step back and gazed at the poster.

'It's striking,' I murmured in complete awe.

'Sam Stone's latest novel,' Clara admired, appearing behind us. 'What a marvellous cover. In fact, I finished reading the book last night.'

'What did you think of it?' asked Aiden.

'Absolutely awesome as usual. It was one of those books I couldn't put down. Hence why I have huge bags under my eyes this morning,' she said, pointing to her face.

'The only downside is, now I'll have to wait months for the release of his next book.'

We stared for a moment longer at the poster before Clara moseyed over towards the children's corner and Aiden began to file the returned books back to the shelf.

Drifting back towards the front desk, I noticed Jenny was still sitting at the computer. She was staring at the screen, twisting her wedding ring round and round on her finger, then she scribbled something furiously in her notepad before snapping it shut.

I walked up behind her and she jumped guiltily.

'Sorry, I didn't mean to make you jump,' I apologised. 'Would you like a cuppa? I'm making one for all of us.'

'That would be lovely.' Jenny looked strange and couldn't meet my eye.

'Are you OK?'

I was shocked to see a tear escape down her cheek. I quickly pulled out a tissue from my pocket. 'Here, take this,' I said softly.

She dabbed the corner of her eyes. 'Thank you. Yes, ignore me. I'm just having a moment – nothing to worry about.'

Jenny was far from OK. I could see the sadness written all over her face.

'Is there anything I can help you with?'

Jenny placed her hand on my knee. 'Honestly, I'll be fine.'

'Well, at least let me make you that drink.'

She nodded her appreciation and I gestured towards Clara that I was going to the staffroom.

Five minutes later, I was back on the library floor carrying a tray of mugs and biscuits. The library was quiet. There was an elderly couple standing amongst the children's books with a toddler in tow, chatting with Aiden, and a couple of younger people wandering the stacks.

I walked over to Jenny and placed a steaming mug of tea next to her. She gratefully cupped both her hands around it as I slid a plate piled high with chocolate digestives over towards her. 'Here, take one. A chocolate biscuit always works wonders for me,' I said, dunking one into my tea.

'Thank you.'

'If you need anything, please give me a shout.'

She nodded.

I carried the tray over towards Aiden, who was kneeling down to show the little boy a book on steam engines. The boy made train noises with an infectious giggle, then launched himself into the pile of brightly coloured beanbags.

'Hi,' I said as I approached. 'I'll pop your drink up here, Aiden,' I told him, placing the mug on a high shelf away from the toddler.

'Thanks, Evie, and while you're here, can I introduce you to Louisa's mum and dad?' he said, gesturing towards them both.

'Pleased to meet you,' I said and smiled, glancing over at the small boy on the beanbag. 'And this has to be Theo, right?' I looked at Aiden.

'It sure is,' he replied with a huge grin across his face.

'Well, there's no mistaking he belongs to you. Two peas in a pod,' I exclaimed, passing him the tray before I knelt down next to the little boy. He looked up at me with huge hazel eyes.

'You are a handsome little fellow, aren't you?' I held out my hand towards him. 'I'm Evie, and I'm very pleased to meet you.'

Theo looked up towards his dad before his wide eyes met mine again.

'Shake Evie's hand,' Aiden encouraged.

Theo shyly grabbed my hand before letting go and hiding his hand behind his back. He had such an adorable face.

'David and Barbara have just popped in to grab a few books for Theo.'

'Here's the ones Theo has picked out,' Barbara said, holding out a pile of books.

'I'll stamp them out in a minute,' Aiden said, handing me back the tray and taking the books from her.

'It was lovely to meet you both – oh and you too, Theo.' Theo gave me a cheeky smile over his shoulder. He was now holding on to the edge of the shelf, happily pulling off every children's book he could lay his hands on and stacking them in a pile on the floor.

Clara was hovering at the back of the room, helping a student. She was reading aloud so the student could type up the information on her laptop.

'Here you go, Clara,' I said, walking over towards them and holding the tray out to her. She took a mug. 'There's a plate of biscuits over there near Jenny if you fancy one.' I turned round to see that the chair Jenny had been sitting in was now pushed neatly under the table. She'd disappeared.

Clara sipped her tea. 'She's just left.'

'Oh, I must have missed her.'

'She did say to thank you for the drink.'

I nodded, letting Clara go back to the student. I walked back to the main desk and swiped the biscuits as I passed. Then I noticed a parcel sitting in the middle of the desk, wrapped up in pink birthday paper bound together with ribbon.

I fixed my gaze on the handwritten label.

It read: 'For Evie Cooper'.

There was nobody nearby. I couldn't work out where the parcel had come from. Clara was still with the student and Aiden was by the door, saying goodbye to Theo and Louisa's parents. The library had been extremely quiet this morning, and in the past ten minutes I hadn't noticed a delivery driver enter the premises or even anyone standing by the desk.

I slid the parcel towards me and turned it over. There was no postage mark so it had definitely been hand delivered.

Scrambling to control my thoughts, I tried to think rationally. Who could it be from? There was only one way to find out and that was to open the parcel.

'What've you got there?'

I looked up to see Clara standing over me.

'I've no idea – I just found it on the desk.'

'Are you going to open it?'

'Yes,' I said, grasping hold of the ribbon but hesitating for a moment.

'Come on then.'

I began to hum as I pulled at the ribbon and ripped open the paper.

Staring back at me was a copy of Sam Stone's new book. I picked it up and flipped it over.

'I don't understand,' I exclaimed, mystified.

'Me neither,' Clara said, taking the book from my hand and fanning through the pages.

Suddenly she gasped.

'Whatever's the matter?' I asked as she thrust the book back into my hands.

Her eyes were wide and she could barely speak. She wagged her finger towards the book.

'L-Look at the front page,' she stuttered.

I flipped it open and stared down at the page, then at Clara. It read:

Dear Evie,
Happy birthday!
Best wishes,
Sam Stone

The writing looked posh, as if it had been written in fountain pen. I gasped.

'What's going on?' Aiden asked, appearing at the side of the desk.

'Evie Cooper here has landed the best birthday present ever. A signed copy of the new Sam Stone novel. Look!'

'How cool is that?' Aiden said, as his eyes darted towards the page.

'How would Sam Stone even know I existed or where I worked?'

'I've no idea. It's a mystery but a very lovely one.'

My mind was racing with all the possibilities.

'Maybe it was Mum?' I looked towards Clara and Aiden. 'Maybe she had a contact with working in the library all those years.'

'That doesn't make sense because she would have given it to you tonight. She would have wanted to see your reaction,' Clara said, taking the book from my hands again and flicking through the pages.

'Very true.'

I couldn't quite believe anyone would send me such a birthday gift, but someone had, and I was going to try my damnedest to find out where it had come from.

CHAPTER EIGHT

Locking the library door behind Aiden and Clara, I smiled at them both, even though inside I was feeling apprehensive. Clara had asked why I wasn't travelling back with her on the bus this evening, but I'd told her I had a few loose ends I needed to tie up before I went to Irene's. That wasn't strictly true though – I was actually about to start the search for my mother. The next bus was due in a little over an hour, which would still give me plenty of time to arrive at Irene's in time for tea, and meant I'd be out of here before the cleaners arrived.

I switched the lights off in the main foyer before I sat down at my desk. I knew the form I had to complete – I'd researched it many times. I brought up the web page and began to read section one, the notes of guidance. There wasn't much information I could provide the Salvation Army with to begin the trace, except my own details and my mother's name, but there was something inside telling me it was worth a try.

I completed as many details as possible and took a moment to check back over the form. My hands were shaking while my mouse hovered over the 'submit form' button. I stared at the screen as I battled with the question – was I doing the right thing? Were some things better left in the past?

I cast my eyes around the room, sighed, then counted to three aloud. My heart was thundering. With one final click I took the plunge and pressed the grey box at the bottom of the screen. The words that appeared next smacked me as hard as a physical blow.

'Your form has been submitted.'

There was no going back. My search was now in the hands of the Salvation Army.

I cupped my head in my hands and exhaled. I felt nervous as hell. Slumping back in the chair, I stared at the screen, paralysed. There was no guarantee they would even be able to trace my mother, or if they did that she would want to be found. But if they weren't able to uncover any information, I wouldn't be any worse off than I was now. Or that's what I kept telling myself. This was my chance to at least try to discover the truth.

Fifteen minutes later, I shut down the computer, grabbed my signed Sam Stone novel and stuffed it in my bag. Maybe Irene could shed some light on how this book had miraculously appeared on the desk. I smiled, thinking of the girls at book club – I couldn't wait to see their reaction when I showed them all.

'Are you still here, Evie? You're working late.'

I looked up to see Gwen and Julie strolling towards me. Gwen was pushing a hoover and Julie was armed with every cleaning product possible.

I smiled. 'I'm just off. It's been a long day. See you soon,' I said, thankful that my voice didn't falter.

I fastened my coat and threw my bag over my shoulder, glancing quickly up at the clock. I was still in plenty of time for the next bus – I'd at least twenty minutes to spare. Pausing briefly at the top of the steps outside the library, I took a deep breath and watched the hive of activity in the market square below. All the wagons and stallholders were busy packing up for the night, and the suits were striding quickly past them, probably wanting to get home as early as possible.

My head was whirling as I walked down the steps. Even though I felt emotional, a huge weight had been lifted from my shoulders. I wouldn't share with my friends yet that I'd begun the search for my mother, and until there was anything to tell, only Irene would be privileged to know my secret.

I arrived at Irene's house, full of emotion as I knocked on the door. I'd so much to tell her, and I was looking forward to spending some time with her. It had only been a few weeks since she'd retired, and it felt strange not seeing her every day at work. I missed her company. I wasn't sure how she would find the change in her daily routine, now that we were properly into the new year, but her broad smile as she threw open the front door said it all.

'Gosh, I've missed seeing you! Come here! Happy birthday!' Irene threw her arms wide and hugged me like I'd just returned from a year's travelling round the world.

'I've missed you too,' I replied, smiling at her overzealous welcome.

'How are you?' she asked, holding the door open for me.

'Great!' I replied weakly.

Irene looked sceptical. 'I'm not sure who you're trying to convince – me or you.'

'OK, you can read me like a book,' I said, unbuttoning my coat as the fresh aroma of home-baked bread hit me.

'Mmm, that smells divine.' I slipped my arm through Irene's as we walked towards the kitchen.

'Home-made bread with fish fingers and tartare sauce just for you, followed by, wait for it…'

'Eton mess?' I exclaimed, putting my hands together as if in prayer.

'Of course.'

'Thank you! Even though, I have to admit, I've had cake for breakfast.'

Irene pulled down the oven door and took out a baking tray. 'If you can't have cake for breakfast on your birthday, when can you?' She smiled, turning the temperature up on the oven before placing the freshly baked loaf in front of me on a chopping board.

With a wicked grin on my face, I leant forward, but before I managed to pinch a little from the corner of the loaf Irene playfully swiped my hand.

'Damn,' I muttered, rolling my eyes.

'Caught you.' She smiled. 'You, young lady, can wait another twenty minutes for your tea.'

'OK, OK, but it just looks so delicious – especially this bit here that seems to be looking straight at me.' I managed to break a little bit off and pop it into my mouth before Irene playfully struck me again, this time with the tea towel.

I shot her a regretful look, then carried on eating with a huge grin on my face.

'Cup of tea or a glass of wine?' she asked, hovering at the fridge door.

'Are you waiting by the fridge door because you're hoping I say wine or milk for the tea?' I replied with a laugh.

'It's your birthday and Friday night – let's go for the wine.'

'Good choice.'

After pouring us both a glass, Irene popped the fish fingers in the oven, set the timer and we went to sit down in the living room.

I sank into the chair and gazed into the fire. Irene sat opposite me on the settee and sipped her wine.

'How've you been today?' she asked.

I looked up and met her concerned gaze.

'It's been a strange day, mixed with different emotions, and I didn't sleep a wink last night.'

Irene nodded.

'I've been thinking a lot recently.'

'About?'

I swallowed a lump in my throat.

'Who I am.'

Irene patted the space next to her on the settee. I wandered over and settled next to her, tucking my feet underneath me.

'This past year, I've been happier than I've ever been before.'

'I know.' Irene nodded. 'But…'

'But…'

'There are questions you need answered – about your mother.'

'Yes,' I replied softly.

'Why now?' Irene took a sip of her wine as she waited for me to answer.

'A number of reasons really.' I thumped my chest. 'In here, I'm aching with sadness. It's hard to explain, but there's a raw pain inside me that never goes away. Though some days it's less painful than others.'

Irene squeezed my knee but didn't interrupt me.

'I think as time is passing, it's beginning to get worse. Over the last few years, I've become more emotionally balanced. My life has settled down. I have stability, I love my job, and that's all down to you.'

Irene took one of my hands and cupped her other hand over the top.

'And then there's Josh and Elle.'

'What do they have to do with anything?' Irene asked.

'They're getting married, embarking on the next stage of their life, and I want the fairy tale, the happy-ever-after too, but I feel I need some sort of closure about my past before I can look forward to my future.'

'I can understand that.'

For a moment we sat in silence, then Irene spoke. 'Have you decided how you're going to go about it all?'

I pulled away from her but held her gaze.

'I've already set the wheels in motion. I sent the form to the Salvation Army after work today.'

'You have?' she asked tentatively.

'Yes, but I'm a little worried about us too.'

'Us? As in you and me? Why?'

I paused for a second. 'Because everyone who's come into our lives in the last few years thinks you're my mum. How are you going to feel when people begin to discover the truth?'

'This is about what's best for you, and whatever happens, I'll be with you every step of the way. You know I will.'

My voice faltered a little, and my eyes filled with tears. 'Thank you.'

'It'll all be OK, you know.'

'I hope so. It's the first thing on my mind in the morning and the last thing I think about before I go to sleep.'

'It's definitely time then,' Irene said encouragingly.

A tear rolled down my cheek. 'I know it sounds daft, but I feel like I'm a jigsaw puzzle that's waiting to be completed, and there are two more pieces to fit in.'

'Two?' Irene prompted.

I hesitated. 'Maybe finding my mother will lead me to discover who my father is too.'

'It might or it might not. Who knows, but you need to prepare yourself for every possible outcome. All we can do is wait. These types of searches can take weeks or even years, and your mother might not want to be found.'

'Or she could be dead,' I blurted.

'That is also a possibility,' Irene admitted. 'But you need to keep an open mind. The only way we're going to discover the truth is if we find your mother, and even then she might not want to talk about it.'

I knew Irene was talking sense, and I might just have to accept not knowing, despite the feeling of abandonment that throbbed deeply inside me every day.

'I know – I do understand what you're saying.' Who was I to judge? I didn't know any of the facts, but my heart ached for answers.

'Have you spoken to anyone else about this?' Irene asked.

I leant forward and took a sip of my wine. 'I've thought about talking to Clara about it all.'

'But you haven't yet?'

I was silent for a moment.

'Once I've crossed that line, there's no going back. She'll know you aren't my mum.'

'Clara isn't a gossip. She'll support you, I know she will. Have a think about it.'

'I will,' I agreed. 'She's going to be moving in with me next week, which will help me out financially too.'

'I think that'll be good for you – not only for the money but for the company too.'

Just then we were interrupted by the oven timer beeping.

'You go and wash your face. I've set the table in the dining room.'

'OK, and thanks, Irene.'

'What for?'

'Just for everything.'

'You don't need to thank me.' She smiled lovingly towards me. 'I'll dish up and then you can tell me all the gossip from work.'

'And you can tell me what you're doing with your days now you aren't up at the crack of dawn.'

After I'd finished touching up my make-up in the downstairs bathroom, I opened the door to the dining room and smiled. Irene had done a superb job of setting the table, and she'd even gone to the trouble of blowing up balloons and attaching them to the back of my chair. On top of my happy-birthday napkin lay a small gift wrapped in shiny silver paper.

A few seconds later, Irene appeared in the doorway clutching two plates brimming with food.

'Wow, there's enough to feed a small army!' I exclaimed, sitting down at the table and staring at the plate in front of me.

The home-made bread was cut into large doorstops, the sandwich piled with fish fingers and crisp iceberg lettuce. I lifted the top of the sandwich and smeared it generously with tomato ketchup, then put the other bit of bread back on top and pushed it down using a little force, which for some reason always seemed to make it taste better. By the side of the sandwich were a handful of thick-cut chips and a freshly prepared salad.

'This looks absolutely delicious, thank you,' I said, picking up my fork and stabbing a chip with it before popping it into my mouth.

'There's a pot of tartare sauce there too. Would you like a top-up?' she said, hovering the wine bottle over my glass.

'Oh go on then. It is my birthday after all.' I held up the small gift on the table. 'Is this for me?'

'It is indeed.' Irene pulled out her chair and sat down opposite me. 'Open it.'

I ripped open the paper to reveal a burgundy box. I flipped open the lid and there sparkling back at me was the most stunning diamond ring.

My voiced cracked with emotion. 'Irene, it's beautiful! Absolutely exquisite.'

I looked up at her and saw that there were tears in her eyes. 'Oh forgive me, I'm being daft,' she said. 'It was my mum's, and I'd like you to have it.'

'I don't know what to say.' I took the ring from the box and slipped it on to the fourth finger of my right hand. I held my hand out towards Irene. 'It fits perfectly.'

'Will you treasure it?' she asked.

'With all my heart,' I answered, overcome with emotion.

'You mean the world to me, Evie. I know you might not have had the best start in life, but I can feel it in here – it's your time now. I was one of the lucky ones. My relationship with my mum was one of love and respect, and even though I'm not your blood, I will always think of you as my own daughter. Thank you for coming into my life.'

I was unable to speak.

'That ring is very special to me, and I'm glad that I can pass it on to you.'

Her kind words had hit me hard. I bit down on my bottom lip, but it was no use – the tears were falling. Standing up, I walked round the table and threw my arms around her. She kissed my head lightly.

'Now let's eat,' she said, smiling up at me, 'before it gets cold.'

I sat back down at the table and sank my teeth into the enormous sandwich. 'Mmm, delicious,' was all I could manage to say while catching the ketchup that was dripping down my chin.

'So how are you finding retirement?'

'At first, it felt like I'd taken two weeks' holiday because it was Christmas, but now it's beginning to hit me, and I have to say I'm missing the place.'

'We're missing you too. It's not the same without you there.'

'I'm keeping myself busy though,' she said. 'I've joined a walking group.'

I raised my eyebrows. 'A what?'

'A walking group.' She laughed. 'I decided I needed to do a little more exercise, and anything too strenuous is beyond me but I do like a stroll. So every Monday and Wednesday morning we meet by the church and go for a ramble – well, that's what they call it.'

'How did you hear about it?' I asked as I devoured my sandwich. 'Sorry, I shouldn't talk with my mouth full,' I said, grinning.

'There was a poster in the butcher's so I thought what the heck, why not. I rambled on Monday—'

'Sounds painful,' I interrupted.

Irene laughed. 'And there was a lovely group of men and women that turned up. They'd all been before on numerous occasions, and I was definitely the new girl. But they made me feel very welcome and the company was great. Most of the walkers live around here, and it was nice to get out in the fresh air and have a chat.'

'Are you going again?'

'Yes, I think I will. It gets me out of the house for a couple of hours.'

'You'll be climbing mountains next!'

'Ha, I wouldn't go that far.'

'I don't believe you for a minute! Walking this week, climbing mountains next week, then you'll progress on to skydiving!'

'My feet are staying firmly on the ground!' she said. 'But tell me about your day. How was work?'

'It was OK. Quite eventful, actually. Clara bought me these gorgeous earrings.' I tucked my hair behind my ears to reveal them.

'Very pretty indeed,' Irene exclaimed. 'And very apt because you work in a library.'

'And Aiden bought me a cake.'

'Aiden?'

'Yes, as in Aiden from Claxton Library.'

'Why was Aiden in our library?'

It made me smile every time Irene called the library 'our library'.

'He's transferred – he's working with us now.'

'He seemed a lovely lad. I've met him a couple of times.'

'He said exactly the same thing about you.'

'Why the transfer?'

'He's split up with his girlfriend and they have a son together. Louisa, the ex, has moved in with her parents, somewhere around here, and Aiden's rented a house nearby so he can still be close to Theo.'

'Sounds like a decent lad then,' Irene said.

'Yes, he is,' I replied. 'On a slightly different note, do you remember Jenny?'

'Jenny?'

'Mim's friend. We've met her a couple of times in the café when she popped in to see Mim.'

'Vaguely, why?'

'Her son, Wilson, is the new UPS guy. And he also happens to be Josh's best friend.'

'Elle's Josh?'

'Yes. He's best man at their wedding.'

'It's a small world.'

We both finished our meals and I clasped my hands over my stomach. 'I don't think I could manage another mouthful. Can we wait half an hour until dessert?'

'Of course!' Irene smiled. 'Let's sit back in the living room. We can tidy these plates away in a little while.'

I stretched out my fingers again and stared at the ring.

'I'm glad you like it.' Irene touched my arm affectionately before I followed her into the living room.

I suddenly remembered the mysterious Sam Stone book delivery.

'I can't believe I've forgotten to tell you this! Look what I have.' I fished inside my handbag and pulled out the book, passing it across to Irene.

'Sam Stone's latest! I was going to ask you about this one. Can you reserve me one at the library?' she asked.

'Yes, of course! But Irene, look at the front page!' My voice cracked with excitement.

I watched Irene's expression change to one of shock as she focused on the birthday message written inside.

'I have no idea where it came from, and judging by the shock on your face, you have no clue either?'

'You have a signed copy from *the* Sam Stone? *The Sam Stone?*' she repeated, just in case I hadn't quite heard her the first time.

'It's an absolute mystery. One minute I'm off taking a cup of tea over to Clara and the next there's a parcel sitting slap bang in the middle of the desk addressed to me.'

'And you didn't see who put it there?'

'No, not at all.' I shook my head. 'And it wasn't posted either.'

'Hand delivered then? Now that is a mystery,' she said, her eyes wide.

'At first, I just thought it was a normal copy of the book, but then Clara spotted the writing.'

'Looks like a posh pen too,' Irene commented. 'Do you think it's fake?'

'Why would anyone send me a book with a fake signature? What would be the point of that?'

'But how does Sam Stone know who you are?' she asked.

We both stared at each other for a moment, mystified.

'I've no idea.'

'Wait until you show them at book club next week!'

'I know. Poor Mim will be hyperventilating – she must be his number-one fan.'

We both took a sip of our wine as Irene kept flicking through the pages of the book.

'What a day it's been for you,' she said.

'Definitely a day full of highs and lows, to say the least – the biggest high being here with you, of course, but a signed Sam Stone, if it's real, comes a close second.'

'Why thank you.' Irene smiled across at me.

'No, thank you, and especially for the ring. I promise I'll treasure it forever.'

'I know you will – I didn't doubt that for a minute.' She took another sip of her wine, then asked delicately, 'What happens now with the search for your mother?'

'From what I read on their website, the Salvation Army will contact me if they manage to trace her, so it's just a waiting game now.'

'Well, I'll be here waiting with you every step of the way,' Irene said, leaning over and clinking her glass with mine.

'Happy birthday, Evie.'

We smiled affectionately at each other. I didn't know what I would do if I didn't have Irene in my life. She was my rock, and I loved her dearly.

CHAPTER NINE

'Steady,' I shouted as the ladder wobbled.

'Whoa, this looks easier than it actually is,' Clara squealed, clinging to the top of the ladder for dear life.

'Why do you think I'm not up there?' I said and laughed, trying to steady her balance.

'What we need is a man,' Clara grumbled, fighting with a piece of wallpaper that seemed to have a mind of its own.

'Ha, we don't need a man. Just think girl power!'

'I am, but it's not doing it for me right now.' Clara ripped the air-bubbled piece from the wall and dropped it to the ground, then climbed back down the ladder in a huff.

We'd spent the whole of Saturday morning dragging every piece of furniture out of the bedroom and the rest of the day stripping off the old wallpaper. Not only had we found what looked like a mouse's tail behind the old chest of drawers, but we'd also discovered layer after layer of woodchip wallpaper papered on top of each other. The idea had been to decorate the room before Clara moved in, but now I thought the pair of us wished we hadn't started it. It would have been easier just to apply a fresh lick of paint and gloss over the skirting boards.

'Urghh, I'm losing the will to live,' Clara declared, slumping to the floor and placing her head in her hands.

'You and me both,' I replied, sliding down next to her.

'It looks so easy! How can it be so difficult to hang a piece of wallpaper straight?'

'Maybe that's why we work in a library and we aren't decorators.'

'I wouldn't mind, but papering the walls is meant to be the easy part! Imagine us trying to cut and measure around the windows.'

'Oh God. I don't even want to think about it.'

'Well, we have two options. The first is that we could give up… and the second is that we give up and drown our sorrows in alcohol.'

I looked at Clara. 'The second option sounds the best one. Shall I nip to the corner shop?'

'Come on, let's both go. We can get cleaned up and grab a bag of chips from the chippy too.'

'Sounds like a plan.'

Clara stood up and kicked the screwed-up wallpaper as the doorbell sounded. She smiled at me. 'Maybe that's our knights in shining armour coming to help us out.'

'Knights? We should be so lucky! It's more likely to be next door, asking if I'll feed their cat while they're away this weekend.'

Clara looked disappointed.

The doorbell went again.

'Coming,' I shouted, bounding down the stairs and opening the door.

There standing on the doorstep with huge grins on their faces were Wilson, Josh and Aiden.

'The cavalry has arrived!' they all chorused.

I was dumbfounded. 'What are you all doing here?'

Wilson thrust his phone in the air. 'We are your knights in shining armour!'

I was a little suspicious that Wilson had just used the exact same phrasing as Clara. I glanced over my shoulder to see her hovering on the bottom stair, looking rather sheepish.

'I'm assuming this is your doing?' I waggled my finger at her.

'We have wallpaper paste, brushes, scissors, gloss, masking tape – oh and not to mention a bag of chips each for the lovely ladies.'

'Thank God!' I exclaimed, ushering them inside. 'But shouldn't you lot be doing something more exciting on a Saturday night?'

'We *were* in the pub but we couldn't leave you to struggle. And then we bumped into Aiden, so we roped him in too.'

'Wrong place, wrong time for you then, Aiden.'

'Luckily for you pair, I've just finished decorating my own house, so I've had a lot of practice.'

I smiled gratefully at them all.

'Here you go – chips! Why don't you pair go and devour this lot while they're still warm and point us in the direction of the room,' Josh said, handing me a white plastic carrier bag. The smell of chips drenched in salt and vinegar was absolutely divine.

'Thank you! You lot really are our knights in shining armour,' I replied with a huge grin on my face.

Without any hesitation, Clara pointed them up the stairs and directed them to the second room on the left. We watched as the three of them disappeared before she whisked me towards the kitchen, smiling.

'You are terrible, Clara!' I said, laughing as I placed the bag on the table and grabbed a couple of plates.

'I know,' she agreed, giggling. 'But they didn't have to come, did they? They could have pretended they were busy.' Clara plonked herself at the kitchen table and began to unwrap the chips.

'True,' I said, rattling around in the drawer for some clean knives and forks and sliding a plate across the table towards Clara. 'Here you are.'

'I didn't actually think they would come,' she said, popping a chip into her mouth.

'Who are you trying to kid?'

Clara looked up with a wicked glint in her eye.

'From what I've seen – or call it women's intuition – but I think *both* Wilson and Aiden have a teeny crush on you. I think you knew they would turn up.'

'Maybe!'

'What are you up to, Clara Lawson?'

She arranged her face into an innocent expression. 'Nothing. I just realised I wasn't cut out for decorating.'

'I think that goes double for me. I wouldn't even climb the ladder!'

Although Clara hadn't moved in yet, I was already enjoying her company. The house had certainly come alive.

Clara leant over to switch on the radio and we both sat listening as we stuffed our faces with chips. The next song to play was Adele's 'Hello', and Clara immediately began to mime along, despite the chips in her mouth. I couldn't help but smile at her. Listening to the lyrics of the first line reminded me of Noah: 'Hello, it's me'. I wondered where he was now.

I'd met Noah on 17 May last year. Irene had asked him to host a writing workshop for students from the local college, and the moment he'd walked through the doors I'd been mesmerised. He'd immediately put me at ease and I'd warmed to him instantly. He'd been down to earth and funny, not to mention handsome, and we'd got on like a house on fire. So much so that I'd prayed for time to stand still.

When the talk had finished, only Noah and I had been left in the room. I'd started to collect the handouts left on the desk, and I'd felt him watching me the whole time. When I'd handed them over to him, my fingers had brushed against his and I'd felt a surge of electricity before I'd pulled my hand away. His eyes had been soft as they'd held my gaze, and I was sure he must have felt it too.

Taken aback, I'd busied myself quickly and grabbed the empty mugs from the desk.

'That was a very inspirational talk,' I'd said, smiling as I worked.

'Thank you,' he'd answered. 'How long have you worked here?'

'Six years.'

'Do you enjoy it?'

'I absolutely love it,' I'd said, beaming.

'Have you ever thought of writing?'

'After your talk today, I'm going to go home and begin writing straight away. Don't they say everyone has a book inside them?'

'They sure do,' he'd replied, grinning. 'Here, take this.'

He'd fished around in the inside pocket of his jacket and handed me his card.

'My card. Just in case you need any help.'

'Thank you.'

'I have to run now, but call me.'

'I will,' I'd replied.

He'd leant forward and cupped his hand around my elbow, then swiftly pressed a kiss to my cheek. 'Thank you for looking after me today.'

'You're most welcome,' I'd replied.

That business card was still pinned to the board in my kitchen. I'd never called him because I had no intention of writing a book, but thinking about him now, I still got the slightest pang in my heart. It was silly really – we'd only spent a few hours together.

'Earth to Evie.'

I saw Clara grinning at me and I met her inquisitive stare.

'What are you thinking about?' she asked.

'Nothing,' I replied, not wanting to mention Noah.

'I completely forgot to ask – did you have a lovely time with Irene last night?' she queried, standing up and putting her empty plate in the washing-up bowl.

'Yes, she gave me the most beautiful gift! A ring – it was her mother's.' I thrust my hand towards Clara to show her. 'What do you think?'

'It's beautiful,' she said, holding my hand up to the light to get a better view.

'I told her you were moving in and she thought it would do me the world of good. Are your parents all right about it?'

'Yes, Mum was a little tearful – again! But it's not as though we've not been here before.'

'How are you feeling about Nick now?'

'Nick who?' She smiled. 'Exes are exes for a reason, and it's time to move on.'

'Well, at least that's something,' I said. 'All we need to do now is finish decorating your room and it's full steam ahead. I wonder how they're getting on up there.'

'Hey, slackers, any chance you're going to switch the kettle on? We are *dying* of thirst,' Wilson said, popping his head round the kitchen door.

'I'm on it!' Clara said, immediately flicking the switch on the kettle.

'You have a lovely house here, Evie,' Wilson said as he cast his eyes around the room.

'Thank you. It suits me,' I replied, offering him a leftover chip from my plate.

Clara smiled. 'Suits me too. How many teas and how many coffees?' she asked as she unscrewed the lid from the tea canister.

'Look at this one – she's already making herself at home,' Wilson teased.

'Let's hope she's as enthusiastic about washing the pots and cleaning the bathroom,' I joked, standing up and placing my empty dishes in the washing-up bowl next to hers.

'We're all tea and one with sugar,' he said to Clara. 'Thanks. I best get back to it. We're already papering the second wall.' He gave us the thumbs-up before turning round and disappearing back out of the kitchen.

'Wilson or Aiden?' I caught Clara's eye and posed the question.

She stuck her tongue out at me in jest.

'I couldn't possibly say! Anyway, isn't it about time you found someone?'

'Me? I'm quite happy by myself.'

'Mmm, why am I not convinced? Come on, you must have your eye on someone.'

'I had a very brief encounter eight months ago –and we are talking brief – and before that all the dates I went on, I just didn't seem to click with them.'

Clara raised her eyebrows. 'Brief encounter?'

'Yes, but there's nothing to tell! He was in my life for one afternoon and that's about it.'

'Are you sure there's nothing to tell?' Clara tried to probe further, spooning a sugar into one of the mugs of tea.

'Absolutely sure,' I replied, wondering why I'd even bothered to mention it and why thoughts of Noah were suddenly creeping back into my head.

'I will delve into this more,' Clara said, eyeing me suspiciously, 'but not before we get these drinks up to the lads.' She grabbed a tray and I followed her up the stairs.

We could hear the boys laughing and joking as we reached the landing.

'Teas are here,' Clara chirped as I rattled the door handle.

'Out!' they all chorused. 'You can't come in until we've finished.'

Aiden appeared at the doorway and pulled the door shut behind him. His sleeves were rolled up and his shirt was covered in splodges of wallpaper paste. 'Thank you,' he said, taking the tray from Clara's hand. 'Now, you pair get yourselves downstairs and relax,' he ordered, standing firm in front of the door so we couldn't see the progress.

'Can we just have a little peep,' I begged.

'No! Now go!' he said, shooing us away.

I caught Clara's eye and we both pulled aww faces.

'You're never going to finish all this tonight,' Clara said, giving him a twinkly smile.

'You'll be amazed at what we can do when we put our minds to it.'

'Are they still here?' we heard Josh shout from the other side of the door.

We put our hands up in defeat. 'OK, we're out of here!' I said, and we giggled all the way down the stairs like a couple of schoolgirls before settling on the couch with a couple of beers.

'Bridget Jones or *Notting Hill*?' I asked, pressing the remote control and scrolling between the two films.

'Definitely Bridget Jones,' Clara replied, taking a swig of her beer.

'Excellent choice!' I said, clinking my bottle against hers. 'Welcome to your new home, housemate!'

'Thank you so much for having me. This is going to be so much fun!'

I smiled warmly at Clara. Perhaps Irene was right – maybe it was about time I let someone else in.

CHAPTER TEN

'Oi! Wake up, sleepy head.'

I could feel myself being lightly shaken. Opening my eyes, I looked up, startled, to find Wilson standing over me.

'Sorry, I didn't mean to make you jump,' he whispered.

'Where's Clara?' I asked, sitting up and stretching my arms out in front of me.

'She's asleep in the chair,' said Aiden softly, nodding towards her. The light from the television flickered across her face. Her legs were draped over the arm of the chair and she was curled up under the blanket that I kept by the side of the settee.

'What time is it?'

'Just gone 3 a.m.,' Josh said, smiling as he checked his watch.

'You're kidding me. It must have been hours since the film finished,' I exclaimed, suddenly feeling wide awake. 'I'm so sorry! I didn't mean for you all to be here this late.'

'This is the first time ever I'll be rolling in at 3 a.m. sober,' Wilson said, smiling as he zipped up his coat and pulled his bobble hat over his head.

'It's all finished, Evie. We hope you like it,' Josh added, touching my arm.

'You're kidding me?' I said again.

Aiden smiled. 'I'm sure you've just said that!'

I was dumbfounded. 'You lot really are our knights in shining armour. I can't thank you enough. *We* can't thank you enough,' I added.

'Just remember – the paint is still wet on the skirting boards and the windowsill, so be careful. Don't put anything on there until it's completely dry. Oh, and we've put the curtain rail back up for you too. Wilson has scooped up all the old wallpaper from the floor and we've taken up the carpet. He's left everything outside the back door. I hope that's OK?' Aiden asked.

'You hope that's OK? You guys are total sweethearts – my heroes in fact,' I said, standing up and beaming from ear to ear.

'We aim to please, but now if you'll forgive me, I really need my bed. I'm taking Theo swimming in the morning and I have to be up in five hours.'

'Yes, go, and thank you all again!' I pressed a kiss swiftly to each of their cheeks before they moved towards the front door.

I watched them stride down the steps and climb into the car, waving as they drove off and disappeared round the corner.

I locked the front door behind me and glanced back round the living-room door to check on Clara, but she was still fast asleep.

I was itching to see the room and couldn't wait any longer. I hurried up the stairs, then paused outside the bedroom door before pushing it open. I gasped with joy – I couldn't believe my eyes.

The room that had once worn an overcoat of dust and woodchip wallpaper and oozed neglect had now been transformed into an exquisite space that could have featured in the latest edition of *Country Living* magazine. Well, maybe that was a little bit of an exaggeration, but the lads had done a magnificent job. The rosebud wallpaper was hung to perfection, trimmed neatly around the sockets and windows. They'd stripped back the multi-coloured carpet to reveal beautiful oak floorboards that had been hidden away, and positioned the bed in the middle of the room with the bedside table next to it. They'd worked so hard, and I couldn't thank them enough. It would have taken Clara and me months to get it looking as good as this.

Suddenly hearing the stairs creak behind me, I swung round to see Clara.

'I must have fallen asleep. Are they still here?' she murmured, still looking half-asleep.

'No,' I said, smiling, 'they left about five minutes ago.'

She stood on her tiptoes and peered over my shoulder. She ran an approving eye over the room and I watched as a huge smile spread across her face.

'What do you think? Do you like it?'

'Do I like it? I absolutely love it! I am so happy!' she squealed, clapping her hands together.

'I can't thank them enough,' I said. 'What a transformation!'

Clara slipped her arm through mine and gave it a squeeze as we admired the room.

'It looks bigger now they've taken up that carpet,' I said. 'And now that mucky pink wallpaper's been stripped away, it has a lovely airy feeling to it.'

'It all looks amazing! All I need now is a rug at the side of the bed and a pair of curtains,' Clara said.

'Are you OK to sleep on the settee tonight and then tomorrow we can go and collect your stuff and move you in officially.'

'I can't wait!' Clara said and grinned, opening her arms and pulling me into a hug.

CHAPTER ELEVEN

Waking up with the sun streaming through the small gap in the curtains made a change. For weeks now, it seemed, I'd woken up to the sound of rain, but this morning everything seemed calm outside. I stretched my arms above my head and yawned before reaching for my phone.

Last night in my dream, I'd kissed a man. It had seemed so real, and as I lay there remembering, I opened up my internet browser and Googled Noah Jones.

This past week had seemed to open up a world of possibilities – maybe life was beginning to show me that I shouldn't keep myself cocooncd inside my own need for self-preservation. I was finally beginning to come alive.

I felt myself flush as Noah's handsome face smiled back at me from the screen.

'For goodness sake, Evie,' I mumbled to myself. Whatever was I thinking? It was only a dream! The poor lad would not be lying in his bed on a Sunday morning Googling me. Still, finding out more about the mysterious Noah was addictive.

'Does Noah Jones have a wife?' I blurted to Siri.

Clara rapped gently on my bedroom door. 'Who are you talking to?'

I shoved my phone under my pillow. 'No one. Come on in. You're up then?'

Clara strolled into the room carrying a steaming mug of tea. 'Brew,' she said, smiling.

'Interesting question,' Siri suddenly piped up as Clara placed my drink down on the bedside table.

'I have found this on the web for "Does Noah Jones have a wife?".'

Clara looked at me with pure puzzlement on her face while I buried my head in my hands and shook with laughter.

'Right, budge up, Evie Cooper. Who is Noah Jones and why do we need to know if he has a wife?'

I bit down on my bottom lip as I tried to stop the smile spreading across my face. Throwing back the duvet, I patted the space next to me before cupping my hands around the mug and taking a sip.

Clara plumped up the spare pillow and lay next to me. Pulling the duvet up around her chest, she giggled, and then said, 'Get talking, Cooper.'

'Damn that Siri!'

I hesitated for a moment, wondering how much to tell Clara – which was silly, actually, as there wasn't really anything to tell.

I reached under the pillow and grabbed my phone, unlocking it and tilting it towards Clara so she could view the picture of Noah.

'His name sounds vaguely familiar, but I don't think I've ever seen him before,' she said, nodding with approval. 'But he is one majorly gorgeous man.'

'He is,' I said and grinned, turning pink.

'So far we've established he's hot and we've established you've Googled him. All I need to know now is why?'

I sighed. 'Honestly, there isn't anything to tell. Eight months ago he came to the library to talk to a bunch of students who were interested in writing for a living. I looked after him all afternoon.'

'And?'

'And nothing.'

'And that was it?'

I nodded.

'But you liked him?'

'I did.'

'And now?'

I smiled. 'He pops into my head quite often.'

'When you think about him or hear his name, how do you feel?'

'Like a jittery wreck.'

'Ha! So, what you mean is the butterflies fluttering around in your stomach go berserk.'

'That just about sums it up.'

'Have you kissed him?'

'No! Don't be daft!'

'Evie!'

'Only in my dreams,' I said and smiled, suddenly realising parts of my body that had been in hibernation for as long as I could remember were beginning to stir, and soon I knew they would be raring to go.

'What are we going to do about this, then?'

'I think I've left it a little late.'

'It's never too late!'

'I have his number.'

Clara bolted upright. 'What are you waiting for then?'

'He gave me it in case I ever needed any help writing a book.'

'Since when have you ever thought about writing a book?'

'Exactly – that's why I haven't rung.'

'Do you know how lame that sounds?'

'What do you mean?' I asked, perplexed. 'Call me if you need help, he said. I've not called him because I don't need help and I'm not writing a book!'

She sighed. 'No man would give out his business card just to help you with your writing.'

'He was a genuine guy.'

'I'm not disputing that. All I'm saying is everyone at that talk was embarking on a writing career, yet he gave his number to you. Think about it.' She nodded knowingly. 'Did he give his card out to anyone else?'

I shrugged.

'Of course he didn't. It's like me saying to Wilson, if you ever need any help delivering your parcels, here's my card.'

I swiped the duvet playfully and laughed. 'That scenario is a bit off the wall.'

'Maybe so, but you get what I mean. Does he live around here?'

'London I think... according to Google.'

'What about Twitter or Facebook? There are always author pages knocking about,' she said, taking my phone off me and bringing up my Twitter app.

'Ah,' she said. 'According to his bio, he does live in London.'

I sighed. 'Miles away.'

'Why aren't you following him on Twitter?'

'For the same reason he's not following me.'

'Well, let's put a stop to that nonsense.'

'What do you mean?'

'You are now!'

'Clara!'

'To be fair, he has that many followers, he might not even notice, but look – he has a brand new book being published next month and he's doing a tour. There are no dates or venues confirmed yet, but maybe we should make the effort and pop along to one of them,' Clara said, smiling at me.

'No! He would have no clue who I was.'

'It's about time he noticed you then.'

'You're starting to worry me, Clara. What are you thinking?'

'Well, look at your profile picture. It screams librarian,' she said, flicking the phone in my direction.

'That's because I am a librarian.'

'Ha! But it's dowdy. There's no colour to your clothes or your cheeks. In fact, it doesn't even look like you've brushed your hair.'

'But that's what I look like,' I protested.

'We need a punchy bio, an up-to-date picture… There are so many filters and apps these days – who actually looks like their profile photo anyway?' she continued, completely ignoring me.

'Me – I do!'

'Then that's where we're going wrong!'

'We?'

'Yes, we! It's a good job I've moved in, Cooper. We need to get your life back on track.'

'Oh God,' was all I could manage to say. But Clara had got me thinking.

We lay in bed for a further twenty minutes, flicking between people's profiles and chatting about anything and everything. The plan for the rest of the day was to nip across to Clara's and transport all of her stuff into her new bedroom. Usually on a Sunday, I'd potter around doing absolutely nothing and count the hours until Monday morning. The feeling of finally starting to share my thoughts with a friend was fantastic, and I was glad again that Clara had moved in.

In the pit of my stomach, I had a feeling that life was going to become a little more interesting with Clara around, and on top of that, in the last twenty-four hours Noah had been permanently on my mind, starting to scratch an itch that I hadn't even known needed scratching.

CHAPTER TWELVE

It was Sunday night and the Royal Oak was heaving.

'Where do all these people come from? Shouldn't they be at home watching telly or something? This place is packed,' Clara said as we weaved through the sea of people towards the bar.

'It's carvery night. The only time you can pile your plate high with as many roast potatoes and slices of roast beef as possible, like food is going out of fashion, and no one bats an eyelid.'

Suddenly I noticed Elle at the bar, chatting to Mim.

'Keep your eye on the prize, I'm just nipping to the toilet,' I said, handing Clara a ten-pound note.

'Eye on the prize?' she queried.

'Yes, the queue. Don't let anyone push in, otherwise there will be arguments.'

Clara grinned at me. 'The usual?'

I nodded before waving across to Elle and Mim, who'd spotted us.

By the time I returned, Clara had been served and was sitting down at a table with Elle and Mim. I pulled up a stool and reached across to pinch one of Clara's crisps.

'Perks of being your landlady,' I said and grinned, popping it into my mouth before Clara could object.

We'd spent all afternoon lugging her belongings from her family home to her new room. I'd never seen so many clothes or shoes in my lifetime, not to mention she seemed to have a different colour handbag for every day of the week. Her mum had joked that Clara could set up her very own boutique, trying her best to hide her tears as she stood on the doorstep and waved us off.

'Shall we fight our way through to the bar again and pay for a ticket for the carvery?' I suggested, suddenly feeling ravenous.

'No need!' Clara smiled as she handed me one. 'It's on Bill – a moving-in present.'

I smiled across at Bill, the landlord, and he caught my eye as he poured a pint for a customer. I waved at him, mouthing thank you, and he nodded in appreciation.

'Are you pair eating?' I asked Elle and Mim.

'Yes, I'm just waiting for them to bring out a fresh tray of roasties.' Mim smiled. 'And I may even be tempted to try a sticky toffee pudding for dessert.'

'She says that,' said Elle, laughing, 'but all she ever does is criticise any desserts made by anyone else. It's never up to her standards.'

We all laughed as Mim playfully swiped her hand.

'So, I believe you kept my fiancé up to the early hours on Saturday night,' Elle said to us.

Clara grinned. 'Yes, sorry about that. It was my fault.'

'They did a marvellous job,' I chipped in. 'You wouldn't recognise the room. This time last week it was a junk room and now it's been totally transformed thanks to them.'

'It'll do Josh good. He needs to get the practice in so he can decorate the nursery.'

Both Clara and I watched as Elle patted her stomach, grinning.

'Aww,' Clara said as I jumped up and moved round the table to put my arms around her.

'Congratulations! How far gone are you?' I asked, noticing her cheeks looked very flushed.

'It's still very early days, only eight weeks. It's not what we would have planned, but we're very happy, though I've started to feel hideously sick all the time. We wanted to keep it quiet a little longer, but I have the slight problem of the hen party fast approaching, and if the bride to be is only drinking orange juice, I'm sure questions will be asked.'

'Oh, of course,' I said, glancing quickly towards the food queue as my stomach let out a huge gurgle.

'Hen party? Did someone say hen party?' Clara grinned.

'Ha! First of all she blags an invite to your wedding—'

'As your plus one and anyway who else are you going to take?' Clara pulled a face and folded her arms, trying her best to look hurt.

'And now she wants to gatecrash your hen party!' I joked.

'You are more than welcome to come, Clara,' Elle piped up.

'We're thinking of having the hen do sooner rather than later,' Mim added.

'Thankfully it's not long to the wedding now, though there's still loads left to organise. Fingers crossed I won't bloom too much in the next couple of months, otherwise my dress may need to be altered.'

'So what are the plans for the hens then?' I asked, one eye still on the food queue, which thankfully was now dwindling.

'We thought maybe just a meal up at the Gatehouse restaurant.'

I noticed Clara's face fall and I gave her a swift kick under the table to encourage her to look a little more enthusiastic.

'I'm sure that'll be absolutely lovely, and you can count us both in,' I said, standing up and clutching my ticket for the carvery. 'Who's coming for food?'

'You three go and I'll wait here with all the coats and bags,' Mim offered kindly as both Elle and Clara followed me without hesitation towards the vast silver trays of food.

Five minutes later we began tucking in, our plates piled high.

'Mmm, I needed this,' Clara murmured, swirling her roast spud around in the pool of gravy on her plate. 'I've worked up an appetite after lugging all my stuff to yours.'

'Yes, me too!' I replied.

'What's been going on in the land of books this week?' Elle asked, slicing up her beef. 'Anything interesting?'

'It's been fairly quiet, hasn't it?' I said, glancing at Clara and wondering why Noah was the first thing to pop into my head again. He was beginning to make a habit of that.

'Well, sort of, apart from the fact we have a new employee – not to mention your unexpected birthday present.'

The weekend had been so busy I'd totally forgotten about that. 'Oh yes, Aiden has joined us – he's transferred from Claxton Library.'

'Very easy on the eye,' Clara chipped in.

'Behave! And I've had a birthday and a mysterious present, which no one seems to be owning up to.'

'Oooh, was it a good present?' Mim asked, intrigued.

Clara smiled. 'You could say that.'

I looked up to see both Elle and Mim staring at me with anticipation.

'So here's the thing…' Everyone folded their arms and leant on the table as if I was going to reveal some massive secret. 'On Friday, my birthday—'

'Get on with it! Elle will have had the baby by the time you finish this story,' Clara demanded, laughing.

'There slap bang in the middle of the desk was a parcel addressed to me.'

Clara rolled her eyes. 'That parcel was only a copy of the new Sam Stone novel.'

Elle and Mim sat back in their chairs.

'Is that it?' Mim asked, disappointed.

'Not quite,' Clara continued, hitting my arm. 'Go on!'

'I was trying until you rudely interrupted.'

'So there's more?' Elle queried as they both leant forward again and waited.

'It was a signed copy from *the* Sam Stone, wishing me a happy birthday.'

Both Elle and Mim gasped.

'Get away! You're pulling our leg.' Elle's eyes narrowed.

'Honestly, I'm not. It's all very bizarre. One minute I'm making a cup of tea and chatting to Aiden and his gorgeous son—'

'Cut to the chase,' Elle said, grinning.

'And the next I'm opening a present from Sam Stone.'

Elle and Mim looked at each other with puzzled expressions.

'Surely it's a practical joke? Someone's faked the signature.'

'That thought did cross our minds, but if it was a joke, no one has owned up to it,' I answered.

'Yet,' Mim chipped in.

'And we've no idea how it appeared on the desk. The library was nearly empty, and neither of us saw anyone put it there,' Clara added.

'Was it posted?' Mim asked.

I shook my head.

'There was a handwritten label,' Clara piped up.

'So it's someone who knows you work in the library?' Mim raised her eyebrows.

'That's what I said.'

'I would die for a signed copy of any Sam Stone book. How lucky are you?' Elle said.

'Very,' I replied, still mystified by the whole thing.

'How can we discover how it got there?' Mim asked.

'I've no idea,' I replied, sucking in air thoughtfully.

'Well, that's easy,' Elle said, and we all looked over in her direction and waited patiently.

'Tweet him.'

I laughed.

Clara's eyes widened as she turned towards me.

'Why didn't we think of that?'

Before I could even answer, she'd grabbed my phone off the table.

'Passcode,' she demanded.

The laugh faded from my voice as soon as I realised Clara was serious.

'Too late, I'm in,' she said, grinning from ear to ear.

Damn.

'Fancy not having a passcode.'

'I've never needed one before!'

Before I had a chance to object, the tweet was sent and the phone placed back on the table.

Almost immediately, the phone pinged.

We all stared at it.

'There you go, he's replied,' Mim said, clearly amused.

'Ha! Very funny!'

Clara glanced at the notification, then looked up at me. She was silent.

'What's the matter?'

She passed me the phone.

I hesitated before I flicked my eyes towards the screen.

Noah Jones is now following you.

I could have sworn my heart missed a beat.

I met Clara's gaze, and we squeezed each other tightly and squealed.

CHAPTER THIRTEEN

Clara and I were on a high. After several drinks we left the Royal Oak and ambled home with our arms linked.

'Why don't you send him a message?' Clara suggested.

'Who?'

She rolled her eyes at me. 'Noah of course.'

'And what am I going to put? "Remember me? We spent the afternoon together."!'

'Ha! That would set the cat amongst the pigeons. Which afternoon was it anyway?'

'It was 17 May,' I said without hesitation.

Clara stopped dead in her tracks and raised her eyebrows at me.

'You actually know the date?' She picked her jaw up off the floor. 'I can't remember what I did last week, never mind eight months ago!'

'Keep walking. I'm sure he won't even remember,' I answered, deliberately avoiding her question.

'Yes, he will. He's followed you back.' Clara squeezed my arm, then did a drunken celebratory dance on the pavement.

I giggled at her antics. 'He probably follows everyone back.'

'We could soon put that theory to the test,' she said and grinned, reaching into her bag and whipping out her mobile phone.

'Let's not, eh?'

'Anyway, what's the plan for the morning?' Clara asked. 'We don't want to be tripping over each other in the bathroom. What time do you normally get up?'

'About six, but you've just reminded me – I'll need to change the times of the water so we both manage to have a hot shower.'

We strolled in silence for a minute, lost in our own thoughts, until I noticed a familiar figure walking towards us.

'Look,' I said under my breath. 'Let's cross the road.'

Clara looked up. 'Oh no.'

'Do not make eye contact – just keep walking.'

Strolling in our direction was Nick, Clara's ex. We hurriedly crossed the road, staring down at the ground in the hope he wouldn't notice us. Even though I didn't say it out loud, I had to admit to myself I could see why Clara had been attracted to him. He was very handsome. It was just a shame he was a total idiot.

'He texted me this morning.'

'Are you kidding me? Did you reply? You've kept that quiet.'

'No, I've not replied to any of his texts, though I've been tempted. He's sent me a few now, but I've made myself remember all the pain he caused me. He just keeps saying he's made a huge mistake.'

'We already know that.'

'Oh, and that he's sorry.'

'And let me guess: if he could turn back the clock...'

Clara nodded.

'It's a bit late for that now, isn't it?'

Clara was silent.

'Isn't it?' I urged.

'Shhh! Oh lord, he's spotted us – he's crossing the road.'

I looked up to see Nick heading straight for us.

Awkward.

'Hi,' he said, hovering sheepishly in front of us on the pavement, his hands stuffed firmly inside his coat pockets.

Silence.

'Hi,' I said, feeling like a fish out of water.

'Have you been anywhere nice?' he asked, doing his best to make small talk.

Still Clara didn't speak.

'Just the pub,' I offered, dodging the sudden glare Clara shot me for providing such information.

More silence.

Nick shuffled his feet and we both stared at him.

'I'll leave you to it then. It was lovely to see you both,' he said, pausing for a moment before he reluctantly moved past us and kept walking. We turned slightly to watch him go and saw him glance over his shoulder at us before he turned the corner. He gave us a half smile and a cringeworthy wave.

'See ya – wouldn't want to be ya,' Clara muttered under her breath as we turned round and continued walking.

'Are you OK?' I asked tentatively.

'What does he expect me to do? Stand there and make small talk or even ask him how he's doing?'

'I'd say by the worn-out, washed-up look on his face that he's not doing too brilliantly.'

'He's regretting what he did,' Clara agreed. 'I know I shouldn't be happy with other people's misfortunes, but I kind of think he's got what he deserved. He's girlfriendless and back home living with his parents – unlike me, who's put all that sorry mess behind me and moved in with you!' She managed a smile.

'Exactly. So, no more stalking him on Facebook to see if he's single.'

'Nope. I couldn't care less. I'm well and truly over him. It's about time I moved on.'

I narrowed my eyes at her, but from the look on her face, she meant every word. In my opinion it was far better being single than dealing with the emotional heartache of a failed relationship.

Just then I noticed a car slowing down next to us. The window rolled down and Aiden beamed at us.

'Do you ladies need a lift?'

'It's a shame you didn't drive past two minutes ago,' Clara mumbled.

'Was that a yes then?' Aiden asked, his hand poised on the gear stick.

'That's a yes, thank you, Aiden,' I said, taking the front seat while Clara clambered into the back.

'Well hello, little man,' I heard Clara say as I fastened my seat belt, and I looked over my shoulder to see two big brown eyes staring back at me.

'Hello, Theo, how are you?'

Theo hid his head in his hands, then peeped cheekily through the crack between his fingers.

'We've not met before,' Clara said, holding her hand out, but Theo kept his face hidden.

'Didn't you meet him when he came into the library?' I asked.

Clara shook her head. 'No, I was helping that student with her coursework, remember? I didn't have a chance. You are a handsome chappy, aren't you?' she said in a rather cooey voice as she tried to tickle his tummy. Theo let out the cutest giggle I'd ever heard.

'Aww.' Clara and I pulled a face at each other.

'What have you pair been up to today then?' Aiden said.

'We've been moving all of Clara's stuff across to her new room.'

'Thank you by the way.' She leant forward and placed her hand on Aiden's shoulder. 'It's very much appreciated.'

He turned his head towards her and I noticed that they held each other's gaze.

'Anytime,' he replied warmly. He looked away as he put the car into gear and pulled away from the kerb, but I noticed him catch her eye again in the mirror once we were on the move.

'And we've just been to the pub for tea,' I said. 'We bumped into Elle and Mim while we were there.'

'I suppose those two must get fed up of cooking after spending all week in the café doing it for everyone else.'

'I never thought of that. What have you two been up to today?' I asked.

'We've been to the zoo,' Aiden replied as Theo let out a huge roar from behind us and we all laughed. 'And we've just had tea.'

'I think he quite liked the lions!' Clara said.

'Yes, and hopefully I've tired him out and given Louisa a chance to recharge her batteries. Even though he's beginning to sleep in his own bed, he keeps waking up early now he realises he can get out of it.'

Clara's voiced jumped an octave. 'How grown up are you, sleeping in a big bed?'

Theo looked up and gave her a huge smile.

'You're wasted working in a library,' I said to Clara, admiring the warm interaction between the two of them. 'You should've become a teacher.'

She looked up and smiled.

'You'd make a brilliant teacher,' Aiden agreed. 'Usually when Theo meets anyone new, he cries – and look at him smiling away. He can't take his eyes off you!'

A moment later Aiden was turning into our street and pulling up just outside the house.

'Thanks for the lift,' I said to him, unclipping my seat belt and reaching down for my bag.

'I'll see you another time,' Clara said, pinching Theo's cuddly toy and ruffling it against his cheek. For a second Aiden and I just watched as she made a fuss of him.

'See you tomorrow, Aiden – and hopefully see you soon, little fellow,' Clara said, smiling, as she climbed out of the car and waved at Theo through the window.

We stood on the pavement and watched them both disappear up the road.

'Mmm, never mind Theo – Aiden couldn't take his eyes off you either.'

Clara smiled at me, quirking her lips upwards. 'Yeah, right.'

'Don't "yeah right" me. You know so – and you have that dreamy look all over your face.'

Clara shrugged. 'I don't know what you mean.'

'You fancy him, don't you?'

Clara raised a perfectly arched eyebrow and her eyes twinkled. 'Maybe. Maybe not.'

'Are you going to do anything about it?'

She gave me a cheeky sideward glance and nudged me in the ribs.

'Who knows! Now let's get that kettle on and we can discuss your next move.'

'My next move?' I asked, following her up the steps.

'Yes! I only have two words for you.'

'And they are?'

'Noah Jones.'

Feeling my heart thumping harder, I twisted the key in the lock and opened the front door.

I smiled at Clara. 'We best get that kettle on then.'

CHAPTER FOURTEEN

On Monday morning, the library was unusually quiet, and Aiden was perched at the front desk browsing through the latest newsletter, which was distributed to the library every week. Clara was helping me file the books that had been returned over the weekend. Neither of us worked Saturdays, so the library was staffed by a number of volunteers, who carried out only the basic duties of stamping books in and out.

'There are lots of new releases coming out,' Aiden said, looking over to us as he flicked through the newsletter.

'Anyone we might know?' I asked.

Clara had mentioned Noah's new crime book was due for publication very soon, and I'd had a flick through his Twitter feed in bed that morning. There'd been a couple of new posts from bloggers eagerly awaiting the new release, which of course he'd retweeted. I'd also studied his profile picture, and according to Google he was only a year older than me. I was in awe of his achievements. Such dedication to write one book by his age, never mind that he was about to publish his seventh. I'd hovered over the private message button a couple of times but then realised how silly I was being. If he'd remembered who I was or wanted to get in touch, surely he would have done. The follow back must have just been a gesture of goodwill.

I'd switched over to my own profile and thought that maybe Clara was right. My profile picture did lack any sort of life.

Aiden interrupted my thoughts. 'Did you recognise any of those names?' he asked, looking over in our general direction. I filed the last book Clara had passed to me as I shook my head. 'I don't think so,' I said, though I hadn't actually heard any of the names he'd said.

'Who is she trying to kid?' Clara exclaimed.

'Huh?' I replied.

Just then we heard a squeal of delight and we all looked over to towards the main entrance.

'Theo!' Aiden exclaimed. 'I would recognise that noise anywhere.' He held out his arms while Theo stumbled towards him. Aiden promptly threw him up in the air and caught him.

'Clara, let me introduce you to Louisa's parents – David and Barbara.'

Clara shook both their hands and smiled politely.

'I hope you don't mind, but we thought we'd bring Theo along to your children's session this morning. Aiden has been singing your praises.'

I don't know whether it was just me that noticed Clara flush pink.

'Mind? Of course I don't mind.' Clara beamed, holding out her hand to Theo as Aiden placed both his feet back on the floor.

'Would you like to help me set up?' she asked Theo, who nodded and grasped Clara's hand tightly.

Aiden watched their every move as they walked slowly behind the desk to grab the story sack before making their way over towards the colourful beanbags in the children's area.

David and Barbara wandered after them, pulling out a couple of chairs and perching themselves beside the beanbags.

'Singing her praises?' I repeated, smiling at Aiden.

'What?' he asked, suppressing a smile as he returned to the desk and started tapping away on the keyboard, avoiding eye contact with me.

'Here they all come now,' I said as the library door swung open and a small army of children ran wildly towards the beanbags.

'She's definitely got a way with the little people,' I added, smiling as I took a book from a customer who'd just appeared at the desk.

Clara's animated voice filtered across the room to us. 'Not only has Rachel the Reading Rabbit come to visit you this morning, but we have another new guest.'

Theo was sitting proudly on her knee.

'This is Theo. Can we all give him a wave?'

Both Aiden and I smiled across the room as the session got underway.

'You like her, don't you?' I asked him.

'I think so,' he answered truthfully, finally looking me in the eye, 'but it's not that simple, is it?'

'Why not?'

Aiden gazed back over towards the pair of them. Theo's face was shining with joy as Clara and the puppet began to read this morning's story.

'Theo will always come first – and then there's Louisa.'

'Where *is* Louisa?' I asked, wondering why her parents had brought Theo along to the session instead of her.

Aiden sighed as he looked back at me. 'That's part of the problem. I think she's struggling a little at the minute.'

'In what way?' I asked cautiously.

'I think it's down to moving back in with her parents. Don't get me wrong – David and Barbara are worth their weight in gold, especially with Theo. We couldn't manage without them, but I don't have to live with them, and I suppose once you've had your own space, it's difficult to live by someone else's rules again and...'

'And what?'

'And she's been hinting that maybe we should give it another go for Theo's sake.'

'How do you feel about that?'

A sad look spread across his face. 'It wasn't working – otherwise we wouldn't have made the decision to separate in the first place. At the moment, I think she's experiencing a whole range of emotions. Theo is happy and settled, and I help out as best I can. Sometimes it's lonely for me at night having no one else around, but as much as I'm very fond of Louisa, it's better this way, and in time it will get easier for both of us.'

'You have to do what's right for you and Theo.'

He nodded. 'I know, but I worry if I started dating so soon that Louisa wouldn't cope.' For a brief moment, his eyes flitted back to Clara.

I touched his arm affectionately. 'What will be will be.'

He smiled at me warmly. 'Thanks for listening, Evie.'

'Anytime,' I replied, grabbing the small ladders and walking towards a group of students who I'd spotted were having difficulty reaching a book.

How lovely was Aiden? It must be difficult for him too, I realised. He'd also experienced massive changes in his life, and to go from seeing your son all the time to just snatching every moment possible with him… it had to be heart-wrenching. In the short term, he was sacrificing his own happiness to ensure Louisa had a chance of becoming happy once more.

The morning flew by and at lunchtime I was perched on a stool in the staffroom, tucking into a cheese and pickle sandwich as I watched the drizzle run down the windowpane. At the moment, all it seemed to do was rain, and I couldn't wait for the summer months to be upon us once more.

I flicked my phone on and checked my emails. There was nothing of any importance, and I sighed. As yet, there was no email from the Salvation Army. I'd had confirmation that they had received my form but nothing else. I knew it was early days – I'd only sent the email on Friday after all – and I might never receive the answer that I was so eagerly waiting for, but it didn't stop me from hoping it would ping into my inbox soon.

'That's a huge sigh,' Clara said, smiling as she entered the room. She reached for the radio and cranked up the volume. 'I love this band!' she declared and danced her way around the table towards the fridge. After grabbing her lunch, she jigged her way back towards the radio and turned the volume down.

I looked at her with amusement.

'Chocolate?' she asked, sliding a bar towards me.

'You know I'm trying to lose a little weight for the summer.'

Clara peered out the window. 'I shouldn't worry. It's only January, and British summertime being what it is, it'll probably just continue to chuck it down.'

'Oh sod it, you're right,' I said, pulling open the wrapper. It was that time of the month when I was craving chocolate.

'So come on, what was that huge sigh for?'

I hesitated for a minute before answering. 'It's just the weather – it gets you down after a while.'

What was the point in talking about an email that might never arrive? When and if I ever received a reply from the Salvation Army, I'd consider sharing that I'd been searching for my mother.

'How cute was Theo this morning?' Clara asked, beaming. 'What a gorgeous little boy he is.'

'You seem to have taken to him.'

'You know he clung on to my leg all the way through that session and Aiden had to prise him off me when it was time for him to go home.'

'Aww, bless him.'

'Louisa's parents were lovely too, and I helped Theo choose some more books to take home.'

'It must be difficult for them all at the moment with all the changes that are going on. David and Barbara must have had a shock when Louisa turned up back home with Theo.'

'Ha, yes, Barbara mentioned that she's permanently on the go, with interrupted sleep, but you do what's best for your kids, don't you?'

Not in my case, I thought, but then I remembered Irene and I smiled.

'How did you feel when Aiden read out the list of authors this morning?' Clara asked.

'What do you mean?'

Clara paused in munching her apple and looked up. 'I knew you weren't listening.'

I smiled. 'Busted! So, who was on it?'

'Who was on it? I'm sure you can guess! But it was the next bit of information that Aiden read out that I thought you'd take notice of.'

'Which is?' I asked.

'Noah Jones will be signing books in *this* city during his tour.'

Clara's words washed over me in slow motion, and I knew my mouth had fallen wide open. *Act natural*, I thought, though my stomach had just burst with a million nervous butterflies.

'Oh God! This city – Becton?' My voice was shaky.

'See, I knew you weren't listening.' Clara was grinning at me.

She was right – my mind hadn't been on their conversation, but it had certainly been on Noah Jones.

'Just because he's going to be in the same city as us doesn't mean we're going to bump into him, does it?' I said.

My mind whirled.

'It does if we go to his book signing,' Clara suggested with a wicked glint in her eye.

'We'll both be working.'

'No, we won't.'

'Why not?' I asked, confused.

'It's on a Saturday.' Clara stared at me, waiting for me to process the information.

'Where at?'

'Venue to be arranged.'

My mind was already mentally flicking through my wardrobe, choosing an outfit.

'So? Shall we go?'

'Let's see a little nearer the time,' I answered, trying to play the whole situation down, even though I was secretly chuffed to bits.

'That's not a no! Yikes! We are going to do this!' She grinned ecstatically.

Despite it having been eight months since I'd set eyes on him, I did want to see him, and I knew that, come rain or shine, I would be going to that book signing.

CHAPTER FIFTEEN

Stepping under the canopy of Mim's colourful hanging baskets, we opened the door to the café and welcomed the warm air and the rich aromas of coffee and cake. As the little bell tinkled above our heads, Mim looked up from behind the counter and greeted us with her usual friendly smile.

There was already a group of women chatting happily in the corner as they flicked through a pile of books, waiting for everything to start. They too looked up and smiled as we closed the door to shut out the chilly night air.

'Tea and cake?' Mim asked as we scrutinised the delights in the glass cabinet in front of her.

'Do you have any Victoria sponge left?' Clara crossed her fingers and closed her eyes as she waited for the answer.

'Of course! Elle put the last three slices to one side, just for you all.'

Clara opened her eyes. 'Thank you. I've been dreaming about that all day.'

'You are most welcome! I can't have disappointed customers now, can I?' she said, grinning as she shouted on Elle, who was clattering about in the kitchen.

'A pot of tea too thanks,' said Irene, rummaging in her bag to find her purse.

'How's life treating you, Irene?' Mim asked as she grabbed a teapot and popped a couple of teabags into it.

Irene smiled. 'Yes, all good. I can't grumble, even though this retirement lark takes some getting used to. My body clock still thinks I should be up at 6.30 a.m.,' she said, grimacing. 'I long for a lie-in!'

'Oh no! Hopefully that'll sort itself out soon.'

'Fingers crossed, because by the time I get to 9 a.m. all my chores are done and sometimes it feels like a very long day.'

'You can always nip across and tidy up our place,' Clara suggested with a huge grin on her face.

'There's nothing like a bit of cheek,' Irene said, smiling across at Clara as she delved into her purse. 'I'll get these – my treat.'

'Thank you,' I said, unzipping my coat and throwing it over my arm.

'Are you sitting in your usual spot? I'll bring the tea over to you,' Mim said as she counted the loose change Irene had handed her.

Clara swung her head around and checked the seats were free. 'Yes, thanks,' she said.

I sank down on to the settee and pulled the signed Sam Stone novel out of my bag, popping it on the table as my gaze flitted around the café.

I noticed Mel and Emma, who'd never missed a book club meet, perusing the pages of a book from the borrow-and-read shelf. They both looked up and waved as they caught my eye from the other side of the room.

Suddenly the kitchen door swung open and Elle appeared, carrying a tray of cakes towards us. 'Here you go, ladies – a slice of the most mouth-watering Victoria sponge, baked today by my own fair hands,' she chirped, setting the tray down on the table.

'I can't tell you how delicious that looks,' I said, making a mental note to do more baking myself.

'Mmm, time for cake!' Clara declared, reaching across the table and taking a slice.

Elle's eyes widened and a smile spread across her face the moment she spotted my book on the table. 'May I?' she asked.

I nodded, and she picked it up, staring at the words on the page.

'Evie, this is simply amazing,' she said.

'I know,' I replied.

'Any clue how it appeared yet? And do we know if it's real?' she asked.

'No and no. It's still very much a mystery,' I answered honestly, shaking my head.

'Whoever put it there won't be able to keep it a secret forever,' Irene said and smiled up at Mim, who had just popped the pot of tea down on the table.

'Wow! This is amazing,' Mim said, taking the book from Elle. 'Oh, that reminds me – I have some news myself.' She was beaming like the cat who'd got the cream.

We all stared at her, then Mim clapped her hands together and gave us a mischievous grin before hurrying back towards the counter and grabbing a slice of cake for herself.

Clara laughed. 'She is such a tease!'

Two minutes later the evening was underway. Mim was sitting at the front of the café, explaining why this week's choice of book had hooked her from the very first page. We all listened intently to each other's points of view and discussed various aspects of the plot. Thirty minutes later, once everyone had had their say, it was time for Mim to choose the next read.

She cleared her throat and we watched with anticipation as she grabbed a cardboard box from the counter and flipped open the lid, a huge smile on her face.

She pulled out a paperback and hugged it to her chest before she turned the cover round for us all to see.

'Ta-dah!' she chirped. 'Here's the book club's next read. This is the new thriller by—'

'Noah Jones,' Clara finished for her.

The hairs on the back of my neck prickled.

'But I don't recommend you take this one to bed with you,' she said, laughing. 'Otherwise you'll be sleeping with the light on. Now I have a copy for each and every one of you here tonight,' she said, grabbing a handful from the box and starting to hand them out.

'Has anyone read anything by Noah before?' Mim asked the group. A number of readers nodded and began reeling off some of Noah's previous book titles.

A flurry of goosebumps ran down my spine at the very mention of his name.

Clara hit my arm playfully and stared at me as Irene looked hard at us both. 'I remember Noah now,' she said. 'He was the young chap that came to do that talk at the library last summer. Do you remember him, Evie?'

I met Clara's gaze and managed a nervous smile.

'Yes, I think so.' I was thankful that my voice never faltered.

'He was a lovely lad, very down to earth. More tea?' Irene offered.

I nodded. 'Thank you.'

'How have you managed to get so many copies?' Clara asked Mim with interest as she took one.

'Well, that's my next bit of news,' Mim said as she shushed everyone. All eyes followed her back across the café as she sat down and clasped her hands together.

'She's going to say he'll be visiting our book club,' I murmured nervously to Clara.

Irene raised her eyebrows. 'What is going on with you pair?'

'Nothing,' Clara replied, and I was grateful for her quick response – I didn't trust my own voice right then.

'Today's big news,' Mim said triumphantly, 'is that Noah will be here in a few weeks' time! How marvellous is that? He'll be in the middle of his book tour then, and on the Saturday he'll be signing books in our café!'

The whole room let out a cheer and I noticed everyone nodding in appreciation as my heart plunged into my stomach.

'How lovely! That's one not to miss,' Irene said, smiling as she read the blurb on the back of the book. 'This looks a really good read.'

'If you bring your copy along on the evening, he will take great pleasure in signing the book for you,' Mim shouted over the excited chatter that had erupted throughout the café.

Clara tipped her face towards me as the reality of what Mim had said hit home.

'You're staring at me,' I said to her, feeling my cheeks redden.

'Sorry,' she replied, holding my gaze for a couple of seconds longer.

My heart was racing now, my mouth suddenly dry.

'Are you OK?'

I sucked in a breath. 'I think so. I know we already knew he was coming to the area, but I didn't think he would be in Mim's café!'

Of course I was nervous about setting eyes on Noah again – that was an understatement – but I was also a little excited.

'It's meant to be,' Clara whispered.

'If you pair aren't going to tell me what all the whispering is about, I'll nip to the loo,' Irene said, standing up.

Our eyes followed her as she weaved her way towards the back of the café and disappeared into the ladies' room.

Mim tapped the side of her mug with a spoon to bring the chatter under control. 'That's not the end of our news,' she said.

'I'm not sure I can take any more surprises,' I murmured as Clara squeezed my knee. 'My heart is already pounding.'

'Not only do we want to wish one of our long-standing members a very happy birthday for last Friday—' Suddenly Irene reappeared and flicked off the lights, plunging the room into darkness as Elle burst through the kitchen door holding the most beautiful cake I'd ever seen. On top of it was an iced picture of Sam Stone's latest thriller. She walked towards me, the candles flickering, and everyone in the room sang 'Happy Birthday'.

'Thank you,' I said, beaming as I blew out the candles and Irene switched the lights back on.

'But *now* we have some news about the man himself,' Mim continued.

'Who?' I heard Mel ask from the other side of the room.

'Sam Stone! It's all explained in this leaflet,' Mim shrieked, unable to contain her excitement. She stood up and quickly circulated a copy to us all.

'A writing competition,' Irene said.

Clara and I both quickly read to the end of the leaflet and looked up at each other.

The leaflet was encouraging any aspiring writers to compose a short story about their life for a national magazine. Sam Stone was going to help the magazine judge the winning entry, and he would meet with the winner himself at a nearby manor house to present them with an award and a copy of the published article.

'Gosh, it's all happening tonight. What do you think about that?' I asked Clara.

'Interesting,' Clara pondered, rereading the leaflet before placing it on the table. 'I'm just nipping to the loo. I won't be a min.'

As soon as Clara was out of earshot, Irene said, 'I think you should give it a go.'

'Me? Why would you even think of me? What the heck have I got to write about?' I asked, taking a sip of my tea as Irene's words whirled around in my mind.

'Your story is a fantastic one.'

'How do you make that out?'

'Against all odds, the girl did well. You could have easily ended up on the streets or bitter about life. But look at you! You're so kind, beautiful… the list is endless. And when your story is written and you win the competition, you can add being a published writer to your many achievements,' Irene said proudly, patting my knee.

'But I don't *need* to play the victim,' I protested.

'You wouldn't be! Why would you even think that? You'd be giving a true account of your life and, not only that, it's an inspiring story with a happy ending. Think about it,' Irene said.

'But we don't know the ending yet, do we?' I said, my voice suddenly cracking as I thought about the search for my mother.

'We don't yet, but you don't need to mention that if you didn't want to,' Irene said thoughtfully. 'Personally I think it would make a very emotive read.'

I stared at the words on the leaflet. 'I'll mull it over.'

'When's the closing date?' Irene asked.

'A couple of months' time,' I replied before slipping the leaflet into my bag.

'That gives you plenty of time, and I'm here to help.'

Something in her tone made me flick my eyes towards her. 'You can do this, Evie – give it a go. What's the worst that can happen?'

I looked up to see Clara wandering back towards us. 'Shush, here's Clara.'

Irene nodded.

Clara returned to the table with a huge grin on her face.

'What?' I said.

'Noah Jones – that is all,' she mouthed back.

I shook my head at her in jest while trying to hide my smile.

'I have no idea what's going on between you two tonight. You're acting like a couple of kids,' Irene said, smiling as she stood up. 'Now I'm going to catch up with Mim before we head off. I'll be back in a bit.' And she took herself off across the café.

I stole a furtive glance at Clara, who was grinning and tapping frantically on her phone.

Within a couple of seconds my phone beeped.

'Clara Lawson, what have you done now?'

'Me? Nothing, why?' She brought her hand up to her chest in mock outrage as she protested.

I stared at the screen of my phone, then flicked my eyes back to Clara.

'You call that nothing?'

'OK, so I've tweeted Noah saying we're looking forward to his visit – and to reading his new book. What's wrong with that?' She smirked. 'Anyway, like we've said before, it's unlikely he'll reply – especially with that many Twitter followers. He probably misses half his notifications.'

'Mmm,' was the only reply I could muster, but I crossed my fingers behind my back and secretly hoped he saw the tweet. But Clara was probably right – his following was huge and increasing by the day. It was doubtful he would notice it.

'And what a night,' Clara continued. 'Who'd have thought our city was going to welcome two of our favourite authors in such a short space of time?'

She pressed a hand to her heart. 'Noah Jones and Sam Stone,' she swooned, fluttering her eyelashes, and we shared a knowing smile – we both couldn't wait to meet Noah and stalk Sam Stone.

'Are you ready for home?' she asked, standing up and sliding her arms into her coat.

'Yes, I think so. I'll just check with Mim to see if she has something for us to take this cake home in. It was such a lovely gesture, but the amount of cake I've been eating recently is no good for the diet.'

Irene was wrapping things up on the other side of the room, giving Elle a hug. Mim bustled towards us carrying a large white cardboard box. 'Here, take this for the cake,' she said, placing it on the table.

'Thanks for the cake, Mim – such a lovely thought,' I said, kissing her cheek. I was genuinely surprised they had gone to so much trouble.

'You are more than welcome! You didn't think we'd let your birthday slip away without any notice, did you?' She touched my arm affectionately before saying goodbye to Mel and Emma, who were fastening up their coats and hovering by the door.

'Are we ready?' Irene asked, grabbing her bag from underneath the table.

'Yes, I think so,' I replied, hearing my phone beep and delving into my pocket.

I stared at the screen for a split second, then looked up at Clara, who was also glancing at her phone. Her mouth had fallen open.

Noah Jones liked a tweet you were mentioned in.

We both squealed at the same time.

Sheer pleasure mixed with apprehension ran through my entire body – and then I saw that he'd replied.

I can't wait to see you all and I hope you all enjoy my latest book. Please let me know!

Nervous butterflies began to flutter around my stomach at a rate of knots as Clara linked her arm through mine and we walked towards the café door with huge smiles across our faces.

CHAPTER SIXTEEN

Clara had spent ages straightening my hair before backcombing it to give it some height. She then pulled it into a tight high ponytail that actually made my eyes water. The living room now felt like the bedroom of a messy teenager, with clothes thrown over the back of the settee, make-up scattered all over the coffee table and the latest Adele album playing on Clara's iPhone.

'I'm nearly done,' Clara said, swiping more blusher across my cheekbones.

'Ta-dah!' she said, turning the mirror towards me.

I did a double take, my pupils dilated and a small noise escaped from my throat.

'What do you think?' Clara asked, standing back and studying my face like she was a professional make-up artist.

'I think I look like one of those ridiculous porcelain dolls that you find abandoned on a dusty shelf in a charity shop.'

'Eww, those things are ugly.'

'My point exactly – and that's where I'm going to end up.'

'Where?' Clara asked, smudging in my eyeshadow with her finger.

'On the bloody shelf!'

'Trust me, no man is going to be able to resist this smoky eye make-up,' she said, cranking up the music. 'You look the business.'

'That's what I'm worried about.'

Clara passed me the mirror and I stared open-mouthed at my reflection, tilting my head from side to side.

'You need to pout like this.'

I giggled. 'You look ridiculous.'

'Go on – give it a try!'

'You'll be advising me to inject collagen next – and Botox,' I said, laughing as I pouted back at her.

'Now it's you who looks ridiculous.'

I swiped her hand playfully.

'If I pouted like that on my profile picture, people would need to slap themselves. They'd think they were watching *Embarrassing Bodies*.'

Clara laughed. 'You'll thank me for this when you have a hot date with Noah.'

I swallowed, feeling a little flutter of pleasure at the mention of his name. 'Pass me some wine. I think I need it.'

'What do you think of these?' Clara held up a couple of dresses.

'Very bright,' I replied, wondering why I'd agreed to let her give me a makeover. I was quite happy with my tattered jeans and Converse.

'OK, grab a couple of outfits and go and get changed in the bathroom.'

Reluctantly, I browsed through the collection of outfits that Clara had laid out on the settee.

'What's this?' I asked, picking up something that resembled a onesie.

Clara laughed. 'It's a jumpsuit. Get with it!'

'It looks like my PJs.'

'They're the latest fashion! They're in every magazine right now.'

'This is exactly why I don't do fashion, and I don't read magazines.'

Hopefully in another hour this torture would be over.

'Go on, take that one first,' Clara insisted, thrusting it into my hand and pushing me up the stairs. 'And do not mess up your hair,' she shouted after me.

Five minutes later, I shouted from the top of the stairs like a sulky teenager, 'I'm not coming down dressed like this.'

Clara popped her head round the corner and stared up at me. 'Wow, you look different – pretty good in fact. I reckon jumpsuits are your thing,' she said with such enthusiasm I nearly believed her.

'Do you now? I feel like I'm wearing a Babygro.'

'Get yourself down here! Let's have a proper look.'

Strolling down the stairs was uncomfortable to say the least. My knickers kept rising up my backside, and I attempted to pull them down for the umpteenth time.

'Stop fidgeting,' she ordered, 'and give me a twirl.'

Unwillingly, I give her a twirl with a forced smile and jazz hands.

Clara bent down underneath the coffee table. 'That outfit will look great with these,' she said, hooking a pair of strappy peach stilettos around her fingers and holding them in the air.

'I'm not sure,' I said, thinking of my flat comfy Converse.

'These are the height of fashion. Pop them on! Luckily for you, we're the same size,' Clara replied, looking hurt.

'Unlucky for me,' I muttered, slipping my feet into the shoes and wobbling from side to side.

'Now walk around the coffee table so I can have a proper look at you.'

Thrusting my hips forward, I began to strut around the table in time to the music, pretending I was on the catwalk. I wobbled as the heel of one shoe got entangled in the rug, and I reached out towards Clara, knocking her glass of wine out of her hand.

'Whoa, OK, maybe let's ditch the heels,' she said, quickly using a make-up wipe to mop up the spilt wine.

Thank God for that, I thought, kicking them from my feet.

'But what about this look in general?'

'I'm the least glamorous person on this earth. I feel like a drag queen, and I look like a drag queen – and not a good one at that,' I said, slumping on to the settee and folding my arms. 'If I have to go to all this trouble to impress Noah, is it really worth it?'

'Trust me, you look amazing. You do trust me, don't you?'

'Hmmm.' I grinned. 'I'm not entirely sure – the jury's still out on that one.'

'Let's take some photos and see how you look.' Clara wasn't taking no for an answer.

'Come on – get posing,' she said as she whipped her phone out.

'I can't, I feel stupid.'

'Tell you what – I'll disappear into the kitchen. Now stand in front of the fireplace,' she demanded.

I had never felt as uncomfortable in my own skin as I did at that moment.

'Tilt your chin up – and the other one,' she said, laughing as I grappled with Clara's phone, trying to get it to focus.

'It's no use, I can't even see all of myself,' I exclaimed.

Clara tutted, then came up beside me, slowly lifting my arm up until the top half of my body came into view on the screen.

'How do you not know how to take selfies?'

'Because I don't need to spend my time posing, pouting and posting pictures just so any Tom, Dick and Harry can give them a like to make me feel wanted. I'm quite happy with people liking me in the real world, for who I am.'

'The lady doth protest too much,' Clara replied, dismissing my answer. 'Now start snapping.'

I took a deep breath and pressed the button.

'OMG, that looks awful.'

Clara peered over my shoulder. 'Mmm, yes, that one doesn't do you justice. Do it like this.' She took the phone from my hand and smiled, then snapped about ten photos before she stopped and stared at them.

'Ooh no, definitely no, don't like that or that one,' she said, deleting them straight away. 'That one's OKish, that one is a no… that's the one,' she exclaimed, and grinned as she pushed the phone under my nose.

'Not bad actually,' I agreed.

'Then we do this, this and this and look!' She twisted the phone back towards me.

'Jeez, Clara, you look like you've just shed ten pounds and have been sunning yourself on a Caribbean island! Where did you get that tan from?' I spluttered, spraying wine from my mouth.

'It's an app. Easy peasy and… posted,' she said. 'Your turn.'

I held the phone up again, feeling self-conscious.

'I can't do this – it feels so unnatural.'

'I'll go in there and top up the wine while you snap to your heart's content.' She picked up the empty glasses and disappeared into the kitchen. I closed the door behind her.

Five minutes later, after the initial awkwardness had passed, I was actually getting into the swing of things and beginning to enjoy myself.

'Can I come back in yet?' Clara shouted from the other side of the door.

'Sorry! I'd forgotten you were still in there,' I said, laughing as I opened the door and took my glass from her.

'Let's have a look at what've you got.' She took the phone from my hand and plonked herself down on the settee.

I looked over her shoulder as she flicked through the photos. 'What about this one?'

'No, I look like a rabbit caught in the headlights.'

'Maybe,' she said, biting down on her lip, 'this is the one?'

I tilted my head to the side to have a proper look. 'Yes, it's not too bad.'

'Not too bad? It's perfect. Let's do this, this and this. Now what do you think?'

I stared at the photo in disbelief. In the blink of an eye she'd made me look fresh and fashionable.

'Where's that wrinkle gone from the bridge of my nose?'

'We don't need that – I've airbrushed it out,' Clara replied like it was the most natural thing in the world.

Just then my phone beeped. 'That's me. I've just sent you the photo,' Clara said. 'Upload it to your profile and let's get this show on the road.'

'Oh God.' I reached for my phone and pressed the Twitter app.

'Go on! Then we can get to work on your bio.'

Almost immediately my phone beeped and Clara and I jumped out of our skins. 'It's only Aiden!' I said, laughing.

Loving the pout!

Clara pouted at me and we both fell about giggling on the settee.

Then my phone beeped again.

'Who is it this time?' We both peered at the screen.

'It's a private message on Twitter,' I said, pressing the small envelope at the bottom of the screen.

'Who's it from?' Clara asked.

'Noah Jones,' I said, laughing.

'Stop teasing me! Now who is it really from?'

'N-N-Noah Jones,' I stuttered.

CHAPTER SEVENTEEN

'Urghh,' I muttered, ripping another piece of paper out of my notebook, screwing it up and tossing it into the wastepaper basket. I stared down at yet another blank piece of paper and attempted to start again. It was 4 a.m., the early hours of Sunday morning, and I was wide awake.

I let out a defeated sigh. This was harder than I'd thought. Where did I start? I had no idea.

After tea, Clara and I had both settled down in our onesies, lit the fire and drunk copious amounts of wine. We'd stared at Noah's message for what seemed like hours – actually, it was hours – and then finally I'd switched my phone off before I could send him a drunken, illegible message back. Drunk messaging was never a good idea! But even though my phone was switched off, I could remember every word of Noah's message.

I hope you can make it to the book signing. It will be good to see you x

'See, there's a kiss!' Clara had exclaimed, jabbing her finger at the screen. 'And more importantly, he remembers who you are.'

As if I hadn't spotted there was a kiss. It was the first thing I'd noticed.

I'd gone to bed around 11 p.m. but couldn't sleep. After tossing and turning for numerous hours, I'd finally pulled my weary body out of bed and staggered back downstairs to make a mug of tea. Then I'd fired up my laptop and reached for my notepad.

Irene's words whirled around in my mind. 'Your story is a fantastic one. Against all odds, the girl did well.' The leaflet about the writing competition was lying next to me on the coffee table. I found myself staring at it, rereading it umpteen times. Irene was right – I'd overcome so many obstacles in my life and there were countless times I could have hit the self-destruct button and veered off the right path. Maybe it would help me if I put my story into words.

I'd battled with crushing disappointment for years during my time at school. They say those days are the best time of your life – well not for me. I dreaded school plays, sports day and parents' evenings. There was no one to watch me and no one interested enough to read my report cards. I never had time to make friends before I was shipped off to somewhere new.

Over the years, I'd read numerous author interviews, the inspiration behind their stories and why they began to write. Authors seemed to be divided into two camps – those who plotted, made wall charts and knew every twist and turn in their book before they put pen to paper, and those who flew by the seat of their pants. I was definitely a fly-by-the-seat-of-your-pants type of girl, and the words from one author interview in particular had always stuck with me: 'Write from your gut.'

I pushed the notepad to one side and stared at the blank screen in front of me before typing: 'My story, where it all began, 20 January 1993'.

Tears welled up in my eyes as I thought about how far I'd come. Irene was right. Entering the competition was more about therapy – I was doing it for *me*. Putting the words on to paper might help release all the feelings that had been bubbling up inside me for years. It was time – it was time to let go.

For a brief moment, my throat became tight and I struggled to think of an opening paragraph. I just didn't know how to begin. I pondered for a second before creeping back upstairs. I opened my wardrobe door, pulled the stool out from underneath the dressing table and stepped up on to it so I could grab a box from the top shelf.

I sat on the bed with the box resting on my knee. Carefully I removed the lid and ran my fingers lightly over the shawl inside – the shawl that had accompanied me through every foster home. I buried my face in it and inhaled. There was a distinctive smell that lingered amongst the stitching. A smell I couldn't describe or recognise. I wrapped it around my shoulders and went back downstairs.

I was ready to begin.

Sitting back down in front of the laptop, I took a deep breath. This was it. *Write from your gut.*

I paused for a moment and then began to tap frantically on the keys, words spilling on to the screen as tears flowed down my cheeks.

When I next paused and squinted at the clock, I was amazed to find it was nearly 9 a.m. I'd been at it for five hours. I gazed at the screen, resting my head on my hands, and began to read over what I'd written.

I couldn't believe it. The words had turned into sentences and paragraphs, and staring back at me was a short story about my life.

Hearing the stairs creak, I glanced up towards the doorway.

'You're up early,' Clara said, breezing into the living room with a smile.

I opened my mouth to reply, but no words came out as I swallowed a lump in my throat.

She paused at the side of the coffee table. 'Hey,' she said softly, 'you look awful. Are you sick?'

I shook my head.

'Have you been crying?'

I looked to the ground and bit down on my bottom lip in an attempt to stop the tears cascading down my face again. I could feel Clara's eyes on me as she walked round the table. She knelt down on the rug beside me and held out her arms. I turned, fell into them and broke down.

She hugged me tight.

'Come on, it can't be that bad.' She stroked my hair softly as if I was a small child.

'Sorry, I'm just being silly.'

'How long have you been down here?'

'Since the early hours.'

'Whatever it is, it's going to be OK,' Clara said in a calm soothing voice.

'It's been a long night,' was all I could say. I didn't have the words to say more.

'You're freezing!' she said, rubbing her hands over mine. 'I'll pop the kettle on, get you something warm to drink, then if you want to you can tell me all about it.'

A couple of minutes later, Clara handed me a mug of hot tea. 'There's two sugars in there,' she said. 'I think you need them.'

I nodded and cupped my hands around the mug, and Clara gave me a reassuring smile. 'Whatever it is, it's going to be all right, you know.'

I smiled at her with bleary eyes.

'Do you want to tell me?' She sipped her tea, but her eyes didn't leave mine.

'I think I probably do.'

I paused for a second and Clara remained silent as I started hugging my knees and rocking back and forth. It was something I used to do as a kid, stalling for time while I tried to work out where to begin.

'I don't know where to start.'

'Try the beginning,' she urged gently.

'There's something I need to tell you about my mum.'

'What about her?'

I hesitated before saying, 'She's not my real mum.'

I watched the look on Clara's face change as my words registered.

'Here, take this and read.' I unplugged my laptop and passed it to Clara. My chest was pounding. She placed her mug on the coffee table and took the laptop from me. 'What is it?'

'Go on – read it,' I answered.

She focused on the screen and began to read in silence. I watched as a tear rolled down her cheek. My chest pounded as I waited for her to finish.

She gazed up at me when she reached the end. For a second she didn't say anything, her eyes brimming with tears.

I watched her compose herself. 'I'm sorry, Evie,' she said sadly, her voice soft.

I handed her a tissue from the box and she dabbed her eyes with it.

'Look at me, stealing your thunder,' she sniffled. 'I had no idea what you've been going through. I think you need a hug.'

My hands were shaking as I took the laptop from her, my lips trembling as I tried to hold it together. I felt drained and battered. We hugged each other tightly, then grabbed our drinks and sat side by side on the settee.

'Evie, you've written that so well. It was so gripping! I feel like I've just stepped off a rollercoaster – my emotions are all over the place.'

'Thank you. I cried writing it. I feel exhausted but also... relieved, in a strange kind of way.'

'Because you've let it all out?'

'Yes. Once I started to write, I couldn't stop. My mind was whirling, and I didn't even notice how many hours had passed.'

'Your life story is truly inspirational.'

'That's one way of putting it, but it hasn't been one I'd have chosen.'

'Was it really difficult growing up?' she asked tentatively.

'I'd see all the other children being dropped off in the playground by their parents. They'd be smothered in kisses and have their friends round for tea. I envied the bond they had. I was never mistreated or anything like that – I was always fed and watered – but I never felt like I belonged. It was more like I was an inconvenience I suppose.' My voice faltered a little.

'Oh, Evie, but look at you now.' Clara squeezed my knee. 'And Irene is the best surrogate mum anyone could ask for.'

I smiled. 'I know – she is. I'm very lucky in that respect.'

'I didn't have a clue. You and Irene even look similar,' she said, sipping her tea.

'I think it's the hair,' I replied, smiling as I twirled a strand round my finger.

'And you have the same surname.' Clara looked puzzled.

I nodded. 'Yes, I changed mine by deed poll.'

'Honestly, I would have never guessed in a million years.'

'Irene suggested I write my story for the competition.'

'After reading it, I think you've got a very good chance of winning.' Clara smiled. 'So have you any clues about your biological parents?'

'No – except for my mother's name. Remember when I didn't come home with you on the bus on my birthday?'

'Yes.'

'That's when I started searching for her. I'd thought about doing it for years, but I don't think I was emotionally ready until now. I'd always thought she might come looking for me… but I also wondered if some things were best left in the past.'

Clara sighed. 'Now there's a thought. There could be numerous reasons she hasn't come looking.'

'Such as?'

'She might be worried about rejection, or that you could be settled, happy and she'd catapult your life into disarray.'

'I suppose.'

'Do you know why she never kept you?' Clara asked tentatively.

I shook my head. 'No, I don't know anything.'

'Did you say you only started the search last week?'

I nodded. 'Yes, my birthday.'

'What happens now then?'

'I sit and wait.'

'*We* sit and wait,' Clara corrected me. 'I'll be here for you every step of the way.' She squeezed my arm affectionately.

'I've had an email to say the Salvation Army have received my form at least. Who knows how long it will take, but you know when you're checking your emails every two minutes, hoping the news you want has landed in your inbox?'

'I know that feeling. I keep checking mine hoping that Harry Styles has finally noticed me on Twitter and thinks I'm sex on legs,' Clara said, smiling.

I laughed. 'I think there's more chance of my email landing than yours.'

'Yep, you're probably right. So, are you really going to enter it in the competition?' she asked, nodding towards my laptop.

'Do you honestly think it's good enough?'

'Do I think it's good enough? Are you serious? Of course I do – it's the best thing I've read in ages.'

'Clara, please keep all this to yourself.'

'Of course – it goes without saying.'

I met her gaze and held it. 'Thank you.'

'Why don't you get yourself back to bed and try to get some sleep? You need to rest. I'll clean up down here.'

I smiled warmly at her. 'Thank you again,' I said, standing up and then hovering in the doorway.

'Clara…'

She looked over her shoulder.

'I'm so glad you're here.'

'Me too,' she replied warmly.

CHAPTER EIGHTEEN

Two weeks later

'Shall I or shan't I?' I asked Clara as we both stared at the computer screen. On the screen was my entry for the writing competition.

'That would be a shall,' Clara said. 'And hurry up or we'll miss the bus.'

'It's now or never,' I teased, stringing it out a little longer.

'For God's sake!' She reached over my shoulder and pressed enter before I could object.

'Clara!'

'Christmas will be here by the time you get round to pressing that button,' she said, laughing. 'Now grab your coat and come on.'

Forty minutes later, we were standing outside the library doors.

'You will remember to keep quiet about my competition entry,' I said, pausing on the top step and glancing over the marketplace.

'Of course, but why?' Clara replied as we noticed Aiden hurrying across the square. He waved when he spotted us and Clara tapped her watch, grinning at him.

'I don't know really, maybe to save face a little when I don't win. If I tell Mim and Elle, the rest of the club will find out and they'll keep asking whether I've heard anything yet and so on and so forth – you know how it is.'

'OK, it's our little secret – just as long as when you win, I can go with you to meet Sam Stone.'

'Ha, OK! But now I've sent it, I'm starting to panic a little.'

'Why?'

'Because it was all so personal – writing about the shawl and revealing Irene isn't my mum.'

'There's no need to panic. Now shush – here's Aiden.'

'Good morning, ladies,' he said cheerfully, bounding up the steps towards us.

Clara narrowed her eyes at him. 'You're full of the joys of spring.'

'Just high on life,' he said and grinned, fishing around in his pocket and pulling out a letter.

'I'm under strict instructions to hand you this.' He passed me the envelope.

'From whom?' I asked, opening the library door.

'All very cloak and dagger.' Clara's mouth and eyebrows twitched with curiosity.

'It's from Elle – an invitation to the hen do,' Aiden replied as I punched the alarm code in. 'It's to both of you.'

We all wandered into the staffroom, hung up our coats and placed our lunches in the fridge.

'Monday mornings do come around a little too quickly for my liking,' Aiden said, tossing his pound coin into the tea-fund caddy. 'Did you two get up to anything interesting this weekend?'

Clara and I exchanged glances and hesitated. We'd spent the weekend putting the finishing touches on my competition entry.

'That silence speaks volumes,' he said, looking at the pair of us.

'Nothing whatsoever,' Clara piped up.

'I thought you'd been out partying, and I was a bit miffed that I never got an invite.'

'Partying? No,' I answered. 'It was just a quiet one for us. Come on, time to open up.'

'I've been invited on Josh's stag do,' Aiden said cheerfully, walking out on to the library floor.

'Where are you going?' Clara asked.

'Unfortunately, I've signed the Official Secrets Act. If I tell you, I'll have to kill you.' He winked as he switched on the computer.

'That sounds more fun than our meal out.'

'You don't *have* to come,' I said. 'No one is twisting your arm.'

She shrugged. 'I suppose it beats staying in by myself – unless I gatecrash the stag do. You wouldn't mind if I tagged along, would you, Aiden?'

'Don't answer that, Aiden. She's only teasing, and remember Elle is in the early stages of pregnancy –she isn't going to want to go clubbing until the small hours.'

'I know,' Clara said reluctantly. 'It's just a missed opportunity in my book.'

'I'm sure you'll have your chance one day and we can party hard then. I'm just wondering who'll be lucky enough to marry you.' I flicked my eyes towards Aiden, who promptly blushed and pretended he hadn't heard.

Clara poked me in the ribs and raised her eyebrows.

'Did you do anything nice over the weekend, Aiden?' she asked, quickly changing the subject.

'I met up with the lads Saturday night. Nothing heavy – just a few beers because I was looking after Theo yesterday.'

'Aww, what did you get up to?'

'We went to the park, fed the ducks and had a picnic, though he spent half the time giggling and trying to throw my sandwiches to the ducks instead of the stale bread. He's developing a little personality of his own now.'

'Bless him,' Clara and I said in unison.

'How's Louisa?'

'Yes, she's OK. She's starting a part-time job today, and now we're both settled, Theo's going to stay over with me a couple of nights a week so we can have some real boy time together.'

'Aww, that's nice.' I glanced up at the clock. 'Has anyone seen Wilson this morning? He's a little late.'

'The traffic didn't seem that bad this morn—' Clara stopped in her tracks as a teary Jenny hurried through the doors towards us.

I knew by the way she was looking at me that something was horribly wrong. Before I knew it, Clara was already round the other side of the desk, draping an arm over Jenny's shoulder and leading her towards us.

'This doesn't look good,' Aiden whispered in my ear.

'Whatever is the matter?' we heard Clara ask softly.

Jenny flashed me a grief-stricken look. 'It's Irene,' she whispered, edging towards me and pulling me into her arms. 'There's been an accident.'

A shiver ran down my spine. Panic mounted inside me.

'What sort of accident?' My mouth had gone so dry I could hardly speak.

'There was a fire. At her neighbour's house. She's alive, but she was unconscious when they pulled her out. I don't know how bad it is.'

'Oh my God,' I whispered as Aiden helped me sit down.

'Wilson noticed the smoke as he was passing and pulled up so he could call the fire brigade – I was following him into town, so I saw the whole thing. They arrived in next to no time and smashed down the door. The house to the left of Irene's,' she added.

'That's Poppy and Hattie. Poppy's a single mum. They've only just moved in,' I said. 'Are they OK?'

'I'm sorry, I don't know. They pulled Irene out first, and as soon as I saw she was alive, I rushed straight over here so I could take you to the hospital. Wilson followed the ambulance in his van.'

'Why was she next door?'

'We don't know.'

Aiden placed his hand on my shoulder. 'You need to go. We've got it covered here. Clara and I can manage.'

I looked up at Clara and Aiden through my tears. 'Thanks,' was all I could manage.

'Will you let us know as soon as there's any news?' Clara asked Jenny.

'Of course. Now where's your coat and bag?' she asked me.

'I'll get those,' Aiden replied, hurrying towards the staffroom.

My legs felt shaky as I stood up. When Aiden came back, he held my coat open so I could slip my arms into it.

Clara kissed my cheek. 'Now go, and text me soon.'

I brushed my tears away and followed Jenny to the door in silence.

'I'm parked at the back of the library,' she said, leading me down the steps.

I let out my breath slowly, my heart hammering in my chest as we reached the car. 'She's going to be OK, isn't she?' I asked.

'She's in the best possible place and they will do everything they can,' Jenny replied as she opened the car door and ushered me inside.

CHAPTER NINETEEN

Jenny parked the car and we hurried across the hospital car park in silence. The wind was strong, the clouds were dark and I could barely breathe. I'd never prayed as hard for anything in my life as I was doing right now. I couldn't lose Irene.

Jenny led the way, and we headed towards the main entrance of the hospital, sanitising our hands before we followed the signs to the reception.

As we joined the queue, I filled my lungs with a calming breath and willed the people in front to hurry. I needed to see Irene and let her know I was here for her.

Out of the corner of my eye, I noticed a tall man in a white coat approaching the desk, and I watched as he walked past us and handed the receptionist a clipboard.

I couldn't wait in the queue any longer, so as he turned to leave, I reached out and touched his arm. 'Excuse me. I'm looking for a patient. She was brought in this morning?'

His eyes were warm and his manner kind. 'What's her name?'

'Irene Cooper.'

'Are you a relative?'

'Yes, I'm Evie – her daughter.'

'OK, if you take a seat over here,' he ushered us towards a couple of empty seats, 'either myself or someone else will get back to you in a moment,' he promised before heading back towards the desk. Jenny picked up a magazine from the table and thumbed through it while we waited.

It felt like hours passed, but he returned just five minutes later and asked us both to follow him.

'If you can wait in here, Irene's doctor will be with you in a moment,' he said before disappearing down the corridor.

'Thanks,' Jenny said as she sat down next to me.

I tried my best to blink away my tears as I swallowed the lump in my throat, but it was no use – I couldn't hold them back and the tears cascaded down my face.

I saw Wilson before he saw me. He was hovering outside the door, but then Jenny stood up and he spotted her.

'I called out to you,' he said, walking into the room, 'but you didn't hear me.' He hugged his mother, then handed me a tissue from his pocket.

'She'll be OK, you know,' he reassured me.

A nod was all I could manage.

'I've parked near the entrance,' he said. 'Irene's neighbours were whisked off too.'

'Poppy and Hattie,' I said.

'Are you OK?' Jenny asked Wilson.

'Just a little shaken up but nothing to worry about,' he replied.

I visualised the scene in my head and my whole body felt numb.

Just then the door opened, and a doctor and nurse walked into the room. All three of us stood up and looked imploringly towards them for news.

'Please take a seat,' the doctor said as the nurse smiled warmly at us.

My stomach was churning, my hands shaking.

'Irene's daughter?' The doctor looked at me.

I nodded and Jenny cupped her hands around mine.

I held my breath, waiting for her to speak.

'Irene suffered a nasty blow to her head, so she's had a couple of stitches, and the wound has been cleaned and dressed. She also suffered a couple of burns to her hands –nothing serious though – and she inhaled a lot of smoke, so her throat will be very sore.'

'But she's going to be OK?' Jenny interrupted.

The doctor smiled. 'She's going to be OK. We've decided to keep her in tonight for observation, and she'll need plenty of rest over the next couple of weeks, but yes, she's going to be OK,' she repeated.

I couldn't describe the relief that swept through my body. My tears continued to fall, and I smiled at Jenny. 'She's going to be OK,' I said.

'She is indeed,' Jenny replied, her own eyes glistening with tears.

'I don't know what I would have done if I'd lost her.'

'She isn't going anywhere.' Jenny hugged me tight.

'How are Poppy and Hattie?' Wilson asked and we all looked up towards the doctor.

'Both are doing fine,' she answered.

'Do you know how the fire started?' Wilson asked.

The doctor shook her head. 'The fire department will investigate and there'll be a full report.'

'Why was she in there?' My eyes were wide as I looked at Jenny.

'We'll have to ask her that.'

I turned towards the doctor. 'Can we see her?'

'You can. If you want to follow the nurse, she'll take you right there.'

'Thank you for everything,' Jenny said, standing up and smiling at them both.

We followed the nurse to a private room at the end of the corridor where we found Irene fast asleep. She looked so pale.

She had a bandage wrapped around her head and her finger was attached to a machine that kept beeping. We settled quietly on the chairs dotted around her bed, and I took her hand in mine.

'Does anyone want a coffee?' Wilson asked.

'Thanks, Wilson, that would be great,' I replied, never taking my eyes off Irene.

'Yes, please. Do you have enough money?' Jenny asked.

Wilson nodded and walked off to find the nearest coffee machine.

'I thought I'd lost her there for a minute,' I said, looking over at Jenny.

Tears were falling down Jenny's face.

'Hey,' I said, standing up and walking around the bed to her. 'She's going to be OK.'

'I know,' she said, hugging me. 'I'm just being daft. I barely know either of you. It's suddenly all spilling out.'

'It's probably the relief.'

We rested our heads together for a split second. 'Thanks for being here for me today, Jenny. It means a lot.'

'Don't be daft. Anyone would do the same.'

'I hope you two aren't spilling tears on my account, Evie,' we heard a hoarse voice whisper from the bed.

'Irene!' I beamed at her with delight. 'You're awake. Don't ever frighten me like that again!' I said, planting a kiss on the top of her head. 'Oh you smell all smoky.'

She smiled. 'I wonder why.'

'Do you remember Jenny? Mim's friend? We met her a couple of times at the café.'

Irene nodded, smiling weakly at Jenny.

'Hi. Do you want me to leave so you can have some time together?' Jenny asked, standing up and opening the door for Wilson, who'd returned juggling three coffee cups.

'No. Stay. It's fine,' Irene said hoarsely.

I grinned at Wilson. 'She's awake!' I said, before turning back to Irene. 'This is Wilson,' I told her. 'Jenny's son.'

'Hi,' she said.

'Wilson is Josh's best man.'

Wilson smiled at her. 'Hey, it's great to see you back in the land of the living. You gave us all a huge fright,' he said, placing the drinks on the table at the side of the bed.

'I'm sorry.' She gave him a weak smile. 'How are Poppy and Hattie? Has anyone heard?'

'They're both fine,' Wilson answered.

'Can you remember what happened?' I asked, rubbing her hand gently.

Irene took a moment.

'I was awake early and realised I'd forgotten to put the bins out, but when I opened the door there was a strong smell of burning. I thought it was Alf in the garden at the back of mine – he's always burning rubbish – but something caught my eye – a flash of light – and when I looked up, I realised it was flames and I just stopped in my tracks.' Irene started coughing then.

'Here, have some water,' I said, pouring her a glass from the jug on the bedside table.

She took a sip. 'My throat does hurt.'

'Don't speak if it's too painful – just rest.'

'I'm OK. It was then I noticed Poppy's car and I realised they hadn't left for nursery. I tried the front door but it was locked, but I knew there was a faulty window round the back. I managed to get that open and unlock the back door, but I didn't know where Poppy and Hattie were so I started shouting. Then I heard a scream from upstairs and I figured they must be trapped somewhere.

'The smoke was beginning to make me feel dizzy, so I grabbed a towel from the kitchen and held it over my mouth. I ran to the bottom of the stairs but the heat was overwhelming. I could see Poppy peering round a door at the top of the stairs, but the flames were getting worse so I shouted for her to shut the door and block out the smoke that was seeping underneath it. I could hear the sirens in the distance, so I knew they'd be there soon.' Irene took a breath and another sip of her water. 'Then I heard a loud creak and the flames leapt over the banister. There was a shower of sparks and what looked like flakes of dirty snow, then a part of the banister splintered off and came crashing down the stairs. I held my hands up to shield myself but it hit me on the head, and then all I can remember is waking up in here. My first ride in an ambulance and I can't even remember it.' Irene managed a fragile smile.

'It could have all collapsed on you at any minute!' I said. 'It doesn't bear thinking about.'

'How did you all know I was here?' Irene asked, holding her throat as she spoke.

'We were driving past on the way to work and noticed the smoke,' Wilson replied.

'And after we realised it was you in the house, I went to the library to fetch Evie,' Jenny added.

'Which reminds me, I need to let Clara and Aiden know you're OK. They'll be worried sick.' I rummaged in my bag for my mobile and sent them both a text.

We all looked up to see a nurse entering the room. 'I've just come to do your observations,' he said, smiling as he took the clipboard from the end of the bed. 'How are you feeling, Irene?'

'My throat is sore and I feel quite nauseous.'

The nurse nodded. 'I can give you something for the sickness. How's the head feeling?'

'It's a little uncomfortable,' Irene admitted.

'Shall we let you get some rest?' Jenny asked, glancing at Irene and then the nurse.

'I think that might be a good idea,' the nurse replied, taking Irene's temperature and recording the result on a chart.

'I can bring you back some toiletries and a nightie,' I suggested.

'That would be great, thank you,' Irene whispered, holding her throat again as her eyes began to droop.

'I'll give you a lift,' Jenny offered, standing up and placing the empty cups in the bin.

I nodded my appreciation and kissed Irene on the top of her head. 'I'll be back soon.'

Jenny squeezed her hand and we walked up the corridor towards the main entrance of the hospital.

'Irene has been very lucky,' Wilson said.

'She has,' I replied, my heart lifting as I pushed open the door to the car park. The love I felt for Irene was overwhelming. I didn't want to think about life without her – and thanks to Wilson, I didn't have to.

CHAPTER TWENTY

'Tea,' I said, placing a tray on the table alongside a plate of biscuits. Irene had been home for a couple of days now. I'd made her up a makeshift bed on the sofa and had brought her lots of books to read from the library.

She kept laughing, saying, 'You fuss more than I do,' but I think she was generally enjoying the attention, and there had been a steady stream of visitors since she'd got home.

Elle and Mim had been horrified to hear about the accident and they'd come armed with what seemed like a year's supply of home-made cake. Poppy and Hattie had also visited, though they'd moved out of their house temporarily while the upstairs was redecorated. The fire was thought to have started from a phone charger.

'Are you OK if I go now?' I asked Irene as I plumped her cushions.

'Honestly, I'm fine. In fact, I'm getting a little bored of lying here. You'd think there was something wrong with my legs,' she said and smiled, taking a biscuit from the tray and dunking it into her tea.

'Enjoy it while it lasts – you'll be back to normal in no time.' I glanced at my watch. 'I must dash. Clara will be waiting for me at the bus stop.'

'You hope.' Irene laughed. 'Have a good day at work.'

I pressed a kiss to her cheek. 'I'll pop back after work and make your tea.'

'I thought you'd have plans tonight?'

'Plans? Why would I have plans tonight?' I asked, puzzled.

'You mean you and Clara haven't had to widen your letter box for today's post?'

I gave her a confused look.

'Valentine's Day!' Irene chuckled. 'I would have thought you girls would have had all the lads falling at your feet.'

'You really have had a bump to the head – it's addled your brain,' I said, laughing as I grabbed my coat and bag and headed towards the door. 'Don't overdo it,' I called on my way out.

I found Clara standing at the bus stop, bopping away to her headphones in a little world of her own.

'Morning,' she said as soon as she spotted me. 'How's Irene?'

'On the mend. I think she'll feel better when the head bandage is removed and she can wash her hair properly.'

'Yes, you always feel cleaner after a good hair wash.'

'Talking of which, I'm sure you didn't go to bed with red hair.'

'There's no fooling you, is there?' Clara said, laughing as she twirled a strand round her finger. 'Fiery red, this one. What do you think?'

'I think it better not be splattered all over the bathroom.'

'Actually, I need to speak to you about that,' she said and giggled, quickly hopping on to the bus and leaving me trailing behind her.

'Any plans for tonight?' I asked as I plonked myself down next to her.

'There are a couple of options I'm mulling over.'

'Which are?'

'I could go out to dinner with David Tennant or, as a back-up, I could attend a film premiere with Gary Barlow.'

'And failing that?'

'I could come to Irene's with you, and we could stuff our faces with fish and chips.'

I laughed. 'Sounds like a plan to me.'

'Have you replied to Noah's message yet?' she asked.

I shook my head.

'Have you stalked him on Twitter lately?'

'Ha, no, I haven't. We were busy with my writing, then there was Irene's accident – in fact, thinking about it, I've not looked for a while.'

'There's no time like the present. Let's have a look at what he's up to today,' Clara said, whipping her phone out of her pocket.

'Noah Jones,' she murmured to herself as she waited for the app to open. 'I spend half my life waiting for Twitter to load,' she said.

I smiled at her impatience. 'I don't think holding your phone up to the window actually makes it load any faster.'

'Little do you know, Cooper,' she said, stretching her hand further in the air and nearly hitting the head of the man in front.

'Right, let's have a look,' she said, tucking her hand under my arm and holding the screen in front of us. 'Here he is – Mr Noah Jones.'

I dropped my gaze to the screen.

'It appears that Noah Jones is spending this Valentine's…' Clara scrolled her finger up and down the screen.

'Probably with his girlfriend,' I said, leaning my head on her shoulder.

'Doing nothing,' Clara said. 'He's not tweeted so far today.'

'That's probably because he's all loved up and hasn't got time to tweet today.' I felt my shoulders sag and all of a sudden I felt sad. Why hadn't I messaged him at the time? I could kick myself.

'Such a pessimist.'

Clara tossed the phone back into her pocket, and we sat in companionable silence until the bus reached our stop.

'Here we are,' I said, standing up and holding on to the metal pole as the bus halted.

'Flipping 'eck,' Clara said as we jumped off. 'Wilson and Aiden are both already standing at the top of the steps.'

I laughed. 'They're probably about to fight for your affections,' I said.

'Don't joke about that.'

'Is there something you aren't telling me, Clara Lawson?' I nudged her in the side.

'Not as such,' she mumbled.

'I know that look. What's going on?'

'Not now – I'll fill you in later,' she whispered as we met the smiles of the two lads waiting for us.

'Good morning,' I sang.

I noticed a sheepish look pass between Wilson and Clara as I put the key in the door, and made a mental note to grill her at the first opportunity.

'I'll put your deliveries on the front desk and then I need to get going. It's manic today,' Wilson said, placing numerous cardboard boxes on the desk and turning towards the front door. 'I'll text you at lunchtime,' he said, touching Clara's arm affectionately.

Once Wilson was out of sight, I whispered, 'Why would Wilson be texting you at lunch?'

Clara shrugged her shoulders dismissively.

'Why do I get the feeling there's something you're not telling me?'

'Shhh,' she said as Aiden wandered out of the staffroom clutching a mug of tea.

'There's a cuppa on the table for you both,' he said, before grabbing a duster and heading towards the shelves.

Luckily for Clara, her interrogation was interrupted by a steady flow of customers exchanging books, and for the next ten minutes the only noise in the library was the thump of the date stamp and the turning of pages.

'Gosh, that was a bit of a rush,' Clara said when we finally got a breather.

'I know,' I said, exhaling as I leant back in my chair.

Almost immediately I noticed a woman walking towards us with a beautiful bouquet of flowers. 'Wow,' I said to Clara. 'Someone is a very lucky girl.'

She jumped to her feet with the biggest grin on her face and stretched out her arms. 'Thanks, I'll take them,' she said.

'Aiden or Wilson?' I mouthed.

Clara flicked me a grin and glanced down at the flourish of pastel-coloured roses and freesias.

She inhaled. 'What a gorgeous smell.'

'Come on, who are they from?'

She pulled out the small white envelope and paused.

'Blooming heck, Clara, you're dragging this out.'

'They aren't for me,' she said, disappointment written all over her face.

'Oh no, have they been delivered to the wrong place?'

She shook her head. 'No, they're for you.' Clara held the flowers towards me.

'For me?' I asked, puzzled, and took the bouquet from her.

I stared at the envelope: 'Evie Cooper'.

'Come on then, open the card.'

I passed the flowers back to Clara and slipped the card out of the envelope. 'It's probably Irene,' I said heartily. 'This is the kind of thing she'd do.'

I read the card and swallowed. 'Very interesting,' I said, feeling myself go all fluttery.

Clara stared at me for a few seconds, waiting, before she took the card from my hand and read the message aloud.

Dear Evie,
Happy Valentine's Day!
Love from
Guess who xx

'Guess who? That's a let-down,' Clara said, clearly disappointed.

'I suppose that's what Valentine's Day is all about – sending anonymous gifts.'

'Blooming annoying though! First the Sam Stone book appears and now these flowers.'

'Do you think they're connected?'

'I never thought of that.'

'Ooh, what have you got there?' Aiden asked as he came up behind us and flicked the duster over the front desk.

'Flowers,' Clara answered, stating the obvious.

'Who from?'

'That's the question,' I said, still mystified. 'We've no idea.'

'You'd best go and put them in some water,' Aiden suggested.

'Have you discovered any admirers today, Aiden?' Clara asked, fishing for gossip.

'No, it's a microwave meal for one tonight unless anyone fancies keeping me company?'

'That sounds like either one of us would do!' Clara said, hitting him playfully.

'Just keeping my options open,' he joked before heading towards the photocopier to help a customer load the paper.

'You should have jumped at the chance,' I whispered to Clara once he was out of earshot.

'Don't! I'm feeling bad enough as it is.'

'Why? What do you mean?' I cast my eyes around the library. No one looked like they needed us, so I said, 'Come with me to put these in water so you can spill the beans.'

Clara trailed after me into the staffroom and I grabbed an old vase from under the sink unit while she balanced on the edge of the table and started swinging her legs like a moody teenager.

'Spit it out then. You've gone all maudlin on me.'

'You know the other night when Jenny went with you to collect Irene from the hospital…'

I was half listening until I heard the words, 'I slept with Wilson.'

My jaw hit the floor. Wide-eyed, I turned to face her.

'I could have sworn I just heard you say you slept with Wilson.'

'That's exactly what I said.'

'Jeez! I wasn't expecting that, I have to admit.'

'I can't say I was either.'

'I'm honestly gobsmacked,' I said, pulling out a chair and sitting down.

'How did that happen?'

Clara raised her eyebrows at me.

'I obviously know how it happens. You know what I mean. When, where and how did it come about?'

'After you and Jenny left, Wilson knocked on the door. He was going to go with you, but he missed you by about ten minutes, so I invited him in and poured him a glass of wine. We sat on the settee and chatted about the shock he felt when he saw Irene being stretchered out of the burning house. I could see he was upset, so I gave him a hug – then before I knew it, we were kissing and one thing led to another.'

'I can't leave you alone for a minute,' I joked. 'And it happened just like that?'

'Yes.'

'And was it just a one-off?'

'He wants to see me again, and I'm feeling really embarrassed about the whole thing,' she said, looking at the floor.

'Why? You're single.'

She lifted her head for a fraction of a second and gave me a vacant stare before she spoke. 'Because I think I actually like Aiden, and now I've gone and slept with his mate. I've messed it all up.'

'Oh, now that is a bit tricky.'

'I do like Wilson – well actually who wouldn't? He's kind, considerate – not to mention easy on the eye – but I don't get that nervous flutter in my stomach—'

'Like you do with Aiden,' I interrupted.

'Like I do with Aiden,' she repeated.

'So what are you going to do?'

'I've no idea. I've made the situation really awkward, and then there are even more complications with Aiden.'

'Which are?'

'He's only recently separated from Louisa, and there's Theo to consider.'

'How do you feel about dating a man with a small child?'

'I hadn't really thought about that until I'd slept with Wilson. It's a whole new ball game to me, but Theo is adorable and I see him as an added bonus.'

I smiled. 'Who wouldn't?'

Suddenly Aiden popped his head around the door. 'Hey, I'm on my own out here and I think these ones are for you, Clara,' he said, holding out a bouquet of twelve red roses to her.

He held her gaze for a moment and I thought I saw sadness in his eyes. She took them from him sheepishly and he hurried back to the front desk.

'Awkward,' Clara said as she breathed in the scent of the roses.

'Beautiful flowers though. Are they from Wilson?'

Clara nodded as she read the card. 'Yes. What am I going to do?'

'Firstly, put those in water, and secondly, if you receive such beautiful flowers after only one night, he's a keeper!' I joked.

Clara rolled her eyes. 'You aren't much help!'

'Come on,' I said. 'We best get back out there.'

When we returned to the library floor, we found Aiden sitting behind the front desk, twirling a biro and looking miserable.

'I'm not sure if it's the flowers or the microwave meal for one that's sent him over the edge,' I whispered in Clara's ear.

'You are *not* helping,' she muttered as we walked towards him.

'Clara, is this your phone in this drawer?' Aiden glanced up. 'It's just beeped.'

'Yes, could you pass it here please?' she asked. 'Thanks.' She quickly flicked me a glance and swiped the screen.

'Clara, I was just wondering whether this evening…'

'Mmm,' she replied, half-heartedly listening to Aiden as she read her text.

'If you were at a loose end tonight, I'd—'

'Oooh, I've been invited out on a date tonight,' Clara interrupted Aiden mid-flow.

Aiden stopped dead in his tracks and didn't finish his sentence. I saw the look in his eyes as his heart obviously sank somewhere past his knees.

'Sorry, Aiden, I interrupted you there. What were you saying?'

He forced a smile and lifted his eyebrows. 'Oh nothing,' he said. 'Have a good time tonight.' He stood up then. 'Will you excuse me for a moment?'

I nodded and watched him walk towards the staffroom.

'He's upset,' I said to Clara, who was busy tapping on her phone.

She looked up, her eyes whirling to follow Aiden as he disappeared into the staffroom. 'Why?'

'Because he was in the middle of asking you out when you blurted out that you had a date.'

'Really?'

I rolled my eyes. 'Yes. Now who asked you out? Wilson?'

'Yes.'

'Aiden obviously didn't want to complicate things for you so he backtracked.'

'Bloody hell,' she said, staring at me. 'What am I going to do now?'

'I've no idea.'

'Today is turning into a huge disaster!' she said, and her voice cracked a little. She opened the drawer and tossed her phone back into it.

'How about we stick to the original plan?' I suggested.

'Fish and chips with Irene?'

I nodded.

'Fish and chips it is then,' Clara said as we watched Aiden walk back on to the library floor and disappear behind the artificial plants on the other side of the room.

'It will all work out in the end,' I whispered.

'I hope so,' she said. 'I really hope so.'

CHAPTER TWENTY-ONE

'Wow, it looks like you girls have been very popular today,' Irene exclaimed as she opened the door.

Clara and I smiled, clutching our flowers and a steaming bag of fish and chips.

'The only deliveries I've had today are the newspaper, a charity bag and a coupon for a free cup of tea from the local garden centre,' she continued, chuckling as she held the door open for us. 'Now pop your flowers in the front room and you can tell me all about who sent them while I dish up the food.'

We did as she said, then kicked off our shoes and hung our coats up before we followed her into the kitchen.

'I can't believe neither of you has a date tonight. What is the world coming to?' she asked, smiling as she poured three glasses of water. 'Will you put out the knives and forks,' she said to me as she started plating up the food.

'I'll do it,' Clara said, heading towards the cutlery drawer.

'How did you both end up here for tea after receiving such lovely flowers?' Irene asked.

'Clara has had two offers…'

Clara swiftly stuck her tongue out at me while Irene wasn't looking.

'Lucky girl,' Irene said.

'Whereas I've had none.'

'You could have had one of mine,' Clara said, grinning as she squeezed brown sauce all over her chips.

'Let me guess, your two,' she pointed at Clara with her fork, 'Wilson and…'

Clara raised her eyebrows, waiting for the second guess.

'Wilson and… please don't tell me it's the ex, Nick,' Irene said, wide-eyed.

'No, of course not,' Clara replied. 'Actually he's not even been mentioned today.'

'Have you had any texts from him?' I asked curiously.

'I wouldn't know because I took your advice and blocked his number, so if he has been texting, he's been talking to himself.'

'I know Wilson sent you some flowers because Jenny popped by to see how I was.'

'What did she say?' I asked before Clara could get a word in edgeways.

'I think she said he's like an excited little puppy every time he leaves for work, knowing the library is his first stop.'

'Oh God,' Clara said, looking at me.

'He's a lovely lad,' Irene said, puzzled.

'Of course he is, but Clara likes Aiden, who was in the middle of asking her out when Wilson texted, inviting her to dinner, and now he thinks she's out with him, not here with us.'

'And where does Wilson think you are?'

'Oh no! I forget to text him back, and I've not even thanked him for the flowers,' Clara exclaimed in horror.

Irene shook her head. 'The youth of today,' she said, laughing, then turned back to me. 'Now, Evie, don't think it's escaped my notice that you haven't said who your flowers are from.'

'I'd tell you if I knew,' I said. 'They were another mystery gift.'

Irene looked surprised. 'Another one? You mean like the Sam Stone book?'

'Yep. But though we know Sam Stone signed his book, there are no clues as to who the flowers are from.'

'You must have an inkling?'

'I haven't.'

'No man in your life at all?' Irene prompted.

Clara coughed, then laughed.

'It's only Irene,' she said. 'I think she'd love to know all about your secret crush.'

'This sounds interesting. Secret crush? Tell me more.' Irene grinned at the pair of us.

'Mouth of the south.' I hit Clara playfully. 'It's nothing.'

'Anyone I know?' Irene asked curiously.

'You could say that.'

'Noah Jones,' I said finally, when Irene continued to stare at me.

'*The* Noah Jones? The *author* Noah Jones? Noah Jones who will be attending book club very shortly?'

Clara grinned. 'The one and only.'

'And how long has this been going on?'

'There's nothing going on,' I said, shocked at the sudden change in my voice – I sounded like a chipmunk on helium.

'I don't understand. Have you seen him recently?'

'The last time she saw him was nine months ago at the library.'

'All right, all right –stop talking about me as if I wasn't here,' I said, but they ignored me.

'He seemed a very nice lad. What are we going to do about it then?' Irene queried.

'I'm still here, you know. You two are completely barmy,' I said.

'Just having some fun while I extract all the information.' Irene smiled at me. 'So you have a crush on the lovely Noah?'

'It's hardly the romance of the century.'

'He has tweeted her recently though,' Clara said. 'I think your new profile pic helped with that.' I rolled my eyes as she giggled.

'What's all this?' Irene asked.

'This bright spark here,' I nodded towards Clara, who brought her hand up to her chest in mock outrage, 'decided my profile picture looked very librarianish and that we needed to jazz it up to gain some male attention.'

Irene shook her head, laughing. 'Librarianish? I'm not sure that's even a word.'

'Here, have a look.' Clara thrust her phone towards Irene, who squinted at the profile picture.

'Is that even you? You look like you've been holidaying in the Caribbean for a couple of weeks.'

'It's done with an app. It's meant to make you look fresh and hip.'

'So we have no idea who your flowers are from, Evie?'

I shook my head. 'Clara did try and do some detective work by ringing the florist, but she said she wasn't at liberty to say!'

'It's still a mystery then?'

We nodded.

A little one-sided smile appeared on Irene's face. 'Well, I think it's about time we tried to figure it out.'

'How do we do that then?' Clara and I leant forward with bated breath, waiting for Irene to answer.

She laughed. 'I have no idea, but does anyone want a cup of tea? A cuppa is always good in a crisis.'

'Go on then, that would be lovely,' I said, wondering how on earth we were going to solve the mystery.

CHAPTER TWENTY-TWO

The next morning the library door opened, letting in a blast of cool air. Wilson walked straight up to the front counter without uttering a word, though he managed a slight smile before placing our parcels on the desk and heading back towards the door. He seemed to be hurting. Clara's rejection must have hit him hard.

'Wilson?' I shouted after him, but he just waved and continued without saying a word. I let him go and vowed I'd go and see him after work tonight to make sure he was OK.

Last night after Clara and I had left Irene's, we'd settled ourselves down on the sofa with mugs of hot chocolate when there had been a knock on the front door. We'd already removed our make-up and changed into our onesies to watch *Pretty Woman*, so neither of us had wanted to answer it.

We'd dithered for a few seconds, sinking further into the sofa, before the knock had come again.

Whoever it was hadn't been for going away.

'It's your house,' Clara had said, grinning. 'You go.'

'Why doesn't anyone knock on the door when we're dressed up?' I'd asked. 'Why do I always have to answer the door looking like a sack of spuds?'

'Cos that's life,' she'd said, giggling as I'd handed her my drink and walked towards the door.

It had been Wilson standing on the step. 'I've been knocking for ages.'

'Sorry, the telly was blaring. We didn't hear you.'

He'd cleared his throat. 'Is Clara in?'

'Yes,' I'd answered.

'Clara, it's for you,' I'd shouted over my shoulder, then smiled at Wilson, who'd appeared a little agitated.

'Hi.' Clara had appeared behind me.

There'd been an awkward silence and the three of us had just stood there.

'Do you want to come in?' I'd asked, ignoring a disgruntled look from Clara.

He'd looked at me. 'If that's OK?'

'Of course,' I'd answered, holding the front door open, and we'd all traipsed into the living room.

'I've interrupted you, haven't I?' he'd said, staring at the paused TV screen.

'It's fine.' I'd smiled warmly. 'The film hasn't started properly yet. Would you like a drink?'

'Yes, that would be great,' he'd replied, perching on the edge of the settee next to Clara. She'd rolled her eyes at me and I'd been relieved to escape the room. The atmosphere had seemed a little tense.

From the kitchen, I'd heard Wilson speak first. 'Did you get the flowers?' he'd asked.

'Yes, thank you – they were lovely. They're over there.'

'You didn't answer my text about dinner tonight. I've been sat waiting, not knowing what to do.' His voice had faltered a little.

'I'm sorry,' Clara had said.

I'd peeped through the crack in the door. Clara had been staring at the wall in front of her. 'It was a genuine mistake on my part. I was about to reply when I got distracted, and before I knew it, it was teatime. I only remembered when I was round at Irene's with Evie, eating fish and chips.'

Wilson had looked relieved. 'You've been at Irene's?' His expression had been earnest, his eyes sparkling with anticipation.

'Yes, why? Where did you think I was?' Clara had asked, making eye contact for the first time.

'Are we OK?' Wilson had asked softly, edging his way up the settee.

He'd looked like he was about to lean across and kiss her, and I hadn't known whether this was my cue to go back into the room or not. Clara had looked awkward, shuffling back in her seat.

Wilson had hesitated for a moment, before saying, 'I wasn't looking for a quick fling, Clara. I'm still not looking for a quick fling.'

My heart had been in my mouth, so I couldn't imagine how Clara must have felt.

'Wilson, you are so lovely...'

'But...'

'Funny and handsome too. But I can't put my finger on it. I'm just not feeling it. I'm so sorry if I've hurt you.'

Wilson had looked down at the floor and put his head in his hands. It had definitely sounded like the end of the road for them, though it hadn't even properly begun.

'Sorry, I feel like a right idiot,' he'd managed to say. 'I shouldn't have come round.'

'Don't be daft – and don't ever apologise for being such a lovely person.'

He'd let out a defeated sigh before standing up and putting on a brave smile. 'If you ever change your mind, please come and find me. I really like you, Clara.'

'I will – I promise,' she'd said.

She'd stood up and hugged him. 'Friends?' she'd whispered. He'd nodded.

I'd stopped watching then, and a couple of minutes later I'd heard the front door shut. He'd left.

'You can come out now,' Clara had shouted towards the kitchen.

'Are you OK?' I'd asked, hurrying into the living room and sitting next to her on the settee.

'God, that was awkward.'

'But you were honest with him, and you didn't string him along, which would have been easy to do.'

'It doesn't mean I feel any better though – I feel like a right cow.'

'I can imagine. Is it just because of Aiden you've turned him down?' I'd asked, sipping the tea I'd just made for Wilson.

'I think it is – which is daft because there isn't anything going on between me and Aiden.'

I'd squeezed her knee. 'Well, not just yet.'

She'd smiled. 'Every time I hear Aiden's voice, it sparks off a swarm of fireflies in my stomach.'

'That's a good sign.'

'It is – except I've probably messed that up now. I shouldn't have gone with Wilson.'

'Don't beat yourself up over that now. It was just timing. These things happen. You're only human.'

'Aiden's probably got enough going on in his life right now – and anyway, he might not even be looking for another relationship so soon after Louisa.'

'That's very true,' I'd said, remembering the conversation Aiden and I had had previously. 'But at the moment, I think he's thinking more about Louisa.'

'Does he want to get back with her?' Clara had asked, horrified.

'No, no, nothing like that. All he's told me is that she's struggling a little bit with the changes in her life – the break-up, moving back in with her parents and generally being on her own.'

'Oh I see,' Clara had said, relieved.

'She has mentioned them getting back together, but Aiden was adamant that wasn't going to happen. There's no connection there except for Theo now.'

She'd nodded, then we'd spent the rest of the night slobbed out with Julia Roberts and Richard Gere.

'What's up with Wilson this morning?' Aiden asked, appearing behind me. 'He doesn't seem his usual cheery self.'

'No, he doesn't, does he,' I replied, wondering whether to tell Aiden about last night. Then I remembered two things. Firstly, Aiden didn't know that Clara and Wilson had had a one-night stand, and secondly it wasn't any of my business. All I hoped was that things could get back to normal as soon as possible.

'And what's up with you?' I asked him. 'You look as miserable as Wilson this morning. Is there something in the water?'

'Mmm, maybe,' he answered, shuffling some papers on the desk.

I'd never seen this subdued side to Aiden before. Since he'd arrived at the library, he'd always had a smile plastered on his face, but then he was entitled to an off day I supposed.

'Do you want to talk about it?' I asked, glancing around the library. Clara was on the other side of the room, helping a pensioner.

'There's nothing I can do about it anyway,' he replied. His voice was cold and distant, and he didn't make eye contact with me.

'About what?' I asked.

He sighed. He looked pale and tired.

'I saw them.'

'Who?'

'Wilson and Clara.'

'Saw them when?'

'Last night – Valentine's Day. He was chatting to her on the doorstep. It was him who sent her the flowers, wasn't it?'

I nodded. 'But it's not quite what you think.'

'Why's that then?'

Aiden had put me in a difficult position. On the one hand, I was loyal to Clara, but on the other, Aiden was standing in front of me with huge puppy dog eyes, hoping I was going to tell him what he wanted to hear.

'They aren't going out together…' I hesitated.

'I've put you on the spot, haven't I?'

'A little,' I admitted.

I began to fiddle nervously with the strap on my watch. 'Clara isn't going out with Wilson. They're just friends – good friends. How's Louisa?' I asked, changing the subject as I noticed Clara walking towards us.

'She's started her new job now, which seems to have perked her up a little. She's socialising a little more and hopefully getting her life back on track.'

'That's good to hear then.'

'What are you two talking about?' Clara asked as she approached the desk.

Aiden and I exchanged a glance before he replied. 'My microwave meal for one last night,' he said, smiling as he leant across the desk to answer the phone.

'Hello, City Library – Aiden speaking. How may I help you?'

There was silence for a moment while the person on the other end spoke.

'Who's calling please?' Aiden asked, looking directly at me. I raised my eyebrows at him. He put his hand across the receiver and mouthed at me, 'It's the Salvation Army for you.'

I froze on the spot. My stomach clenched with pain, and I felt my whole body heat up a notch, but I pulled myself together enough that I could take the phone from him and put it to my ear.

'What's going on?' I heard Aiden whisper to Clara, but she just shrugged and perched herself on the desk next to me. Both of them stared at me.

'Hello,' I managed to say, my voice shaking. My heart was thumping, and my pulse throbbed in the side of my head. All I could think was – had they traced my mother?

'Hello, is that Evie Cooper?'

'Yes, speaking.'

'This is Ann Blears, and I'm ringing from the Salvation Army. Are you OK to talk?'

'I am.'

'I phoned your mobile and left you a message, but I thought I'd try this number too.'

I quickly took my phone from my pocket. It was switched to silent and there was a missed call and a voicemail from a number I didn't recognise.

'Can I just confirm some personal details with you?'

Ann took me through a serious of security checks.

The seconds ticked by and I became increasingly desperate for them to cut to the chase. And then just when I thought Ann's checks were never going to end, the words I'd been waiting for came down the phone.

'Evie, we're pleased to tell you we've found your mother.'

Goosebumps broke out on every part of my body, and I clasped my hand to my mouth.

For a moment, I couldn't speak as I digested the information. I took a deep breath. 'Does she want to see me?'

I closed my eyes, waiting for the answer.

'Yes. Your mother has written you a letter, and we'll post it to you first class today. You'll be allocated a caseworker – Emily Kirk – and she'll liaise with you both. All the details will be in the letter.'

Ann gave me some more information about my mother and I listened intently. At the end of the call I thanked her and placed the receiver down.

Clara placed her hand on my knee but didn't speak.

'What was that all about?' Aiden asked tentatively. 'You look like you've seen a ghost.'

I couldn't speak. Clara cupped her hands around mine – they were shaking.

'Shall I make myself scarce?' Aiden asked.

I tried to compose myself, but it was no use. The emotional impact hit me like a high-speed train and I placed my head in my hands. The tears fell and I sobbed. I couldn't believe it.

'Come on, stand up,' Clara said, gently placing her hand beneath my elbow and leading me into the staffroom, away from prying eyes.

'I'll stay here,' Aiden suggested and Clara nodded at him.

She sat me down on a chair and passed me a tissue. I looked up through my blurry eyes. 'Thanks,' I managed to say as I watched her switch on the kettle and make two mugs of tea.

'Are you OK?'

The adrenaline was pumping through my body as I locked eyes with Clara. 'They've found her,' I whispered. 'They've found my mum.'

'Does she want contact?'

'Yes,' I breathed. 'She's written me a letter.'

I fell into Clara's arms and she hugged me tight.

CHAPTER TWENTY-THREE

The sunshine streamed through the window into Irene's living room. I was curled up on the settee, my feet tucked beneath me.

'Here, grab this,' I heard Irene say. I managed a smile as she handed me a mug of tea and perched on the settee next to me.

My eyes met hers. 'How are you feeling?' she asked softly.

'Numb, curious, apprehensive, excited, physically sick, all mixed together.'

'Do you know how long she's been looking for you?' Irene asked.

My tears were threatening to fall at any moment. I squeezed my eyes together and took a deep breath.

'They said her request was logged on the same day as mine.'

'It's fantastic that she wants to meet you.'

'Do you think she filed her interest on that day because it was my birthday?'

'Most probably.'

'That goes to show she's never forgotten me,' I said, and Irene wrapped her hands around mine. I could feel the emotion rising inside me and my breath caught in my throat.

'She's never forgotten you,' Irene whispered.

'Why now though? Why after all these years has she only just decided to come looking for me?'

'That's a question you'll have to ask her. Maybe it's the right time in her life too. Everything happens for a reason,' she said before asking, 'Do you know what the next step is?'

'She's written me a letter.'

'Hopefully that might answer some of the questions whirling around in your mind.'

I nodded. 'And then they suggested that once I'd read the letter – if we both are agreed – they can arrange a meeting for us.'

'How are you feeling about that?'

'Terrified.'

'Do you have any more information about her?'

'No, but the letter's in the post.'

'Well, hopefully that'll come soon.'

'Tomorrow – they've posted it first class – but I'm not sure I can wait that long.'

'It'll be here before you know it,' she said. 'What are you going to do about work tomorrow?'

I sighed. 'I feel like I've let Clara and Aiden down by coming home today.'

'Don't be daft – they'll understand,' she said. 'Does Aiden know the reason you left today?'

'He will now. I've told Clara it was OK to tell him.'

Irene nodded. 'Good call.'

'They've also rung Jane. She usually covers on Saturdays but she's gone in today to help them out, which is extremely kind of her at such short notice.'

'Maybe she'll be able to do the next few days as well, in case you need more time off.'

Irene put her arms around me and held me tight.

'Everything will be OK,' she promised, whispering in my ear.

'What're your plans for the rest of the day?' I asked, pulling away.

'No plans whatsoever. I've a few errands to run but they can wait. Why, what are you thinking?'

'I'm thinking maybe a walk and lunch?'

'That sounds great. We could walk into town. There's a new bistro opened on the corner of the High Street.'

'Perfect. I'll go and wash my face and clean myself up, and let's pray today goes quickly.'

Irene smiled warmly. 'Tomorrow will soon be here.'

'I know you shouldn't wish your life away, but this is one of those times when tomorrow can't come soon enough,' I said.

CHAPTER TWENTY-FOUR

After we left Irene's house we walked the long way through the park to town. The weather had begun to change in the last couple of days, and even though there was still a slight chill in the air, the first signs of spring were beginning to burst through.

The entrance to the park was impressive, with two stone statues framing the wrought-iron gates. A narrow path led us through the oak trees, and the sun filtered through the branches to dapple the ground before us as we walked along.

'I love it when the daffodils begin to come through,' Irene said. 'It gives everywhere that first burst of colour.'

'It definitely lifts your spirits,' I replied as we stood for a moment watching two squirrels chase each other along the path.

We walked a little further. 'Even the pond looks like it's come alive this morning with the sun reflecting on the water,' Irene said, and we leant against the railings and watched a young family throw bread to the ducks.

'Do you think you'd like children one day?' Irene asked tentatively.

In the past, I'd vowed that I would never have children. Even though my childhood wasn't my fault, and I wasn't my mother, there had always been a voice in the back of my mind that said I wouldn't be good enough. But as time went on and I grew older, my thoughts had begun to change, and I knew in my heart of hearts that if I ever did bring children into the world, I would do everything possible to give them a loving, stable upbringing.

'Maybe,' I replied, 'but I need to find a lovely man to settle down with first, and they're hardly queuing round the block right now.'

'It'll happen when you're least expecting it. It did for me,' Irene said with a chuckle, obviously remembering Neville.

I smiled at Irene. 'Mint choc chip ice cream has a lot to answer for.'

She grinned. 'It certainly does! I put on half a stone that summer visiting the ice-cream van.'

I linked my arm through Irene's as we began to walk again. 'But it was worth it.'

'I didn't think I'd have a chance in a million years, especially when I found out Hazel Clarke had her eye well and truly on him.'

'Who was she then?'

'A local girl – and one of *those* girls.' Irene raised her eyebrows.

'What girls?' I asked.

'The ones that've been round the block more times than a Mr Whippy van.' Irene chuckled at her own joke.

'Neville was helping his dad that summer. I can still picture his cheeky smile from the van window as he popped his head out to see what he could get us. Every time I saw him, I had swarms of butterflies, but I always played it cool. I didn't think he'd even look in my direction.'

I laughed. 'Playing it cool is overrated.'

'The van was always parked over there.' Irene pointed to a clearing behind a well-tended garden. 'That garden hasn't always been there. It was once a huge paddling pool, and that's where my friends and I spent most of our summers. I used to set up camp under that tree so I could watch Nev in the van.'

'Do you miss him?'

'Every day. It feels like there's a massive void in my life. People say it gets easier in time – and time's a great healer – but it still seems very raw to me.'

'I can't imagine.'

'Sometimes my dreams about him are so vivid that when I actually wake up, it takes me a minute to realise it was only a dream.'

I squeezed her arm.

'We had a wonderful life together, and I treasure that time. My heart will never soar for anyone else like it did for Neville.'

We ambled along in silence; no doubt, Irene was lost in her memories. I stopped as I saw a familiar figure in the park, giggling as a woman pushed him back and forth on the swing. His small hands gripped the rope for dear life and, for a moment, I just watched them from a distance.

'Who's that?' Irene asked, glancing over to where I was looking.

The woman gave Theo one more huge push on the swing before perching on a bench next to someone I didn't recognise. He placed his arm around her shoulder and nuzzled her neck.

'That's Theo, Aiden's son, and I'm assuming that must be Louisa.'

'Who's the man?'

'I have no idea but they seem close.'

The man whispered something in her ear and Louisa threw her head back and laughed. They seemed very at ease in each other's company. A few seconds later, he pulled Louisa towards him, cupped his hands around her face and kissed her deeply.

'Oh my,' I muttered, thinking about Aiden, who'd been so convinced she'd react badly if he started dating again. From where we were standing, though, it looked like she'd well and truly moved on.

'Well they don't look like just friends,' Irene commented.

'No,' I said, just as Theo suddenly caught my eye. A huge grin spread across his face and he pointed straight at us.

Louisa stood up and stared our way.

'I think we'd better introduce ourselves,' Irene said. 'Otherwise she'll be wondering how Theo recognises you.'

I waved at Theo as we wandered across the park towards them all.

'Hi,' I said, making eye contact with Louisa. 'I'm Evie – I work with Aiden at the library. And this is my mum, Irene.'

'Lovely to meet you both.' She flicked her eyes towards the man, but he just smiled awkwardly and stayed sitting on the bench.

'Hello, little man,' I said, moving over to Theo and giving the swing a little push.

He let out an infectious laugh. 'More!' he shouted as I gave him a couple more pushes.

'Are you not in work today?' Louisa asked.

'Day off,' Irene said, thinking on her feet.

'It's a lovely day for it,' she said, glancing up at the blue sky.

'Yes, indeed, the weather certainly makes a difference. Anyway, we'll leave you to it. Enjoy the park,' I said, blowing a kiss at Theo before nodding at the man. 'Lovely to meet you, Louisa.'

'You too,' she said and sat back down on the bench.

We could hear Theo's giggles petering out as we walked away.

'Was it just me or was there an uncomfortable atmosphere?' Irene asked when we were finally out of earshot.

'I didn't know whether it was just my imagination.'

Irene shook her head. 'She didn't introduce us to her friend.'

'Who clearly wasn't a friend – which is very strange because Aiden said she'd suggested they give things another go.'

'Really?'

'Yes, really. He wanted to ask Clara out, but he hasn't because Louisa has been very down about all the changes in her life, and he didn't want to cause her any more upset.'

'How lovely of him to put his life on hold and sacrifice his own feelings, but judging by what we've just witnessed, there's no need,' Irene said, shooting a glance over her shoulder. I followed her gaze to see the three of them strolling towards the entrance of the park.

'Do you think I should say something to him?'

'I think you're going to have enough to deal with over the next twenty-four hours.'

'Hmm, yes, I think you're probably right.'

CHAPTER TWENTY-FIVE

I stared at the clock. I'd been awake for most of the night. I'd known I would be. I was willing the time to pass quickly, but of course, it felt like the longest night ever. All I could think about was Sarah Thomas. I wondered what sort of night she'd had, knowing her letter was on its way to me. What sort of life did she have and where did she live? Did she have a family of her own? Did I look like her? There were so many questions. Only time would tell.

Clara gave me a huge hug when she left for work and told me to ring her the minute I had any sort of news.

'You'll be OK?'

'Yes,' I replied, forcing a brightness into my voice that I didn't feel. I saw her out and then stood on the step with my arms folded, my head resting against the door frame. It was only when she waved and disappeared round the corner that I went back inside.

I wasn't hungry, but I made a bowl of cereal and forced myself to eat it. When I'd finished, I began to flick through my phone. I could do nothing but wait.

There was a knock on the door, and I jumped out of my skin. I wasn't expecting anyone and it couldn't be Clara – she had her own key.

I hurried over to the door, and when I opened it, I found Irene smiling back at me.

'What are you doing here?' I asked, ushering her inside.

'You didn't think I'd let you wait on your own, did you?' She kissed my cheek before settling herself down on the chair in the living room.

'You look absolutely exhausted,' she said, sliding her handbag under the coffee table.

'I am,' I admitted. My eyes felt heavy and I had an anxious feeling swimming in the pit of my stomach.

'I take it you didn't sleep?'

'Not a wink.'

'Have you eaten?'

'I've managed a few mouthfuls of cereal but I don't have much of an appetite.'

'Understandable in the circumstances.'

I hovered at the window and stood on my tiptoes, trying to get a glimpse of the postman. I needed that letter to be delivered now.

'It's like waiting for a kettle to boil,' I mumbled.

'Try and relax. The postman isn't going to get here any quicker. What time does he normally come?' she asked, her voice calm and soothing.

I shrugged. 'I'm usually at work during the week, but at weekends it can be any time before lunch.'

She smiled. 'Let's hope they get a shift on today.'

I nodded.

'Are you going to Elle's hen-party meal next week?' I asked, spotting the invitation behind the clock on the mantelpiece.

'Yes, I've already been online and checked out the menu. The feathered beef has caught my eye! It sounds delicious.'

'I've not had a chance to look yet, but Clara and I are going to grab a taxi if you want to jump in with us.'

'Yes, please. I might as well.'

I turned on the TV, and Irene and I sat there for a bit, watching the news.

'It's always doom and gloom, isn't it? I think they should make it the law that one day a week, they only report good news – to give the country a bit of a lift,' Irene suggested.

'I think that sounds like an excellent plan.'

Suddenly the letter box clanged and I jumped out of my skin. I swallowed a lump in my throat and locked eyes with Irene as we heard the post drop on to the mat.

Neither of us moved.

'I daren't look,' I said, feeling my heartbeat quicken, and nausea surged through my body. 'I actually think I'm going to be sick.'

'Take some deep breaths,' Irene said. 'And just get it in your own time. There's no rush.'

'You're right. I've waited this long – another few minutes isn't going to make a difference now.' I was staring at the living-room door. I didn't know what I was expecting to happen, but once I began to read the letter, everything would seem so much more real, and where would I go from there? I bit down on my lip to stop it trembling.

Finally, I exhaled, got to my feet and smoothed down my top. 'I think I'm ready.'

Irene stood up and put her arm around my shoulder, squeezing gently. 'It's going to be all right,' she said. 'I'm here for you.'

I stumbled towards the front door with her following.

We both gazed down at the mat. Lying on top of it was a free newspaper, a bank statement and an envelope with the Salvation Army logo printed on it, staring back at us.

I took a deep breath, scooped the letter up from the mat and walked back into the living room.

Irene perched on the settee next to me. 'Do you want me to make myself scarce?'

I shook my head. Whatever I was about to discover, I wanted Irene by my side. 'Please stay.'

She nodded but remained silent. I stared at the envelope for a while longer before sliding my finger under the edge and tearing it open. Inside I found a smaller envelope and a document from the Salvation Army outlining the details of when Sarah Thomas's request was logged and when they'd received the letter. The caseworker I'd been allocated was indeed Emily Kirk, and she would take care of any further correspondence or liaisons. I was scared witless.

I picked up the smaller envelope and placed it on my lap. The writing was small and neat.

Opening it carefully, I pulled out a sheet of cream paper and stared down at the words written on it, but I was finding it hard to focus.

Irene touched my arm and I jumped – I'd forgotten she was there for a moment.

'Do you want me to read it to you? Would that make it easier?'

I passed the letter to her without saying a word and waited for her to start reading.

Dear Evie,

I'm struggling as to how to begin this letter, and even as I write, the pain is twisting in my heart. Since the day we parted, you have always been in my life, my head, my heart, and not a day has passed without me thinking of you. I never thought I'd have the chance to write this letter to you, and I pray you can forgive me one day.

During the early nineties, I was in a stable relationship with a lovely man called Matt Harrison when my life took an unexpected twist. My parents – Jane and Mike Thomas – were tragically killed in a boating accident in the south of France, and from that moment on my life seemed to spiral out of control.

At the time, I worked three jobs trying to make ends meet while Matt worked on his novel. He spent every hour he could tapping on his keyboard, waiting for that publishing deal. He was going to take the world by storm, but he never got a break and money was tight. Dreams weren't paying the rent.

We lived in a dingy flat in one of the less salubrious areas of Morley. Music would pound above our heads and we could hear arguments through the wafer-thin walls at all hours of the night.

Some months, we had to skip the rent – and even meals at times. After a while, I began to resent the fact that I was working myself into the ground, out all hours, and I became more and more depressed.

At first, I was taking antidepressants I'd been prescribed by the doctor, but they weren't enough. My relationship with Matt was falling apart, and I began to siphon off the rent money to buy stronger drugs from a dealer who lived in the flat above us. As time went on, I became more and more in debt and then it was too late. I was an addict – I couldn't live without the pills.

Matt had no idea. He was too caught up in making a career for himself. He didn't notice my mood swings, and I began to steal to keep the dealer off my back, but eventually I racked up a debt I couldn't pay back.

I have agonised all my life on whether I should share this next bit of information with you, but I think the time has come to be as truthful as I possibly can.

Irene looked up at me. 'Do you want me to go on?'

I nodded.

Irene continued to read.

After a late shift, I was walking back upstairs to the flat when I was grabbed and dragged by my hair to the flat above ours. I was gagged and held at knifepoint for over an hour while the dealer beat me. Then things got much worse. He held a knife to my throat and raped me on the floor as Matt typed his manuscript below. That was the day I left. I couldn't face Matt; I was too ashamed, and I never saw him again. I lived on the streets for nearly nine months, visiting soup kitchens and begging for food wherever possible, but stealing anything and everything to feed my addiction.

The evening of 19 January was bitterly cold. I was slumped against the doorway of a café. It was after hours and the shutters were down. There wasn't a soul in sight when I started to experience pain like nothing I'd ever felt before. It was only when I got the urge to push that I realised I was about to give birth. There was a light on in the flat above the café and I screamed and banged on the door so loudly that the owner appeared. She had a baby on her hip, which she promptly took back upstairs, but when she came back a few minutes later, she was armed with blankets and a pillow and made me up a makeshift bed on the floor of the café. If it wasn't for her, I dread to think what would have happened. She rang for an ambulance but you were almost here.

Irene took a breather and looked across at me. 'How are you doing there?'

I couldn't speak. To hear about the tragic death of Sarah's parents – my grandparents – was one thing, but discovering my father could be a rapist was on a completely different level.

'I think I'm going to be sick,' I said suddenly, rushing out of the room towards the bathroom.

Ten minutes later, after splashing cold water on my face and cleaning myself up, I returned to the living room. Irene had made two mugs of tea. 'I've put you a couple of sugars in there,' she said softly, treading carefully.

'Thank you,' I exhaled. 'Can you please carry on? I need to get this over and done with,' I whimpered, hugging my knees tightly like a small child.

She did as I asked.

All through the labour, I prayed and prayed you would be OK. I knew there was a possibility you'd have to be weaned off the drugs I'd taken.

You were born in the early hours of 20 January. From what I could see, you were perfect – chubby even, which was a good sign considering I'd barely eaten for months.

You cried the moment you made an appearance and I was relieved. The lady gave me clean clothes – we were of a similar build – and she cleaned you up and wrapped you tightly in a shawl. I held you in my arms and hugged you tight while she made me some food.

She asked me my name and I told her – Sarah Thomas.

The lady disappeared upstairs to check on her own child and it was then that I decided I couldn't take you back on the streets. You deserved a better life.

I scribbled a note on the order pad to look after my beautiful baby – Evangeline. I told her you might need medical attention due to the drugs I'd taken and that I loved you. I laid you down on the floor and kissed you.

As I paused at the door, I could hear the sirens in the distance. I knew you were going to be safe. My heart was breaking, but I knew I was making the right decision. I couldn't take you with me. I needed to get myself clean. I came back to you one more time and whispered, 'I love you,' before disappearing into the night. But I never forgot you, and I celebrate your birthday every year.

It took me a while to get my life back on track. One cold evening, I'd ventured into a shelter and was recognised by one of the volunteers – an old friend of my mum's. She kindly took me in and looked after me. She transformed my life, got me clean and helped me to find a job. Then I met a wonderful man named Adam. We have one boy together, and now, after all these years, I've finally shared my past with them both. It's been a traumatic time for them too, but hopefully one day we'll all meet and we can make a fresh start.

When you've had time to digest all this, I hope you can find it in your heart to forgive me – and please don't ever feel guilty about your existence. You are the one beautiful thing to have come out of such tragic circumstances, and I am truly sorry for everything you've been through.

I have no idea how to finish this letter, but I hope it's not the end – only the beginning for the both of us.

All my love,
Sarah x

Irene and I sat in silence. My head was whirling. The circumstances were more extreme than I'd ever imagined. At the time, Sarah had known how hard it would have been for me if she'd kept me, and I could feel a terrible sadness bleeding through the room.

'I always thought the hardest part was not knowing, but now I have to deal with what I do know.'

Irene patted my hand. 'I think Sarah's been very brave to share all this with you. She could have kept it to herself but instead she's been completely honest. To even come to terms with such a violent crime proves to me that Sarah Thomas is a remarkable woman.'

'Who do you think my father is? What if—'

'Don't even think about that at the minute. One step at a time.'

'If the dealer is my father, do you think evil is embedded in my genes?' I locked eyes with Irene.

'No, of course not. His crimes have nothing to do with you. Being conceived by rape doesn't define you as an individual – and anyway there's every chance that Matt is your father.'

'How difficult must this be for Sarah if I'm a reminder of a violent crime?'

'I think she sees herself as a survivor, not a victim, and don't forget – she came looking for you too. She's even confided in her family about you.'

'Yes, you're right,' I said weakly.

'She was scared that night, and if she'd confessed all to Matt, would he have believed her? It would have been a lot for them to deal with.'

I took the letter from Irene and flicked my eyes over it.

'Where do you go from here?' Irene asked tentatively.

'I think I want to meet her,' I answered honestly. 'I think I have to. I'm going to contact the caseworker.'

Irene nodded. 'Whatever happens, I'm always here for you, Evie.'

'Thank you.'

CHAPTER TWENTY-SIX

As the time turned 6.45 p.m. I heard the front door slam and Clara traipse up the hallway.

'Hi honey, I'm home,' she shouted, poking her head round the living-room door and giving me a smile. 'I could murder a cuppa.'

'How was work?' I asked. I was curled up in the corner of the sofa, Sarah Thomas's letter resting on my lap.

'It was OK, a little busy around lunchtime but nothing to worry about. Oh, I have some news but not as interesting as yours by the sound of it.'

I hadn't filled Clara in on every detail in the letter. I'd texted to let her know it had arrived and that my mother wanted to meet me, but I'd thought the rest could wait until she was home.

'How are you feeling?' she asked as soon as she'd sat down beside me.

'Battered, bruised, anxious, sad, happy – this afternoon, I think I've experienced every emotion possible.'

'Is that it then?' she said, nodding towards the letter.

'Yes.' I handed it to her. 'I think it's best you read it yourself.'

'Are you sure?'

'I'm sure,' I replied as Clara took the letter from me and began to read.

I watched as her eyes widened and her jaw fell open, then I left her reading to make us some tea.

'Oh goodness, I don't know what to say,' Clara said when I came back with the drinks.

I sipped my tea and smiled at her wistfully. 'Me neither, if I'm truly honest.'

'Sarah's life seemed to spiral out of control in such a short space of time – it must have been losing her parents so suddenly and the constant worrying about money. I wonder what happened to Matt Harrison. At what point did he realise she was never coming home?'

'It's too awful to even think about. Goodness knows what must have been running through his mind. Did he think she'd run off with someone else?'

'Maybe. I wonder if he tried to look for her,' Clara said. 'He might even have filed a missing-persons report.'

'Who knows? It wouldn't have been that hard to disappear in those days, before everything was online and so easy to trace. And her state of mind must have been so unstable, dealing with such a violent crime, drug addiction… and to run like that. She would have been constantly looking over her shoulder, petrified in case the dealer hunted her down.'

'How would you feel if the dealer was your father?'

The question hung in the air between us.

A lump formed in my throat and Clara's eyes searched mine. I shrugged, not knowing what to say. If he was my father, he would have no clue about my existence, which I was grateful for.

I exhaled. 'At least some of the missing pieces of the jigsaw have been slotted together.'

For a moment we just sat there, then Clara broke the silence. 'How do you feel about her leaving you?'

'At the time, she had good reason. She must have felt so alone in the world.'

'It seems like there usually are extreme circumstances in these kinds of cases. It's never straightforward.'

'Yes, you're right,' I agreed.

'There's no address on this letter,' Clara exclaimed, flipping it over.

'Yes, I know. Her address is deliberately kept off the letter in case I make the decision not to make any further contact.'

'So, at this stage we don't have any idea where she lives? I'm assuming it must be this country?'

'I'm assuming that too.'

'At least Sarah has finally found happiness. She has Adam and a son, and you've found happiness with Irene. What a huge burden she's carried around with her all these years.' Clara shook her head sadly.

'I know.'

'So what happens now?' she asked tentatively, and I flashed her a smile.

'Tomorrow I'll ring my caseworker and ask her to set up a meeting between us.'

'All systems go then?'

'All systems go,' I repeated.

We finished our tea, then Clara's phone pinged from the table.

'Aww,' she said, glancing at her message.

'That reminds me, what's your news?'

'Aiden asked me on a date.' Clara beamed from ear to ear. 'That's him texting now.'

'About blooming time!' I answered and we both laughed.

CHAPTER TWENTY-SEVEN

'How do I look?' Clara asked, flicking her hair over her shoulder before placing her hand on her hip and twirling to the side.

'I'd say dressed to impress.'

'You don't think this lipstick is a little too much? It's not my usual colour.'

'It's a little on the bright side but, as usual, you manage to carry it off.'

Clara pouted at me, then blew me a kiss, and we laughed.

Tonight was Elle's hen party, and I was looking forward to seeing everyone.

'The taxi is picking us up in half an hour – don't you need to get ready?'

'Hey, cheeky!' I threw a cushion at her. 'I am ready.' I was standing there in a ditsy floral dress that fell to my ankles, a cute cardigan and my ever-so-faithful white Converse.

Clara flicked her eyes up and down my outfit. 'You need to show a bit of flesh and pop some heels on.'

'I am absolutely fine the way I am. Did you ever find out where the boys were off to on the stag?'

'No,' Clara replied, 'I couldn't get Aiden to spill the beans.'

'Talking of Aiden, it's your date tomorrow, isn't it?'

'Yes, we're going to the cinema, but he was a little strange when he asked me…' Clara paused.

'Strange in what way?'

'He told me not to tell anyone.' She raised her eyebrows.

'Why ever not?' I asked.

'The only explanation he offered was that Louisa is struggling with life and he doesn't want to upset her.'

I wondered if this was my cue to come clean about what I'd seen in the park. 'Why would it upset Louisa if you went on a date with Aiden? They aren't together any more.'

'He kind of said that she keeps suggesting they give it another go and that she still has feelings for him.'

'Really?' I asked, amazed.

'Don't sound too surprised – he is quite a catch, you know.'

'It's not that.'

Clara was fiddling with a loose thread on the hem of her skirt, but she looked up to meet my gaze. 'What is it then?'

'I may be speaking out of turn but…'

'Go on.'

'Irene and I saw Louisa at the park. I've never clapped eyes on her before, but Theo recognised me and we wandered over to them.'

'What's so unusual about that – little kids like going to the park.'

'It was the fact she wasn't on her own.'

'What do you mean?'

'She was sitting on the bench kissing another man, and when we went across to introduce ourselves, she didn't introduce him.'

'Gosh, that's a little bizarre.'

'It's possible that Louisa isn't struggling as much as she's making out.'

'Mmm, do you think she's trying to make Aiden feel guilty for whatever reason?'

'It's possible, but who knows what goes on in other people's heads.'

I glanced at my watch and saw we still had a few minutes before the taxi was due. 'Changing the subject, we need to keep an eye on Irene tonight.'

'Of course! How's she doing? She's had her check-up at the hospital, hasn't she?'

'Yes, she's finally had the bandage removed from her head and the all-clear given, but I just need to make sure she doesn't tire.'

Clara nodded, just as I noticed a car pulling up outside.

'Here's the taxi,' I announced, swigging the rest of my drink back as Clara did the same. 'Let's get this show on the road!'

When we were settled in the back seat of the taxi, Clara asked, 'Have you written a letter back to your mother yet?'

'Umpteen times. I thought starting the search was hard enough but it was easy compared to the letter!'

'Did you mention your father at all?'

I shook my head. 'I thought it was best to stay away from that subject.'

'Probably for the best.'

'I kept mainly to the facts – that my childhood wasn't the best, but since I met Irene, my life has become settled and filled with love. I told her I'm happy, that I share a house with my best friend and I work in a library. The only emotional part to the letter was when I told her I didn't blame her, or hold any grudges, and that I understood she did what she thought was best at the time.'

'It must be difficult writing to a stranger who's your mother.'

'It was a strange feeling when I ended the letter, but I did agree to a meeting.'

'We don't know what part of the country she lives in yet, do we?'

'No, but now I've agreed to meet her and she feels the same, our caseworker Emily will try to find neutral ground somewhere in-between us both.'

'I suppose where Sarah lives will determine how soon the meeting can take place. Are you nervous?'

'Petrified more like. I never in a million years considered that she would be searching for me too. It's all moved very quickly. I honestly thought it would take years and here we are in a matter of weeks.'

Clara smiled. 'It all happens for a reason,' she said.

After collecting Irene, we travelled to a popular French bistro on the edge of town. It was the perfect place for Elle's hen do, sophisticated yet inexpensive, with traditional, hearty food and a stunning art deco interior.

'Oh look, there's Josh, Aiden and Wilson standing outside the bistro,' Irene said, handing the taxi driver a tenner as we climbed out.

'I wonder what they're doing here,' Clara said, trying her best to pull her skirt down and make it look longer than it actually was.

'There's no point trying to cover up now,' I whispered.

'I just feel a little self-conscious. I wasn't expecting to see my ex standing with my future date on the street.'

'Ex is pushing it a bit – you only had a one-nighter with him.'

'Shush! You know what I mean.'

'Hi, Irene – girls,' Wilson said, avoiding eye contact with Clara altogether and leaning forward to kiss Irene on the cheek. 'How are you feeling now?' he asked her.

Was it my imagination or was Aiden avoiding eye contact with Clara too? There seemed to be a strange atmosphere lingering in the air.

'I'm absolutely fine,' Irene replied. 'Looking forward to a lovely meal with great company.'

'We've just been for a quick drink with Elle, Mim and Jenny, and there are a couple more girls from the book club – they've only just gone inside.'

'Perfect timing!' I smiled, then cleared my throat. 'Now I think you men need to disappear,' I said, shooing them away. 'This is a girls-only night.'

'Ha, we know when we're not wanted,' Josh said, grinning as he patted Aiden and Wilson on the back. 'We're off anyway! We can't have you women cramping our style.' And with that they disappeared up the street.

I looked up at Clara, whose jaw was hitting the floor. 'Was that just my imagination or have I been mugged off?' she asked me.

'Mugged?' Irene asked with a puzzled look on her face. 'I didn't see anyone pinch your handbag.'

'Mugged off – it means ignored, left hanging,' I explained, but judging by the look on Irene's face, she still had no clue what I was talking about.

'I was, wasn't I?' Clara said.

'I'll go in and find the others. What would you two like to drink?'

'Shall we share a bottle of wine?'

Clara nodded, still looking perplexed as Irene disappeared inside the restaurant.

'What the hell was all that about? Did you see Aiden's body language?'

It wasn't like Aiden to be so aloof – in fact it was very out of character. He'd stood to the side of Clara with his feet planted firmly on the ground, his hands stuffed in his pockets, and had mostly been looking in the opposite direction.

'I'm confused. Yesterday he was asking me out on a date and now he's completely ignoring me in public. What's that all about?'

I really had no idea. 'Do you want me to text and ask him?' I offered, not knowing what else to say.

'Oh God, it's Wilson, isn't it? They've been talking. Do you think he's told Aiden we spent the night together? Aiden will never come near me now.' Her eyes were wide, worry written all over her face.

It was a thought that had already crossed my mind. 'Let's not worry about that now. There's nothing we can do about it,' I said, looking through the window to see Irene holding up a wine glass and madly waving at us to come inside the bistro.

'We best get ourselves inside – otherwise they'll be talking about us. So, forget Aiden, forget Wilson – it's nothing that can be sorted now so don't let it spoil our night. Tonight is about Elle.'

'Agreed,' Clara said reluctantly as she followed me into the restaurant.

An hour later, after the most gorgeous gourmet meal, I was fit to burst. I really couldn't manage another morsel.

'Dessert, anyone?' Elle grinned, patting her stomach. 'I'm taking advantage of this eating-for-two lark!'

'Not sure what my excuse is,' I said and laughed, tapping my own tummy.

I glanced over at Clara. She'd been particularly quiet throughout the whole meal. She'd only played with her food but she'd drunk copious amounts of wine and hadn't stopped fiddling with her phone.

'Hey, are you OK?' I whispered.

'Not really – I feel sick to my stomach.'

'Why, what's going on?'

'I'm not sure, but Aiden won't answer my texts, and look,' she said, twisting her phone towards me.

I looked at the screen and read Aiden's latest tweet. It was a photo of him with his arm wrapped around a random girl in what looked like a club, captioned, 'Who could resist a night with these babes?'

Admittedly, it didn't look good, but on the other hand it was a stag party, so surely there were going to be a few dodgy pictures tweeted that would be deleted first thing in the morning when common sense had prevailed once more.

'It'll just be a party of girls who've walked in off the street and noticed they're a stag party. It doesn't mean anything. A quick photo, maybe a beer and they'll be on their way.'

'Do you think so?'

'I know so. We can get to the bottom of this tomorrow. Aiden has to be in touch at some point –he's invited you to the cinema.'

'That's true.'

'So sit tight, turn your phone off and come and join the party.'

'It's not exactly rocking, is it?'

I shot Clara a stop-blooming-moaning look. It was about time she got into the spirit of things.

'I think you'll find Mel has some news but you've been too preoccupied to listen.'

Clara looked up. 'Anything interesting?'

Mel and Emma from book club were sitting at the opposite end of the table, grinning like Cheshire cats. Mel was clutching a leaflet and held it up for Clara to see. 'Ta-dah!' she cried.

'A ladies' night?' I queried.

'Who's up for seeing Dangler Dan in all his glory?' Emma squealed.

I rolled my eyes. 'Dangler Dan? Such a classy name for a stripper.'

'Did someone mention a stripper?' Suddenly Clara came alive and grabbed hold of my arm like an excited child. 'Did I hear you correctly?'

I giggled. 'Put the girl out of her misery!'

'You didn't think this was it, did you?' Elle laughed, sticking her tongue out at Clara. 'A sophisticated meal followed by cups of coffee and mints?'

'Well, I did wonder!'

'I may be pregnant but I've not developed baby brain yet!'

'I knew you wouldn't let us down, girl. The full monty, now that's more like it!' Clara exclaimed, clapping her hands together.

'I'm not sure if it's the full monty,' Mim added quickly. 'More like a local lad trying to earn a few extra quid by taking his kit off.'

'Please tell me you're being serious.' Clara flicked her gaze round the table and looked every one of us in the eye.

'Yes!' the whole table erupted.

'And if you look outside now, you'll see our carriage awaits!' Mim announced.

We all turned towards the window and gasped.

'Only the best for my daughter,' she said, smiling as she handed her credit card to the waiter. 'And tonight's meal is on me!'

One by one, we thanked Mim before swigging down the rest of our wine.

'Now let's get this show on the road!'

We all grabbed our bags and walked excitedly out of the bistro.

'This night might not turn out so bad after all,' Clara said, smiling as she pulled down her skirt and climbed into the back of the limo.

CHAPTER TWENTY-EIGHT

The limo pulled up outside the club, where already there was a queue of shrieking girls with their arms linked, tottering on heels and scantily dressed.

'They'll catch their death dressed like that,' Irene said, gripping the lapels of her coat tighter. 'It makes me cold just looking at them.'

'Ha!' I laughed. 'You know you've definitely reached the next stage of your life when leaving home without your coat is not an option.'

We joined the back of the line and chatted amongst ourselves as the queue slowly began to move.

'So it's going to cost me ten pounds to watch some bloke get his kit off on a Friday night,' Emma said, laughing as she rummaged through the loose change in her purse.

'He'll be worth it,' Clara said, snapping her purse shut and clasping her money in her hand like her life depended on it.

'I've never been to this kind of show before,' Mim admitted, with a twinkle in her eye, 'but I'm kind of looking forward to it. I really enjoyed watching *The Full Monty* at the cinema.'

Elle smirked. 'I can't believe I'm actually queuing up with my mother to watch this kind of show!'

Inside the foyer, we could hear the music blaring out from a room at the far end.

There was a woman sitting behind a dated oak booth. She was lacking a smile, and her hair was harshly scraped into a bun and secured by a black velvet scrunchie. Electric blue eyeshadow covered her lids and thick red blusher striped her cheeks.

'Are you sure we aren't coming to watch *Rocky Horror*?' Clara whispered in my ear.

'That's next month,' I said, nodding to the tatty poster pinned up behind the woman in the booth.

'You must be over eighteen to enter. Prepare for nudity. No touching the act and no photography allowed,' she intoned as she blew a bubble with her gum and slapped a pink ticket down on the counter. 'Ten pounds please.' She held out her bony hand.

Once we'd paid we were soon fleeced out of another fiver for hanging our coats in the 'cloakroom', which was actually an aluminium rail on wheels – no expense spared, probably from the pound shop.

'Are we all ready?' Clara asked, clapping her hands together. 'Let's go find out what Dangler Dan has to offer.'

I giggled. 'Name me two facts about Dangler Dan.'

'One he dangles, and two he's called Dan,' Clara stated as we all fell about laughing.

Mim pushed the doors open and we all filed into a sweaty room that was a sea of pink feather boas and flashing deely boppers, which were bouncing along to the song 'I Predict a Riot'.

'If it wasn't for our pregnant hen, I could cause a riot.' Clara giggled.

'Behave! Actually, have you see Elle? She looks rather pale,' I said.

'I'd say grey. No doubt she's very tired.'

We all glanced towards Elle.

'I can hear you! Honestly, I'm fine, really. I'm just grateful that you haven't made me dress up in a stupid outfit or pinned learner plates all over me.'

'There's time yet – let's see what I have in here,' Emma said, grinning as she rummaged inside her bag.

We all laughed at the look of horror on Elle's face.

Jenny touched her arm. 'She's only joking.'

'Phew! Thank God!'

'Are we up for a bit of karaoke later?' Mel grinned, swinging her hips.

'NO!' everyone cried.

After we managed to fight our way to the bar, we stood in the corner of the room and leant against the wall.

'I think I need to sit down,' Elle said, fanning herself with a beer mat while Mim grabbed a chair from a nearby table.

'Here, have this.'

'Are you OK?' Jenny asked with a concerned look on her face.

Elle nodded. 'Yes, it's just a little hot in here.'

'It's going to get even hotter when Dangler Dan makes an appearance,' Clara said, grinning as she took a swig of her beer.

We all jiggled on the spot to the music until it stopped suddenly and the lights dimmed. There was a loud cheer and then the crowd began chanting, before an unruly group of women surged towards the stage.

'Maybe it's that tiny they need a closer look,' Clara said, laughing as she grabbed my hand and pulled me towards the crowd.

I giggled. 'What are you doing?'

'Copping a better look.'

I flicked a glance over my shoulder. Jenny, Irene, Elle and Mim were still standing at the back of the room, while Mel and Emma had totally disappeared.

'Where have those two gone?' I asked, standing on my tiptoes and trying to spot them over a sea of deely boppers.

'Forget them. Come on!' Clara grasped my hand and snaked her way through the crowd until we managed to land a prime spot right at the front of the stage.

'Why are we waiting, why-y are we waiting,' the crowd sang, the whole room vibrating as everyone stamped their feet.

'So will Dangler Dan be a fireman, a construction worker or a—'

As the music struck up and the curtains lifted, I said, 'Policeman!' I laughed at the helmet tipped over his eyes and the huge truncheon in his hand. He'd packed his muscly upper half into a very tight shirt and his thighs were bulging through his trousers.

'Now that's what you call orgasmic.'

'I have to admit he's rocking that look.' I nodded approvingly.

'He is undeniably a damn fine-looking man.' Clara was straining her neck to get a better look.

He began to slowly unbutton his shirt and when it finally hit the floor, the girls went wild.

'Jesus Christ, the hormones in here are on fire. If he's not careful, they'll be carrying his charred body from that stage before this song finishes.'

He turned to face the crowd. 'Off, off, off,' they screamed as he launched his hat into the crowd.

As the hat sailed over us our eyes followed it, then we covered them as a group of girls pushed and shoved each other to claim the prize.

'Jeez, it's carnage – they were nearly fighting!' I exclaimed.

'Look!' Clara pointed and the pair of us burst out laughing. Emma gave us the thumbs-up from the side of the stage. She was just standing there, proudly wearing the helmet.

'I might have known!'

We looked towards the stage again, then immediately back at each other, as if we'd both had the same thought.

'He reminds me of someone,' I said to Clara, shooting a glance towards the stage.

'I know, me too. Who though?'

'I can't quite put my finger on it, but I'm sure it'll come to me soon.'

Then my breath caught in my throat. Oh my! My mouth went dry.

'Do you see who I think I see?'

Clara gasped. 'I think I do!'

The incredibly attractive man from the 425 bus was now standing in front of us wearing nothing but a red thong.

'It looks like he's been reunited with his rucksack!'

Dan – aka the man from the bus – moved to the front of the stage, and the women started shoving each other, their hands thrust forward trying to grab hold of his leg. His eyes twinkled at every girl in the room.

'Look at them – they're falling at his feet.'

'It's like he's seducing them with his eyes.'

'And the rest!'

Dan hooked his finger under the red thong and pulled it down slowly, gently teasing the crowd. 'They're like a pack of wild animals!' I said.

He turned his back towards us and glanced over his shoulder. My eyes caught his and one side of his mouth lifted in a sheepish smile before he shot us a cheeky grin. We both squealed, laughing.

'I think he's recognised us!' Clara shrieked.

'I think you might be right!'

The crowd were still yelling 'OFF, OFF, OFF.'

I knew I was gawping, but I couldn't help myself.

Dan faced the screaming girls and whipped off his thong. I'd never heard noise like it. The lights went down and the room fell into darkness. It was at that moment that I felt something being thrust into my hand as boisterous applause filled the room and the lights snapped back on. The stage was empty and Dan was gone. The crowd began to disperse in every direction.

'What have you there?' Clara asked, looking down at my hand.

'A card,' I said, flipping it over and reading it. 'A business card – Daniel Jones, Entertainer.'

'He was definitely that. Where did you get it?'

'Someone put it in my hand when the lights went out.'

Clara waggled her eyebrows at me. 'There's some writing on it,' she said, squinting at the handwriting.

'What does it say?'

'Meet me at the stage door in twenty minutes.'

Clara grabbed hold of my arm and squealed, 'Evie Cooper! Grab your coat – you've pulled!'

CHAPTER TWENTY-NINE

Once the performance had finished, another set of doors at the back of the room was flung open. They led to a disco, which was now open to the general public.

'Shall we go for a dance?' Clara asked, grabbing her drink.

'It would be rude not to, but where is everyone?' I asked, spinning my head round.

'What do you mean? This place is packed.'

'I mean, where are Elle, Mim, Jenny and Irene?'

Clara pointed. 'There's Mel and Emma through there, they're already in the disco.'

We both giggled at Mel, who was snogging the face off some bloke she'd managed to pin against the wall. Emma was standing with his mate, throwing peanuts into the policeman's helmet.

'I actually think I need some air.' I suddenly felt a bit hot and bothered.

'Ha! You just want to see if Mr Dan appears at the stage door in erm… ten minutes' time now. The clock is ticking,' she said, tapping her watch.

'Don't be ridiculous,' I said, grinning as I delved into my bag, searching for my phone.

She winked. 'I bet he doesn't give his card out to just anyone.'

'I bet he blooming does!'

'Yes, you may be right,' Clara said, laughing.

'Six missed calls from Irene!' I exclaimed, alarmed, quickly swiping the screen so I could read the text message she'd sent.

'What does it say?' Clara asked, looking over my shoulder at the screen.

'Nothing to worry about, thank God. She and Mim have taken an early dart.'

'Aww, that's a shame. So, that leaves Elle and Jenny unaccounted for.'

We both scanned the room but we couldn't spot either of them in the mass of writhing bodies.

'Maybe they're in the toilet.'

'Possibly.'

Feeling a tap on my shoulder, I spun round to see a panic-stricken, pale-faced Jenny standing behind me.

'You need to come with me right now.'

Clara and I both stared at her. 'Whatever's the matter? Jenny, you look awful.'

'It's Elle. Hurry.'

We ran towards the foyer, where we found Elle leaning against the wall, clutching at her stomach.

She cried out. 'The pain is getting worse.'

'Is it the baby?' I asked.

All Elle could manage was a nod.

'OK, deep breaths and don't panic. Clara, phone an ambulance.' I tossed her my phone.

'I've tried to ring Josh but the phone keeps going to answerphone,' Elle wept.

'He's probably in a club somewhere with no signal. Don't worry, we'll find him.'

Clara strode over to the hatch and asked the cashier the full address of the club, relaying the information down the phone. Once the ambulance was on its way, she hung up.

'Jenny, can you try Wilson and leave him a message – and Clara, try Aiden too.'

They both nodded.

'I think I'm going to be sick,' Elle blurted.

'OK, do you think it would help if we moved you outside or are you more comfortable here?'

'I need some fresh air.'

'We can manage that,' I said softly. 'Jenny, can you grab a chair from over there so Elle will be able to sit down outside, and we need the coats from the cloakroom.'

'I'll sort the coats.' Clara disappeared towards the coat rail.

'Please don't leave me,' Elle wailed. Her head was bent low and she was doubled over in pain.

'I'm not going anywhere, and you are going to be fine.' I wrapped my arm carefully around Elle's waist and we began to walk her towards the exit. I sounded much calmer than I felt. Once we were outside, we waited for Jenny to appear with a chair.

'Here's Jenny and Clara now.'

Jenny placed the chair in a doorway further down from the entrance to the club and Clara wrapped a coat around Elle's shoulders.

'The ambulance won't be long now.'

Elle perched on the edge of the chair and we all stood on the pavement in silence, praying everything was going to be OK.

'The pain is getting worse,' Elle whimpered.

I glanced up the road for any sign of the ambulance but I couldn't see anything. I squeezed Elle's hand.

'I wish it would hurry up,' Jenny whispered in my ear.

'Any news from Josh?' I asked.

Clara checked the phone and shook her head. 'No, nothing as yet.'

'Does anyone know which club they've gone to?'

'No,' Clara answered.

'Please don't let me lose the baby, please don't let me lose the baby,' Elle was muttering over and over.

I watched in horror as her face crumpled and all the colour drained from her skin. She gripped the side of the chair and began to sob.

'I think I'm bleeding,' she whispered.

We all looked at each other in horror.

Just then we heard voices filtering through a door behind us.

'What's this place?' Jenny asked, looking up at the sign above our heads.

'Stage door,' I said as the phone in Clara's hand started ringing.

'Quick, it's Josh!' Clara exclaimed, pushing the phone into my hands. 'You speak to him.'

I put the phone to my ear and my mouth went dry. 'Josh, it's Evie.' My eyes filled with tears and I took a breath. 'We're waiting for an ambulance. It's Elle – she's started bleeding.'

'Oh God. I'm at a club on the other side of town. I'll flag a taxi and get straight to the hospital.'

I ended the call.

'Josh is going to meet us there,' I told Elle reassuringly after I'd hung up.

'At last!' Jenny exclaimed. 'I can hear the sirens.'

At first they seemed miles away but they soon began to get louder and louder.

'They're nearly here – not long now. Hang on in there,' I said.

Elle couldn't speak; she just clutched at her stomach.

'Mim! We haven't phoned Mim!' Clara cried, taking the phone back and quickly scrolling through my address book. 'I'll ring her now.'

'It's here,' I said, relieved to see the ambulance speeding down the road towards us. Jenny stood on the edge of the pavement, waving her arms frantically to tell the paramedics where to stop. A crowd had started to gather around us, and there were hushed whispers as the ambulance drew to a halt beside us. They switched the sirens off but the blue lights still whirled.

The doors swung open and a paramedic made his way over to Elle.

'She's pregnant,' Jenny said immediately.

'And I think I'm bleeding,' Elle sobbed.

His manner was calm as he asked Elle a series of questions before taking her blood pressure and strapping her to a chair.

'I think I'm losing my baby,' Elle said, grabbing my hand. I walked alongside her.

'You're in the best possible hands,' I reassured her. 'Try not to worry.'

'Please can you come with me in the ambulance?' Elle asked.

'Of course. I'm going nowhere.'

The paramedic lifted her into the back of the ambulance and started hooking her up to a machine.

I turned back to Jenny and Clara. 'If I go in the ambulance, are you OK to follow in a taxi?'

'Yes, of course,' they said in unison. 'We'll follow you there.'

'Can you pass me my bag and my coat?' I asked, nodding towards the chair on the street. The stage door behind it had been flung open, and a group of girls who were hovering nearby started squealing as Dan stepped through it on to the street. His eye caught mine, then his expression quickly turned to one of concern as he clocked the ambulance.

'Are you ready?' the ambulance driver asked me, ushering me inside. I snatched my coat and bag from Clara and as I glanced backward, I noticed someone else standing next to Dan. My eyes locked with Noah Jones's and I held his gaze. What on earth was he doing here? Where had he come from?

Despite how worried I was, seeing Noah standing only a few steps away from me made my heart flutter.

'Evie,' I heard him shout, but then the ambulance door was slammed shut and we sped off towards the hospital, sirens blaring.

CHAPTER THIRTY

As soon as we arrived at the hospital, they whisked Elle off up the corridor and into a room out of sight. She'd spent the whole journey with her eyes shut tight and hadn't spoken. I'd kept hold of her hand and when we'd arrived, her eyes had locked with mine. They were full of pain, and I think we both already knew that she'd miscarried.

Clara and Jenny arrived five minutes after us and found me slumped in the corner of the waiting room, gripping a cup of coffee. Mim was on her way and Josh hadn't arrived yet.

'I don't know what to say,' Clara said softly.

Jenny shook her head. 'Me neither.'

We all looked exhausted. 'Josh should be here in a second. Has anyone heard from him since he jumped in the taxi?'

'He's here now,' Clara exclaimed as Josh rushed through the doors, quickly followed by Aiden and Wilson.

Immediately I stood up and stretched out my arms. Josh hugged me tightly. 'Where is she?' he demanded. His cheeks were flushed and he was close to tears.

Aiden and Wilson lingered behind him.

'They've taken her through to a separate room. I'll let the nurse know you're here,' Jenny said, patting his arm and hurrying over to the reception desk at the far end of the room.

'How is she?'

Tears brimmed in my eyes. 'She's in a lot of pain. One minute she was OK and the next…'

'I feel so helpless,' he said.

Jenny hurried back over to us. 'The nurse is coming now and she'll take you to Elle. In fact, here she is.'

We watched Josh disappear up the corridor.

'This is not a good end to the night.' Wilson kissed his mum on the cheek and slumped into a chair.

'It's awful, isn't it?'

None of us knew what to say. All we could do was wait. We sat in silence for twenty minutes before Jenny said, 'Why don't you boys get yourselves home? You aren't going to be able to do anything here, and if there's any news, we'll be in touch.'

Aiden began flicking through his wallet. 'I've got enough cash to get us all home. What do you think?'

Wilson gazed up from his chair. 'I'm not sure. I feel like we need to stay.'

'Honestly, that's very kind but there's no need. Go home and get some rest. Mim will be here shortly and it doesn't need all of us hanging around.'

Clara rubbed a weary hand over her face. 'I'm feeling tired too. Would anyone mind if I travelled back with the boys?'

'No, not at all. You three go.'

'Aiden, Wilson, is that OK with you?' Clara asked.

'Of course,' Wilson replied, but Aiden still seemed to be a little frosty towards her.

'There's a taxi rank just outside. Clara, grab your coat.' Aiden turned towards me. 'And please contact us as soon as there's any news.'

'I will – I promise.'

I stood up and hugged each one of them briefly before they wandered outside into the cold early morning.

'This is awful, isn't it?' Jenny sat down next to me, her eyes glistening with tears.

'Are you OK?' I asked. 'Shall I get us another coffee?'

'I'm fine. I feel like I'm drowning in coffee.' Jenny paused. 'I wouldn't wish this on my worst enemy.'

'I don't think you could have many enemies.' I tried to sound brighter than I actually felt.

She shook her head gently. 'You don't understand.' A lonely tear ran down her face and she brushed it away with the back of her hand.

'Jenny, are you OK?'

'Yes, honestly. I'll be fine. I experienced something similar many years ago, and the pain never goes away,' she said.

I rested my hand on her knee.

We sat in silence for a minute and my heart went out to both Jenny and Elle. Then the door at the end of the corridor opened and we heard footsteps padding towards us. My eyes met Josh's and immediately I knew it wasn't good news.

He stood in front of us. His voice was soft. 'She's lost the baby.'

I squeezed my eyes shut as Jenny stood up and wrapped her arms around Josh. They both sobbed.

'I'm so sorry to hear that,' she whispered. 'I'm so, so sorry.'

Once Jenny pulled away, I stood up and hugged Josh tight. 'How is she?' I asked tentatively.

'She's finally drifted off to sleep.'

'How are you feeling?'

'Numb,' was all he could say as he perched on the edge of the chair.

'Shall I get you a coffee?' Jenny asked.

He nodded and she walked off down the corridor towards the coffee machine.

Josh handed me a pile of leaflets. 'Do these things really help?' he asked.

The leaflets contained information on dealing with miscarriage. 'It's something you can discuss with Elle when she wakes up,' I said.

He nodded.

'They don't know why it happens – it just does.'

I leant forward and held his hand as he spoke. 'They just said that most miscarriages early on are caused by abnormal chromosomes in the baby. If a baby has too many or not enough, it won't develop properly. We didn't plan to have a baby so early on, but that doesn't mean I hadn't got my head round being a dad.'

'I know,' I said sympathetically.

'I had everything planned out in my head. It didn't matter whether it was a boy or a girl. Every Sunday we'd be at the park feeding the ducks, playing on the swings. We'd travel to the coast and build the biggest sandcastles and dig the deepest holes that we could climb inside. We'd bake cakes, wash cars and I'd even thought about getting a dog. But now...' His voice petered out and he looked down at the floor.

'It's not the end, Josh,' I said warmly. 'In time you and Elle will be the most wonderful parents and you'll be able to do all those things you've dreamed about.'

'I know. It's just such a shock, seeing Elle lying there, and I can't do anything – I can't ease her pain.'

'Does she know she's lost the baby?'

He nodded. 'The doctor said that when she wakes up, she'll probably go through a few different emotions – shock, sadness, even anger. She might be tired, or have trouble sleeping...'

'People grieve in different ways,' I told him.

Jenny returned from the coffee machine and handed him a cup.

'Thank you for looking after her and calling the ambulance,' he said.

'Don't be daft. You don't have to thank us.'

'I do. I really appreciate it, but honestly you've done enough, and there's nothing more anyone can do now. Get yourselves home.'

'Do you want us to fetch you anything?'

'No, I'm fine. Mim should be here any second, and she's picked us up a few bits and pieces – in fact here she is now.'

We all looked up to see Mim hurrying through the doors of the hospital.

When she reached us, she threw her arms around Josh, tears rolling down her face. 'I'm so sorry for you both.'

I locked eyes with Jenny, who softly patted them both on the back and nodded towards the door. We slipped away quietly, leaving them in a tight embrace.

CHAPTER THIRTY-ONE

When I woke up the next morning, my mood was sombre and my thoughts immediately turned towards Elle and Josh. It had been such an awful end to what should have been a lovely evening.

From the taxi, I'd sent a text message to Irene. She'd replied instantly, devastated by such sad news.

Jenny and I had travelled home in silence – there was nothing more we could do or say. When the taxi had pulled up outside my house, we'd hugged each other and said goodnight.

Clara had left the living room light on for me, which I'd switched off before wearily climbing the stairs to bed. I'd peered round her bedroom door to check if she was awake, but she'd been fast asleep, her head buried under her duvet. I'd wondered if she'd got to the bottom of Aiden's frosty behaviour and whether their date would go ahead, but that would have to wait 'til the next day.

I'd been awake for around ten minutes when I heard a gentle rap on the door.

'Come on in,' I said, sitting up in bed. Clara popped her head round the door with two mugs of tea in hand.

'Morning. I thought you might like one of these, but I didn't know if you'd be up just yet.'

'I've not been awake long but thank you.' I clasped the mug with both hands.

Clara perched on the edge of the bed. She looked exhausted. 'Did you sleep OK?' I asked.

'Not really. I tossed and turned most of the night thinking about Elle and Josh.'

'I know. It's so sad, isn't it?'

Clara nodded and sipped her tea.

'I'll text Josh in a little while to see if there's anything we can do, but in situations like this, you always feel helpless. It'll be something they need to deal with together.'

'It's such a shame. They're such a lovely couple. Hopefully this will only make them stronger.'

I nodded. 'How was your journey home with the lads?'

Clara sighed. 'Strained.'

'Oh, Clara,' I said.

'Aiden ignored me for most of the journey and just fiddled about on his phone. I tried to make small talk but that's exactly what it was – I'd ask a question and he'd answer. Other than that, we travelled home in silence.'

'What was Wilson doing at this point?'

'He was resting his head against the window and snoring. The taxi dropped him off first…'

'Which just left you and Aiden in the taxi alone.'

'Yes, so I asked him outright why he was being a moody git.'

'You didn't say it quite like that, did you?'

'No, but I was tempted! I asked what was wrong, and it was just like we'd feared.'

'He knows you slept with Wilson.'

Clara nodded. 'Yes. It turned out Wilson had confided in Josh that we'd spent the night together and that he wanted to see me again. Then last night in the pub, Josh had asked Wilson how we were getting on.'

'In front of Aiden?'

'Yes, which was a little unfortunate, and as you can imagine, Aiden wasn't very impressed with me.'

'Christ on a bike! And I thought it was women that were meant to be the sensitive ones? It's not as if you were going out with Aiden – or anyone else for that matter.'

'I tried to explain it was just one of those things, a spur-of-the-moment decision, but he wasn't buying it and made a quip about being easy as the taxi pulled up outside the house. So I threw him the dirtiest look ever before getting out and slamming the door shut behind me. I didn't even offer him any money for the ride.'

'Quite right, too!'

'Half of me wonders if Aiden's really worth it anyway – especially if he's this moody and we haven't even been on a date yet.'

I sipped my drink. 'It'll be a jealousy thing. From his point of view, he would have been looking forward to the date today and then bam – he discovers that you and Wilson have had sex. But what he needs to realise is that if you wanted to be with Wilson, you could be – you're both single and there's nothing stopping you from being together. Except for the fact that you prefer Aiden.'

'If he carries on like this, he'll miss his blooming chance.'

'I bet he'll be in touch this morning.'

'You reckon? I've got a feeling he's stubborn and it'll be down to me to text.'

'Let's just wait and see.'

'And anyway, Evie Cooper,' Clara said, leaning forward and picking up the business card from my bedside table, 'I think we need to have a chat about this card and the sudden appearance of Mr Noah Jones last night.'

I could feel the grin spreading across my face.

'Funny you should say that…'

'What have you got to tell me?' she squeaked.

'Ha! Honestly, absolutely nothing!'

'Look at his business card! Noah and Dan have one thing in common,' Clara said, handing it to me. 'Their surname!'

'Brothers?'

'Now you come to mention it, they do have a similar look about them.'

'I couldn't believe it last night when I spotted Noah standing next to Dan on the pavement. I thought I was imagining it.'

'He must be back in the area for his book tour.'

'Let's have a look at his posts from last night,' I said, grabbing my phone from the bedside table.

'Did he tweet last night? What's his latest one?' Clara asked.

I searched for Noah's profile, then scrolled down his feed.

'His last tweet says… "The boys are back in town". There's a photo of him and Dan in what looks like a pub.'

Clara took the phone from me and studied the screen. 'That's the club we were at last night. Look – that's the same bar.'

'He must have met his brother after the show for a beer.'

'He shouted my name just as the ambulance doors shut. What happened after it pulled away?' I asked.

'A group of girls surrounded him and Dan, then Jenny and I jumped in a taxi and followed the ambulance to the hospital. I didn't see what happened to them. I think you should message him – after all, he did shout for you.'

I pondered for a moment. 'OK, let's message him and see what happens.'

Clara grinned. 'I knew you'd come to your senses.' Her fingers flew over the screen. 'All sent!' she said with a wicked glint in her eye.

'Hang on! I've not told you what to write yet!'

'I've kept it simple! All I've written is "I thought I saw you last night".'

Thankfully what Clara had written wasn't too bad and I was mid-gulp when the phone beeped with a notification.

Clara looked up, amazed. 'Jeez, that's quick by anyone's standards!'

'Surely that's not him?'

Clara handed me the phone back. 'Yes, it is!'

I flicked my eyes over the screen. It read:

Yes, it was me. Are you OK? What was with the ambulance? Love Noah x

I thought for a moment and then typed:

Yes, all OK. The ambulance was for a friend.

'You can't leave it there,' Clara insisted, reading the message. 'You need to ask him a question to keep the conversation going.'

'Hark at you, Miss Relationship Expert! I'll just add "What were you doing there?"' I did. Then I hit send.

'Good plan – we might find out if our suspicions are true and he is, in fact, Dangler Dan's brother.'

The phone pinged once more. 'Well?' Clara asked impatiently.

I took a minute to read his message. 'He says that he hopes my friend is OK, and yes, he's in town visiting his parents. He was at the club last night to see his brother and apparently, he noticed me from backstage during the performance.'

'This is sounding very good,' Clara interrupted.

'And he gave Dan the business card to put in my hand when the lights went out.'

Clara raised her eyebrows. 'And?'

'And that's all he's said.'

'Blimey! What do you think about that then?'

I lifted my hair off my neck and twisted it into a bun, then let it cascade back over my shoulders as I pondered.

I bit down on my lip and then a huge grin spread across my face. I couldn't hide the fact I was pleased.

'You know what I think?' Clara said. 'I think he has a little bit of a soft spot for you.'

'And what gives you that impression?'

'Call it women's intuition – I'm tuned in to that sort of stuff.' Clara handed me the phone back.

'Are you really?' I grinned at her. 'OK then, how am I going to reply to that message?'

'Let's just go with it. Why don't you ask…' Clara was thoughtful for a second, 'why he would get Dan to give you a business card?'

'Mmm, I'm not sure about this.'

'OK, how about "It was good to see you last night, if only for a split second"? Go on – stop dithering.'

I locked eyes with Clara. She wasn't taking no for an answer. She gave me a stern look, and I was just about to protest when she leant forward and tried to grab the phone off me.

'OK,' I said, finally typing in a message and pressing send.

We both stared at the phone like it was about to explode – and then there was nothing.

I sighed. 'See? We've frightened him away now.'

'It's been a couple of seconds! He might have nipped to make a drink or to the loo. He might even be working.'

'On a Sunday?' I replied, swallowing my disappointment.

'He's a writer, isn't he? He might be up to his eyes in edits or something.'

'More like back to bed with a girlfriend for lazy Sunday sex.'

Clara tutted and rolled her eyes dramatically at me. Then we both jumped out of our skins as the phone beeped.

'Ha! This time it's my phone,' Clara said.

'Life must have been so much more straightforward when there wasn't technology and you physically had to go and knock on someone's door to ask them for a date,' I mused.

'I'm so glad those days are gone! My dad would have chased everyone away with a shotgun. No one would have been good enough for his precious daughter.'

'Your dad doesn't own a shotgun – and anyway, who is it?'

'Aiden,' she said, slowly swiping the screen.

'And it says?'

'"Do you fancy the cinema today at 1.30 p.m.?"' Clara read. 'See!'

Clara ignored me. 'There isn't even an apology.' She turned the phone towards me and exhaled.

I took it from her and reread the text. 'OK, here's the thing – this is a man apology.'

'And how do you make that out?' She looked at me as if I'd just said something absolutely ridiculous.

'Because he's texted first – and not only that, he's brushed over the subject because he knows he was acting like a prat last night!'

'Seriously?'

'Yes, seriously! He's slept on it and, OK, I'm no relationship expert, but I don't think men are very forthcoming with their feelings. This is his way of saying, "I was hurt, we weren't to-gether and I overreacted, but I really like you".'

'A simple sorry would do.'

'As the saying goes: men are from Mars and women are from Venus. Just accept the blooming invitation! You know you want to. You can give him a hard time about it later!'

'But what will you do this afternoon?'

'Me? I'm going to have a long soak in the bath and then cook up a magnificent roast for when you get home. Then you can tell me all about your date.'

'You are *so* good to me!'

'I know – and don't you ever forget it.'

'I won't, and to prove it I'm going to knock us up a couple of bacon butties to keep us going, and then you can help me choose my outfit.'

'You need an outfit for the cinema?' I asked. 'But it's dark!'

Clara raised her hand to her chest. 'One must look good always,' she projected in a dodgy Shakespearean voice.

'Come on then – let's get breakfast,' I said, throwing back the cover and jumping out of bed as my stomach rumbled.

'Your phone just beeped again,' Clara said.

It was a response from Noah:

It was good to see you too x

I resisted the urge to jump up and down on my bed – just. Instead, I screamed into my pillow while Clara squealed, 'Oh my lord!'

CHAPTER THIRTY-TWO

Slumped on the settee in my faithful old trackies and sloppy sweater, I was half watching *Back to the Future* while continually staring at Noah's last message. It all seemed very surreal. Over our bacon butties, Clara had said the tweet was a good sign. Even though I knew I'd be very nervous seeing him again at the book signing, I also couldn't wait. But I wasn't going to turn up dressed to impress like Clara had tried to insist – I was simply going to be me and wear what I felt comfortable in. There was no point pretending to be something I wasn't.

I heard Clara bounding down the stairs. 'Close your eyes!' she shouted.

I squeezed them shut obediently and waited.

'Ta-dah! How do I look?'

When I opened my eyes, I saw Clara had plumped for a hoody, jeans and Converse, which was not her usual attire.

I did a double take, then studied her look intently.

'Oh no, what's wrong? I don't like that look on your face,' she said, placing her hands on her hips and giving me a worried smile.

I sucked in my breath, then smiled. 'You've taken me a little by surprise, I have to admit. It's not your usual sexy knock-'em-dead kind of look.'

'Ha, that's where you are mistaken!' she said, laughing as she unzipped her hoody to disclose absolutely nothing underneath but a black satin push-up bra that showed off her ample cleavage.

Clara gave her shoulders a little shimmy.

'Wow.' I whistled, impressed. 'That's my girl! I knew you wouldn't let me down!' I marvelled, giggling at her.

'But,' she said, zipping her hoody back up, 'he isn't going to know what assets I'm hiding under here unless things get steamy – and then I'll knock his socks off. In the meantime, I will sport a toned-down look and leave it to Aiden to make a move.'

'Very good plan. Put the ball in his court.'

'Exactly,' she said, grabbing her bag off the chair.

'What time are you leaving?' I asked, just before a car beeped outside.

'That'll be him now.'

'Well, have a fantastic time, and I hope everything isn't as fraught as last night.'

'Thank you.' She hugged me quickly, then the front door slammed shut and she was gone, with a spring in her step.

It was now early afternoon and I'd promised Irene I would nip over for a cuppa in the next hour or so. I'd already grabbed a quick conversation with her this morning just before she'd popped over to Mim's with a bouquet of flowers for Elle.

I decided to go over now so I'd have plenty of time to prepare dinner for Clara getting home, so I switched off the TV, grabbed my coat and headed out the door.

I inhaled the afternoon air and glanced up at the turquoise sky. It was much warmer today. Heavy rain and thunder had been predicted for later, but at the moment, I was enjoying the calm before the storm.

Ahead of me was a couple walking hand-in-hand. They were all cosied up, laughing together, and in the blink of an eye my thoughts whizzed back to Noah. It was good to see you too, he'd said. My pulse began to race thinking about it, and the thought of going to his book signing left me feeling a mixture of trepidation and excitement.

By the time I reached Irene's house, there was a massive smile etched on my face. I rang the bell and waited. I could hear her chit-chatting away to someone as she approached the door.

'You wait there,' she said firmly and I wondered if it was a child she was speaking to.

The door opened. 'Good afternoon,' Irene chirped brightly, then immediately crouched on the floor.

'What are you doing?' I asked, perplexed. 'Have you lost something?'

She smiled up at me. 'Not quite,' she said, then all became clear. Behind her, I heard a tiny yelp and then I saw, sliding towards me on the wooden floor, the cutest ball of chocolate-coloured fluff I'd ever set eyes on.

'Oh my life!' I shrieked, bending down and scooping the tiny pot-bellied puppy up into my arms. 'He's absolutely gorgeous,' I said as I stepped into the hallway.

Irene stood up and grinned. 'Let me introduce you to my new companion – Buddy.'

'Well hello there, Buddy! Aren't you cute? How long have you had him?' I asked, juggling the puppy in my arms as I unfastened my coat.

'Approximately three hours – and my life has never been so chaotic!' But she smiled affectionately at him as I followed her into the living room. She perched on a chair and I settled on the floor with the energetic whirlwind tugging at the cuff of my hoody.

'Where did you get him? He's so adorable.'

'One of the ramblers' daughters breeds Labradors, and I couldn't resist. I need a bit of company in the day, and he's the perfect excuse to venture out in the fresh air.'

'It's those paws – they're huge! He'll grow into them one day I suppose... and those eyes – look at those, Irene. I'm already in love.'

'Yes, he does have the knack of making you fall in love with him instantly.'

'Ouch,' I yelled, my voice jumping an octave. 'And not forgetting those razor-sharp teeth.'

Irene laughed.

I scooped the puppy up again and held him in front of my face. 'We do not bite Auntie Evie – otherwise you'll have nowhere to stay when Irene goes on holiday.'

I realised my voice had gone all gooey, and I buried my face in his fur as he let out a tiny bark like he understood my request.

When I put him back down on the floor, he scampered towards his teddy bear and grabbed it with his teeth. I giggled as I began to pull the bear and he tugged back with a surprising force. His bum waggled in the air and he growled softly as I dragged him around the floor.

'How was Mim this morning?' I asked Irene tentatively.

'She hadn't slept and was a little subdued. Elle can come home later this afternoon, and Mim said she's coping well and still looking forward to the wedding.'

'That's good to hear.'

'Where's Clara this afternoon?'

'At the cinema with Aiden, thankfully.'

'Thankfully?' Irene asked.

'It was a little touch and go for them last night. Josh let slip that Clara and Wilson had shared a moment together, and Aiden wasn't too impressed.'

'Oh dear, but they were both single.'

'That's what I said, but I suppose it doesn't stop him feeling hurt.'

'And what about you?'

'Me?' I asked.

'Isn't it about time you sorted yourself out with a date?'

'I think I have enough going on in my life at the moment, don't you? And with all of Clara's dramas…' I rolled my eyes.

'So, nothing to report at all?'

'No. Why are you narrowing your eyes at me?' I held Irene's inquisitive stare.

'Because last night you and Clara couldn't get to the front of the stage quickly enough.'

'Ha, well funny you should say that and it's not what you think.'

'Shall I pop the kettle on and you can tell me all about it?'

'Go on then,' I answered, suddenly realising my hand wasn't being pulled any more. I looked down to see Buddy had climbed on to my lap and was now curled up fast asleep.

I stroked his head softly until Irene came back with the drinks.

'So, young lady, what is it I'm not thinking?' She eyed me suspiciously.

'Dangler Dan is not his name.'

'You don't say!' Irene laughed. 'Funnily enough, I never thought it was – unless his mother really didn't like him.'

'You'll never guess who he was!'

'Nothing springs to mind… pardon the pun!' Irene chuckled.

I flashed her a smile. 'Dangler Dan's surname only happens to be Jones – he's Noah's brother.'

Irene crossed her legs and leant forward. 'Well, well, well. Gorgeous author Noah?'

'The one and only.'

'Well, fancy that, as my old mum would say.'

'Out of all the strip joints in all the world, can you believe that not only was the bloke that left his bag on the bus Dan Jones, but he's also Noah's brother. And that's not all!'

'Mmm, intriguing.'

'While Clara and I were watching the show, Noah was watching us from behind the curtain backstage. At the very end, when the lights went out, I felt something being thrust into my hand.'

'What was it?'

'A business card with a message scrawled on the back – "Meet me at the stage door in twenty minutes". Obviously we weren't going to go.'

Irene laughed. 'Obviously.'

'But then we happened to be outside the stage door when the ambulance pulled up, and Noah appeared as the paramedic shut the doors. He shouted me but then the ambulance pulled off.' I managed to manoeuvre my arm without waking Buddy up and took a sip of my drink.

'So was it Dan or Noah that wanted to meet you at the stage door?'

I pressed my lips together to stop a smile escaping but it was no good. 'I think it was Noah.'

'Because…'

'Because we were messaging each other this morning.'

'This all sounds very promising.' Irene gave me one of those looks that meant she knew best.

'We'll see,' I said, trying to play the whole thing down. What I actually wanted to do was bounce on the settee like a child and whoop as loud as I could, but being in my early twenties, I didn't think I could get away with it.

'So what are you going to do about it? Keep talking, meet up?'

'I've no idea, but I'll go to his book signing and see what happens,' I replied with a big grin on my face.

Buddy had begun to snore lightly. 'What's the timescale with this little one? How soon can you take him out for a walk?'

'He's had his first batch of injections and his second lot are tomorrow. Then normally another two weeks after that, though he can roam around in the back garden in the meantime.'

'I bet you can't wait.'

'I can't, but apparently they don't need that much exercise when they're puppies. I've thought about taking him to obedience classes, though – look...' She grinned as she held up a chewed shoe.

I laughed.

'Anyway, thanks for the drink but I best go – I promised I'd cook Clara a roast dinner for when she gets back from the cinema, and I need to nip to the shop for some potatoes on my way home.'

'You can't have a chicken dinner without roasties,' she said. 'Fingers crossed the date goes without a hitch.'

Her eyes turned to Buddy. 'Aww, look at him,' she said, smiling. He was asleep in the crook of my arm.

'I know – so cute.'

I reluctantly handed him back to Irene and she laid him down gently inside his puppy pen and closed the door.

'I'll come over after work on Tuesday with Clara if she's free. I'm sure she'd love to meet Buddy.'

'That'd be great.'

After kissing me on both cheeks, Irene stood in the doorway and waved me off.

'It's going to rain,' she shouted after me. 'Hurry.'

The sky had indeed darkened, and a second later the heavens opened.

'I will,' I bellowed, picking up speed and burying my hands in my pockets. I reached the shop in record time.

By the time I'd paid for the potatoes, the rain had worsened. I sheltered under the jutted-out roof of the shop doorway and watched the rain bounce off the pavements. People were racing along the street with their coats over their heads, trying to keep the drenching to a minimum.

I stood hedging my bets about whether to wait a moment longer or make a dash for it, and I was just about to run for it when I sensed someone standing next to me.

'Hey,' came a male voice.

I looked up to find the gorgeous eyes of Noah Jones staring back at me. I did everything in my power to stop myself from gasping aloud.

'Hey back,' I said, my eyes not leaving his. My heart was thumping so loud that I worried he might hear it.

'It looks like you're deciding whether to make a run for it or not.'

'You read my mind,' I replied. Our eyes were still locked. I was glad he couldn't read my mind because then he'd know I wouldn't be running anywhere in front of him. He didn't need to see my backside jiggling all over the place.

Noah clutched on to his umbrella as we watched the rain batter off the cars parked next to the shop. He was dressed casually in a tight white T-shirt, faded jeans and Converse. I was doing my very best not to stare at his toned abs or breathe too deeply – the aroma of his aftershave was already making me weak at the knees.

'Where are you going?'

'Home,' I managed to say.

'Is it far from here?' he asked casually.

'About five minutes.'

'Come on then. I'll walk you,' he said. 'This rain doesn't look like it's giving up anytime soon.'

'Are you sure?'

'Absolutely. Here, come closer.' He extended his arm and draped it around my shoulders. His hazel eyes bore into mine, and I could feel my entire body trembling.

He was definitely striking, and I felt myself blush.

'OK, it's that way.' I pointed up the street and stepped out of the doorway.

Just then we saw a flash of lightning and our eyes flicked upwards. Thunder rolled across the dense black sky, and somehow the rain got even heavier. Then another jagged bolt of white split the sky.

Noah took the bag of potatoes from my grasp. 'Are you ready to make a run for it?'

'As ready as I'll ever be. We're going to get drenched!'

'That's half the fun.' He looked at me from under his dark eyelashes and we exchanged mischievous grins. Instantly my stomach fluttered.

We took off up the street, the rain bouncing off the ground around us, but despite Noah's umbrella, my shoes were sodden in seconds.

A second burst of thunder, even louder than the first, rumbled across the sky and I flinched. Noah passed the umbrella to me and grabbed my hand. We both glanced at the angry storm clouds above and he began to run faster, pulling me along behind him.

Neither of us spoke as we ran. We reached the steps of my house in six minutes flat. Not that I was counting.

There was a huge crack as lightning flashed above us again, 'This is me,' I said, bounding up the steps and fumbling in my bag for the key. 'Would you like to come inside?'

Noah was soaked to the bone. Little droplets of rain fell from his hair and a smidgen of chest hair curled over the top of his T-shirt. I fought the urge to wipe the raindrops from his forehead. Our height difference meant I'd been holding the brolly too low for him, so he'd had to run most of the way without its protection.

He hesitated for the slightest of moments. 'That would be great, but only if you have time?' he said, flashing me the most gorgeous smile.

There was something about the way he smiled at me that made my heart skip a beat.

'Yes, I have time.'

'Then I'd love to,' he said.

It took a second for his answer to sink in. 'You would?' My face broke into a smile.

His eyes glinted with amusement. 'Yes – that's a yes. Now open that door! In case you haven't noticed, I'm drenched.'

'No, I hadn't noticed,' I said, giving him the most sparkly grin.

He smiled back and I glowed inside.

Once we were in the hallway, I took the potatoes back. 'You're soaked,' I said, trying not to notice the way the wet T-shirt was clinging to his torso.

'That was a downpour and a half,' he said, smiling as he raked his hand through his hair and swept his wet fringe from his eyes. 'Am I OK to kick these wet shoes off?'

'Of course! And let me get you a towel – then I'll pop the fire on. It's the least I can do. Go in there and make yourself comfortable.' I nodded towards the living room. He disappeared through the door and I stopped to risk a hesitant look in the hallway mirror. Jeez – my hair was limp, my nose red and my mascara smudged. This was definitely not the look I'd wanted for meeting Noah again. I hurried upstairs to brush my hair and touch up my make-up, then grabbed a towel from the airing cupboard.

When I walked into the living room, Noah was kneeling down in front of the fire, which he'd already managed to light.

'Here, take this,' I said, handing him the towel. 'Would you like a cuppa?'

'You read my mind!' He grinned, rubbing the towel over his arms. 'One sugar please,' he called as I skirted round him into the kitchen and switched the kettle on.

While I waited for the water to boil, I peeped back through the gap in the kitchen door. It was so surreal – the man who was on my mind all the time was currently sitting in my living room. I watched as he stood up and peeled the wet T-shirt from his body before drying himself off with the towel and holding the T-shirt towards the fire.

I bit down on my lip; I couldn't take my eyes off him. His body was perfect, his muscles toned to perfection, and it was one of those moments when I regretted eating chocolate biscuits for breakfast. I couldn't quite believe he was in my living room and my stomach was full of butterflies.

When I wandered back into the room clutching two steaming mugs of tea, he started slipping the T-shirt back over his head. As he did so, I made sure to keep my eyes on the fire, which was now crackling away.

'I hope you don't mind – I was a little sodden.' He smiled and the corners of his eyes crinkled.

'No, not at all,' I said, placing his mug on the table and deliberating over where I was going to sit. I was feeling very nervous.

I decided it was best to perch on the chair next to the fire. He looked sideways at me, and my heart melted. I had no clue what to say.

'How's your friend?' he asked, sitting down on the rug and stretching his legs out in front of the fire.

'Friend?' I asked, dazed.

'Saturday night – the ambulance.'

'Oh, yes, sorry. Unfortunately she suffered a miscarriage.'

'I'm so sorry to hear that,' he said sadly.

'It was her hen party too – she's getting married very soon. It had been such a fun evening up until that point.'

'I noticed you were all very entertained by my brother.' He cocked an eyebrow at me.

I blushed.

'I'm teasing you! Anyway, tell me all about you. What's happened since I saw you last? Are you still at the library?'

'Yes, I love it there, but Irene has retired now. I miss seeing her every day, but she's only up the road. And look how well you're doing – another book out soon,' I said, quickly changing the subject.

'Yes, that's why I'm here – visiting Dan, catching up on the family and attending a few book signings. Is this your place then?' he said, switching the conversation back to me.

'Yes, all mine.'

'Boyfriend? Husband?' His eyes caught mine.

The question hung in the air for a split second.

'No boyfriend, no husband – just Clara, my housemate,' I answered, thankful my voice didn't falter. 'She's just recently moved in with me after splitting from her boyfriend. She moved back with her parents for a while, but I think once you've made that step to move out, it's difficult to live by their rules again.'

We were silent for a couple of seconds while we both sipped on our tea.

'Are you originally from around here?' I asked as a shiver ran down my spine.

'You're cold,' he said. 'Here – sit by the fire.' He moved up on the rug. I hesitated for a moment, then settled next to him. The heat from the fire was inviting, and I rubbed at the goosebumps on my arms.

My eyes lifted towards him and I held my breath, praying he couldn't read my mind. I thought he was perfect.

'Yes, originally I am from around here,' he said, answering my question. 'My parents still live here, and so does Dan obviously.'

'Where do you live now?'

'I moved to London a while back.'

I knew that, of course, from his Twitter profile, but I didn't want him to think I'd been stalking him. 'And how long have you been there?' I asked.

'I moved just after I saw you last. I thought it would be cool to say I'm a writer living in London. I thought I'd spend most of my days wandering through the city and parks, finding inspiration wherever I walked. Or maybe writing in bistros next to the Thames while sipping cappuccinos.'

'And is that not what you do?'

'Hell no, it's all too expensive. I pretend I'm living the dream when actually I'm skint and living in a bedsit with only four walls for company most of the time.'

I laughed. 'So rock 'n' roll!'

'I know, but please don't tell anyone!' he said, smiling. 'And how is Irene? Your mother, right? Is she enjoying retirement?'

'She's actually my foster mum. She's good, and she is very much enjoying retirement. She's just got herself a small bundle of fluff to keep her company.'

'A puppy?'

'Yes, a chocolate Labrador called Buddy.'

'A handful I'm sure.'

'But a cute handful.'

This was the first time I'd admitted to anyone new in my life that Irene wasn't my real mum.

'So you said, Irene's your foster mum?'

I hesitated for a moment. It would be so easy to share the news about my mother.

'I didn't mean to pry,' he said. He must have thought I was upset with him.

'You're not. I mentioned it,' I said, pulling my knees up to my chest and wrapping my arms around them.

'Are you OK?' Noah reached over and squeezed my hand gently, giving me a reassuring smile.

'I am. I'm just going through a very emotional time at the minute. Yes, Irene is my rock – my whole world in fact – but a few weeks ago I started the search for my biological mother.'

Noah's eyes widened. 'And?' he asked. 'Any news?'

I nodded, not trusting myself to speak for a moment. Noah sat in silence and sipped his tea, waiting until I was ready.

'I was given up at birth and passed between foster families. For years I battled with my own demons – feeling like I was never wanted – and I never stayed in one place long enough to make any real friends. It was Irene's love and care that saved me. That sounds dramatic, I know, but it's true.'

'It must have been tough.'

'It was. I learnt to go under the radar at school, and I struggled. It was Irene who discovered I couldn't read.'

'You couldn't read?' Noah asked, wondering whether he'd heard me correctly.

'Yes, that's right. It wasn't that difficult to hide. I'd changed schools that many times that no one ever noticed, and I learnt to get by.'

'Gosh, Evie, I can't imagine what you've been going through all these years,' he said, touching my knee.

'Irene is a very special person. If it wasn't for her…' I quickly brushed away a tear. I always got emotional thinking about Irene's kindness and love for me. 'She taught me to read, and she's helped me to overcome so many barriers in life – I will be eternally grateful for that.'

'It sounds like everyone needs an Irene in their life.' He smiled warmly at me.

'They sure do. Anyway, shortly after I started the search for my mother, the Salvation Army confirmed they'd found her. It came as quite a shock – I'd convinced myself it would take years to track her down. She wrote me a letter explaining why she had no choice but to give me away. I always wondered what type of person could give up their newborn baby, but when I read the letter, I realised I shouldn't ever have judged what I didn't understand.'

'I think that's something we're all guilty of from time to time, but life is never simple.'

'Sarah Thomas – that's my real mum – started looking for me on the same day I started my search for her.'

'What a coincidence,' Noah said softly.

'It was 20 January – my birthday.'

'It sounds like she never forgot you.'

'In her letter she said that not a day goes by without her thinking about me.'

'So, what happens now?' Noah asked.

'We've both agreed that we want to meet up.'

'How are you feeling about that?'

'Scared, excited, nervous, physically sick. What if she doesn't like me?'

Noah smiled warmly at me. 'Evie, who on earth wouldn't like you? You're beautiful, warm, funny… the list is endless.'

I felt myself blush. 'Thank you. It's all just a waiting game now,' I said as his words whirled around in my mind.

'Come here.' Noah stretched his arms out and I fell into them, resting my head on his shoulder.

He wrapped his arms around me and hugged me.

'I think you needed that,' he whispered in my ear, before he kissed me lightly on the top of my head.

'I think you might be right.' I pulled away and felt his hand drop to the small of my back. We stared into the dancing flames of the fire and sat in silence for a moment, both lost in our own thoughts.

'That's enough about me now,' I said finally. 'What about you? What's next?'

'It's mainly work, work, work. When I'm not writing, I'm editing, and when I'm not editing, I'm promoting.'

'That sounds very busy.'

'It is.'

'So it's all work and no play?' I asked, lifting one shoulder and playfully bumping it against his.

His eyes sparkled. 'No play at all lately.' I realised that his eyes weren't leaving mine.

His hand brushed against mine on the rug and my whole body tingled. Then he dipped his head towards me, and I thought he was going to kiss me.

He moved a little closer and I could feel his breath on my face. His lips lingered next to mine – and then his phone beeped. He pulled away.

'Damn it.' He gave me a warm smile as he grabbed his phone from his pocket and swiped the screen.

'Damn it indeed,' I said, feeling the tension ease for a second as he read his message.

'Double damn it! I should currently be sitting down for a Sunday roast with the family.'

'Double damn it indeed.' I pressed my lips tightly together to hide my smile.

'This conversation isn't over, Cooper, but I have to go.' He stood up and disappeared into the kitchen with his empty mug.

'I was just thinking the same thing,' I murmured when he was out of earshot.

Through the open door, I saw him hover by the kitchen table for a moment, and I wondered what he was doing.

'You've still got it,' he said as he stepped back through the door. His eyes met mine and sparkled. He'd spotted his business card pinned to the board in the kitchen – the card I'd kept for over eight months. He held it in his hand and leant against the door frame. His gaze met mine, and neither of us faltered. He walked towards me and I forced myself to breathe calmly. When he got close to me, my whole body started trembling and I knew I was blushing. My fingers itched to stroke his stubble and my heart was beating so fast I thought I was going to explode. I hadn't felt desire like this before – nothing had ever come close.

'You have my number, so ring me. No excuses, and failing that...' He tapped the card lightly on my nose, then flipped it on to the table next to my phone.

'Failing that, what?'

'Then I'll see you at the café for my book signing on Saturday. Promise me you'll come.'

'I will,' I replied softly, meaning every word.

'It's a date then.'

I watched the vision of loveliness that was Noah disappear into the hallway and could feel myself grinning like a loon. I bit down on my lip, and a couple of seconds later the front door shut behind him and he was gone.

'It's a date,' I squealed as I rolled on to my back and kicked my legs in the air like an excited child.

CHAPTER THIRTY-THREE

I heard muffled shouting from the hallway as I stretched and sat up.

'Evie, are you home?' Clara bounded into the living room and plonked herself down on the settee. 'I've shouted you twice! Who's been having a sneaky kip in front of the fire?' she grinned. 'That's a sign of old age, that is.'

'What time is it?' I asked, glancing towards my phone. After Noah left, I'd poured myself a glass of wine and snuggled down under a blanket on the rug with a book. I must have dozed off soon after.

'Five o'clock, and I'm ready for my roast. I've worked up a right appetite.' She winked.

'Ha! So the casual look with only the push-up bra underneath worked a treat?'

Clara hitched her chest up to her chin and we both laughed.

'Well, I have bad news about the roast,' I said guiltily.

'Which is?'

'I fell asleep before I could make anything.'

'You're kidding me?'

'Afraid not. I've been kind of preoccupied this afternoon,' I said with a huge grin on my face.

Her eyes shot up. 'Sounds intriguing! I'd best pour myself a glass of wine then and we can swap Sunday afternoon stories.'

'Go for it!' I grinned. 'And you might as well grab the take-away menu from the drawer while you're in there.'

'Pah! You had one job this afternoon, Cooper,' she shouted jokingly from the kitchen.

A couple of seconds later Clara was back and had stretched herself out on the rug next to me.

'So how was the film?' I asked.

'Not really sure,' Clara said as she took a sip of wine.

Our eyes met and we both burst out laughing.

'Which suggests to me that you spent the whole time snogging in the back row.'

'Don't look at me like that!'

'What happened to playing it cool?'

'Apparently, he likes the casual look.' Clara winked. 'And when Renee Zellweger was getting her kit off, he began to get a little amorous. You know how it all starts – he pretends he's stretching his arm and it sneaks around the back of your chair.'

'Then he begins to play with your hair.'

'And pulls you in closer, kissing you lightly on the top of your head.'

'Then your eyes meet and your lips linger closely together.'

'And you go in for the kill! That's basically what happened.'

'So, the question remains – are you going to see him again?'

'Yes, of course I am. Tomorrow morning, 9 a.m., at work!'

'Apart from work, silly!'

'Nothing was arranged as such, but I felt it in here.' Clara thumped her chest.

I could hear the excitement in Clara's voice, and I was truly happy for her – she deserved a little bit of happiness after her disastrous relationship with Nick.

I thought I was doing a grand job of keeping my feelings to myself, but as visions of Noah seeped back into my mind, I couldn't help the smile spreading across my face. I shifted on the rug and tucked my feet underneath my body.

'I think it's about time you told me what you're smirking at,' Clara said, giving me an amused look.

'Well – oh, Clara, it's quite a story! First I took a quick trip to Irene's – and oh my gosh, I was introduced to the newest member of the family,' I said in a high-pitched voice. 'He's this big,' I continued, gesturing with my hands, 'with gigantic eyes and the largest paws you've ever set eyes on.'

'A puppy?' Clara squealed.

'Yes, the most gorgeous chocolate brown Labrador called Buddy.'

'I want to meet him now,' Clara shrieked. 'I love puppies.'

'I've said we'll nip over after work on Tuesday, if that's OK with you?'

'More than OK! So, were you too preoccupied cuddling a ball of fur to remember the dinner?'

'I did actually go to the shop to buy potatoes, and I had every intention of starting the dinner when I got back, but the heavens opened and there was a massive thunderstorm.'

'And?'

'And secondly… I bumped into Noah.'

Clara bolted upright and stared straight at me. 'HA! Ha! You had me there for a moment.'

I didn't say anything.

'Hang on. You're not joking, are you?' she said, studying my face.

I grinned. I couldn't help myself. 'We both got soaked in the thunderstorm, so I invited him inside, and after peeling the wet T-shirt off his perfect body, I let him spend the afternoon drying out in front of the fire,' I said casually.

'Oh my gosh! Seriously?'

'I may have exaggerated a little. I didn't peel his T-shirt off – I gave him a towel and made him a brew – but I couldn't take my eyes off the way it was clinging to him! And I might have caught a sneaky peek when he pulled it off.'

Clara sat up straighter. 'Marks out of ten for his body?'

I caught my bottom lip between my teeth. 'He was *off* the scale!'

Clara squealed and clapped her hands together. 'Wow! You've had Noah Jones sat on this rug, drenched to the skin, on a Sunday afternoon?' She narrowed her eyes at me and leant forward on the settee. 'You best get talking, Cooper. I want to hear all the details.'

'I was sheltering in the shop doorway when he appeared from nowhere and offered to walk me home.'

'Just like that?'

'Pretty much. The rain was pelting down, and I didn't have a brolly but he did. But we still got soaked, so I asked him in for a drink.'

'Then what?'

'Then we chatted, and I even told him about my biological mother.'

'Really?' Clara stared open-mouthed at me.

'Yes, I know – it just came out. We were chatting about families, and in the moment, it just felt right to share my news. But then things got a little more interesting.'

Clara gave me a cheeky sideward glance. 'In what way?'

'He nearly kissed me but his phone beeped.'

Clara laughed. 'Bad timing.'

'Indeed.'

'So will you be seeing him again?'

I blushed. 'I said I'd go to the book signing at the café, but we couldn't really talk about it properly. He had to leave in a hurry.'

'Aww, why?' Clara asked, fiddling with her phone.

'He'd forgotten he had a family dinner. But he did see I'd kept his business card from eight months ago and told me to ring him.'

Clara grinned. 'This all sounds so promising! Raise your glass and let's have a toast.'

'What are we celebrating?'

'Life in general.'

'I'll drink to that.'

'Cheers!'

And we smiled as we clinked our glasses together.

CHAPTER THIRTY-FOUR

'Come on, Evie, hurry up. We're going to miss the bus at this rate,' Clara shouted from the bottom of the stairs.

I was staring into the bathroom mirror. After we'd caught up with each other's news yesterday, my mood had dipped to an all-time low. Noah had made me feel completely at ease. I'd bared my soul to him, and I really wanted to see him again, but once the book tour was over, he'd be heading back to London. I knew in the grand scheme of things that it was silly to be worrying about it. London wasn't that far on the train, and it wasn't as if he'd even asked me out on a proper date, but I really liked him, and the thought of him leaving made my heart ache.

Last night I'd lain in bed and counted the seconds as they ticked by. I'd been desperately hoping he would send me a message about how lovely it was to see me again, but nothing came. Eventually I'd placed my phone down on the bedside table and drifted off to sleep. Now I felt exhausted, and the only thing I was looking forward to was my bed tonight.

My mouth was dry and I croaked, 'I'm coming,' before sighing wistfully and heading downstairs.

'You took your time,' Clara said impatiently, holding open the front door while I grabbed my bag and my coat.

'There's still plenty of time, and anyway I've never known you this keen to get into work before,' I said, even though I knew that this time we were really cutting it fine.

On the bus, it was safe to say I wasn't in a talkative mood, and I just gazed out of the window and watched the houses whizz by.

'Right, come on – what's up with you?' Clara probed. 'You are most definitely not your usual self.'

'Nothing, honestly. I just didn't get much sleep.'

'Would that have anything to do with Noah?'

I sighed. 'It's silly really.'

'Come on, tell me.'

'I really like him – and I mean *really* like him.'

'And what's the problem with that?'

'The distance. If we did start seeing each other, would it just be limited to weekends?'

Clara raised her eyebrows at me. 'Are you seriously worried about that?'

I nodded.

'It's early days yet. You take one day at a time, and don't forget he's a writer.'

'What's that supposed to mean?'

'Surely he can write anywhere. It's not as though he works in an office and has set hours.'

'I hadn't thought of that,' I said, mulling over Clara's words. If something were to happen with us, would he really consider moving home?

'That's because you're too busy thinking of all the reasons why it wouldn't work.'

'Sometimes I wish I was more like you.'

'What do you mean?'

'You're so confident around men – you have them falling at your feet.'

'Don't be daft. Focus on each day and what will be will be.'

'One day at a time.'

'One day at a time,' Clara repeated.

* * *

Half an hour later Clara and I jumped off the bus and walked across the market square. I tilted my face up towards the sunshine. 'Heaven, I do like it when the weather begins to warm up.'

'It certainly makes everything seem a lot brighter.'

'Good morning, ladies.' Aiden appeared behind us, rustling two white paper bags.

He grinned. 'One for you and one for you.'

'Oooh, what's in there?' Clara exclaimed, taking her bag from him and peeping inside. A wide grin spread across her face.

'A warm pain au chocolate, fresh from the bakers.'

'You big softie,' I said, nudging him in the ribs. 'Thank you. You've just lifted my mood no end.'

'Why, what's up?'

'Oh nothing,' I said, noticing Wilson hurrying up the steps on the other side of the library.

'Look, you pair go on in,' I insisted, thrusting the keys into Clara's hand. 'I just need a quick word with Wilson.'

Clara raised her eyebrows at me.

'Go on,' I shooed. 'And stick the kettle on. I'll be there in two minutes.'

Aiden and Clara disappeared inside while I stood on the top step and waited for Wilson. He strode towards me, juggling a number of packages. I wanted to make sure he was OK after being so subdued the previous week. He caught my eye, and I waited for his expression to change when he saw me but it didn't. He looked glum, disheartened and exhausted. There was no smile forthcoming.

'Hey, you,' I said as he finally reached me.

'Hey back.'

'You OK?'

Wilson gazed over my shoulder.

'Clara's gone inside if that's who you're looking for?'

He shook his head. 'No, not really,' he said solemnly.

'Here, let me take those from you,' I said, reaching forward and taking the packages. 'If you want to talk about it, you know where I am.'

Wilson looked for a second as if he was about to say something, but then didn't.

'I'm a great listener, you know.'

Wilson managed a half smile as a group of students filed into the library. 'I'm sure you are.'

'Is it Clara?'

He shook his head. 'No, we've just got a lot of family stuff going on at the moment.'

'Well, you know where I am if you need anything.'

He touched my arm affectionately before turning round and striding down the steps towards his van. My heart melted for my friend – he looked so worried.

Just as I was about to walk through the library door, I heard a shout behind me – 'Evie! Evie!' – and I spun round to see Irene hurrying across the market square. She was waving something frantically in the air. I stopped and waved back at her.

'What are you doing here so early?' I asked when she reached the top of the steps. 'We've only just opened up.'

'Never mind that,' she said, ushering me inside.

'Whatever is the matter?' I asked, wondering what all the urgency was about.

'*This* is the matter.'

Irene thrust a white envelope into my hand.

'Where did you get this?' I asked, looking down at the envelope.

Irene tapped it with her finger. 'I'm no Sherlock Holmes, but it has the Salvation Army logo on the envelope. Do you think this is it?'

I couldn't take my eyes off the envelope. 'Where did you get it?'

'I've been up for hours. Buddy is absolutely adorable, but he's just like a baby. He's howled all night and I've hardly slept a wink.'

I smiled – Irene did look exhausted. 'I've not known many babies that howl.'

'You know what I mean! In the end, I kept him company in the kitchen and spent most of the night cooking. I nipped to yours first thing, but you'd already left for work so I let myself in and popped you a casserole in the fridge for later. When I was leaving, this was lying on the mat, so I drove here as fast as I could and abandoned the car on the High Street.'

My eyes met hers. 'Come on let's go in the staffroom. Shall I open it now?'

She nodded, smiling at me. 'Yes, I feel like I'm all of a whirl.'

Never mind Irene feeling all of a whirl – my heart was thundering in my chest, and I could barely breathe. Was this the moment I found out where my mother lived and the date we would finally meet? My pulse was racing as I tore open the envelope.

Aiden popped his head around the door. 'Are you doing any work today?'

'Out,' Irene replied with a stare that Aiden didn't argue with. He disappeared as quickly as he'd appeared.

'Sorry, did I sound a little abrupt then?'

'We'll explain later. They'll just have to cope for a moment.' I quickly scanned the letter. 'It's from Emily, the caseworker. She's identified a meeting place.'

'And?'

I gasped. *No, surely not*, I thought as I reread it.

'What is it?' Irene urged. 'What does it say?' She touched my hand.

'I have to admit I wasn't expecting that.' My voice was shaky and my palms sweaty.

'Go on.'

'My mother is here.'

Irene glanced towards the door in amazement. 'Here?'

'No, not here as in the library.'

'Where then? What do you mean, Evie?'

My mind was in overdrive before the words left my mouth. 'My mother lives in Becton.'

'You're kidding me?' Irene picked up the letter and began to read.

'Saturday – she wants to meet you on Saturday.'

My stomach lurched. I felt sick with nerves.

'In the small coffee shop on the edge of the park,' Irene added.

'It's all moving so quickly.'

'You don't have to do this unless you're 100 per cent sure.' Irene tilted my head up to face her.

I nodded, then rested my head on her shoulder for a brief moment and gazed out of the window. I had no words to describe my feelings, though I could feel the emotion rising inside me.

'You're crying,' Irene said, pulling a tissue from her pocket.

'I don't know why,' I replied, dabbing my eyes.

'Whatever happens, I'm here for you.' Irene kissed my head lightly.

CHAPTER THIRTY-FIVE

I spent the rest of the week in a blind panic and barely lifted a finger either in the library or at home. Both Clara and Aiden were patient with me, and I tried my best to keep busy, but my mind wasn't on the job.

I wondered if Sarah Thomas was as nervous as I was. I didn't have a clue how I was going to react when we finally came face to face. I'd rehearsed what I was going to say numerous times, but when push came to shove, who knew how any of it would play out. I couldn't believe she only lived a stone's throw away from me, and I wasn't sure whether that was a good thing or not. What if Sarah didn't turn up – or even worse, she didn't like me? What would happen then? I supposed the only thing I could do was take one day at a time.

It was Thursday, which meant we'd be going to book club later. It would be the first time we'd seen Elle since her miscarriage. I'd bumped into Josh at the shops earlier in the week and he'd said she was coping very well and throwing her energies into all things weddingish, which sounded like a good thing.

Of course, Noah had crept into my mind numerous times over the past few days – usually at night when I was lying staring at the ceiling. My Google search history was full of him, and I'd played our last meeting over and over in my mind. He seemed to like me, but then he hadn't contacted me since, and I was confused by the whole situation. He'd told me to call him, but did that mean he wouldn't get in touch unless I did?

I glanced at my watch: 6 p.m. Clara was meeting me at book club tonight. She'd gone out for tea with Aiden and Theo, and he was dropping her off at the café afterwards. I was meeting Irene at the bottom of the street in about ten minutes' time and we were going to make a quick stop at the cemetery on the way to book club. It was the anniversary of Neville's death, and even though I'd never met Irene's husband, I felt he'd always been a part of my life since Irene had taken me under her wing.

I grabbed my bag and coat, and headed up the street. I noticed two figures standing on the corner. I didn't think much about it until I got a little closer, then I realised one of those people was Irene. She spotted me and waved. I noticed the other figure – a man – quickly kiss her on her cheek before disappearing out of sight.

'You look nice,' I exclaimed.

'New coat,' she said, grabbing her lapels and giving me a twirl. 'I thought it was about time I treated myself.'

'It really suits you.' I looked the coat up and down before changing the subject. 'Who was that, then?' I asked.

'Mmm, just someone.'

'What do you mean, "just someone"?'

'We need to talk.' She linked her arm through mine and we began to walk.

'I'm all ears,' I replied as we strolled up the road towards the churchyard.

A little smile appeared on Irene's face, then a look of anguish. 'Is everything OK?' I asked.

Irene took a deep breath and exhaled sharply. 'I need advice.'

'*You* need advice? That makes a change.'

'That was Jack,' she said.

'Jack?'

'He's a friend of mine.'

I stopped walking and stared at Irene. 'A friend as in a friend?'

'That's what friend usually means.'

'Would you like to tell me about Jack?'

'I think I would.'

We walked in silence for a minute while Irene gathered her thoughts.

'Come on! The suspense is killing me.'

'Jack is one of the ramblers, and we seem to have hit it off quite well.'

'Aww, Irene, that's lovely but judging by the look on your face, you don't seem that ecstatic about it.'

'It's Neville,' she answered as we pushed open the rusty gates to the graveyard. The last time we'd visited, it had been Christmas Eve. The day had been misty and the sudden drop in temperature had given the whole place an eerie feel. Today, however, the cemetery was an array of colours – bright flowers lit up the graves, and daffodils danced along the edges of the paths. Spring was most definitely on its way.

'Can we sit on that bench over there for a minute while we talk?'

'Of course,' I answered, walking towards it.

'Jack – he's a lovely man, a widower, so we have that in common. He has a grown-up daughter, Jessica, who's one of those theatrical types.'

'Theatrical types?'

'Yes, she's currently touring the country with *Mamma Mia*.'

'I love that film – it's one of my favourites. Is that the production that's on at Becton Theatre at the minute?'

'Yes, that's the one.'

'So let's change the subject back to Jack,' I said, smiling.

'It's too difficult.'

'What is?'

'Because Neville was the love of my life, and I've started to get close to Jack but…' She tried to put on a brave face but there were tears sliding down her cheeks.

'But?'

'I have these pangs in here, like I'm betraying Neville.' Irene clutched her chest and I placed my hand on her knee.

'No one will ever replace Neville,' I said softly, 'but I'm sure he wouldn't want you to grow old alone – or be lonely for that matter.'

'I still feel like I'm being disloyal.'

'Aww, Irene, that's just not the case. It's OK to move on. It doesn't mean you've forgotten him – you still have all those wonderful memories.'

'It's just so hard.'

My heart ached for her.

'Tell me about Jack then – what's he like?' I soothed, patting her arm.

Irene's eyes swept to me and suddenly I could see a spark in them. She smiled. 'He knew today would be difficult for me, so he popped by this morning with a bunch of flowers.'

'That's lovely.'

'We met in the walking group. When his wife died, he joined the group to make new friends and to get a little exercise. He's funny, kind and thoughtful. We have loads of things in common. We both like to eat out and go to the cinema, and we've even talked about joining the bowling club. It's just so easy – there are no awkward silences when we're together.'

'Good-looking?'

Irene blushed. 'I think so.'

'I think I best look this Jack up for myself!'

Irene chuckled.

'I don't want you to grow old by yourself,' I told her. 'I think you should grab this little bit of happiness while you have the chance.'

Irene smiled at me. 'I suppose you're right.'

'How does Jack feel?'

'He says one day we will be rocking together in the old people's home,' she said, giggling as she rummaged in her bag for a packet of sweets. 'Here, have a pastille. I always find the black ones are the nicest.'

I took a sweet as I said, 'Jack sounds like he wants to be part of your life then.'

We sat for a moment, staring across the cemetery. 'Do you want to come to the grave with me?' I asked.

She shook her head. 'I just need a moment by myself, you go. I'll wait here for you.'

'OK, if you're sure. I won't be long.'

Irene's eyes welled with tears every time she mentioned Neville, but she smiled at me. 'Take as long as you want,' she said.

I stood up and pressed a kiss to her cheek as she pulled a tissue out of her pocket and dabbed her eyes.

The sun shone down and the air smelt fresh and fragrant. I hoped that one day I would find a love as true as Irene and Neville's – they had been soulmates.

I turned and wandered towards the beautiful bouquet Irene had laid on Neville's grave that morning and, for some reason, it was Noah I was thinking of as I stopped to pay my respects.

CHAPTER THIRTY-SIX

'Right ladies, calm your rabble down.' At the front of the café, Mim clapped her hands together and all eyes turned towards her. 'Two minutes until we start, so get yourselves settled.'

We were sitting in our usual seats by the window, sipping tea from beautiful vintage teacups.

I glanced out at the road and spotted Aiden's car pulling in to the bus stop opposite. He leant over and kissed Clara on the cheek before she clambered out of the passenger side and waved at Theo.

'Aww, she's all loved up,' Irene whispered, noticing her too.

I sighed wistfully. 'That makes two of you.'

'That's a huge sigh.' Irene placed her teacup down on the saucer and looked at me.

'I want to be all loved up,' I said, thinking of Noah.

'Sometimes life will twist and turn in a direction when you least expect it.'

'I wish it would hurry up and twist then,' I said solemnly.

The bell tinkled and Clara burst through the door and sat herself down next to us. She had a huge smile plastered on her face.

'Dare we ask what you're smiling at?'

'Just life! That's all!' she said, hooking her arm through mine.

I could hear the happiness in her voice. 'I'm made up for you.' I squeezed her knee. 'You deserve to smile again after everything Nick put you through. It'll just be me that's left on the shelf.' My eyes flicked towards Irene and I raised my eyebrows.

'What's that look for? What have I missed?' Clara asked, leaning forward.

'She's only gone and landed herself a fella,' I said, motioning to Irene.

Clara's eyes widened and she grinned. 'Tell me more, Irene, tell me more!'

'His name is Jack and we met rambling.'

'Apparently, he's very thoughtful, kind, generous and easy on the eye.'

'When are we going to meet this lovely man? We definitely need to give him the once-over, don't we, Evie?'

'Absolutely!'

'Well, actually I've not mentioned it yet, but Jack has invited us both out for a meal with his daughter Jessica.'

'She's currently starring in *Mamma Mia* in Becton, the theatre not far from the library. They're on tour,' I interrupted.

'Oooh, I love *Mamma Mia*,' Clara said. 'Maybe we should try to get tickets. I love a night at the theatre.'

'The last show's on Friday,' Irene informed us.

'What, tomorrow?' I asked, and she nodded.

'That's a shame, maybe next time.'

'Jack's booked a table on Sunday, Evie, if you'd like to join us?'

'Try and stop me. It would be lovely to meet them.'

Mim clapped again and we all turned towards her.

'I'm so glad you're chuffed for me,' Irene whispered and gave me an affectionate hug.

'Always,' I said.

CHAPTER THIRTY-SEVEN

The following morning, Friday, I was perched behind the desk in the library with lunchtime fast approaching.

I flicked through the pages of a book I'd been trying to read for ages, but the words just weren't sinking in. I'd reread the same passage numerous times now so I finally gave in and closed the cover. Maybe it was just the mood I was in. The only thing I could think about was that this time tomorrow, I'd be face to face with my mother, and I couldn't lie – I was absolutely petrified.

I smiled at Clara and Aiden, who were standing together, thick as thieves, in the far corner, before glancing up at the clock.

'Auntie Clara!' I looked over to see a vision of chubbiness toddling towards Aiden and Clara. Clara caught my eye, and I mouthed 'Auntie Clara?' at her. She grinned as she caught Theo mid-leap before swinging him around.

'Stop,' he said, giggling.

Barbara was hurrying after Theo, smiling.

'I'm so sorry,' she said to Aiden. 'He's not let up all morning. We were at playgroup over the road and he spotted the library.'

Clara placed Theo's feet firmly back on the floor before bending down in front of him. 'Would you like to come to the staffroom with me? We can see if we can find a biscuit in the tin, that's if your dad hasn't eaten them all.'

She chuckled, and Theo squealed.

'I've got an emergency supply of chocolate buttons in my desk if that helps,' I said.

'Even better,' Clara replied, smiling down at the little boy.

'Here you go,' I said, handing over the packet.

Clara scooped Theo up and sat him on the desk. His legs dangled over the edge as he plunged into the packet with a huge grin on his face.

'How was playgroup this morning?' Aiden asked, quickly pinching a chocolate button while Clara distracted Theo with a new dinosaur book that had come in that morning.

'That's the other reason we're here, isn't it, Theo?'

Theo's eyes went wide and sparkled.

'Tell me more,' Aiden said, laughing as he sat beside his son and pretended to dangle his legs off the desk too.

'Do you want to ask Daddy, or shall I?'

Theo pointed towards Barbara with a cheeky grin.

'I know it's short notice but the playgroup is holding a small craft fair in the church hall tomorrow to raise money for some soft play mats. Theo and I will be baking some cakes and selling them on a stall, and we were wondering whether you'd like to come along.'

'I'll be there, matey.' Aiden ruffled Theo's hair. 'What time?'

'About two?'

'Perfect – and make sure you save me plenty of cakes!'

Theo smiled. 'And Auntie Clara too!'

Clara's cheeks flushed. 'I'm so sorry he's calling me that. I don't know where he got it from,' she said, her eyes switching to Barbara. Aiden looked at her with amusement.

'Don't apologise on my account,' Barbara said, smiling warmly. 'This little man thinks the world of you and so does his father.'

Now it was Aiden's turn to blush.

'Will Louisa be there too?' Aiden asked.

'She's popping in about threeish, after she's been to the shops.'

Aiden looked at Clara and raised his eyebrows. 'Would you like to come?'

Theo glanced up, his eyes wide with hope as he waited for Clara to answer.

'Is that OK with you?' she asked Barbara, clearly not wanting to step on anyone's toes.

'It would be lovely to see you,' Barbara replied with a broad smile.

'Then I'd love to come!' Clara held out her arms and Theo launched himself straight off the desk into them. He giggled as he wrapped his arms tightly round her neck.

'You've got yourself a huge fan there,' Aiden said, grinning at them both before he turned towards me.

'I'm flattered,' Clara said, quickly dipping into Theo's buttons and popping one into her mouth.

'What about you, Evie? Would you like to come?' Aiden asked.

'I would love to,' I said, beaming, 'but I've got to be somewhere tomorrow.'

Clara handed Theo over to Aiden before touching my arm affectionately. 'We'll buy you a cake.'

'Now that sounds like a very good plan. Could I have a chocolate one with loads of multi-coloured sprinkles?'

'Yum,' Theo said, patting his tummy.

'Right, we better go, Theo. Granddad will be waiting for us.' Barbara took his hand and smiled at Aiden. 'We'll see you tomorrow. We've got a lot of cakes to bake this afternoon, don't we, Theo?'

'Yes, chef!' Theo blurted and saluted.

Everyone laughed.

Barbara smiled and gave Theo a high five. 'We've been practising that all morning at playgroup!'

'I'll walk out with you,' Aiden said, following Barbara and Theo as they started towards the entrance.

'See you tomorrow,' Clara called after them as Theo glanced over his shoulder and gave Clara a cheeky grin.

'He is so adorable, isn't he?' Clara perched on the edge of the desk and looked at me.

'He is indeed, Auntie Clara!'

Clara smiled, but then her face turned a little more serious.

'I can come with you tomorrow if you like. Aiden would understand.'

'Thank you, but Irene is going to be there.' Tears blurred my eyes. 'Look at me, I get emotional just thinking about it.'

Clara placed her arm around my shoulder.

'I'll be there when you get home.'

'Thank you. Everyone should have a friend like you, Clara Lawson.'

CHAPTER THIRTY-EIGHT

My stomach performed a double somersault as I took one last look in the mirror.

'You look gorgeous,' Irene said, and Clara nodded.

'What do you wear when you meet your mother for the first time?'

I glanced down at my clothes. In the end, I'd opted for jeans with a smart but casual blouse.

'I don't think she'll be looking at your clothes,' Irene said softly, tucking my hair behind my ears as if I was a small child. I'd never felt so sick or nervous in my whole life.

I stared in the mirror one last time.

'Right, I think I'm ready,' I said in a wobbly voice.

'Come here.' Clara stretched out her arms and hugged me tight. 'I'll be back here for 5 p.m., waiting to hear all about it.'

I nodded.

'And don't forget we've got Noah's book signing later.'

I hadn't forgotten. Today was going to be an emotional day on so many levels.

'Here,' Irene said, handing Clara her front door key. 'I hope Buddy doesn't drive you too insane.'

'I can't wait to look after the little ball of energy. I've even worn long sleeves so those sharp little fangs don't leave any war wounds.'

We all gave a small laugh, which lightened the mood a little. Clara was puppy-sitting for a few hours, and then Aiden was picking her up from there.

Clara pressed one last kiss to my cheek before she grabbed her coat and disappeared through the door.

I smoothed down my blouse and slipped on my shoes. 'Right, I'm ready.'

My head and heart were ready for whatever was going to be thrown at me in the next couple of hours. Despite my fears, this was something I needed to do.

We ambled slowly towards the high street. It was a glorious day and unseasonably warm – the sky above was blue and dotted with fluffy cotton-wool clouds. The shops had beautiful floral bunting draped in their windows, and hanging baskets filled with pink fuchsias and purple petunias framed the doorways. There were bursts of colour everywhere you looked, and the whole world felt brighter somehow.

I took a calming breath and looked towards Irene.

'You just tell me where you want me to sit and I'll wait for you,' she said warmly. 'Take as long as you need – there's no rush.'

We walked through the gates of the park, which was busier than usual. There was some sort of Scout fundraiser going on and two large gazebos housed refreshments while smaller tables laced with floral tablecloths had tombolas, a bottle stall and a hook the duck game.

We watched people bustling around as we walked, Irene no doubt lost in her own memories for a moment.

Then out of the corner of my eye, I spotted a familiar figure.

'Oh no,' I said, unlinking my arm from Irene's and pushing her swiftly behind a crowd of people who were walking in front of us.

'What are you doing?' she asked, bewildered.

'Look.' I motioned towards a picnic blanket laid out on the grass. 'What's he doing here?'

Irene glanced over. There was Wilson, sprawled out on a rug with a flask, reading a book.

'Maybe he likes to frequent parks and read in his spare time?' she said.

I raised my eyebrows at her. 'I wonder how long he'll be hanging around? I hope he doesn't spot us.'

'Isn't it the café at the other end of the park we need?' Irene asked as we veered off the main track and hurried across the grass before he spotted us.

I cast a look over my shoulder but Wilson hadn't moved – he was engrossed in his book.

'Yes, how long have we got?' I asked anxiously.

'Twenty minutes or so,' Irene said. 'How are you holding up?'

'I'm about to crumble,' I replied. My insides were twisting and I could have quite happily thrown up at any moment.

'Shall we have a short walk around the gardens?' She smiled. 'I've got something to show you.'

I nodded, not trusting myself to speak.

We wandered past the pond, where a group of excited children were pointing to the proud mother leading her six fluffy ducklings across the water to the bread they'd thrown.

'Where are we going?' I asked, following Irene towards a small courtyard at the far side of the grass. I wasn't familiar with this area of the park.

Irene glanced over her shoulder and I noticed a glint in her eye. 'I'm going to transport you back forty years.'

'Isn't this someone's house?' I asked as we walked up a winding path at the side of a cottage.

'It was.'

'Who did it belong to?'

'In my day, this place used to belong to the park ranger – Mr Preston if I remember rightly. He was employed to maintain the gardens in the park. It's been empty for a fair few years, but I believe it's about to be auctioned off.'

I stared at the old brick cottage. 'It's absolutely beautiful, full of character – and look at that clematis twisting round the porch.'

'It is indeed,' Irene replied, standing still for a moment.

The garden behind the cottage was equally stunning. Daisies peeped through the pea-green grass and the blossom on the trees added a beautiful splash of pink. Irene pointed to a nest in one of the trees and a chattering blackbird peered back at us.

'Look at this place – it's like something out of a novel,' I exclaimed in awe.

Irene gave me a warm smile. 'It's a very special place.'

She began to walk across the grass and I followed.

She steered me towards a gate at the bottom and twisted the wrought-iron knob. Behind the gate was an overgrown vegetable patch and a small potting shed, but Irene led me towards a cherry tree, and I jumped as a squirrel ran out in front of me.

At the foot of the tree, groups of crocuses had burst from the ground, and golden daffodils danced in the breeze. Everywhere I looked was teeming with life.

Irene turned towards me and smiled. 'Look,' she said softly, nodding towards the trunk. Her eyes welled with tears.

'Aww, Irene,' I breathed, tracing the shape of it with my fingertip. There carved in the tree was a heart with the words 'Neville loves Irene' etched inside it.

'I lived and breathed the bones of that man. He's in here, you know,' she said, thumping her chest. 'He was taken too soon, but I still feel him. Some days I even have a conversation with him. It's daft I know, but he was my one true love and will be until the day I die.'

I draped my arm around her shoulder and gave her a squeeze. We stood in silence, then Irene traced the heart and a lone tear ran down her cheek. She brushed it gently away.

'Memories hey – bloody good memories too.'

I wondered why she'd never shown me this place before. 'He sounds like he was a very special man.'

'He was the best kind. I truly wish you could have met him.'

'Me too.'

'We tried for children, you know. It was agonisingly painful when all our friends were falling pregnant and we didn't. We were constantly being asked when we were having children. Some marriages wouldn't have survived the heartache month in, month out, but the love we shared was one in a million. *Neville* was one in a million.'

Irene turned towards me and held my gaze. 'You were the daughter we never had. He would have been so proud of you, Evie.'

I swallowed a lump in my throat as tears welled up in my eyes.

'And whatever happens today, just remember I'm here for you. It will never change anything between us! I love you.'

'I love you too.'

My heart soared. What would I have done without Irene?

A few seconds later, she kissed her fingertips and pressed them to the heart on the tree, then we turned and walked away. The moment had finally come.

It was time to meet my mother.

CHAPTER THIRTY-NINE

We walked slowly towards a bench not a million miles away from where I was meeting Sarah Thomas.

'Shall I wait here?'

'Yes, this will be perfect. Thank you, Irene.' It wasn't too near the café but it wasn't too far away either.

Irene placed her bag down and clutched at my elbows with her hands. I could feel myself shaking.

'Try and relax. Just remember she wants this as much as you, otherwise she wouldn't be here.'

I nodded, but a wave of panic swelled inside me. How was I going to get through this? My mouth had gone so dry that I could barely speak. I hastily kissed Irene on the cheek, then exhaled.

'I'll see you soon.' My voice was barely a whisper.

A bolt of fear shot through me as I left her behind. After a few steps, I glanced back over my shoulder. She was perched on the edge of the bench, her hands tucked between her knees, and she gave me an anxious smile.

I took a deep, shuddering breath. 'Stay calm, stay calm,' I said repeatedly in my head. How could I possibly stay calm? I was oblivious to everything around me, and in a trance, I put one foot in front of the other and walked towards the café. The only thing I was aware of was my own thundering heartbeat.

I squinted up ahead and noticed a woman sitting at one of the tables outside the café. My pulse was throbbing in the side of my head as I continued to walk. I didn't know whether Sarah would be waiting inside or out.

I stumbled on the path and a twig snapped under my foot. The woman sitting at the table twisted towards me.

My breath caught in my throat. What was Jenny doing here? We locked eyes.

'Hi,' Jenny said, 'have you been to the fair?'

'No, have you?'

Jenny shook her head. 'I'm just grabbing a pot of tea.' She hugged her cup. 'Would you like one?'

'I'll nip inside and get myself a drink,' I said, not sure what to do or say.

I hovered for a second and glanced inside the café. There was a couple sat opposite each other drinking tea and a trucker dipping a piece of toast into a runny egg, but I couldn't see anyone else.

'Would you like anything else?' I asked Jenny.

'No, thanks, I'm OK.'

I went inside and grabbed a cuppa in a dreamlike state, then wandered back outside and sat down next to Jenny. She kept staring into the distance and seemed a little jumpy.

'I've just seen Wilson near the entrance to the park. He's sitting on a blanket reading,' I said, sipping my tea.

She nodded. 'Yes, I know. He's waiting for me.'

'Are you OK?' I asked. It seemed a bit strange that she was sitting here alone when he was in the park too.

'I'm waiting for someone,' she said. I heard a tiny wobble in her voice. 'What are you doing here?' she asked.

'I'm waiting for someone too,' I said slowly.

As soon as the words left my mouth, my stomach whipped itself up into a frenzy. We stared at each other for a split second. I studied her face. The way she bit down on her lip when she was anxious – she looked just like me. Surely she couldn't be…

I forced myself to breathe calmly. We sat in silence, my mind whirling. I had no idea what to say. Was she really here for the same reason as me? Every part of my body broke out in goose-bumps and I shivered. Surely not – it had to be a coincidence.

Get a grip, Evie, I told myself. *This isn't Sarah Thomas. You know this person.*

I had a quick look around but there was no one else in sight.

I hesitated, then whispered two words very softly. 'Sarah Thomas?'

As soon as the words had left my mouth, there was no taking them back. Instantly, her head swung towards me and my eyes searched hers as the words registered. I was doing my very best to hold on to my tears. I tried to blink them away, but it was no use – they began to cascade slowly down my face.

'Yes.'

'I think that someone you're waiting for might be me.' My voice faltered. 'Are you my mother?'

The question hung in the air. I didn't understand. Sitting next to me was Jenny Hughes. Her son was Wilson Hughes, my friend. It just didn't add up.

My heart ached as I waited for her to speak. She cupped her hands around my cheeks. 'Evangeline Thomas, my beautiful baby.' She let go of her tears and sobbed.

'My mother!' I gasped.

We both stood up and fell into each other's arms, clinging to each other for dear life.

'I'm so sorry! I'm so sorry for everything!'

'There's nothing to be sorry for. I've found you now.' My tears soaked into her jumper.

'And I'm never letting you go,' Jenny whispered.

CHAPTER FORTY

Five minutes later Jenny held my hands and we sat staring into each other's blurry eyes. I forced myself to stay calm and stop speculating – the question needed to be asked. I took a deep breath and broke the silence. 'Your name isn't Sarah Thomas. It's Jenny – Jenny Hughes.'

Her eyes slid briefly from mine and she let go of my hands. 'My real name is Sarah Thomas, but when I needed a fresh start, I changed it,' she whispered. Her bottom lip was quivering and my heart fluttered with nerves. I took two or three breaths before speaking again.

'Fresh start?'

'Oh, Evangeline, I don't know where to begin.'

It was strange hearing someone call me by my full name. I'd always been known as Evie.

I noticed a shadow of disappointment pass across her face and she blinked fresh tears away. 'I let you down. I let everyone down.'

'Don't say that. The past is the past – we can't change it,' I said warmly.

She took a deep breath. 'My name was Sarah Jennifer Thomas. Jennifer is my middle name; Thomas is my maiden name.' Then she hesitated.

'Do you want to tell me about it?' I asked, cautiously even though I was desperate to hear everything she had to say.

'Yes, I think I do.'

She took a deep breath.

'Matt Harrison was my childhood sweetheart, the one I wrote about in my letter. He didn't deserve the way I treated him. But our life was difficult – money was sparse and I was tired of working so many jobs, out until all hours of the evening. He was a lovely man – handsome too – but I started to resent him…'

Jenny's face was full of anguish but she carried on.

'Worse, I began to doubt him. The other women made me feel insecure.'

'He had affairs?'

'No, not to my knowledge, but people saw him as a pillar of the community. Women fell at his feet. They thought being an author brought you lots of wealth. Little did they know we lived in a dingy flat and had to miss meals here and there!'

For a brief second, my mind flicked towards Noah.

Jenny took a deep breath and continued, 'Whenever he ventured out of the flat, they'd hang off his coat-tails, buzzing round him like bees round a honey pot, and they were always giving him flirty looks when they thought I couldn't see. He began to change – he enjoyed the attention and would always give them the time of day. Sometimes if we were out, he'd spend more time chatting to them than me. "This is my audience," he would say. "These are the people that are going to buy my books." ' Jenny sighed. 'All they wanted to do was to entice him into bed, and it was only a matter of time before it happened. It began to grate on me. I was the one keeping a roof over our heads so he could live his dream. Then it all spiralled out of control when my parents died. Like I told you, they were killed in a boating accident off the south of France. When the news came through, my whole world just shattered. I felt so alone and began to slip into a deep depression.'

'Oh, Jenny,' I said, snaking my arms around her shoulders and hugging her tight.

She pulled away and stared at the ground. 'I stopped caring about life. I barely slept, and I didn't give a damn about my appearance.'

'That was the grief,' I said softly.

She nodded and dabbed at her tears.

'The drugs the doctor prescribed weren't strong enough and I fell into bad company.'

I didn't want to hear what was coming next. I didn't want Jenny to relive that pain. 'It's OK – really it is. You don't need to carry on.'

She nodded gratefully and took a moment.

'Words can't describe the pain and guilt I felt after the attack. I was in debt, and I knew if I didn't run...' She shuddered, her voice shaky, then wiped her tears away with the back of her hand. 'I panicked, so I just disappeared.'

'Do you know what happened to Matt?'

She shook her head regretfully.

'I haven't even gone looking for him. I've thought about him often over the years, but what would it achieve? We were besotted with each other once, but I'm married to Adam now and we have Wilson. Matt's most likely married with a beautiful family of his own. He deserves that. Some things are just better left in the past, but I would like to apologise to him for the hurt I caused. That was unforgiveable.'

As Jenny took a few steadying breaths, we sat and watched a young mother walk by. She was pushing a pram and making cooing noises at a newborn baby, who was gurgling away inside. We both smiled at the excited toddler running alongside the pram, pointing towards the swings in the play area of the park.

'I missed out on all that,' Jenny said sadly. '*We* missed out on all that,' she corrected. 'You smiled at me, you know. I know people would say you were too young to smile, but you did.' Jenny broke down completely, no longer able to maintain eye contact with me. 'I'm so sorry,' she wept, over and over again. She looked exhausted. 'You have to believe how difficult it all was.'

'I've wanted to hate you for years,' I blurted out.

Jenny's face crumpled in pain. 'Oh, Evangeline,' she said, touching my knee.

'It's OK, Jenny – honestly it is. Now I understand it all a little better. I know it was impossible for you at the time. Taking a baby on to the streets… I dread to think where I would have ended up – where both of us would have ended up.'

It was Jenny's turn to listen, and she grasped my hands as I began to talk.

'I just existed from day to day. My earliest memory of all time is at primary school.' I swallowed a lump in my throat. The memory was so clear it felt like yesterday. 'The class had baked biscuits for Mother's Day – small heart biscuits that we'd decorated. The school invited our mums in for the afternoon, and I had to watch as everyone's mothers started to file into the classroom. Everyone's except mine. They all looked so happy, praising their children for making such wonderful biscuits. No one came for me. The memories of that foster family are so vague,' I said, scrunching my eyes in an effort to remember, but there was nothing.

There was a strange tension in the air, and Jenny looked me straight in the eye. 'My heart ached for you every birthday, every Christmas, every Mother's Day. Don't ever think it didn't.' She squeezed my hands. 'I'm so glad you're here,' she murmured.

'I always felt like I never fitted in. I felt alone, and it wasn't until I met Irene that my life began to have some meaning.'

'I thought Irene was your real mum. I just had no idea. Why would I?' Jenny's gaze met mine. 'Mim never mentioned that she wasn't.'

'Mim wouldn't have realised. Irene and I only met her a couple of years ago, when we started going to book club. We never told anyone. I felt more secure that way. I only told Clara recently when I started to search for you. If it wasn't for Irene...'

'She's one in a million,' Jenny whispered.

'She is.' My voice faltered as I held back more tears.

'I will be eternally grateful to her. You were my little angel. For years, the only thing that kept me going was the hope that we'd be reunited one day, and not a day's gone by that I haven't thought about you. You've always been in my heart,' Jenny said.

The two of us sat in silence for a few moments, lost in our own thoughts.

'So why come looking for me now?' I asked.

Her eyes met mine. 'It was the right time. I'd gone to press that button so many times, but I was scared.'

'What were you scared of?'

'Rejection. I talked it over so many times with Adam and Wilson. If I'm honest with you, Wilson was so apprehensive when Adam and I told him the truth.'

'Why?' I asked.

'Because Wilson is adopted, and you're my biological child.'

'Wilson's adopted?'

Jenny nodded. 'Adam and I were unable to have children together.' She took a breath. 'Wilson went through a difficult period a few years ago, and we didn't want him to feel anxious or rejected, if that makes sense?'

I nodded. 'Has Adam always known about me?'

'Yes, from the outset. As soon as I knew we were serious about each other, I told him I had a daughter. He's been brilliant. He knows when I need a cuddle or when I need space. He's the one who finally gave me the strength to start the search.'

'He sounds like a good man.'

'He is.'

'That day in the library…'

'Your birthday,' she said.

'You were using the computer.'

'That's when I started the search,' she confirmed.

'I sat at the very same machine when I started my search. I always thought I'd know instantly if I ever stumbled across my mother, but there you were – so close by – and I didn't have a clue.'

'The night of the hen party…' Jenny paused.

I sneaked a glance at her. Her eyes were closed and her hands were clenched in her lap. She suppressed a sigh.

'It brought it all back, didn't it?'

She nodded. 'I know I never miscarried, but when we discovered Elle had lost her baby…' Jenny fought back the tears. 'It was the same feeling I had when I left you in the café that night.'

I touched her knee affectionately. 'Jenny,' I murmured, 'I just don't know what to say.'

'I'd love it if you would be a part of my family and get to know us better.'

'I'd love that,' I said, meaning every word.

CHAPTER FORTY-ONE

'Does anyone want to tell us what's going on here?'

Our eyes darted up to see Wilson and Irene standing before us. Wilson looked at us blankly. He was clutching tightly on to his rug and book.

For a second, Jenny and I were lost for words.

Irene touched his elbow gently. 'I think it might be better if you sit down,' she suggested. Irene's gaze met mine, and I knew she'd already guessed the situation without any of us saying anything.

'I don't want to sit down.' A flash of anxiety crossed Wilson's face and his eyes flitted between Jenny and me.

'I can leave you to talk privately,' I offered, shooting a look in Irene's direction before I turned back to Jenny.

'I think that might be for the best,' Wilson said before Jenny had a chance to speak. My skin prickled with fear at the tone of his voice. I could see the turmoil in his eyes – right now he wasn't sure what to think.

I felt for Wilson. This wasn't going to be easy for him, finding out this way. Jenny and I were only just coming to terms with the discovery ourselves.

'No, I want Evangeline to stay – and you too, Irene.' She smiled softly at Irene, who acknowledged her wish with a slight nod.

'Evangeline? But your name is Evie. I don't understand. You were coming here to meet—' Wilson stopped in his tracks. Both

Irene and I knew what he was going to say, but he didn't finish his sentence – he didn't want to out his mum's secret.

'Evie is short for Evangeline. How about we walk back to my house?' Irene suggested. 'It's not too far and I'll put the kettle on.'

I stood up, feeling a little out of sorts, and shuffled from foot to foot waiting for Wilson to answer.

'Come on,' Jenny replied, following my lead and linking arms with Wilson.

'It's you, isn't it?' Wilson exclaimed, as the penny finally dropped. I couldn't tell by the look on his face how he was feeling about it. Wilson had become my friend over the last couple of months, and in an amazing twist of events, his adopted mum was my real biological mum. I knew I had to tread very carefully. I had no idea what had happened to Wilson's real parents – the only reason I knew he was adopted was because Jenny had just told me.

'Yes, Wilson, Evie is my daughter.'

'But Irene's your mum. Irene Cooper – Evie Cooper.'

His eyes widened, and he stopped walking and stared at me. His face had turned completely white.

'My real name is Evangeline Thomas. Irene is my foster mum, and I changed my name by deed poll a few years back so we'd have the same surname.'

'Are you OK?' Jenny asked tentatively.

'I'm not sure.' He flashed his dark eyes and gave me a sideward glance. I wasn't sure whether he thought I was the enemy at this moment in time, so I held my breath and stayed silent and let Jenny handle the situation.

'Come on, let's walk and talk,' she said. 'I could do with a very strong cuppa.'

There was a knot of tension in my stomach as we all began to walk up the path. I had no idea how any of this was going to pan out. What if Wilson couldn't accept the fact that I was Jenny's biological daughter? What if he began to resent me? I began to feel panicky.

Irene must have seen the look on my face. 'It'll be all right. It's just the shock. Trust me – you'll see,' she whispered.

I nodded, not daring to speak.

As we walked, my eyes met Wilson's and he looked at me aghast. He turned away without speaking, and I bit back my disappointment.

We walked the rest of the way in silence, my stomach in turmoil.

By the time we reached Irene's house, the tension had eased a little. As soon as the front door opened, Buddy came bounding towards us. He was attacking his cuddly toy and wagging his tail.

'My gosh, he's grown,' I exclaimed, scooping him up off the floor and cuddling him.

'He's gorgeous!' Jenny exclaimed.

'Oh, he is – especially when he's asleep,' Irene said, chuckling.

We all settled in the living room and Irene soon rustled up a tray full of mugs and a teapot. 'Be a love, Evie, and grab that plate of biscuits from the kitchen for me?'

I nodded and fetched the plate, Buddy close on my heels, his nose twitching. 'These aren't for you, little man. Here, have one of these instead,' I said, throwing him a chew from the barrel on the sideboard. He snatched it out of the air and scampered off towards his playpen.

After the tea had been poured, I was at a loss about what to say. Wilson had sat next to Jenny on the settee, and Irene was perched on the arm of the chair next to me.

'What are you thinking, Wilson?' Irene asked softly.

All eyes turned towards him.

He shrugged. 'I dunno.'

I felt so helpless; I'd never have wanted to cause Wilson pain.

'Actually, I never wanted this day to come. And why does it have to be you? I wanted to dislike you, but how can I?' He suddenly sounded angry and his eyes blazed at me.

I felt my face heating up and began to fiddle nervously with the strap on my watch.

'Why would you want to dislike Evie?' Irene asked.

Wilson paused and looked towards Jenny. She touched his knee and waited for him to speak.

He narrowed his eyes and flicked them in my direction. 'Because things were just fine the way they were.'

'But they weren't, were they?' Irene said gently. 'We have two people sitting in this room that have carried heartache all their lives. They've suffered every birthday, every Christmas wondering where the other one was and who they actually were. The jigsaw needed to be completed for Jenny and Evie.'

Jenny brushed a tear from her cheek. 'I'll tell you what I think, shall I?' she said, taking control of the situation. 'I've waited for this day to come since Evie was born. For years, I've lived with the guilt of leaving her behind, of not knowing what happened to her. Every day the pain got worse and worse. Some days were better than others; some days I couldn't even bring myself to get out of bed. And some days I just existed.'

Jenny paused, and we all sat in silence for a moment as she gathered her thoughts.

'There was a part of me that was always lost,' she continued, 'however…' She turned towards Wilson and took both of his hands in hers. 'I love you. This doesn't change anything between us. I can heal now – I can build a relationship with Evie. *We* can build a relationship with Evie. Our family is complete.'

Wilson stared into his mum's eyes and held her gaze. Irene and I watched on in silence, and I swallowed a lump in my throat.

'I love you too,' he said, kissing her softly on the cheek. 'I'm sorry. I'm being an idiot, aren't I? This isn't about me. It's about you two.'

Jenny squeezed Wilson's hand. 'This makes me complete, and I'm sure Evie feels the same way. Now I feel like I can start being me again.'

Wilson nodded. 'I know, Mum, and honestly, I'm really happy for you – and you too, Evie.' He stood up and turned towards me with his arms opened wide.

Relief swept over me and I wrapped my arms around him. I looked over his shoulder at Irene and she caught my eye, mouthing, 'I love you,' and wiped away a tear.

Just then Buddy started barking and began to pull on Wilson's shoelace. We all looked down and laughed as Buddy tugged and tugged, his bottom waggling from side to side.

Wilson grinned. 'Come here, you little monkey,' he said, sweeping him up and placing him back on the rug amongst his toys.

'Does anyone want another drink?' Irene asked.

Jenny shook her head. 'No thanks, Irene.'

Irene stood up and began to place the empty mugs on the tray.

'Here, let me take those.' Wilson paused for a second and looked over towards where I was sitting.

'Come on, sis, we can wash these up,' he said, his eyes warm.

'We can,' I said, genuinely touched by his words. 'I've always wanted a brother.'

I saw a smile pass between Jenny and Irene as we left the room together, heading through the hall and into the kitchen.

I stood next to Wilson as he ran the water into the washing-up bowl and began to wash the mugs. I grabbed the tea towel and looked out of the kitchen window, racking my brains. I had no idea what to say, but Wilson broke the silence.

'I kind of get the feeling they're talking about us in there.' He glanced towards the sitting room.

I hadn't had a chance to talk to Irene properly alone yet. On our way back to the house she'd linked her arm through mine and murmured, 'Is it everything you expected?'

'I'm a little shocked but happy,' I'd replied, and we'd left the conversation there.

'Are you OK?' I asked Wilson.

He suppressed a sigh. 'I knew this day would come and, to be honest, I was dreading it.'

'Why?' I asked, taking a mug from him and drying it.

He put the cloth in the bowl and turned towards me. 'Because without Mum and Dad, goodness knows where I'd have ended up, and even at my age, I wasn't ready to share them with anyone else.'

He looked shattered and exhausted. It had been a big day for both of us.

'Pull up a chair,' he said, closing the kitchen door properly.

I sat down and clasped my hands on the table in front of me. He sat down opposite and swallowed.

'Is everything OK, Wilson?'

His voice was barely a whisper as he said, 'Jenny and Adam aren't my biological parents.'

The pain was visible on his face, so I reached across the table and took his hands in mine. I squeezed them tight.

He paused and took a breath. 'I was taken into care when I was younger. I'm going to say this quickly, Evie, to get it over and done with.'

'It's OK, Wilson. You don't have to tell me if it's too painful.'

'I want to – I need to – but only Jenny and Adam know the truth.'

'It won't go any further, I promise.'

'My early childhood wasn't one I would wish on my worst enemy. My biological mum and dad married young, age seventeen. As much as they thought they were love's young dream, they weren't ready to play happy families – and believe me, we were far from happy.

'My father was the kind of person you'd dread meeting down a dark alley. He was short-tempered, drank too much and dabbled with drugs. My mum was timid from what I can remember. I think she might have been scared of him – I remember her flinching sometimes when he came near her.'

Wilson took a minute to compose himself.

'Take your time,' I said softly.

'I can remember the night I was taken into care. We were travelling back from somewhere, and I was sitting in the back of the car. We'd stopped off at the chippy – I can remember eating a cone of chips – then they began to argue. I can't remember what the argument was about, but my father was goading her, calling her a whore. I think something inside her just snapped, because she threw a hot pie in his face, followed by a bag of chips. The car screeched to a halt – I can remember the tightness of my seat belt as it cut into my neck – he was yelling at her and grabbing her hair. He dragged her out of the car, and I screamed and screamed, but they didn't come back. The next thing I knew, there were blue flashing lights everywhere and my seat belt was being unclipped by a lady who took me away.'

'What happened to your parents, Wilson?'

'My father is serving time in prison and my mother…' He took a deep breath. 'She took her own life just before his trial.'

I was devastated by this revelation. I stood up and wrapped my arms around Wilson's shoulders as he stayed sitting at the table. He cupped his hands around mine briefly before pulling away. I had no idea what to say. The only words I could muster were, 'Oh, Wilson, I'm so sorry.'

I kissed the top of his head lightly and walked over to the kitchen cupboard, rising up on my tiptoes to fish inside. I knew Irene kept a small bottle of whisky in the back of the cupboard – for medicinal purposes, she claimed. I poured Wilson a glass and slid it over the table towards him. 'Drink that.'

He didn't argue and slugged it back in one go. 'Urghh,' he said, shaking his head and placing the glass back on the table.

'Evie, please don't tell anyone,' he begged.

'Of course I won't – I promise. This is your business, Wilson, and not mine to tell.'

'Thank you.'

'You cope so well – honestly I wouldn't have had a clue.'

'That's all down to Mum – she's been wonderful. She's been there for me every step of the way.'

As soon as the words left his mouth, he apologised. 'Oh God, I didn't mean for that to sound like it did.'

'Don't worry – I know what you meant, and I'm glad she has.'

'I'd often hear her crying late at night, when she didn't realise I was listening. That's why I finally confronted her. I was scared I was about to relive my past.'

'How? I don't understand.'

'I used to hear my mum – my real mum – crying late at night, and the memories were so vivid, I started waking up at night in hot sweats. My imagination began to run wild and I started to think my dad, Adam, might be—' He stopped.

'Oh, Wilson.'

'It's daft really. Dad is my rock too. I don't know how I could think such a thing. Anyway, that's when they told me what was going on. I already knew you existed, but that was the night they told me they'd started the search for you.'

'You know I'll always be here for you, Wilson – anytime. I mean that from the bottom of my heart.'

He smiled. 'I know.'

'This is just the beginning – a new beginning for us all,' I said, as he stood up and walked towards the sink. He splashed cold water on his face, patted it with the towel and blew out a long breath.

'What a day,' he said. 'And wait until you meet Dad. He's fantastic.'

'Why didn't he come to the park today?'

'He wanted to, but Mum insisted this was something she needed to do by herself. She thought if she turned up with a mob it could frighten you away. But I followed her, and she only spotted me when she reached the park.'

'I can't wait to meet Adam too,' I said.

He grinned. 'Come on – let's get back in there. They'll be wondering where we've disappeared to.'

We gave each other a quick hug and opened the kitchen door.

Buddy bounded up the hallway to us. 'Where does he get his energy from? I could do with some of that!' I grinned. The puppy rolled on to his back and Wilson rubbed his tummy.

Just after we'd both sat back down in the living room, we heard the bell ring, and Clara popped her head round the door. 'It's only me. Hope you don't mind – the front door was open.' She scanned the room to see four pairs of eyes staring back at her. Aiden stood behind her, peering over her shoulder.

'No not at all, come on in,' Irene said.

'I've brought cake like we promised!' She smiled, waving a paper bag in the air.

'No Theo?' I asked.

'Louisa turned up just as we were leaving, so she's taken him home. We nipped back to ours, but as you weren't back yet, we thought we'd come and check on this little man,' she said, handing the cake to me and scooping Buddy up in her arms. He gave her a playful woof and licked her face.

'Aiden, don't stand out there – come and sit down,' Irene insisted, gesturing to the empty chair in the corner.

'Thank you. How come you've all ended up back here?' Aiden asked Wilson. 'Have you been having a party without us?'

The whole room fell quiet.

'Have we missed something?' Clara asked, noticing the change in atmosphere. She perched on the edge of Aiden's chair and popped Buddy back on the floor.

'Oh here – take this, Irene, before I forget.' Clara dug into her pocket and pulled out Irene's front-door key.

'Aww thanks. Was he good for you this morning?'

'He certainly has a zest for life, that's all I'll say.' She grinned down at Buddy, who was currently trying to gnaw the leg off the coffee table.

'Anyway, no one's answered Aiden's question – how come you're all back here? I thought you were—' Clara broke off and glanced over towards me.

I blinked. I wasn't sure what to say. I looked at Jenny, then Wilson, and back again. It was only a matter of time before Clara found out the truth.

I swallowed and Jenny nodded. I took that to mean that it was up to me to share the news if I wanted to. I turned back to Clara and blew my fringe out of my eyes. 'Well, here's the thing.'

Clara arched an eyebrow.

'Today I met my mother.'

'I know that, silly! How did it go? What is she like?'

'So many questions,' Aiden said, shooting her a warning glance.

'And how have you all ended up here?'

'OK.' I took a breath. 'Sarah Thomas was absolutely lovely and it went very well.'

'Phew, that's a relief. I've been worried about you all morning. Will you be seeing her again?'

'I think that's a dead cert.'

'Things did go well then. Will we get to meet her anytime soon?'

'You already have,' I said and smiled, waiting for the penny to drop.

'Huh?' Aiden said.

'Who? When? Where…?'

Jenny coughed slightly and Clara's voice petered out as the realisation hit her. She stared at Jenny with wide eyes.

'You?' she asked, amazed.

Jenny gave her a warm smile. 'Yes – me, Clara.'

'B-B-But I don't understand,' she stammered. 'Your name's Jenny.' She turned to me. 'I thought your mum was called Sarah?'

'My name was Sarah Jennifer Thomas. I started using my middle name many years ago, and Hughes is my married name.'

Clara was shaking her head in amazement. 'Wow! Just simply that – wow!' she exclaimed, standing up. 'I'm so pleased for you both!' She hugged me, then Jenny.

'Which makes you and Wilson brother and sister,' Aiden added, leaning across to shake his hand.

I locked eyes with Wilson. He could tell them he was adopted if and when he was ready, but until then I would respect his privacy.

'It does indeed.' I gave Wilson a quick wink. He stood up and opened his arms wide, and I fell into them.

'Thank you,' he whispered in my ear.

'It seems to have been quite a day for everyone,' Clara said, smiling as she checked her watch. 'And it's not over yet.' She tapped the watch with her finger and gave me a pointed look.

I swallowed.

'We need to grab a quick tea and head over to Mim's,' she said to me, then looked around the room. 'Is anyone else coming to the café to meet Noah tonight?'

The very sound of his name made my stomach do a double somersault.

'Are you coming, Irene?' I asked.

She shook her head. 'No, I've been out all day and feel rather tired. I'm going to curl up with Buddy instead, but please say hello from me.'

'Will do,' I said, feeling my cheeks flush with anticipation.

CHAPTER FORTY-TWO

An hour later, Clara and I were sitting on the sofa, stuffing our faces with takeaway pizza in front of some mind-numbing TV.

'How long have we got before we need to leave for Mim's?' Clara asked before sipping her wine.

'I think it starts at 6 p.m. and finishes at 8 p.m. Shall we aim to get there around 7 p.m.?'

'Perfect! We can get ready after we've finished this,' she said, sinking her teeth into a thick slice of double pepperoni. 'How are you feeling about tonight?'

'Nervous!'

'No wonder. It's already been quite a day – and it's not over yet!'

'I know.'

'I'm sure your phone just beeped, by the way,' she said, closing her empty pizza box.

'Did it? It's over there in my bag. I'll get it in a minute. I just want to sit here for a bit – I feel stuffed after that.' I sank back on to the sofa and patted my stomach.

'So how are you feeling about today?'

'I can't even begin to tell you how I felt when I spotted Jenny sitting outside the café.'

'I can imagine,' Clara replied, tucking her feet underneath her.

'At first I just thought it was a coincidence, until she said she was waiting for someone.'

'How did the penny drop for you both?'

'I said her real name and the shock on her face said it all.'

'Oh, Evie, I bet you were shocked too.'

'I was. It's all so surreal.'

'I know. It's a very emotional situation.'

'She's invited me round for tea next week to meet Adam, which I'm really looking forward to.'

'That'll be nice. And Wilson? Is he OK?'

'He is now. He was shocked at first. He'd been so apprehensive about Jenny searching for me, but I know Wilson and I are going to be just fine.'

'That's good then.'

'We've finished this already!' I exclaimed, pouring the dregs from the wine bottle into my glass. 'We'd better not open another one or I'll end up falling asleep, and we won't get to Mim's.'

'We don't want that! We need to be there tonight!'

I hauled myself up from the sofa and took the empty pizza boxes into the kitchen.

'And how's it going between you and Aiden?' I called from the kitchen.

'It's going great,' she admitted. 'Except Louisa seems a little…'

'A little what?' I asked, reappearing in the doorway.

'I think she's a little what you'd call high-maintenance. I've only met her today, but she was there with another man and acted really stand-offish towards me.'

'Ah! The new boyfriend?'

'Yes, Aiden was a little taken aback. He said even up to last week she'd been hinting that they should get back together. Then Barbara let slip that Louisa and the new man had been together for weeks.'

'I bet it's a jealousy thing. It sounds like a case of "I don't want you, but I don't want anyone else to have you either".'

'That's exactly what Aiden said.'

'He's not daft!'

'Well he isn't, is he? He's going out with me!'

I grinned at her.

'But it really is going well with Aiden.'

I saw a flush come to her cheeks. 'You're falling in love!' I exclaimed.

'I think you might be right,' she swooned, and we both shrieked.

I was glad Clara had moved in with me. At first, I'd been a little worried I'd feel like my space was being invaded, but I loved it. I loved the company, our chats and our girls' nights in. Finally, I felt like my life was all coming together, and I couldn't ask for a better best friend.

'That was your phone again.' Clara nodded towards my handbag.

'Oh! I forgot to look at the last message,' I said, reaching towards my bag.

I stared at the screen. 'It's Noah!'

'What did he say?'

'"Hope to see you tonight."' My heart fluttered.

Clara clapped her hands together. 'Come on! Let's go and make you look drop dead gorgeous – not that I'm saying you aren't already drop dead gorgeous,' she added quickly.

'And the second text is from Irene: "I hope tonight goes as well as today."'

'Aww, that's nice of her.'

'Right, what are you going to wear?'

'Jeans and a nice top, and maybe those boots with the little heel?'

'Yep, come on then, let's get ready and go and bag your man.'

I laughed. 'Now that would finish off my day just perfectly.'

CHAPTER FORTY-THREE

Clara knocked on my bedroom door. 'Are you ready?'

I was feeling nervous but excited.

'Ready as I'll ever be,' I answered, opening the door. 'Well, how do I look?'

'Absolutely gorgeous! It's just started to rain so I've ordered a taxi. It'll be here in a minute.'

'Great – I'll grab my coat and my bag.'

Just then we heard the taxi beep outside and my heart gave a little bounce.

'Where to?' the driver asked as we climbed into the back of the cab.

'Mim's café – do you know it?'

The driver nodded, put the car into gear and began to drive up the street.

I turned towards Clara. 'Why do I feel so nervous?'

'You know why, silly – because you like him.'

I grinned sheepishly at her as my excitement threatened to bubble over.

Suddenly the car screeched to a halt and the seat belt tightened around me.

'Jeez!' Clara exclaimed, as I gasped.

We both peered through the wet windscreen and saw numerous flashing lights ahead. The cars on both sides of the road were at a standstill.

The taxi driver turned towards us. 'Looks like an accident up ahead. The road's been closed.' He picked up his radio and spoke into the receiver. The voice on the other end confirmed that one of the other drivers had just reported the accident and the tailback.

I glanced down at my watch, then looked at Clara. 'What are we going to do now?'

Just then, a policewoman knocked on the window, and the taxi driver wound it down.

'Excuse me, sir, but you might want to turn off your engine. There's been an accident up ahead and I think you might be sitting here for a bit.'

The taxi driver nodded and immediately switched off the engine.

'And if you could all stay inside the vehicle, please, that would be helpful,' she added before moving on to the next car.

Clara attempted a feeble smile. 'Don't worry,' she said. 'I'm sure we won't be here too long.'

I pressed my face up against the glass and saw a fire engine and an ambulance a little further up. Then I shuddered. 'It looks like there's a motorbike on the ground,' I said.

'Oh God,' Clara said. 'And someone will probably be waiting for them to come home…'

A huge wave of sadness washed over me.

There was suddenly a lot of commotion up ahead and I wound down the window to see what was happening. The firefighters had gathered round an upside-down car and there was some muffled shouting before a shower of sparks suddenly burst through the air.

'They're cutting into a car,' I said. 'Someone must be trapped.'

We sat in silence for nearly an hour, watching the emergency services care for the wounded and the wreckage of the car being towed from the road.

'What time is it now?' I asked anxiously.

'Just before 8 p.m.'

'Damn. The book signing was finishing at 8 p.m.'

'Why don't you text Mim and let her know what's happened?' Clara said. 'See if she can keep Noah there a little while longer?'

I rummaged inside my bag, then smacked my hand to my forehead. 'I've left it sitting on the sofa!'

'And mine's flat,' Clara muttered crossly.

'The police are letting people through now,' the taxi driver piped up.

We looked out and saw the group of onlookers that had gathered being allowed through the police barrier.

'Yes, we're definitely on the move,' I said.

'I think it'll be quicker to walk now we're allowed out of the car. What do you think? It's only round the next corner.'

'I agree – the cars aren't even moving yet.'

Clara glanced towards the meter before delving into her purse. She thrust the correct change into the driver's hand and we jumped out of the taxi.

Though the car had been towed away, the crushed motorbike was still lying at the side of the kerb.

'It's awful,' I muttered, averting my eyes as we passed and checking my watch.

'Come on – quickly!' I said to Clara. 'It's just gone eight. We might still make it.'

We weaved in and out of the crowds and soon reached the end of the road. We could see Mim's café in the distance.

I sucked in my breath. 'The lights are still on,' I murmured, suddenly feeling excited but apprehensive too. Just then the coffee shop plunged into darkness, and Mim and Elle appeared on the street. I noticed Mim holding the door open and Noah stepped out on to the pavement beside her.

'That's lucky – he's still here. Just!' Clara exclaimed, picking up speed.

But I stopped dead on the pavement.

'Look,' I said, nodding towards the shop. Mim and Elle had taken flight up the road, but there, standing on the pavement beside Noah, was a girl. I watched as he put his arm around her shoulder and the girl leant towards him. She kissed him on the cheek then wrapped her arm around his waist.

Clara swivelled towards me, her eyes wide. 'What do you want to do?'

I heard them laughing, and my heart dropped like a stone.

They dashed towards a taxi that had pulled in at the side of the road and jumped into the back seat together. There was a split second where I wanted to shout out to him, but I was paralysed – and what would have been the point?

The taxi driver revved his engine and they disappeared out of sight. Noah was gone.

I felt a lump form in my throat as Clara whispered, 'Oh, Evie, I'm sorry.'

CHAPTER FORTY-FOUR

The next morning, it all came flooding back to me the minute I woke up. Even if I squeezed my eyes shut, the image of Noah jumping into the back of the taxi was clearly visible in my mind – urghh.

After we'd caught a taxi home, Clara and I had stayed up to the early hours, drinking every drop of alcohol we could lay our hands on and deciding that no man was ever going to make me feel that way again. Now I was regretting the late night and the copious amount of alcohol. Every time I moved my head, my brain slammed into the back of my skull. How the hell had I let Noah get under my skin so much? I barely knew him.

I picked up my phone from the bedside cabinet and brought up his Twitter feed. There were numerous posts thanking readers for turning up to his book signing and then there it was – a picture of him and her in the back of the taxi with the words:

About to paint the town red.

My heart constricted at how gorgeous he was, then I remembered he was just like every other man you read about in the agony-aunt pages of women's magazines – a two-timing rat – or nearly a two-timing rat in his case. I enlarged the picture so I could see the huge smiles spread across both of their faces.

I quickly unfollowed him. I wasn't a masochist.

I snuggled down under my duvet and tried to block him from my mind.

Clara tapped on my bedroom door. 'Hey, are you up?'

'Yes,' I groaned.

'Here, I thought you might be needing these.' She walked into the room and put a couple of headache tablets into my hand and a cuppa on my bedside table.

'Thank you. How are you feeling this morning?' I asked, popping the pills in my mouth.

'Let's just say I've not woken up full of the joys of spring. In fact, I've barely had any sleep at all,' Clara said, heading back towards the door. 'I've put us some bacon under the grill. We need a little sustenance to soak up the alcohol.'

'Mmm, bacon butties are just what I need,' I said as she disappeared down the stairs.

I sipped my tea and glanced at the clock. I was supposed to be meeting Irene, Jack and Jessica in a bistro on the edge of town later, and I hoped that once I'd had some food and a shower, I'd be feeling a little more human.

'Bacon butties are ready,' Clara shouted from the bottom of the stairs. Quickly I wrapped my dressing gown around my body. 'Mmm, that smells good,' I called back, following the smell down the stairs.

Clara was jigging away to a song on the radio when I stepped into the kitchen. 'Where have you got all your energy from?' I murmured as she slid a plate of bacon butties across the table towards me.

'I have no idea,' she said, smiling. 'Brown or red?' she asked, hovering by the fridge door.

'Always brown please.'

Clara brought the sauce over and sat down opposite me, and we began to tuck into our breakfast.

'So this afternoon you're meeting Irene's new fella?' she said, catching the oozing sauce on the plate as she bit into her roll.

'Yes, Irene can't wait to introduce us.'

'Where are you going to?'

'The Nifty Vault, that lovely bistro on the edge of town.'

'Hugely expensive,' said Clara, raising an eyebrow.

'And posh,' I answered, wrinkling up my nose. 'I have no idea what to wear.'

'We can sort out your wardrobe after we've finished these.'

'Irene said that Jack wants to treat us all. I'm just hoping I feel better after I've had a shower. At the moment, my head feels like it's not attached to the rest of my body and I'm not in the best of moods.'

'I can tell. You'll feel better after you've had something to eat. Did you contact Noah at all?'

I paused, then shook my head. 'No, what's the point? I deleted him from Twitter.'

'You mean business then?'

I nodded. 'Let's not mention him again.'

Clara nodded back.

'And anyway, I've more important things on my mind.'

'Which are?' Clara asked, taking the last bite of her roll.

'Meeting Irene's new man and today's dress code. What shall I go for? Jeans, dress or a skirt?'

Clara glanced up towards the kitchen window. 'Blue sky and barely a cloud. How about that lovely floral dress with your navy cardigan and ballet shoes? That would be perfect.'

'Mmm, yes, I think you might be right,' I said, mulling the outfit over in my mind.

'I'll wash these up – you go and jump in the shower.'

'Thanks,' I said, handing Clara my empty plate and climbing back up the stairs towards the bathroom.

A few hours later, I was walking down the street towards the bistro. Irene had called to say she was already inside with Jack, and Jessica was arriving any minute. I pushed the door open and almost immediately there was a waiter by my side. It was a quaint little place with an olde-worlde feel about it. The lighting was dimmed, and flickering on each crisp white tablecloth was a tea light. I spotted Irene in the corner and she gave me a cheery wave as I followed the waiter towards her table. He pulled the seat out and I sat down.

Jack stood up and shook my hand.

'Let me introduce you. This is Evie and this is Jack,' Irene said, gesturing to each of us as she spoke.

'Pleased to meet you, Jack.'

'Jessica won't be long – she's just texted,' Irene said, picking up the bottle of wine. 'Would you like a glass?'

I placed my hand over my glass. My stomach turned even at the word wine. 'Just water for me please. It was something of a heavy night.'

'You can tell me all about that in a minute, but I hope you don't mind, I was telling Jack about you meeting Jenny yesterday.'

'No, I don't mind at all. I'm going over for tea this week to meet Adam too.'

'That'll be lovely.'

'It will, I'm really looking forward to it and I can't wait to meet Jessica.' I said, studying Jack's face, which was kind and gentle.

He smiled. 'Here she is now.' He nodded towards the door, then stood up to welcome her with a huge smile on his face.

I swung my head round towards the entrance of the bistro. My jaw dropped, and I gasped.

The girl walking towards us was the same girl who had jumped into the back of the taxi with Noah last night.

Jessica was stunningly beautifully. She floated over to our table in the most elegant teal mini-dress, which gathered softly around her neck. She wore a tiny black cardigan and ballet shoes and her long brown curls bounced past her shoulders as she walked.

Visions of her and Noah seeped into my mind again, and I suddenly wished I could be anywhere else on the planet except in this bistro.

Jessica fell into her dad's arms and they hugged tight.

Irene smiled across at them and then looked over at me. 'Are you OK? You've gone white.'

'Of course,' I mouthed back. A complete lie.

Irene had already met Jessica, so after they'd airbrushed each other's cheeks with kisses, it was my turn to be introduced. She shook my hand and looked at me with a confused expression on her face.

'Have we met before?' she asked, taking the chair next to me.

'I don't think so,' I managed to say, thankfully without my voice faltering.

'It'll come to me,' she said. 'I never forget a face.'

I wanted to forget a face. I wanted Noah Jones's face to be eradicated from my mind, but no – he was in there again. I didn't seem to be able to get rid of him.

'Here, I've got you a *Mamma Mia* programme,' Jessica said, smiling across the table at Irene. She delved into her bag and popped it on the table.

Irene beamed. 'I hope you've signed it for me.'

'Aww, I can do,' she said, whipping out a pen and scrawling her name across the photograph of herself.

I actually felt a little light-headed.

'Can you excuse me for a moment?' I stood up and forced a smile at everyone.

'Are you sure you're OK? You look so pale,' Irene said with a concerned look on her face.

'I'm fine, I just need to use the ladies' room,' I replied, scanning the room for the toilets.

Once inside, I leant against the basin and stared at my reflection in the mirror. I couldn't believe Jessica was the girl who had had her arms wrapped around Noah last night, but I needed to pull myself together – for Irene's sake at least.

I heard the door open behind me and looked up to see Irene hurrying through.

'Are you sick?' She stood beside me, waiting for me to answer. 'I'm worried about you.'

'I'm not feeling very well. I think I might have had too much to drink last night with Clara.'

'Oh, you girls!' Irene exclaimed. 'But I can't blame you. It was such an anxious time yesterday, discovering Jenny was your mum. No one could blame you for having a few too many last night.'

I nodded, thankful she hadn't somehow found out about Noah. That would have been just awful.

The toilet door swung open once more, and we turned to see Jessica standing in the doorway.

'The waiter's asking if we're ready to order, and Dad asked me to come and check if everything's OK.'

Irene gave me a warm smile. 'Yes, we're ready. We're just coming,' she said, patting my elbow and heading towards the door.

I gave Jessica a weak smile and quickly began to touch up my make-up. Jessica didn't follow Irene back to the table but leant against the washbasin waiting for me.

'I've been racking my brain since I got here. I was sure I knew you from somewhere, and it was only when Irene mentioned you worked in the library that I realised who you were.'

Now I felt even worse, 'Yes, I think I know your boyfriend.'

'Evie. Yes – Evie. He's mentioned you a few times in the last couple of weeks. It's such a small world – such a coincidence you're Irene's daughter.'

My stomach twisted with embarrassment.

'It is,' I agreed, feeling foolish that Noah and Jessica must have had conversations about me – and, not only that, he'd had the cheek to sit in my living room and pretend he was single.

'Irene mentioned you travel all over the country performing in theatre productions,' I said, quickly diverting the conversation.

'Yes, I love it! It can be a little difficult though when your loved one is on the other side of the country. It does get lonely.'

'I bet,' I replied, brushing down my dress and managing to avoid eye contact. 'But you must be proud of his success too.'

'Believe me, his choice of career has nearly split us up on numerous occasions.'

I was quite taken aback by Jessica's response and was just about to ask why when Irene popped her head back round the door. 'Hurry up, you two. Jessica, your dad is getting a little impatient.'

'That's because he's hungry.' She smiled. 'He's always been the same. Nothing changes!'

After we'd ordered our food, I sat quietly at the table listening to Jack and Irene talk about their latest ramble. It was lovely to see the interaction between the pair of them. Irene's eyes were bright as they spoke and it was clear Jack was a welcome addition to her life. The only problem for me was that it meant Noah was always going to be hanging around, and I was going to find that difficult.

As I ate, I listened to Jessica talk excitedly about being cast in an upcoming production of *Les Misérables*. Jack's face beamed with pride as she spoke.

'She was always one for dancing around as a child.' He smiled. 'She would sing at every opportunity. All my Saturdays were spent going from ballet to tap, drama to singing.' He looked at Jessica fondly.

'And it was all worthwhile,' Irene said.

'So when do rehearsals start for your next production?' I asked Jessica.

'I have a couple of weeks off before the rehearsals start, then it'll be full on, all the way up 'til Christmas.'

'Christmas?' Irene exclaimed. 'That seems like a million years away.'

'It'll be here before we know it,' she replied.

'How does your other half cope with all your time away?' Irene asked, eating her last mouthful of food and placing her knife and fork down on her plate.

'He's learnt to cope with it. He knows I love my job, and I love him. We just get on with it as best we can. We had a lovely night out last night after Noah's book signing. We met up with the cast of *Mamma Mia* for a few farewell drinks. I thought I'd be a little tired today but I'm bearing up!'

'Evie, Jessica's boyfriend…' I met Irene's gaze and I knew I couldn't hold it in any longer. 'Noah Jones,' I blurted.

My stomach lurched and I felt physically sick. Jessica was so beautiful, warm and funny. Why had I ever thought he would look in my direction?

Jessica burst out laughing. 'Dad wishes.'

'At least Noah has a respectable job.'

'Pah!' Jessica stuck her tongue out at him playfully. 'Dad thinks I'm about to marry the black sheep of the family.'

'I wouldn't go that far. I just wish he didn't feel the need to take his clothes off for a living.'

I looked between the pair of them, utterly confused.

Irene smiled at me. 'Jessica's going out with Dan. The guy from Elle's hen do – Noah's brother.'

I reached across the table, grabbed Irene's glass of wine and took a huge gulp. 'You're going out with Dan?' I asked, picking up my jaw from the floor.

'Yes, for my sins!' She smiled. 'He's my lovable rogue.'

'Definitely a rogue.' Jack grinned at his daughter.

'As you can see, Dad would have preferred me to date the sensible brother.'

'His job prospects are definitely more appealing.'

'Don't listen to him, Evie. Dan and my dad get on just fine – in fact, when they get together, they act like a couple of kids.'

'Indeed we do,' Jack confirmed. 'I just like to tease my daughter from time to time.'

'So does Noah have a girlfriend?' I asked casually.

'Noah? No. He's young, free and single,' Jessica answered as the waiter appeared at the side of the table with the bill.

I brightened up instantly, relief surging through my body.

'My treat,' Jack said, taking the silver plate from the waiter.

'That's lovely of you, Jack. Thank you.'

'Jack and I need to get back to Buddy. I can't leave that little rascal alone for too long. He's already chewed his way through my slippers and a new pair of trainers – not to mention the leg of the kitchen table.' Irene rolled her eyes as the waiter came back to the table with the payment machine.

We all laughed.

Jessica glanced down at her watch. 'I've got another forty minutes or so until Dan picks me up. Are you in a rush, Evie, or have you got time to stay for another drink?'

'I've nothing planned.'

'Fantastic, let's move over to that little table by the bar then. Those chairs look a lot more comfy.'

We stood up and hugged Jack and Irene as they left the bistro, then ordered a couple of glasses of wine. I felt like I could manage one now.

'I shouldn't really drink in the afternoon,' Jessica said with a twinkle in her eye. 'It usually sends me to sleep.'

'Me too,' I agreed.

We settled into the seats by the bar, and I swallowed. 'I've got a confession to make.'

Jessica chuckled. 'Sounds ominous.'

'When you arrived, I was a little subdued because I recognised you from last night.'

'Last night?' Jessica asked, puzzled.

'Yes, my friend Clara and I were on our way to the book signing last night when we got stuck in a taxi. There'd been an accident and the road was closed. When the police finally let us through, we hurried up the street towards the café and that's when I saw you both.'

'Who?'

'You and Noah. It's silly now, but you had your arms around each and you were rushing towards a taxi...'

Jessica threw her head back and laughed. 'Oh, Evie! Noah was gutted you hadn't turned up! He kept checking his phone, but there was nothing.'

'I'd left it at home,' I said, feeling like a fool.

'I gave him a quick hug outside the café to cheer him up, and he put his arm around me to shield me from the rain.

'Noah's done nothing but talk about you for the last couple of weeks. It's funny really, we never usually get that much time all together with me touring, but with the show being in Becton for the last few weeks and Noah's book tour bringing him this way, we've had some fantastic nights out. I know Dan's missed him a lot since he moved to London.'

'Noah talks about me?'

Jessica nodded. 'Yes, we had a family get-together last weekend. When I say family get-together, I mean I appeared for an hour or so in-between the Sunday matinee and the evening performance. A couple of my old college friends were coming to watch me in the evening performance, but they had to cancel at the last minute. There was that terrible storm, remember? One of the trees near them got struck by lightning and it ended up blocking the road. Anyway, Noah saw I was disappointed and he'd never seen me on stage, so he asked if he could come and watch. It took us thirty minutes to drive to the theatre, and the only thing he talked about on the way there was you!'

'Really?' The corners of my mouth lifted in a smile.

'Yes, really! He definitely has a soft spot for you.'

A glow of happiness began to rise up inside me.

'In the end, we jumped into a taxi. He was hoping you'd come out with us last night. We were meeting Dan – he'd been working on the other side of town. Well, if you can call it working. I think he enjoys his job a little too much.' She grinned.

'I wish I'd called out to him now.'

'Honestly, he was miserable all night, and he was even worse this morning.'

'Why? What happened this morning?'

'He noticed you'd deleted him from Twitter.'

'Damn! I'd forgotten I did that! I was just so upset.'

'You two need your heads banging together.'

Just then Jessica's phone beeped. 'That'll be Dan, he was going to text me after—' Jessica stopped mid-flow and looked up at me with wide eyes.

'After what?' I asked, staring at her.

'After he dropped Noah at the train station.'

'Why is he dropping Noah at the station?' I asked, though I wasn't sure I wanted to hear the answer.

'He's going home – back to London. He said there was no point hanging around after you didn't show up.'

My heart plummeted.

Suddenly Jessica picked up the phone. 'Dan, it's only me. How long until Noah's train leaves?' I watched Jessica balance the phone between her ear and shoulder, then glance at her watch.

She hung up the call and stopped the waiter. 'Could you order me a taxi please?' she asked with urgency.

'There's one outside if you'd like me to hold that for you?'

'Yes please!' Jessica turned towards me. 'His train leaves in twenty minutes, and he's on platform two. You need to hurry.'

For a split second, I felt like time had stood still.

'Go!' she said, thrusting my coat and bag at me. 'I'll pay the bill.'

A mixture of panic and fear surged through me as I stood up. 'Really?'

'Yes! Now go,' she ordered, pushing me towards the door. 'Go and get your man.'

I stuffed my flailing arms into my jacket and pecked Jessica quickly on the cheek before I hurried towards the taxi.

'Let me know how you get on,' Jessica called after me.

'Will do,' I shouted back, but as soon as I was in the taxi, I realised I didn't have her number.

Fifteen minutes later the taxi pulled into the train station car park. I paid the driver and glanced at the huge clock hanging from the red-brick wall. I had five minutes until the train left. I followed the signs to platform two, running as fast as my legs could carry me, weaving in and out of the other people until I hit something solid and suddenly found myself stumbling to the ground, the contents of my bag spilling everywhere.

'I'm so sorry,' someone said as a hand thrust towards me.

An apologetic man pulled me to my feet. I bent down and began to scoop up the contents of my handbag.

'Sorry again!' he called as I hurried off without giving him a second glance.

I spotted Noah just as I reached the platform, and my heart soared with relief.

Then suddenly time seemed to stand still, and I was rooted to the spot, watching in horror as Noah climbed on to the train.

'Noah!' I yelled at the top of my voice, suddenly finding my feet and sprinting up the platform.

The doors of the train shut and the whistle blew.

The train began to move.

Quickly I fumbled inside my bag and called Clara. She picked up after a couple of rings. 'Clara, are you at home?'

'Yes, why? Are you OK? You sound a little—'

'Never mind that,' I interrupted. 'I need you to go into the kitchen and text me Noah's number. His card is on the pin-board.'

'Is everything OK?'

'Yes, but hurry.' I hung up and willed the phone to beep.

As soon as the number came through, I heaved a sigh of relief and rang him immediately.

'You have reached the voicemail of Noah Jones.'

Damn.

Noah was gone.

CHAPTER FORTY-FIVE

An hour later, I slumped down on the settee and kicked off my boots, sighing loudly.

'That's a loud sigh. What's up with you and what was all that about before?'

Startled, I looked up to see Clara standing in the doorway.

'Blooming hell, Clara, you sneaked down those stairs quietly! You frightened the life out of me!'

'I was cleaning the bathroom,' she answered, 'hence the Marigolds.' She sat on the edge of the chair and looked over at me. 'So come on, what's going on?

'It's Noah.'

'I kind of gathered that,' she replied.

'The girl last night – the one with her arms wrapped around him – she only turned out to be Jessica – Jack's daughter.'

'Shit a brick, Jack as in Irene's new Jack?' Clara exclaimed, sliding into the chair. She raised her eyebrows at me.

'Yep.'

'So are they going out together?'

'Ha, that's what I thought. I felt sick to my stomach until I found out she's actually with Dan, not Noah.'

'Dan? As in Dangler Dan?'

I nodded.

'Lucky cow!' She laughed. 'So why are you looking so glum?'

I took a deep breath. 'Because he's gone back to London.' My chin stiffened and my lip wobbled. 'I think I've missed my chance. When we didn't come to the book signing last night, he thought I wasn't interested, and then this morning I deleted him from Twitter.'

'Oh no.'

I sighed. 'Dan had taken him to the station and when Jessica told me what had happened, I jumped in a cab and headed straight there. When I got there, I saw him standing on the platform.'

'You saw him? What did he say?'

I shook my head. 'Nothing. He climbed on to the train and before I could reach him, the train pulled out of the station.'

'Oh, Evie, what a disaster.'

'That's when I rang you for his number, but it went straight to answerphone, and I… I couldn't just leave him a message. What would I have said?'

We were interrupted by a knock on the door.

'That'll be Aiden,' Clara said. 'He was going to come round after he dropped Theo back with Louisa. I'll get the door.'

I nodded but I was already lost in my own little world, thinking about everything that had happened in the last twenty-four hours. I'd met my mother, found out Wilson was my brother, got to know Jack and Jessica – and Noah had disappeared back to London. My head was spinning.

'Is it Aiden?' I shouted to Clara.

'Not quite.'

I looked up with a sharp intake of breath, and the skin on the back of my neck prickled as our eyes locked. 'Hey,' I said, my heart racing. There standing in the doorway was Noah, a lopsided grin on his face.

'Can I come in?'

'Yes, of course. Where's Clara?' I asked, straining my neck to see if she was behind him.

'She's given us some space. Her words, not mine,' he said. 'She grabbed her trainers and jumped into a car that had just pulled up outside.'

'Aiden,' I said.

Noah sat down on the chair opposite me. He was a vision of total gorgeousness.

'What are you doing here?' I could barely speak.

Breathe Evie – in, out, in out.

'A couple of things really. I heard you shout me as I got on the train, but by the time I realised it was you, the doors had closed and the train was off. Then once I got a signal I got texts from both Jessica and Dan telling me not to get on the train.'

I looked down. 'But you were on the train. How did you get here?'

'I jumped off at the next station and got a taxi here.'

My pulse ramped up a notch. 'You did that for me?'

I lifted my head and found he was looking at me with the most kissable smile I had ever laid eyes on.

'I did. Did you want me for any particular reason?' he asked softly.

I hesitated and he just waited for me to speak.

'Did you want me to want you for any particular reason?' I said, smiling coyly as I scanned his face.

His eyes locked on to mine. My heart pounded with anticipation.

Noah stood up slowly and came over to sit next to me on the settee. I began to tremble; my heart was beating so fast I thought it might explode.

'I'm hoping you feel the same way I do,' he said.

I nodded.

'Come here,' he said, stretching his arms towards me.

I snuggled into the embrace and rested my head against his chest.

'Jessica explained what happened,' he murmured before he tilted my head upwards and brushed my lips gently with his fingertip. 'You are beautiful, Evie Cooper,' he said and leant his head against mine. 'I remember the first time I ever set eyes on you – 17 May, nine months ago.'

I gasped. 'You remembered the date.'

'Of course.'

I lifted my hand up to his chin and stroked his stubble.

'I thought maybe you'd get in touch after you'd received your flowers.'

'Flowers?' I asked, surprised.

'Valentine's Day.'

'They were from you?'

'They were.' He gave me a sheepish grin. 'I suppose it was daft to think you'd guess they were from me after all that time. I should've been less mysterious.'

I smiled at him. 'I had no idea who they were from but they were beautiful – thank you.' My heart swelled with happiness.

Noah lowered his lips towards mine. I couldn't wait any longer, and I grasped his hair as our lips locked, gently at first, then harder.

'Evie…' He pulled away slowly but his gaze stayed locked on mine. 'I wanted you the minute I set eyes on you.'

'Me too,' I murmured, willing him to kiss me again. 'But I'm wondering…?'

'What?' he asked, puzzled. 'I'm not after a quick fling, if that's what you're worried about?' For a fleeting moment, he looked hurt.

'I didn't mean that, silly.' I squeezed his arm and took a deep breath. 'You live in London and I live here.'

'One day at a time.' He grinned. 'I have a very good feeling about this.'

I blushed. Did he really just say that?

'One day at a time,' I repeated, bursting with happiness.

'But I do have to go back to London tonight. I've a meeting with an agent tomorrow lunchtime.'

'How about early morning?' I asked hopefully. I didn't want to let him out of my sight.

'Mmm, I think I could be persuaded.' He dipped his head and brushed his lips against mine.

I took him by the hand and led him slowly upstairs. I couldn't wait a moment longer to be wrapped up in his arms.

The moment I shut the bedroom door, he pressed his body against mine, his hands in my hair, and kissed me like I'd never been kissed before. I ran my hands under his shirt, gasping at the smooth warmth of his skin.

He pulled away and stroked my face. 'Are you sure about this?'

I nodded, not trusting myself to speak.

He picked me up and lowered me gently on to the bed, his hands sliding under my dress to caress my thighs. I closed my eyes and basked in the pleasure, willing his hands to move to my breasts. I could feel the hardness of him against my thigh as I hitched my dress up over my head and threw it on the floor.

'You are just perfect,' he whispered, kissing my neck and then easing down the cups on my bra.

I shivered. 'Stop talking and kiss me again,' I said.

'You don't need to ask me twice,' he said, lowering his lips to mine.

I woke up at 3 a.m. entwined in Noah's arms, and an overwhelming feeling of happiness surged through my body. He was fast asleep. I traced his lips with my finger, thinking how perfect he looked, and kissed him gently before snuggling back into his chest.

'Mmm, what time is it?' he murmured.

'Threeish,' I whispered. 'You've got another couple of hours before you need to go.'

'Another couple of hours you say? Who needs sleep?'

I laughed as he wrapped me up in his arms again. I was the happiest girl on the planet.

CHAPTER FORTY-SIX

'OH MY GOSH! Look at that smile on your face!' Clara exclaimed, pouring milk over her cornflakes and grinning up at me.

'I have no idea what you mean,' I said.

'Don't give me that! I heard all the whispering before the front door closed this morning – oh and the kissing sounds.' She laughed, puckering up her lips.

'Behave!'

'I take it it all went well?'

I nodded. 'Noah and I…'

'Yes?' she urged.

'Noah and I are officially a couple,' I said, beaming as I grabbed myself a bowl of cornflakes.

'About blooming time! That's brilliant! I'm made up for you, Evie! It's only taken how long?'

I laughed. 'Nine months!'

'Come on! Spill the beans – tell me what happened. I was surprised to see him standing on the doorstep, I can tell you,' she said, shovelling the last of her cornflakes into her mouth.

'He'd heard me shout on the platform, but it was too late – the train doors had closed and it had started moving. Once his phone got a signal, he got messages from Jessica and Dan telling him not to get on the train. So he jumped off at the next stop, grabbed a taxi and came straight here.'

'Aww, this is so romantic. It's like something that happens in the movies.'

'I have to keep pinching myself. I can't believe this is happening to me.'

'What'll you do about the distance?'

'I was a little worried about that, but he said we should take it one day at a time, and he's right. What will be will be.'

Clara squealed. 'Oooh, I think he's definitely a keeper. This is all *so* romantic.'

'Are you seeing Aiden tonight?' I asked, sprinkling a little sugar over my cornflakes.

'No, his dad is staying with him this week, and he doesn't get to see him that often. He said Theo is very excited.'

'You'll get to meet him though, won't you?'

'Yeah, hopefully. Aiden mentioned something about meeting up next weekend before he goes home. A meal out or something.'

I grinned. 'Long may all this happiness continue for both of us.' I hugged Clara as my phone beeped.

'Aww,' I said, reading a text from Noah.

'Gosh, it must be love if he's already texting you. He only left a couple of hours ago!'

I beamed. 'I'm saying nothing!' We'd already made plans to get together this coming weekend and Friday couldn't come quick enough.

'Right, I'm in the bathroom first,' Clara said, bounding towards the kitchen door. 'You can daydream out the kitchen window while you wash the dishes.'

'Cheeky!' I shouted after her.

A few hours later, Clara was entertaining the little folk with Rachel the Reading Rabbit, while Aiden rearranged the crime-fiction shelf and I trawled through my unread emails. Unless I wanted to speak to Russian women online or lift saggy skin without surgery, there really wasn't anything interesting in my inbox.

A shadow fell over my computer and I looked up to see Jenny. She smiled. 'Good morning.'

'Morning! What a lovely surprise! I wasn't expecting to see you.'

Jenny had a sense of calm about her and she looked rested. 'I was passing and just wanted to make sure you were OK after Saturday.'

'That'll be the maternal instinct in you,' I teased.

'You'd better believe it!'

'Yes, all good here. Are you OK?'

She nodded. 'Yes, but I have to admit I couldn't sleep on Saturday night. Everything was whirling around in my head. It's so surreal. It's you – and you're here.'

I smiled. 'Some things are just meant to be, I guess.'

'And then last night I slept through for the first time in as long as I can remember.'

'That's great news!' I said and smiled as another email pinged into my inbox.

I stared at the screen and moved the mouse over the message as I quickly scanned the words.

'What night would you be free to come over and meet Adam? He's really looking forward to it.'

Jenny's words faded in my ears as I devoured the email before me.

'Evie, what's the matter? You've gone white!'

I sat back in my chair and gasped. 'I don't believe this,' I muttered.

'Clara! Aiden!' Jenny shouted over to them. Clara was just wrapping up her reading session.

'Everything OK?' Aiden asked, hurrying over.

'I don't know,' Jenny replied.

'Evie?'

I stared up at the three of them, then swivelled the computer screen towards them.

'Holy bloody moly!' Clara screeched at the top of her voice.

'Shhh! You can't swear – it's a library!' Aiden said, grinning.

My stomach whirled with excitement.

I got to my feet unsteadily and threw open my arms. 'Oh my God! Group hug!'

We all hugged and jumped up and down like excited toddlers.

'You won, Evie! You won!'

'Is this real?' I yelped happily. 'I've won! I don't believe this is happening.'

There on the computer screen was an email from the organisers of the writing competition. Sam Stone had chosen my story as the winner out of thousands of entries, and this Saturday I was invited to attend a presentation and a three-course dinner at a very swish manor house not too far away.

My chest was heaving as I tried to catch my breath. 'I need to phone Irene!'

Clara and Jenny beamed at each other, their faces lit with delight.

'I can't believe it! Not only have you won but you're going to meet Sam Stone! *The* Sam Stone – the *legend* that is Sam Stone!' Clara shrieked.

I was absolutely stunned.

'Your story's going to be published in a magazine too!' Clara clapped her hands in excitement. 'I'm so chuffed for you, my clever friend.' And she beamed, kissing both my cheeks.

'It's fabulous news, Evie,' Aiden said, grinning.

'Aww, and look,' Clara said, running her finger across the screen. 'You can take four guests with you.'

'I missed that part!' I exclaimed.

Clara's eyes twinkled as she put her hands together and prayed.

My heart was in a spin. Irene, of course, was my first choice, followed by Clara, but then I had two invites left. Clara would love to be able to take Aiden, and I would want Noah there, but there was Jenny too.

She was standing in front of me, smiling from ear to ear. 'I'm so proud of you, Evie. You deserve this.'

'Thank you.'

'Am I OK to share the news with Wilson?'

'Of course,' I said, and Jenny pulled out her phone and popped outside to call him.

'Would you like to come with me, Clara?'

'Would I ever,' she squealed. 'Try and stop me!'

Then I paused.

Aiden placed his hand on the small of my back. He must have read my mind because he gave me a knowing look and said, 'Invite Jenny. Don't worry about me. I'll look forward to hearing all about it when you get home.'

'Are you sure?' I asked.

'Yes, of course – but on one condition.'

'Which is?'

He grinned. 'Take lots of photos!'

'I will, I promise. Thanks, Aiden!' I said. 'Now pass me the phone. I need to tell Irene my news!'

Aiden slid the desk phone over towards me, and my hand was shaking as I punched in the number. I shuffled from foot to foot, willing her to hurry up and answer it.

'Hi,' she said at last.

'It's Evie,' I gasped. 'I have news! Fantastic news!'

'Shush, Buddy, calm down,' I heard her say. He was barking excitedly about something.

'News? Did you say news? What is it?'

'Are you ready for this?' I paused. 'I've only gone and won that writing competition!'

There was silence while Irene digested what I'd said, then she squealed so loud that Buddy began to bark again.

'Evie, I am absolutely delighted for you! You never cease to amaze me! I'm so proud of you!' Irene gushed.

'Thank you! I have to go now as I'm at work, but Irene…'

'Yes, Evie,' she said, catching her breath.

'I love you.'

'I love you too!'

CHAPTER FORTY-SEVEN

The bell tinkled over my head as I walked into Mim's café, and I felt like a celebrity as everyone cheered and gave me a rapturous round of applause. There were balloons in every corner of the room and congratulations banners pinned across the wall. News of my win had circulated quickly and tonight's book club was packed to the rafters, which Mim told me was all down to me.

Mim herself had become something of a local celebrity following my win; the likes on her Facebook page had doubled and established authors were knocking down her door to come and do a talk. The local newspaper was also popping along tonight to photograph Mim and me and some of the other book-club members. After all, if it hadn't been for her telling us all about the competition in the first place, I never would have entered.

Elle was standing behind the counter. As soon as she saw me, she beamed and hurried over.

'Congratulations, Evie! Well done on your story, but how jealous am I that you get to meet the man himself on Saturday? You must be so excited!'

I was very excited about meeting one of my idols but also extremely nervous. The organiser of the event had given me a ring on Monday evening to talk me through the night. The presentation would begin at around 7 p.m. Myself and two runners-up would each be presented with a plaque, then Sam Stone would give a small speech about why my entry had stood out before reading a small extract and presenting me with the published magazine article. Then we would sit down and enjoy a three-course meal with champagne. I was so nervous about my story being read out to a room full of people I didn't know.

I'd barely slept on Monday night after discovering I'd won the competition. Something had been playing on my mind and around 3 a.m. I'd sent Noah a text to see if he was awake. I'd been surprised when he replied straight away. He'd been up writing the synopsis for a story that had come to him that evening and he'd wanted to get it all down on paper before he forgot it. He'd ended up phoning me and we'd spoken in hushed whispers so we didn't wake Clara.

Noah had been absolutely over the moon that I'd won and even more excited when I'd asked him to attend the presentation with me.

'What's worrying you,' he'd asked. 'Why can't my budding superstar sleep?'

I'd explained the situation to him and he had understood exactly where I was coming from – I was worried about Jenny. She'd accepted my invitation to the presentation, happy tears pricking her eyes. But when I'd found out that Sam Stone would be reading an extract from my story, I'd been worried how Jenny would react. The story was about my life – my unhappy childhood, and how I'd been abandoned – and it had been written with such raw emotion. I didn't want to hurt Jenny – she'd suffered enough.

'You need to tell her and give her the choice to attend,' Noah had said. 'You can't let her walk into the room and listen to the extract without being prepared. That would be unfair.'

Noah had been right of course.

The very next day, I'd plucked up the courage to ring Jenny. It was the first time I'd actually dialled her number and I'd been feeling very apprehensive about how she would react. She'd listened in silence and never interrupted as I'd explained what my competition entry was about.

'Evie, I'm very proud of you and very grateful you've told me in advance, but I'm fine with it,' she'd said. 'What happened has made us the people we are today, and we can't change the past. I'd still like to come, if that's OK with you?'

It was more than OK with me and I'd felt like a huge weight had been lifted off my shoulders as soon as I'd told her.

We'd gone on to joke about how excited everyone else was about meeting Sam Stone – whereas she didn't like dark crime books and wouldn't know Sam Stone if she fell over him.

Noah had laughed when I'd told him how nervous I was about meeting Sam. I'd read every one of his books, but according to all the research I'd done, he was a recluse – there were no photos of him online and his private life was just that: private – so I was truly honoured that he'd be making the effort to present me the award personally.

'He's just a normal bloke you know,' Noah had said. 'He eats, drinks and goes to the loo just like the rest of us.'

Well, everyone here in the café didn't think Sam Stone was a normal person – he was God in the world of crime writing.

Irene, Clara and I sat in our usual seats in the window and Mim dashed towards us clutching three plates of Victoria sponge.

'Just for you, my dear, and on Saturday, you let Mr Stone know if he wants to sample any of my finest cakes free of charge, he can just pop over on Sunday.'

She winked at me, and I laughed. 'I'll be sure to let him know.'

Mim hurried back to the front of the café and clapped her hands. Silence fell and everyone turned towards her.

'Tonight I would like to welcome our very own published writer, Evie Cooper,' she announced. Everyone turned towards me and clapped again.

I smiled gratefully around the room, then caught Irene's eye. She wiped away a proud tear and squeezed my knee.

'Thank you,' I replied once the applause had died down.

'Evie will be attending a very special ceremony on Saturday evening where her plaque and published article will be presented to her by the bestselling crime author… Mr Sam Stone.' Everyone in the café let out a whoop and laughed. 'So tonight we have a little change to our proceedings. Firstly, I want to know – if you had one question to ask Sam Stone, what would it be, and secondly, Evie has agreed that she'll read us a short extract from her winning entry ahead of Saturday.'

Everyone turned back to me with admiring looks and clapped again. I felt my stomach twist. Aside from my moment with Noah – and he had been a special case – this would be the first time I'd be letting anyone I wasn't close to learn something about my past. It was a huge step forward for me.

'We're also expecting the local paper to turn up in the next hour to take some photos and interview Evie,' Mim added.

I grinned at Clara. 'That's why you have a full face of make-up, isn't it?'

'You know me so well.'

'So,' Mim continued, 'if you could ask Sam Stone one question, what would it be?'

Immediately Emma's hand shot up. 'How many times a day do you check your rankings on Amazon? You know, to see how well your book is performing?'

Everyone laughed.

'I'm sure Sam Stone has no need to check his rankings,' I said. Funnily enough, I'd asked Noah that question when we'd last talked on the phone. I wasn't sure whether to believe him when he'd said every hour on the hour.

My heart soared when I thought about him. Since he'd gone back to London, we'd spoken on the phone every night for hours. The conversation just flowed so naturally – we were so at ease with each other, and I felt like he'd been part of my life for years.

'Any other questions?'

'Have you ever had a crazed stalker on social media?' a woman who was new to book club asked from the corner of the café.

Again, I thought of Noah. He'd been telling me last night about a blogger who'd become overfamiliar on Twitter. Every time he tweeted, she liked it immediately, like she was obsessed. She'd even begun making up nicknames for him.

Then Clara piped up. 'I know one question you need to ask him.' She stared at me.

'Which is?'

The whole room fell silent.

'How did he know it was your birthday, and how did a signed copy of his book end up on your desk at work?'

'Yes!' Mim cried. 'Don't forget to ask him that!'

With everything that had been going on recently, I'd totally forgotten about the signed Sam Stone book, but it was definitely something I was going to slip into the conversation when I met him.

After much more joking about, it was time for me to read the extract.

Mim shushed the room and all eyes turned to me.

I swallowed and took a deep breath. I prayed my voice didn't wobble as I began to read.

'"The winter brings another cold and dreary night. It's times like this I wish I could melt away like the snow outside. I want to stop the ever-present pain.

'"It's late now and I huddle in my bed. All I want is a hand to hold, but no one comes. The sense of abandonment I feel is raw and the darkness swirls around the room. Night-time is always the worst.

'"Then I hear hushed whispers and the creaking of the stairs. The door opens slowly and light seeps into the room. I am bustled from my bed again, bundled in a coat that's way too big and told to wait by the door. It is the middle of the night. I watch as the headlamps of the car snake up the road and stop outside the house. The only thing in my grasp is my shawl. An owl hoots as a hand clutches mine and leads me towards the car. I don't look back.

'"*She didn't fit* are the words that echo all around me, my sunshine stripped from me again. Why does no one love me? Maybe I don't deserve to be loved.

'"Loneliness is my only dependable friend."'

Tears blurred my eyes as I stopped reading and I swallowed a lump in my throat. The whole café sat in complete silence, and when I finally looked up, there wasn't a dry eye in the place.

Someone started to clap and the whole room mirrored the sound, then suddenly everyone was on their feet.

'I'm sure I speak for everyone at book club when I say we are super proud of our very own Evie Cooper,' Mim called across the room, smiling at me through her tears. 'Teas and cake on the house for the next hour,' she announced.

Everyone clapped some more as Irene mouthed, 'Thank you' to Mim.

'I think I need something a little stronger,' I whispered.

'That is why I am *so* your friend,' Clara said, whipping out a hipflask from her bag. She glanced at my teacup, which was empty, and poured some whisky into it.

'Drink up,' she said. 'Do you want a drop, Irene?'

'Without a doubt,' she replied, sliding her cup towards Clara.

'Here's to Evie,' Clara said, smiling.

'Here's to Evie,' Irene agreed, and we clinked our cups together.

CHAPTER FORTY-EIGHT

I checked the overhead display board as I stood waiting on platform two. Noah's train had been delayed by around half an hour. The butterflies were already racing around in my stomach – I'd been waiting for this moment all week.

The station was alive with the hustle and bustle of Friday-night commuters. Everyone jumping off the trains seemed to be in a hurry, and there were several people around who looked like they were also waiting eagerly for loved ones to arrive.

I perched on the edge of the bench and dug my hands deep into my pockets. Tomorrow I'd be attending the presentation at Crossley Manor Hall and the nerves were really beginning to kick in. I'd found out the editor of *Women's Writing* magazine would also be attending to present me with the copy of my published story alongside Sam Stone.

I smiled as my thoughts turned to Clara. After we'd got home from book club the previous night, we'd cracked open a bottle of wine and talked clothes. Clara had dragged every item of clothing she owned from her wardrobe and laid it out all over the living room. I'd been aghast when she'd said she didn't have anything to wear and maybe it wasn't too late to trawl the internet and purchase something with next-day delivery.

'Clara, you have everything from a little black dress – actually three little black dresses – to ball gowns, jumpsuits and skirts,' I'd said.

'But, this is a very special occasion! Not only do I want to do you proud, but there might be an opportunity to get a photo with Sam Stone!'

I'd laughed. 'I knew there was an ulterior motive.'

'Penny for them?' My thoughts were interrupted by a voice I knew only too well, and I looked up to see Noah.

'Eek! That thirty minutes went quickly!' I said, scooting off the bench and jumping straight into his arms.

'I've missed you,' he said, kissing me before grabbing my hand and leading me down the platform.

'What a week it's been,' he joked, swinging my hand. 'I leave you alone for five minutes and you end up winning competitions and getting your face plastered all over the local press.'

I grinned up at him. 'It's so surreal! Last night I went to the book club and honestly I felt like a celebrity.'

'Everyone is so proud of you – including me.'

'Thanks, Noah,' I said bashfully.

It was a fifteen-minute walk back to my house from the station and we chatted all the way. I'd told him briefly on the phone about my dinner date at Jenny's a few nights previously but now he wanted all the details.

Meeting Adam for the first time had been nerve-wracking, but he'd been absolutely lovely and had instantly made me feel welcome. I'd sat next to Wilson at the table and felt a real sense of belonging. After the meal had ended, Wilson and I had loaded up the dishwasher and retired to the living room, where we'd sat with Jenny and Adam and talked about everything and anything.

It was then that Jenny had asked me to help her choose her outfit for Saturday night.

'Come on, Wilson, let's leave the girls to it,' Adam had said, and they'd headed out to the pub for a pint.

I'd followed Jenny upstairs to a spacious bedroom that had been decorated in a soothing palette of white and duck-egg blue.

'Wow, look at those views,' I'd exclaimed, in awe of the acres of fields and the beautiful church in the distance.

'Yes, it's fabulous, isn't it? How are you feeling about tomorrow?' she'd asked as she'd laid outfits out on the bed.

'A little nervous. I'll be glad when the presentation is over and we can just enjoy our food.'

'What do you think of this?' she'd asked, holding a dress up against her. 'I don't want to be overdressed or underdressed.'

'No, that one's too stuffish – if that's even a word,' I'd said, laughing.

'What about this one?' Jenny had held up a pair of black trousers with a spotted bow-tie blouse.

'Hmmm.' I'd hesitated. 'Maybe. I'm not sure though – it kind of looks like something you'd wear to an interview.'

'Yes, that's exactly what Adam said!'

We'd both laughed.

'This one?'

'That's the one,' I'd said, smiling as Jenny had held up a navy chiffon dress that gathered softly around the neckline and fell to just below her knees.

'Perfect,' she'd said. 'I have a red cardigan that I can dress it up with and a matching handbag.'

'All sorted.'

'What are you wearing, Evie?' she'd asked then.

'I've borrowed a little black dress off Clara. Honestly, she could open her own boutique with the amount of stuff she hoards.'

Jenny had laughed. 'I'm a bit like that with shoes,' she'd said. 'You can never have too many shoes.'

The rest of the evening had gone swimmingly and we'd arranged to meet outside the venue on Saturday night before we went into the presentation.

'Here we are,' I said to Noah as we reached the house, bounding up the steps and unlocking the front door. He followed me into the hallway and tossed his holdall on the floor before giving me a sheepish look.

'I'd probably be better hanging up my shirt and trousers for tomorrow night. Otherwise I'll end up having to iron them again.'

'There'll be a few spare coat hangers in my wardrobe – go up and help yourself.'

Noah kissed me on the tip of the nose and disappeared up the stairs.

Clara had left me a note on the table. She'd gone round to Aiden's for tea and to meet his dad but had invited us to join them in the pub afterwards if we fancied it.

'What do you want to do?' I asked Noah when he came back downstairs, handing the note to him.

'I'd rather curl up with you on the settee and maybe get a takeaway? Come here.'

He pulled me towards him and lowered his head to mine. He kissed me and instantly my heart started fluttering.

'How do you do that to me?' I said, blushing. 'You make me go weak at the knees.'

'Glad to hear it,' he replied, his eyes locking playfully with mine. 'You have exactly the same effect on me.' And he grinned as he pretended his legs had given way and pulled me down on to the settee with him.

I giggled as he put his strong arms around me and nuzzled into my neck.

I swiped at him playfully.

'Let's order our food first, then you can take full advantage of me afterwards.'

He grinned. 'Sounds like a plan,' he said, sitting up and spotting the signed Sam Stone novel on the table.

'So what was the story behind this again?' he asked, picking it up and flicking open the cover.

'It was my birthday and it just appeared out of nowhere on the desk at work. It was bizarre! There was no one around and Clara and Aiden hadn't seen anyone loitering.'

'It's a fantastic read and I bet signed copies are like gold dust.'

'Have you ever met him?' I asked.

'No, he's a writer that seems to stay out of the public eye. I do follow him on Twitter, but he rarely tweets.'

'Yes, I did tweet him after I received the book, but I never got a reply.'

'That doesn't surprise me.'

'Let's get the food ordered. I'm starving!' I said, walking into the kitchen.

'Your phone just beeped,' Noah called after me.

'It'll be Clara. She'll be checking in to see if we're going to the pub. Just swipe the screen and look. I've not got a passcode.'

I scooted back into the living room armed with numerous menus and tossed them on to the coffee table. Noah was staring down at the phone screen.

'Is it Clara?' I asked, sitting down next to him.

His eyes met mine and he passed the phone to me.

'Oh my!' There in my notifications list was a mention from Sam Stone himself.

Looking forward to meeting the talented @EvieCooper tomorrow!

'Someone definitely has a fan!' Noah exclaimed.

I couldn't reply. I was too busy picking my jaw up off the floor.

CHAPTER FORTY-NINE

'How do I look?' I asked Clara and Noah nervously.

They both swung their heads towards the living-room door and their eyes locked on me.

'You look amazing! Now come on – the taxi's been waiting outside for nearly five minutes!' Clara exclaimed, grabbing her sparkly handbag from the table.

Noah looked gorgeous in a crisp pale blue shirt. He walked over to me. 'Absolutely beautiful,' he said, tilting his head down to me.

I held my hand up in front of his face. 'No kisses until after the presentation,' I said, laughing. 'I don't want my lipstick smudging. Now we'd better go – Clara's already in the taxi, and we need to pick up Irene en route.'

Thirty minutes later the taxi passed through the enormous wrought-iron gates of Crossley Manor Hall.

'Wow, look at this place!' I said, staring out of the window at the magnificent building in front of us. It looked like something out of *Downton Abbey*.

'What a fantastic venue,' Clara agreed.

The car pulled up right outside the entrance, and the driver came and opened the door for us.

After we'd paid, Irene spotted Jenny standing at the entrance, beaming in our direction. I gave her a wave as we wandered over, and Noah grabbed my hand and gave it a little squeeze.

'Are you nervous?'

I nodded. Although I was a little jittery about meeting Sam Stone, that was nothing compared to how I felt about reading my story to a room full of strangers. I was sure there were a number of worthy winners.

After I hugged Jenny, we sauntered into the impressive entrance hall, where we were met by the event organiser, who was looking extremely smart in his suit. He was clutching a clipboard and after he checked our names, we were ticked off the list and shown into a room just off the main foyer.

Waiters circulated with free drinks, and after we'd all taken a glass from a passing tray, my eyes swept the room. There were rows and rows of chairs laid out in front of the stage, and standing in the middle of the stage was a microphone on a stand. It was when I spotted that that my nerves really began to kick in and I gulped back my glass of fizz.

'Hey, steady,' Noah whispered. 'You don't want to be tipsy on stage. Wait until after the presentation.'

I knew he was right, but I just needed a bit of courage.

'Evie Cooper?' The man who'd ticked our names off the list was hurrying towards us.

'Yes,' I managed to say, my voice a little shaky.

'If you and your party would like to follow me, you have the opportunity to meet Sam Stone before you go up to collect your prize.'

Clara clapped her hands together. 'This is better than meeting Santa Claus.'

We followed the man towards an oak door at the far end of the room. Then the door opened, and I had to look twice.

Clara gasped.

'What the bloody hell are you doing here?' she asked Aiden.

He met Clara's gaze and began to stutter. 'Oh— Oh God. You shouldn't have seen me just yet.'

We all stared at Aiden in shock.

'Don't be mad at me.'

He too was dressed for the occasion in a suit and tie.

Clara clamped her hands on her hips. 'Why would I be mad at you? What have you done? Please don't tell me you did something dodgy to blag yourself an invite.'

He smiled. 'Not quite.'

'Aiden, is there anything else you need?' the event organiser asked.

'No, I'll take it from here. Thank you.'

'What's going on?' I heard Jenny whisper to Irene, who shrugged.

'Aiden, spill the beans! This is all so weird!' Clara exclaimed, giving him a gentle pinch and a kiss on the cheek to hurry his explanation along.

'It's not really that weird,' he said, giving us all a cheeky smile as he motioned us to step through the door. 'I'd like you to come in and meet Sam Stone – my godfather.'

'Your godfather?' Clara cried.

We all gasped and stared at Aiden open-mouthed.

'You're kidding us, right?' Noah shook his head in disbelief.

'No. He's my father's best friend.'

'You kept that quiet,' Clara trilled at the top of her voice. 'And your dad never said a word last night!'

'He was sworn to secrecy!'

'Why the blooming heck didn't you say?'

'Because I knew one day you'd all meet him and your faces would be an absolute picture!'

He was right. There, standing in the middle of the room with a smile, was Sam, and Clara and I could only stare.

'Which one of you is the talented Evie Cooper?' Sam asked, walking over and stretching his hand out.

'That'll be me,' I said, rather shyly shaking his hand.

'I'm very pleased to meet you. Your competition entry touched me, and I'm not ashamed to say it actually brought tears to my eyes. I could relate to it in so many ways. It was a fantastic journey, full of raw emotion, and it deserves to be published.'

'Thank you,' I whispered, completely awed. 'This is Clara,' I managed. 'My best friend.'

Clara's smile couldn't have been any wider. 'Fangirl moment,' she squealed, shaking his hand. 'I'm your biggest fan, I've read all your books, and I've loved every one of them,' she went on without taking a breath.

Everyone laughed.

She turned to Aiden. 'And I can't believe you never told me! What a cool godfather to have!'

Aiden smiled at her. 'I would have in time.'

'So that explains where the signed book came from?' I blurted.

All eyes flicked between Sam and Aiden, and Aiden grinned.

'Guilty as charged,' he said. 'I knew Sam was your favourite author and I wanted to spill the beans so many times, but I'd planned to bring him to the library this week because he was up with Dad visiting me – they also live relatively close to each other near the coast, you see. But then you won the competition.'

I swiped Aiden's arm playfully and rolled my eyes.

'This is Noah, a fellow author,' Aiden continued with the introductions.

'Yes, I've heard of you,' Sam said, shaking Noah's hand. Noah stared back at him with wide eyes.

'And this is Irene.'

'Hello,' Irene said, politely shaking his hand.

'And— Where's Jenny disappeared to?'

We all spun around but Jenny was suddenly nowhere to be seen.

'That's strange,' Noah said, whipping his head back towards the door. 'She was here a minute ago.'

'She can't have gone far,' Aiden replied, 'but unfortunately it's time to take our seats. The presentation is about to start.' He glanced at his watch.

'Would it be OK if Sam and I came and joined you at your table for the meal afterwards?' Aiden asked me, putting his arm around Clara's waist and walking us all back towards the door.

I smiled. 'That would be lovely.'

'I've got to go this way now,' Sam said. 'I'll look forward to chatting with you all at the meal.'

Once we were through the door, I scanned the main room, but it seemed Jenny had disappeared altogether.

'Where do you think she's gone?' I murmured to Noah.

'I've no idea. Maybe it all got a little too much for her? It has been a hell of a couple of weeks.'

I nodded, but I wasn't convinced. Something wasn't right – I could feel it in my bones.

We all made our way towards the chairs in front of the stage, and one of the organisers directed us to seats in the front row.

'You need to save one for Jenny,' I whispered to Irene. She placed her bag down on the seat next to her and we studied the hordes of people filtering into the chairs behind us, but there was still no sign of her.

'She must have nipped to the loo.'

'What a time to disappear!'

A few moments later, a man came on stage and switched on the microphone. The whole room hushed and all eyes focused on where he stood.

'Jenny needs to hurry up! Otherwise she's going to miss it,' Irene whispered.

'I've just texted her but I've not had a reply.' Clara switched her phone to silent and put it back in her handbag.

'Please put your hands together and welcome the bestselling author Mr Sam Stone.'

The whole room erupted in rapturous applause and Sam strolled on to the stage.

'I think Sam Stone is a very romantic name. He sounds like a movie star,' Clara whispered, all gooey-eyed.

Aiden placed his hand on her knee and squeezed it. 'It's not his real name, you know.'

'What?' Clara swung towards him.

Just then Jenny appeared from nowhere and slumped into the chair next to Irene. She looked ghastly white.

'Sam Stone is a pseudonym – he doesn't write under his real name.'

'Gosh! What's his real name?' Irene whispered.

'Matt Harrison,' Jenny said, locking her shocked eyes on mine.

CHAPTER FIFTY

My eyes didn't leave Jenny's, the words 'Matt Harrison' whirling round and round in my head.

She nodded at me – it was him. I was absolutely flabbergasted. Goodness knew how Jenny was feeling, her past hurtling back into the present when she least expected it.

My heart went out to her. She must have had the shock of her life walking into the room to find Matt standing there. No wonder she'd disappeared.

I had no idea what was going to happen next.

'What are you doing? Get yourself up on stage, girl,' Irene whispered urgently, leaning across and tapping me on the knee.

'Evie, go!' Noah nudged my arm.

I glanced up to find the whole room clapping and Matt, standing on the stage, looking over in my direction. I was rooted to the spot.

Aiden stood up and gestured for me to follow him to the side of the stage. I'd been that shocked by Jenny's revelation that I hadn't even heard the kind words Matt had said about my story, or the moment he'd asked me to come up and collect my prize.

Finally, I stood up. I saw relief wash over Matt's face as my wobbly legs began to carry me to the steps beside the stage. Everyone was on their feet clapping. I noticed Irene dabbing at her eyes, proud tears running down her cheeks.

Then my eyes flicked to Jenny. Her eyes were darting between Matt and me.

Matt shook my hand and presented me with the plaque. Then we welcomed the editor of *Women's Writing* to the stage, and she handed me the magazine I was featured in and a framed copy of the story.

After a lot of handshaking and once the room had stopped applauding, Matt cleared his throat. 'I would now like to read you an extract from Evie's story.' He smiled at me and paused for a moment. He must have seen how anxious I was and thought he'd help by reading the story for me.

I just stared at him. I couldn't help but notice that I looked like him – in fact, the resemblance was striking. I had his eyes, my nose curved in the same way and his smile mirrored mine. 'It's OK,' he whispered, placing his hand over the microphone. 'I've got you.'

I glanced back over to Jenny as he started reading.

I could feel myself shaking and saw Jenny was on the brink of tears. Noah was glancing anxiously between us and mouthed, 'What's wrong?' at me, but of course, I couldn't answer.

Everyone else in the room was listening to Matt, and, aside from the odd gasp, there was complete silence as the words of my story spilt from his lips.

I wanted to leave the stage and wrap my arms around Jenny – I could see how much she was hurting, but I was stuck.

Matt continued to read but then his words began to slow, his eyes flicking in Jenny's direction, and I knew he'd recognised her. He couldn't know who I was, but there was no doubt in my mind when I looked at him: Matt Harrison was my father.

CHAPTER FIFTY-ONE

As soon as the presentation was over, I saw Jenny run from her seat, Irene quickly following her. The moment Matt walked me off stage we were greeted by a sea of journalists, who wanted to photograph us for numerous papers and magazines. We were held up for nearly fifteen minutes while I was interviewed, and Matt stayed by my side the whole time. I could barely breathe, never mind smile as the cameras flashed at us.

'Who's that woman you're with?' Matt asked as soon as the photographers had moved on to the other award winners.

'Jenny,' I replied.

'Jenny,' he repeated. 'Ah, my mistake.' His eyes darted towards the back of the room but Jenny and Irene had disappeared. 'I thought it was someone I used to know.'

'She used to be called Sarah Thomas.'

Matt stopped dead in his tracks.

'She's my mother.' My voice faltered and my lips quivered.

'Hey, congratulations, lovely one.' Noah pecked me on the cheek and took the framed story from my grasp as we reached him.

I didn't answer. Instead, Matt and I just stood in silence, staring at each other.

'Are you guys OK? You look like you've seen a ghost,' Aiden said. We both glanced at Aiden, then back at each other.

And still neither of us spoke.

'What's going on?' Aiden asked.

I tried to keep my emotions under control as the full enormity of it hit me – I'd just found my father.

Matt strained to see over the crowd, which was full of fans clutching his latest book, hoping for a photo and an autograph. We could hear them calling his name and squealing with delight as he looked in their direction, but he didn't even see them.

It was Jenny he was searching for.

He turned back towards me, raking his hand through his hair. 'We need to find her.' Matt's voice had lowered to a whisper.

Noah simply stared at me.

My pulse quickened, and I dashed after Matt as he took off through the crowd, leaving Noah, Clara and Aiden wondering what the hell was going on.

CHAPTER FIFTY-TWO

Ten minutes later, we had searched everywhere. Jenny and Irene were nowhere to be found and both of their mobiles had been switched off.

Matt let out a defeated sigh and sat down on a settee in the foyer. 'I need to ask you something.'

I knew what was coming.

'The story you've written – was it true?' Matt's eyes searched mine.

I nodded, swallowing the lump in my throat.

'But your writing suggests you're looking for your real mum so does that mean Sarah... Jenny is an adoptive mum?'

I shook my head.

'I don't understand, Evie.'

I took a deep breath. My legs felt like they were going to buckle, so I sat down next to him.

I could feel the emotion rising inside me as I said, 'Irene is my foster mum. I've only just been reunited with Jenny. It's a long story.'

Matt dropped his head into his hands and, for a moment, he was silent.

'How old are you, Evie?' he asked finally, his eyes gleaming with unshed tears.

My throat became tight, then my tears fell. I didn't know how to answer, but I knew I had to tell the truth. 'I turned twenty-three in January.' As soon as the words left my mouth, I could see him doing the maths.

'You're Matt Harrison,' I said bravely. 'The man Sarah loved – the man she disappeared on.'

A tear ran down his face. 'She told you?'

I nodded.

'I loved that woman with all my heart. I couldn't understand what had happened. She just never came home. You hear of people going out to buy a newspaper and never coming back. I thought she must be dead. I filed a missing-persons report, and I searched and searched, but there was no trace of her anywhere.' Matt was clearly distraught.

'She was my first love and not a day goes by that I don't wonder what happened to her. And then after all these years, she appears out of the blue. We need to find her!'

My chest was pounding and I took a deep breath. Where the hell were they?

I stood up and stared out of the window at the gently lit grounds. It was then I spotted two familiar figures sitting on a bench. 'There they are,' I said.

Matt was up and out the door in seconds, hurrying across the grounds towards them with me hot on his heels.

They looked up and spotted us immediately. Jenny's face was stained with tears, and Irene's arm was draped around her shoulder.

'Hello, Sarah,' Matt gasped, out of breath, as he stopped in front of her.

'Hi.' She managed a weak smile.

Irene squeezed her knee and stood up. 'Come on, Evie. We need to leave them to talk.'

I hesitated, then followed Irene's lead.

'How are you?' she asked tentatively.

'I'm not sure.' My voice was shaky.

I stopped walking and Irene took both my hands in hers. 'I think Matt Harrison is my father.'

Her eyes locked with mine. 'I think he is too.'

We hugged each other tight.

CHAPTER FIFTY-THREE

One month later

'Are you ready?' Noah called up to me. 'The taxi's here.'

'I'm coming,' I shouted, hurrying down the stairs into the living room.

'Evie!' Theo came running towards me and I scooped him up in my arms and planted a huge kiss on his cheek. He giggled.

'Well look at you, Theo! How handsome do you look in your suit and bow tie?' I exclaimed, putting his feet firmly back on the floor.

Theo grinned and held out his fist, which I bumped with mine.

'You look gorgeous,' Noah said, kissing me on the cheek with a smile.

'I'll second that,' Aiden said.

'Where's Clara?'

'You'd think it was her getting married, the amount of time she's taken to get ready!'

'Oi, Aiden, I heard that!' Clara said, laughing as she popped her head round the kitchen door. 'I'm ready!'

Theo ran to the kitchen door and squeezed his hand into Clara's. She promptly ruffled his hair, and he beamed up at her.

The last month had been such a whirlwind. After the presentation, Jenny had finally confided in Matt what had happened all those years ago. Matt had been completely devastated by what Jenny had endured.

Despite the resemblance between us, Matt and I had taken a DNA test, just to be sure, and of course, the results had been positive.

Overnight I'd gained a dad, and the jigsaw puzzle was finally complete. Matt lived a half hour away from Aidan's dad, on the coast, and had invited Noah and me up for a weekend at the end of the month, which I was looking forward to immensely. I couldn't wait to get to know him better.

'Where to?' the taxi driver asked as we all climbed in.

'The small church on the other side of Marbury.'

The driver nodded and we were on our way.

'What a fantastic day for a wedding!' Clara exclaimed, staring out of the window at the blue sky.

As we arrived, we could hear the church bells pealing, and we spotted Josh standing next to Wilson by the doors. They both looked handsome in their top hats and tails, sporting the widest smiles.

It was such a romantic setting, perfect for a spring wedding. Daffodils danced along the edge of a large pond that sat in front of the church, and as we wandered over the bridge, we could see a family of ducks paddling below.

'Such a stunning place,' I said as we reached Josh and Wilson.

'It's a perfect venue – very English countryside,' Noah agreed, shaking Josh's hand. 'Congratulations mate.'

Josh grinned from ear to ear. 'Thanks! I've got to get inside in a moment – apparently the bride's on her way!'

Suddenly Mim appeared from inside the church. She looked gorgeous in a duck-egg blue outfit with matching hat.

'Irene and Jack are already inside with Jenny and Adam,' she said, smiling in my direction. 'And you, Josh, need to disappear inside now.'

'We know, it's unlucky to see the bride,' Josh and Wilson said in unison before bursting into laughter.

'So whose turn is it next?' Josh asked, playfully casting his eye between myself and Clara.

'Time will tell,' Clara replied, sticking her tongue out at him.

'Oh no!' I said, spotting Elle's car approaching. 'Get inside now,' I cried, pushing Josh through the door.

Mim beamed proudly at her daughter as Elle stepped out of the car on her dad's arm, and we all gasped.

She looked beautiful. Her dress was an elegant cream A-line, with a crystal-encrusted lace bodice and cap sleeves, and a chic tulle skirt. It was simply stunning.

We all gave her a wide smile before hurrying into the church to take our seats. The church too was beautiful, decorated to perfection with bursts of ivory roses lining the pews.

All eyes turned towards the doors as the wedding music began to play, and Elle glided up the aisle, her dad as proud as punch beside her.

Josh beamed at Elle as she approached and there wasn't a dry eye in the place.

'I do love a good wedding,' Clara sobbed as I passed her a tissue. I caught Jenny's eye, and she smiled across at me before turning towards Wilson, who was sitting on the front pew. Wilson had done her proud today, and I caught a special look between her and Adam before he draped his arm around her shoulder and kissed the top of her head.

Once Josh and Elle were pronounced man and wife, Josh cupped his hands around her cheeks and kissed his bride. The whole church erupted in cheers and the bells rang out. After they'd signed the register and walked back down the aisle and out the door, they were showered with a rainbow of confetti, and they stood holding hands and beaming at us all from the steps of the church.

'Right, ladies, this is your time,' Elle said with a smile.

She turned her back to us before counting loudly to three and launching her bouquet in the air.

Everyone's eyes followed the blast of colour as it flew towards us, and I darted forward so it landed straight in my hands.

Everyone cheered.

'You know what that means, don't you, Evie?' Noah winked at me.

I grinned. 'I sure do,' I said, wrapping my arms around him.

'I love you, Evie.'

My heart soared. 'I love you too.'

He tilted his head and kissed me on my lips.

'Eww, Evie that's naughty!' Theo cried, making slurpy kissing noises.

There was a ripple of laugher as I scooped Theo up in my arms and smacked the noisiest kiss on his cheek.

Theo's giggle was infectious.

'Photo time,' the photographer shouted, and we huddled together for a group shot on the steps of the church.

'I hope you'll marry me one day,' Noah whispered in my ear.

I beamed at him. 'You can count on that, Noah Jones.'

A LETTER FROM CHRISTIE

Dear all,

Firstly, if you're reading this letter, thank you so much for choosing to read *Evie's Year of Taking Chances*.

I sincerely hope you've enjoyed reading this book. If you did, I would be forever grateful if you'd write a review. Your recommendations can always help other readers to discover my books.

I can't believe that I've had five books published over the past two years; writing for a living is truly the best job in the world.

The characters of Evie, Clara and Irene have been a huge part of my life for the last four months, and I will be sorry to leave them behind. I have, without a doubt, enjoyed writing every second of this book.

The inspiration for this novel came when I visited a quaint vintage café in a town called Cannock in Staffordshire. The café was owned by a lady called Mim, whose infectious smile and love of reading sparked the idea behind this story.

I want to say a heartfelt thank you to everyone who has been involved in this project – my family, friends, publisher, book bloggers and readers. I truly value each and every one of you, and it's an absolute joy to hear from you all via Twitter and Facebook. If you'd like to keep up-to-date with all my latest releases, just sign up at http://www.bookouture.com/christie-barlow. Your email address will never be shared and you can unsubscribe at any time.

I would love it if you all could keep in touch!

Warm wishes,

Christie x

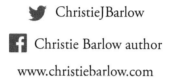

ChristieJBarlow

Christie Barlow author

www.christiebarlow.com

ACKNOWLEDGMENTS

Without a doubt, the hardest part of writing a book is always the thank yous. The list of people who have accompanied me on my writing journey so far is truly endless, and I thank you all from the bottom of my heart. This book was a team effort and huge love to everyone at Bookouture for turning this story into a book.

As always an enormous thank you to my family: Christian, Emily, Jack, Roo, Mop, Mum, Dad and my mad cocker spaniel Woody. I couldn't do the job I love so much without the support of you all.

A special mention of gratitude to Cathy Bramley, Katie Fforde, Sharon Sant and Samantha Tonge who, despite their busy schedules, have always been on the end of the phone or email in the past six months. Thank you, ladies, you rock.

Being a writer has provided me with many opportunities, and I've got to meet some fantastic individuals along the way. These include Dawn Crooks, Claire Knight, Lorraine Rugman, Sarah Hardy, Joanne Robertson, Annette Hannah, Noelle Holten, Rachel Gilbey, Petra Quelch, Kate Moloney and Rebecca Pugh. You all came into my life as book bloggers but now I would class each and every one of you as a friend. Your constant sharing of posts has never gone unnoticed, and your support for my writing is truly appreciated.

My new famous friends, Lisa Hall and Bella Osborne, merit a special mention – thank you for rescuing me in London!

Many thanks to my wonderful friends Anita Redfern, Nicola Rickus, Sarah Lees, Catherine Snook, Louise Speight, Bhasker Patel, Alison Smithies, Ann Blears, Bev Smith, Lucy Davey and Susan Miller, who check up on me on a regular basis to make sure I'm still alive and well in my writing cave.

Last but not least, *Evie's Year of Taking Chances* would never have been written if it wasn't for Marie 'Mim' Deakin, whose vintage café and book club in Cannock provided the inspiration behind this story. Thank you, Mim – and not forgetting you bake the most delicious Victoria sponge cake too.